everyone nervous. They were the oppressive right hand of Dario Villano's government and always on the lookout for anyone who threatened the peace and status quo of the Neo-Caesar's city.

I had to navigate twice across the traffic lanes, once almost being run down by a hauler, and passed by an abandoned green information kiosk. The six-sided shacks were prevalent in the heart of City Center and, like the fountains, had become casualties when the end of tourism had plunged most of the city into poverty.

I pulled my mobiterm out of my pocket to check the time and felt proud that I was only twenty minutes late. Probably thirty by the time I got there, assuming there would be security. After four years in and around the Roman underground, it was a personal best. My world did not put much stock in punctuality.

I had no messages. Probably because I had no friends and tended not to give my enemies my number.

I looked up just in time to see the large man slam into my mobi, sending it skidding into the street. Pain shot up my arm from my broken left pinky. I had tried to wrap and splint it that morning, but I hadn't paid a lot of attention when they taught us field medicine. I had been too busy learning how to jump out of gravjets, resist torture and kill people.

"*Harami!*" I swore after him, but he didn't look back or understand me or give a shit. I didn't blame him. We were all just trying to cut our path through the world. No one was going to help us, but there were plenty of people in the way, and sometimes those people got trampled. I knelt to grab the device while at the same time trying not to get bowled over. The Romans forced to go around me spit words like *bitch* and *Paki* at me. I snatched the mobi, stood back up and carried on. I looked for damage but couldn't tell. This

✝

mobiterm was already obsolete when Alba sold it to me two years before. It was nicked and scratched and in some ways flat-out broken: the speaker was blown out and due to crack and bleed in the screen it had been a year since I had seen the first three characters of any message. But I couldn't exactly walk into a shop and order a new one. All comm-gear was registered with the government, and hacked gear was expensive. It was another thing in my life that would have to wait.

I pulled a small packet out of my breast pocket. My finger was killing me. I placed two (*better make it three, take the edge off*) insta-tabs of chryo under my tongue to dull the pain.

Minutes later I arrived at the southwest corner of the Grand Hotel. The St. Regis. Halfway up the block from me was the front entrance, but I took a right down a shaded walkway running along the building's short side. I saw the worn bronze awning first, then the two dark green-uniformed men standing on either side of a set of green, wood and glass double doors. Both carried Chinese-made *Fángbào* CPC rifles. Heavy gear. About as nasty as a non-make-dead weapon could get. As I approached, their fingers tightened on their triggers. The men were very serious about whatever it was they were paid to be serious about.

I stopped in front of them. There was an awkward beat before they figured out I wasn't going away. They exchanged a look before the taller of the two let out a sigh and spoke:

"What do you want?"

"My name is Virata Das," I said. "I'm here to see Admiral Moreno."

The idea seemed preposterous to the guard. "You are, are you?"

"Ask your boss," I suggested. "Now."

The guard sneered at me. "We don't take orders from Pakis."

Will you take my boot down your throat? I thought. "Please," I said.

He raised his non-trigger hand to his temple and gave it a tap. Tiny blue script, scrolling heads-up information, flashed across the surface of his left eye. The guards were hired muscle, for sure. They weren't Legion, and no municipal *carabiniero* could afford gear like that.

"They say to let her in."

"Then let me in."

"What did I tell you—"

The shorter guard interrupted, "Let her in, Beppino."

They let me in. Six red carpeted stairs led up to a small antechamber, with old-old looking paintings on the walls and claw-footed couches. At the far end was a glass door. I went through it and found myself in a small, well-lit room with an open lift waiting for me. The touchpad inside had only one option. The magnets activated, and the car began to climb, not stopping at any numbered floors along the way. Its only purpose was to get one to and from the Imperial Suite that topped the Grand Hotel.

The lift stopped, and the doors slid open, revealing six armed and severe-looking men standing in an ornately decorated sitting room. They wore the same uniforms as my friends downstairs. Straight lines of utilitarian green in a parlor of crimson and gold frill.

I laced my fingers behind my head as they patted me down. I didn't carry a weapon. To get caught by The Legion with any kind of unregistered piece was trouble, and I wasn't the kind of person that got things registered.

The door to the next room opened, and a man in a suit emerged. He was tall for a Roman and well groomed. Probably past fifty, with rod-up-his-ass posture and a gleaming bald scalp. He walked with the assistance of a black cane topped with a brass sphere, although the hitch in his step seemed mild to me. In slow Italian he introduced himself as Orso Cola, the Admiral's assistant, and asked if I needed anything.

"No, thank you," I responded.

"Did you have any difficulty finding us?"

"No. Just left my place and walked north."

"The Admiral is waiting for you."

"How should I talk to him? How's his Italian?"

"He has been in Roma since before you were born."

"So better than mine." In the army I had been given subconscious flash-training on all of the Romance languages. So when I washed up in Roma, it only took me a few months to become functionally fluent.

He smiled. "Would you prefer English? Your Italian is quite passable, but he so seldom gets to converse in his native tongue."

"No, that's okay. When in... yeah. Don't worry about it."

He led me through the door and into the suite. It was as gaudily furnished and decorated as the antechamber and twenty times the size of the cube I called home. Maybe thirty. It smelled like flowers and antibac gel. There was music playing. Old music, the kind with words. A whining voice sang slowly and earnestly:

Summer has come and passed.
The innocent can never last.
Wake me up when September ends.

Whatever that meant.

Along one wall were a dozen two-dimensional photographs framed in molded gold. A princess called Grace. White men with their names written beneath their faces in script: Clinton, Ilysasov, Gere, Mercier. A dark-skinned man named Nwosu and a dark-skinned woman named Winfrey. Another Clinton, a white woman. A Chinese called Du.

The other two I recognized. Xian Hao was a late twenty-first century scientist who had made the first tentative contact with intelligent extraterrestrial life. Since then, we had been having a cryptic long-distance conversation with what we assumed was an advanced alien race. We had no idea what they were saying, and we were pretty sure they had the same dilemma.

We had already discovered life on other worlds: first the microscopic fossils on Mars, then the millions of nonocular, silicon-based "blackfish" under the icy surface of Europa. But Xian had proven that we weren't alone as thinking, intelligent beings, even if the others were eleven light years away. I always found it comforting to know that if we truly fucked things up down here, there was something out there that still had a chance.

My father had been an admirer of Doctor Xian and spoke of him often.

The other picture was of Sagni Dubashi, who had been the Prime Minister of India during the Shame of 2020 and the ensuing global, genocidal war. My father had hated him and I never met anyone who felt otherwise.

Here comes the rain again.
Falling from the stars.
Drenched in my pain again.
Becoming who we are.

"Do people think that staying in a room where an extraordinary person once slept will somehow transfer their greatness to them? Relevance by osmosis?"

The man speaking sat on one of the room's six sofas. Admiral Jonah Moreno, I presumed.

"As long as they change the sheets often enough," I said. "I wouldn't worry about anything transferring to anybody." He looked about seventy, with a full head of fine black hair, parted on the left. His skin was wrinkled and worn, but free of any molds, lesions or growths. A mouth full of polished white teeth hid behind his thin, pink lips.

"You're Admiral Moreno?"

"No."

"Where's Moreno?"

"There is no Jonah Moreno," he said. "Not anymore. He lives on when it behooves me to not use my given name."

"Which is?"

"My name is Caden Kennedy. I'm sure that means nothing to you."

"Less than zero-zero. Who was he?" I was intrigued by this man who wanted me to make dead for money.

"An old friend. Well, a rival. Of sorts. From a long time ago. We were two very different boys with one common interest."

"A woman."

"A girl."

I wasn't able to dig up any information on an US Navy man named Moreno. "He was an Admiral?" I asked.

He smiled. "No, but I feel naked without a title in front of my name."

"What's your real title?"

"Senator. United States of North America. Deceased."

"Deceased?"

He shrugged. "Officially, yes. I'm sure that seems odd."

Not to me it doesn't, I thought.

"And your real name again?"

"Kennedy. R. Caden Kennedy."

"Why are you telling me this?" I asked. "It's a pretty lousy cover if you go telling strangers about it."

"Once I explain everything to you, you will understand why it's useless for me to hide such information from you." He motioned to the sofa opposite him. "Please. Come sit with me."

Ring out the bells again.
Like we did when Spring began.
Wake me up, when September ends.

When I got closer, I got a better look at him. He was much older than I first thought. Much older. His eyes were devoid of crow's feet, but his full lashes were obviously synthetic. As was the hair on his head, his teeth and maybe even his tongue, which looked natural but had an odd tint to it. His pupils were dead like dulled onyx. He breathed shallowly, as if it would hurt to pull the air deeper. He was a barely together machine adorned with sparkly new buttons and knobs. He wore a gray hooded sweatshirt, unzipped to his navel, a plain white T-shirt underneath. At the bottom of his distressed denim pants were narrow old-time sneakers, black canvas with rubber heels and toes. The bright red, loosely drawn laces were only nominally tied.

I sat, crossed my hands in my lap, tried to look attentive. *Don't fuck this up.*

He picked up a small tin from the end table and used two fingers to pop open the lid. He held it out towards me. The candies inside were brown and green striped discs. I

CHAD J. SHONK

shook my head. He shrugged, took out a piece for himself and popped it in his mouth.

As my memory rests.

But never forgets what I lost.

Wake me up when September ends.

As he set the tin on the sofa beside him, he said, almost to himself, "They're called Bombas Bocas. They're from back home, from one of the Mexican states. They don't have them here. I'm not even sure they make them anymore. I smuggled some over years go. Each one I eat is precious to me because my supply is finite. I do not eat them idly."

He was telling me I should have indulged him and taken the damn candy. And I knew I should have. *You're already fucking this up.*

Kennedy rolled the candy around in his mouth, savoring it. He closed his eyes, and we sat silently until it had dissolved entirely. He swallowed, and the simple act seemed to cause him pain. After it had passed, he smiled. As he opened his eyes, he asked, "Looking at me, how old would you say I am?"

A dozen ways to crack wise came to me, but I stayed quiet. I could tell the difference between a man who wanted a conversation and a man who just wanted to talk.

"I am a hundred and forty-six years old."

He said it with no humor, no slyness, no hint of bullshit. He meant it.

Even ignoring the cosmetic augmentations he looked half that, and I had never heard of anyone living that long. He would have been worldwide famous. Who was this guy?

He continued, "In my grandfather's generation a centenarian was a rarity, a man to celebrate. The product of either careful living or luck."

"Or both."

10

"Or both. What do your friends call you?"

What friends? I thought. "Rata," I said.

"Rata."

"Can I call you Caden?"

He ignored me. "Just so you know, Rata, I will be offering you money to murder a man. But it's one of the few things I've never done in my long life, and I believe I'll have to work my way up to it. If that is alright with you."

I nodded. In the name of the criminals I owed, I had made threats, broken bones, caused terrible confession-inducing pain. But not made dead. I hadn't killed anyone since the war. Not since Neu Berlin.

Wake me up when September ends.

The music stopped. The Senator smiled and sat forward, resting his creaking elbows on his thighs. He ran his hands down both sides of his artificially hairless cheeks. He seemed on the verge of tears, but I doubted his ducts worked anymore. "I seem to be having a hard time. Why don't you tell me about yourself, Virata Das?"

"I'm not as loose with my self-data as you are."

"Then let me guess. You live in The Esquilino, but your name suggests to me you are not of the *Yatiim*. Indian?"

"Bengali."

"And the Paks let you be?"

"I keep my head down."

"I'm old enough to remember when there actually was a Pakistan," he said.

He can't be, can he? This is ridiculous.

"I like your jacket." He pointed to my chest, to the faded badge above my pocket. "You served."

"No. I bought this from a hockshoppe on Via Cavour."

"No, you didn't."

"Jump Commando. Ninth battalion."

11

"What theater?"

Fuck do you care? I thought. "All of them," I said.

"Saudi? Russia? Germany?"

"All of them," I said again with a touch more force.

"I would guess you are fifty-five years of age?"

Pushing aside my vanity, I calmly told him I was thirty-eight. Give or take.

"Sorry. I have lost my ability to guess the age of young people. It has been so long since I have looked my age. Thirty-eight. Have you ever been in love?"

"I don't see how that's any of your—"

"I remind you that you are here for an interview. If I ask you a question, let's just assume it's fucking pertinent. Have you ever been in love?"

"Not so far. I don't believe in fairy tales."

"Good. That's good."

"It is?"

"I've seen four world wars come and go. I was given a college deferment in the first, was too old for the next one and legally dead for the last two. Not that I wanted to fight in any of them. I'm just curious. So when you were killing and trying not to get killed in the name of your country, did you think often of death?"

Sometimes. All the time, I thought. "Not a whole lot of time for that," I said.

"'Learned men do not grieve for the Dead or the Living.'" He was quoting something, I could tell, but I had no idea what.

"Excuse me?"

"Those words are from your book, are they not?"

"I don't read a lot of word-fic. It puts me to sleep after five minutes."

"'Never have we not existed, and never in the future shall we cease to exist.' It's from the Gita."

Great. One of those. "That one knocks me out before I get it loaded." *I wanted to get off the topic.*

"I've always found myself drawn to the Indian traditions. The food, the music, the art..."

If you called me up here to quench your Tandoori Fever, you've got the wrong girl, you old bastard, I thought.

"Really? That's fascinating." I said.

Don't. Fuck. This. Up.

"The religion is of course nothing more than a toxic mythology, but aren't they all? I don't believe in fairy tales, either."

Kennedy began to stand for the first time since I had been there. I stood and offered my hand, and he took it. He arched his back, and I heard the bones cracking, but once he was upright, he had remarkably good posture for someone born in the twentieth century. When he walked, he took deliberate but steady steps. He approached the wall of portraits and looked at them while not looking at any of them.

"When I was forty-one, as a consequence for having my father's weak genes, my heart exploded while I was speaking on the floor of the Senate. At least that was what it felt like. All this time and I still remember. Cardiac arrest, but that seems like such a clinical term for being ripped apart from the inside by a spiteful and parlous fiend. It hurt like a motherfucker."

He paced back and forth in front of the photographs, pretending to study their faces as he spoke. I felt my attention wavering between his story and my throbbing little finger.

"When I woke up, the docs told me I had been dead for eight minutes. Even in my medicated haze, I realized the magnitude of that fact. Do you know what happened in those eight minutes?"

How much more of this will I have to sit through before he gets to the job?

"Nothing. I did not see the Heaven the nuns told me about in church. I was not reborn into the cycle of *samsara*, nor did I find the release of *nirvana*. There were no virgins waiting for me. I did not commune with my lost loved ones. I was, for those four-hundred eighty seconds, nullified."

I had abandoned the beliefs of my parents, of my people, any beliefs, when I was a teenager, but hearing it stated so concretely chilled me.

"I decided then that I would never allow myself to die."

I would have laughed, but he had done a pretty good job of it so far.

"Do you know why I have lived for a century and a half and you most likely will not?"

A fistfuck of dollars?

"It is because I am very rich and you are not. Not one of my organs is factory issue except my brain, and even that has been tinkered with. As we speak, my fourth heart is being printed, soon to be nurtured in a nutrient bath and held in stasis until I need it. Most of my bones have been reinforced with polymers to prevent decay. I have nanobiotic antibodies that patrol my blood for any signs of disease or infection.

"I replaced a religion with a philosophy. This philosophy is called Transhumanism. Are you aware of it?"

"No."

"I'm not surprised. It was an idea ahead of its time, furthered by a man who did not live to see it come true."

He came back and sat down. I could see the gears turning behind his eyes. Maybe he was finally getting to the point. "Despite the stagnation that has maligned the world over the last hundred years, there have been some remarkable things achieved. But they are only available to the wealthy, and that is a horrible shame. Without great personal wealth, a person has no chance to ever see two centuries."

He looked at me. Directly in the eyes. For the first time.

"Would you, Miss Das, be interested in some personal wealth of your own?"

I'd settle for getting my bike out of hock, I thought, but I sat up a little straighter in my chair, shaking off the dullness I had sunk into during his speechifying.

"Six weeks ago, my wife of eighty-three years was murdered in front of my eyes," he said, as coldly and flatly as he could.

The first thing that struck me was the terrifying thought of being with the same person for eighty-three years. But I was pretty sure that wasn't the important part.

"I am so sorry."

"Thank you. She was everything to me, my partner in every way. Beautiful. Intelligent. And strong. Stronger than I could ever hope to be. We held the same ideals, the same goals. We had spent a mortal's lifetime together working to conquer the unnecessary certainty of death with the power of science."

This was the part when I was supposed to start playing like I knew what I was doing. Asking questions. "Tell me what happened."

They had been taking a spring *passeggiata,* a long, slow, near-ritualistic stroll through Roma's city center. It was something Italians had been doing with their evenings for

✝

centuries, and after fifty years the Kennedys no longer thought of themselves as foreigners. The Senator had worn a white silken suit, and his wife, Amelia, donned a powder blue dress that ran down to her ankles, with a yellow scarf around her neck to cut the evening breeze.

When they emerged from their house, they must have been striking: a vigorous hundred and forty-two year old man and his beautiful hundred and nineteen year old wife. Orso had driven their luxury e-cart to the Piazza Navona, where they always began their night walks. As was tradition, Kennedy had walked with his hands behind his back, the fingers of one gently wrapped around the wrist of the other. Her right arm slipped under his left. She had been having a little trouble with one of her synthetic hips, the Senator noted to me, but he hadn't minded keeping her steady as they strolled.

"She had been doing the same for my heart, for all of me, for the better part of a century," he said to reinforce his melancholy. I bit my lip and sighed in an attempt to avoid rolling my eyes.

Strolling had become more popular over the previous decades because of the lack of tourists. Everyone out walking was Roman, or at least lived in the city-state, and understood the need to slow down every once in a while, even during the darkest of times.

The oblong plaza had been a racetrack in the old-old days, but that night the people circled it very, very slowly. The Kennedys stopped at one of Navona's three famous fountains and reminisced about how beautiful it had been when they first arrived in Roma, when the water was flowing to it. The air was crisply biting, so Caden had draped his coat over Amelia's shoulders. They sauntered west and out of the *piazza,* towards what was left of the old

Italian Senate building. It had been burned during the Civil War, and the rubble was left as a reminder ever since. While they stood alone, they could hear the bustle of Navona behind them.

"I was just about to ask Amelia what she thought the American Capitol, which had been my office for fifty years, looked like now, when I felt her entire body convulse. I felt her... I looked over, and her eyes were wide open in terror, and blood was dripping from her lips like spittle. I didn't know what to do. I needed her to tell me what to do...

"As she sunk to her knees, I went with her, feeling that if I let her fall it would be the end. She was mumbling as I lowered her to the ground as gently as I could. Her eyes... they... her eyes they rolled back into the back of her head; her whole body was trembling. Shaking. I didn't know what to... She would have known what..."

"It was only then that I became aware of the man. Maybe three yards from us. Dressed in a blue suit so shiny it reflected the streetlights. Everything else was white. His bow tie. Slacks, jacket, shoes. And he wore a top hat. Also white. A fucking top hat.

"And he was pointing a pistol at me. One of this place's stupid laser guns. He stepped forward, and I saw that he was trembling and there was sweat dripping from the tip of his bulbous nose. He looked terrified. He took aim, his finger twitched, there was a flash, and I dove into darkness."

I hadn't expected that. "But it didn't take," I said.

"I couldn't have been down for more than a minute. When I woke up, he was gone. Amelia and I were lying in the street. No one had seen what had happened, or, if they had, they hadn't bothered to come to our aid.

"Amelia was quiet and still. I crawled to her." He vaguely mimicked the motion with his arms, probably not aware that he was doing it. "I wiped the blood from her lips, sure she was just unconscious. I had survived. The weapon hadn't been lethal. We had been spared.

"But I couldn't wake her. All of our efforts to conjure ourselves immortal were dashed upon the cobblestones of Piazza Madama. I looked into her eyes, their emerald hue already starting to fade, for a full minute before I closed them. She was... I couldn't believe... I couldn't understand why the gun had taken her life but spared mine. In the moment, I wished it hadn't."

Hacking a commercial weapon to make dead sapped the batpack pretty quickly, but an average retail piece could easily deliver three or four killing stings, unless the mod was shoddy. It seemed that once he had blown his load killing the woman, he only had enough juice left in the stinger to send the Senator down for a quick nap.

I waited a beat to press on, then asked, "Did he take anything?"

"I gave her a necklace the day we left America. Buried inside a platinum sphere was a sample of her DNA suspended in amber. He ripped it from her neck."

"Anything else? Money?"

"A few thousand yuros. Our mobis. My pockets were turned out, even the ones that were empty to begin with."

"So it was a robbery?" I asked.

"In every sense. He stole *everything* from me." It turned out his ducts were functional. He reached again for the tin of candy, but changed his mind. I was having a hard time finding sympathy for a woman who managed to fend off death for a hundred and twenty years. My father had made it to fifty-nine. And my brother never got to see his tenth birthday. Maybe Amelia's extra years were supposed to have been theirs.

18

He looked at me, wanting me to speak. His gaze drifted to my left hand. "What happened to your finger?" I regarded my makeshift splint. Considering what he was hiring me to do, I was sure the story wouldn't have upset him. But I didn't feel like telling it.

"You want me to find this man. And kill him."

"Yes."

"How much?"

"Three million."

I tried to keep down the wave of excitement pulsing through me. "That's a lot of denarii."

"Three million yuros."

"Oh." Denarii were worthless outside the walls of Roma. Yuros spent anywhere and were worth twice their Roman counterparts.

"I am told that is a lot. Is it too much?"

I would have done it for a hundred grand, I thought. "I don't think so," I said.

"It's my first time purchasing mortal retribution. I'm afraid I don't know the market value."

"Here's to uneducated guesses."

"But there is more to it."

Chodu...

"I'm not hiring you to kill this man. I am hiring you to avenge my Amelia."

"I'm not sure I get the difference."

"I am not so blind as to call this justice. That is not what this is. It is revenge, and I want to feel its satisfaction. I want to know what it's like to pull the trigger, to watch him fall. I want to tell him why he's dying, explain to him what he's taken from me. I want him to know that nothing waits for him beyond this world but annihilation. I want him to fear. I want him to cry. I want him to beg.

19

‡

"But I am an old man, and this is not a task for me. I don't think my body could take it. I don't think my heart or mind could either. Which is why I need you.

"In order to help me, my pain must become your pain. My grief must become your grief. My wrath must become your wrath.

"I don't need a detective, Miss Das. I'm not looking for a bounty hunter.

"I need a proxy."

PROXY

‡

II: THE ESQUILINO

THE DAY BEFORE I MET THE ANCIENT dead-but-not-dead Senator, I was in a joint on Via Mamiani eating a lunch of stewed lentils that tasted nothing like the food back home but held enough of a familiar whisper in the spicing to make it a mild comfort. Despite shedding most of the superstitions and trappings with which I was raised, I had never developed a taste for meat, synthetic or otherwise.

I had been there many times. There was an unspoken understanding between me and the Paks who ran the place: I pretended not to notice that their food was shit, while they would ignore the fact that I was Indian.

Once upon a time, I learned in school, there had been a place called Pakistan. They were our neighbors and, in fact, were once part of the same nation. They looked like us, spoke like us, ate like us. But they believed in different things than we did. Their God was a frightening monolithic despot; ours were a blasphemous parade of animals and mutants.

A hundred and forty years ago, there was a war that had been a long time coming. Both sides had been bickering over the same patch of land for a century, and finally shots were fired, ordinance exchanged. Other countries were pulled into the conflict. Global war. World war. When the bombs stopped falling and the dust cleared, millions were dead, borders were altered all across the Middle East, and there was no longer a place called Pakistan.

But all this time later, there were still Pakistanis. They were known worldwide as the *Yatiim*, the Orphans. They lived in places like Paris and London. Cities. They formed communities, enclaves and neighborhoods. In Roma, they found themselves on Esquilino, one of the city's seven ancient founding hills. Over time they created a city within a city, a place of their own where they raised their children and built mosques.

Their leaders called this home the *Yatiim Khaanah*. The Orphanage.

Most of the people, inside and out, called it Pakitown.

Generations ago, the goal of every Pak would have been to go home, to reclaim what the Greater Republic of India had taken from them. But that dream had faded. The land of their great-grandfathers was a distant myth, like Eden or Babylon or Atlantis.

The diner was long and narrow, just a counter and a kitchen. I sat near the coin register and was the only customer. Down the line of stools was Hala, the owner. His feet up on the bar, his attention on the screen of his mobiterm. His glossy, flawless mobiterm. A brand new 78-S. Molecular bio-security. China-grade AI emulator. Voice-to-voice communication, a new feature that absolutely no one had asked for. High end. Expensive.

He also wore a thick and heavy-looking gold watch on his right wrist, the kind without any display except for a pair of tiny sticks spinning like tire spokes. They had come into fashion recently because of their ancient feel. I couldn't tell whether it was really from the old times or a cheap replica. If it was real, it would have cost more than his new-new mobi.

"What's with the new gloss on your wrist, Hala?"

I talked at full volume and realized I had never spoken at more than a whisper in the place. My voice echoed off the plexi windows and the low ceiling. He looked at his wrist and made a face like he had forgotten it was there.

"It's just my watch. I've had it a long time."

I shook my head. "I've been coming here nine months, and I've never seen it once."

"Sometimes I don't wear it."

Guys like Hala always wore their gold. He wouldn't have left a piece of gleam like that at home. Not ever. How else was everyone supposed to know how flush he was? I put down my spoon. The lentils were only half gone, but I was tired of waiting.

Get this over with.

"What are you doing?" I asked. Pulling his legs down from the counter, Hala looked around and realized we were alone in the room. "You can't ask a man like him to cut you slack when you wear a new gold watch and buy pricey new gear," I said. "He's not going to stand for that, and either you know that and don't care or you're an idiot. But you do know what you owe."

Understanding, Hala stood. I matched him.

"Listen, bitch. You tell your boss—"

"You knew what you were doing when you borrowed it."

He hocked and spit on the floor.

I had known there was only one way this was going to go. It was what Bijan wanted anyway. Still, I had hoped...

Before I flexed a muscle in his direction, he bolted. With me between him and the main entrance, he ran for the back door. I followed him, slowly, deliberately. There was no rush. He wasn't going anywhere.

Hala grabbed the knob, turned and slammed his shoulder into the door. It opened, but just a little before the polymer cord caught, the rope I had set up before coming inside. He looked back at me and tried the door again. Nothing but a sliver of light and a stressed rattle. He failed a third time, and then I was on him.

Cornered, he sneered at me. "Bhindi cunt."

Hala held his hands in front of him like he knew how to fight, but he didn't. Unfortunately for him, I believed in fighting everyone like they were trained killers. No such thing as taking it easy. End it as fast as possible.

When he took a step closer, I slipped in and brought my fist down like a hammer, split his guard and broke his collarbone. Before he could register it, I drove a knee into his balls. He grunted and doubled over. I grabbed him by the neck, stood him up and drove him back into the wall, my right hand wrapped around his throat. His right arm dangled uselessly at his side. Wheezing. Eyes wide. He was surprised.

Men were always surprised by my strength.

"You can't borrow money from Bijan Antonius and not pay your *hafta*. You know that, but here we are."

He tried to speak. I squeezed a little harder.

"You knew what kind of man he is. If I clean out your register, is there going to be enough for your last three *haftas*?"

I loosened my grip enough for him to slowly shake his head.

"How about just one?"

His voice came out a strained whisper. "No."

I let go of his neck. He groaned, rubbing his neck, pained, trying to breathe.

"And yet you have enough money for clean new gloss?"

"It was my father's—"

I grabbed him under the chin and knocked his head against the wall again.

"If it isn't new, you should have hocked it a long time ago." I reached down, unclasped the watch and slid it off his dead arm. Pocketed it.

I pressed into his collarbone break with two fingers. He screamed. I let the pain take him for a while, then let up. "Now I know I've already broken something, but Bijan wants more. Luckily for you, he wasn't specific."

"Please," he managed to get out.

"I'm not emotionally involved in this, you understand? Not one way, not the other. I'm like you, deep in hock, but I got a skill to trade." I said. "He'd take your joint, but it's not worth a fucking thing on account of you being a shitty cook." Somebody had to tell him.

"I'll pay next week."

I dug my fingers into his shoulder once again. He gritted his teeth, trying not to scream again. Tears started drooling down his cheeks.

"Yes, you will, but that doesn't get you out of this."

✝

I didn't want to hurt him anymore than I already had. I hadn't wanted to in the first place, but there wasn't anything I could do about it. When you dealt with bad guys, bad things happened. That's how I found myself brutalizing stupid and careless men for a dangerously delusional coin shark.

"I have to break something else. If Bijan sees you on the street and you're not limping, I'll be the one in trouble. But I want to be fair. Which one of your knees do you use the least?"

He was about to say something when his eye line shifted for a split second and then came back to me. The flit let me know his cousin Rida had finally gotten out of the kitchen and into position behind me. Stealthily, at least he thought.

I knew he was left-handed from watching him work the register for months. I knew he had no formal combat training. I knew he was a little taller than me.

So I knew exactly where he was holding the stinger.

Before he set his feet, before he knew I knew he was there, I spun left. Grabbed the body of the pistol with my right hand and used the momentum to pull him off balance. As he leaned into it, I came across my body and up into his jaw with the open palm of my other hand.

He staggered back, stunned, leaving the pistol in my hand. A ZIP!-brand hold-out. They could have bought a hundred of them for one of Hala's gold watches. It was bargain-priced gear. Cheap polymer. Unreliable plasma system. Shit weapon.

I tossed the stinger over the counter and deep into the kitchen. Rida tried to say something in Urdu, but his jaw was fucked, and it came out mumbled. With a growl, he rushed me. I sidestepped him, but the counter and stools kept me from clearing entirely. He hooked an arm around my legs and pulled me down with him.

I stupidly broke my fall with my hands, and when my left landed, the fingers splayed. Pain shot up my arm as my pinky overextended and popped. My arm folded under me. I hit the floor face first, and then he was on my back, trying to get a grip around my neck.

I reached behind me with my good hand and felt around for his face. Found it. Stuck my thumb in his mouth, got a good hold on his already-broken mandible and twisted.

He roared like an animal and rolled off me. I scrambled away and flipped myself so I was tail down, ready to repel him again. But he was lying still on the floor. Passed out from the pain.

I looked at my hand. My finger was fucked, broken, bent back at the lower knuckle.

Hala kicked my back in between my shoulders. I had figured him as out of commission, but the adrenal rush of fear and violence could trump almost anything.

It was a poor kick. I spun around on my ass and grabbed his ankle. He screaked and crashed to the ground. I twisted until I heard a crunch. When I stood, he was still awake but barely. I surveyed him as he writhed. The ankle and the collarbone would be enough damage for Bijan.

I stepped over Rida on my way out and thought about leaving a double on the counter to pay for my lentils but caught myself.

Trying to swagger out of here like this is something to be proud of? Do not enjoy this, Rata.

This is not what you do.

Not who you are.

Sooner or later, though, I was going to have to come to terms with the fact that it was.

I left the restaurant and cut through the park, headed for the church. I tried to straighten out my little finger, but the pain made me light-headed. I managed to make it stick out a little less grotesquely, but it was already turning purple. I routed my walk home through the Maggiore Market. The bazaar filled the *piazza* surrounding a massive basilica and had started to expand south down Via Merulana. The oldest church in a city flush with them, it cast a wide shadow with its two domes and tower. The Catholics had held onto the building as long as they could, but as tourist money dried up and Pakitown became more and more hostile and sovereign, maintaining the basilica, no matter the historical import, became untenable. In exchange for ceding the land and the structure, the last Pope of Roma had demanded the removal of the church's Christian mosaics, some of them over a thousand years old. They carried them off a piece at a time, along with any other gold, jewels and religious artifacts, and reassembled them in another cathedral located in friendlier, whiter, territory.

Since then, every cross had been replaced by a golden crescent, and the obelisk in the *piazza* had come to fly the green and white flag of old Pakistan.

The church now served as the hub of The Esquilino. Warehouse. Market. Meeting hall.

I waded through the morass of people. Everything was for sale at Maggiore if you found the right table or cart. There had probably been a point when there was a difference between the black market and the regular market, but that time was long gone. Windowsill-grown vegetables were sold next to stolen public Ether-terms next to wooden blocks for children next to smuggled Chinese opium next to clothes next to discreetly attired whores next to prayer beads next to untraceable weapons. The merchants of The Esquilino cared little for decorum; if someone wanted to buy it, they would sell it.

A table offering off-system tech gear caught my eye. The peddler showed me his selection of hacked mobiterms, used stingers and solos, and low-level external bio-jacks. He tried to sell me a wrist unit that fed antiviral nanobots into your blood through two prongs that dug deep into your flesh. What he didn't say was that the rig was six generations out of date and that the strain of nanos it used had a one in twenty-five chance of turning on you and ripping you apart from the inside. Hardly worth the hundred denarii he was asking.

I never bought stuff from guys like him anyway. You never knew what you were actually buying, if it worked and if someone was going to come looking for it. I had my own sources for illicit gear. But it was fun to browse, and the longer I took getting back to my flat, the better.

I found a chem merchant and asked for a packet of low-dose chryocane tabs.

"This is the stuff they give kids. I've got some pharma-grade nitro," he offered, thinking I would be drawn to the more powerful make-numb. It was much more popular on the street. Pure and potent nitrocodone. I knew it well.

"Just the chryo."

He shrugged and handed it to me, and as soon as he did, I wanted to hand it right back. There was a reason I didn't keep any of the stuff at my place. But the pain in my finger was too great to ignore. The over-the-counter chryo wouldn't make it go away, but it would round it off at least a little. After paying him most of my coin, I bought two pears and few grams of bread from a produce cart with what I had left. I ate while I walked home, saving one fruit for dinner.

The four-story building where I kept my gear was just off Merulana on a street named after a centuries-dead political philosopher. Number 13 was an old building in a block of contiguous old buildings. It was an ugly brown and orange, so similar to rust than I expected it to crumble any day. Wished it would.

I swiped my thumb over the scanner, and the door unlocked. I wanted to go upstairs right off, but I had to check in.

Bijan's apartment was the foremost room on the ground floor, and his door was always open so he could see into the lobby. He didn't want anyone coming and going without him knowing it. He was sitting on the sofa, typing on his living-light table, wearing his white toga, which looked even whiter against his dark brown skin—although over the last year Bijan's skin had been gradually growing lighter. I was sure it was intentional, but had no way of knowing for sure. His garment's borders were trimmed in dark green silk; his sandals were kicked off onto the ground. The bleach job on his hair had gone past blonde all the way to white.

He looked ridiculous.

Bijan always looked ridiculous.

His flat was the largest in the building, the only apartment that still had its original floor plan. The rest had been carved up into cubes like the one I lived in. He had a den, a bedroom, a full-sized kitchen and, to everyone's envy, his own water closet.

The floors were tiled, with mosaics laid into them. Some of old-old Romans, dressed like Bijan tried to, carrying swords, riding in chariots. One was a depiction of the Pakistani Exodus, the only indicator in the entire place of his actual heritage. Most of the mosaics, though, were of people fucking, in every position, in every gender combination imaginable.

His furniture was all white. The walls were painted to look like stone, and the couch was flanked by faux-marble columns. The plastic pillars went from floor to ceiling. Against the far wall was a small stone seraph pissing into a pond. It was probably the only running fountain in the city.

The centerpiece was a meter-tall pedestal on which sat a bust of an ancient Roman. He claimed it was an original piece from the old-old days, but I was sure it was a replica. It was a likeness of Marc Antony, Bijan's hero, the man he wanted to be. Modeled himself after. I had always found it telling that Bijan didn't want to be the Caesar himself, but the Caesar's man—not the boss, but the man standing next to him and a little behind. He identified so strongly with Cleopatra's last lover that he had changed his last name from Wur to Antonius. He asked people to call him Antonius or Antony. He probably would have taken Tony. People would oblige when speaking to him, at times, to placate his temper, but behind his back it was still Wur. Or Baby Wur, to emphasize the fact that, while he may have acted it, Bijan wasn't the biggest cock in Pakitown. As much as he wanted everyone to think of him as a man of old-old, he was still a Pak gangster who wore a dress and talked like a *gandu*.

Bijan would have been a handsome man if I had never met him or not known anything about him. But I had and I did. A lot of people in The Esquilino had both a landlord and a coin shark. Having them as one and the same was not ideal, but at least I only had to worry about one asshole at a time. Bijan owned the two blocks from Via Merulana to Via Ferruccio.

I waited for him to speak. He didn't like being interrupted. He entered in a few more characters and swiped a few fingers around the screen. On the glass rested his ever-present sidearm, a hefty WWV-era LPC, chrome with real gold highlights and modded to kill. Nothing old world about it.

Without looking up, he asked, "Was my message delivered with the appropriate relish?"

"Yeah. He'll have it next week."

"I would not wager upon the word of a plebeian, but I do hope that this is the last time he ever has to lay eyes on you. His next indiscretion will hastify his end. Were there spoils?"

"Free lunch."

"What were the fruits of the violence?"

I held up my wounded hand, "I think I broke my finger."

He looked up from the console. Leaned back into the plush of the couch. Rubbed his sweaty hands in the folds of his toga. "I care not one fuck about your finger. What ills hath you wrought upon my debtor?"

"I broke his collarbone. And his ankle."

"You were too kind."

"I also crunched his nuts something awful."

Bijan winced but then nodded in approval. "A man's cock and balls are his temple. You have desecrated holy ground." He smiled. "I approve."

"His cousin's most likely at the clinic being fitted for a synth jaw."

"Likely they will seek my patronage to fund the procedure."

He smiled, but I couldn't smile back. I had to work for him, but I wouldn't play gangster with him.

It would be so easy to kill him, I thought. *Without his vacuous affections and fancy stinger, he's just a forty-five-*

year-old street tough who has never fought anyone who could truly fight back. But his younger cousin Sarkis is the real boss of The Orphanage, and he would find me.

I guessed I could have fought him too, but then what? Wage war with The Sindeketa? The *Yatiim* mafia would find me. Eventually I would grow tired, slip and lose.

I could have left, but to where? Every city had a Bijan, and every person like me ended up owing them. The outcasts. The desperate. The invisible. The deserters.

I had seen a lot of places both during and after the war. When I ended up in Roma, I had decided that it would be my last stand. I would come out ahead, or I wouldn't come out at all.

"Did they draw arms?" he asked.

"Rida had a ZIP! 46 behind the counter."

"Tsk. That shall be another ten thousand denarii for assaulting my surrogate."

Bijan had an arbitrary fining system that baffled everyone. I'd been fined for being late on a payment, being early on a payment, breaking someone's ankle when it was supposed to be their knee and being an "insolent plebe." Next to all the money I owed him, though, the pittance due for each offense felt like spare change.

"What was its fate?"

"Left it. It was cherry. Registered. Worthless. But I brought you this."

I handed him Hala's gold watch. There were a few specks of blood on the face. He looked at it. Petted the gold band.

"It is a fine piece of treasure." With a smirk, he held it out to me. "Here. It shall be yours."

Hocking a hunk of gleam like that wouldn't have given me enough coin to pay off my debt, but it would have made it so I wouldn't have to borrow any more for a while. I'd always suspected that Bijan had a soft spot and a hard-on for me. It was about time it worked to my advantage instead of just making me nauseous.

Before I could fire off an order to the muscles in my hand, he snapped it back.

"I jest. You are dismissed."

"Okay."

"Okay what?"

"Okay, *Dominus.*"

"Better. Now be gone."

I felt stupid for even thinking Bijan would try to help but couldn't blame myself for hoping. Desperation had made me an impulse optimist; something good had to happen sometime.

I climbed the stairs to the third floor. As I came down the hall, I saw that the bathroom was unoccupied. My lockpad confirmed my print, and I entered the three by three by three–meter cube that was my room. I took out the packet of chryo I had bought and took two tabs (*better make it three, to jump-start it*) and placed them under my tongue. They dissolved almost instantly, and I waited for the pain in my finger to lessen.

I looked at the remaining chryocane and wondered if there were enough of the low-dose tabs left to kill me. If I emptied them all into my mouth, the gelatinous sheets releasing the chems into my blood, would it be enough? I was sure it would be. The quantity would surely overpower the quality.

There was little for me outside. No friends. No prospects. I only left to eat or when Bijan sent me to do something. Sometimes I would wander Roma's streets, but never for long. When darker notions visited me, darker

34

notions such as swallowing fifty tabs of chryo to end it all, I would let them in, roll them around in my head a little, play them out and then let them go. I was either too strong or too scared to go through with it. Probably a little bit of both.

I grabbed my towel and found that the bathroom was still empty. I activated the lock behind me. Our building was a rarity in the neighborhood because it had hot water, one advantage of living in the same building as Bijan. Once the temperature peaked, though, you only had three or four minutes before you were caught in the freezing rain.

I stripped and stepped into the shower, pulling the curtain closed around me. "Hot water" may have been too generous a term, but lukewarm felt like slipping back into the womb when coming in from the cold and grime. I held my busted finger under the spray. It hurt at first, but the water quickly merged its efforts with those of the chryocane to muffle the pain a little.

I looked at my crooked and purple digit. When I got back to my cube, I would try to splint it, wrap it, and then what? What was I going to do the next day? And the day after that? There would always be people Bijan needed leaned on, but that wasn't getting me any closer to getting square with him. That work was just so he wouldn't have me killed for missing my *hafta*. It was up to me to come up with the balance.

I had spent my first several weeks in Roma sleeping on a bench in the shantytown that used to be the Circus Maximus. The large oval field was once a place where emperors would look down to watch festivals, parades and chariot races. Now it was a collection of makeshift tents, homeless, sick, chem-heads and whores.

I didn't sleep for the first two nights. Not out of fear. No one there had been a real threat to me. But the noise. The yelling, the coughing, screaming, moaning. Crackling campfires. The pounding of makeshift drums. Off-tune singing. The occasional fight. Desperate and filthy fucking. Children crying.

On the third night, and on every night after that, I slept soundly.

Soon I found work. The only work available for someone who was off-system and needed to stay that way. Distributing. Collecting. Burglary.

I never killed anyone; I never sold myself.

The work had been steady for a while. I had a long streak of luck, bouncing from one dirty deed to another. I left the bench. Found myself a flat. But soon my luck dried up. So did the denarii.

I started borrowing from my landlord, the second most powerful criminal in Pakitown. Just one bad move in a lifetime of bad moves.

The water began to lose its heat. I shut it off. I found that I was looking forward to the pear I had back in my cube. The first one hadn't even been that good, mealy and flavorless. But I had hopes for the remaining one.

Something good had to happen sometime.

I stepped out of the shower, grabbed my towel and found a man waiting for me.

Kalb was a mutt of a man who had inherited the worst physical traits from each tribe in the stew that was his bloodline. His nose was crooked, his ears too big, his eyes too small. He was lanky and wobbled a little bit when he walked. When he spoke, he whistled through a gap where a tooth once was.

I wrapped my towel around my body quickly but not in a rush. It wasn't anything he hadn't seen before. In addition to scaring, beating and killing people for Bijan, Kalb was also the building's maintenance man. With his prints he was able to get through any door.

"Get out."

"I'm sorry. I didn't know you were in here," he said in a flat tone that didn't even bother to hide his lie.

"You say that every time."

"It's just me. You can relax."

"You can leave."

His eyes scanned me, barely covered and still dripping wet. I wanted to reach out and crush his windpipe. I could have done it. I could have dropped my towel and, while he was ogling my tits, closed on him and broken his face in six places. Dug my thumbs into his eyes and not stopped until I pierced his tiny, ineffectual brain.

He was a dim-witted tool, but he was Bijan's dim-witted tool. It was easy to understand why he kept him around. He was a moron and didn't question anything. He was also in debt way farther than me and had no hope of getting out of it.

"Get out, or I'll tell Bijan."

"Bijan don't care. You're not his girl."

"*You're* going to be his girl if you don't get the fuck out of here."

It took him a long moment to register the threat to his manhood. "You're not nice."

"I can live with that."

"You should be nicer to me."

"I should be a lot of things that I'm not. Like dressed."

"I don't mind."

I stared at him. He had about fifteen seconds before I forgot who he worked for and pretended his balls were wine grapes.

Ten seconds.

Five seconds.

"I'll go." He opened the door and stepped into the hall. "You really need to loosen up, Rata."

"Go fuck yourself."

"Just thought we could have some—"

I kicked the door closed a millisecond after it would have crushed his hands on the frame. He yelped, and I heard him head away down the hall.

I leaned my back against the door, holding the towel even tighter around my chest.

I need to get the hell out of here.

The second pear turned out to be worse than the first one. I added the grocer to the sizable list of people in Roma that I didn't trust.

I threw on a fresh tank and shorts and lay on my mattress and waited for it to get late enough to fall asleep. The porous walls told me that one of my neighbors was fucking someone or something and that the other was going through some sort of hypnometh freak-out. A chorus of grunting, screaming and crying.

Someone knocked at my door.

No one knocked at my door.

"Go away, Kalb!"

Another knock. I let out a frustrated sigh and stood.

"Kalb, so help me, I will—"

"I be not Kalb, Virata."

I opened the door. It was strange to see Bijan anywhere but the ground floor. I wasn't sure I ever had. He had pulled on a pair of pants under his toga.

"You have scheduled audience… with Kalb?"

"Hardly. He walked in on me while I was showering again."

His gaze made me aware that my shirt was clinging to my damp skin. "I have made it quite clear to him that such behavior was bad form."

Bad form for the formed bad.

"I wouldn't be surprised if the *rākṣasa* had a camera hidden in there."

"I had it removed the moment it was discovered." I wanted to think that he was joking, but he clearly was not. He looked at my freshly bandaged finger. I had used a plastic knife as a splint.

"Shit, bitch. You really did fuck up your finger." Every once in a while, he slipped out of his forced person and showed a little of the Pak thug underneath the dress.

"What are you doing up here?"

"This is my house. It is not even beholden upon me to knock."

I stepped out into the hallway.

"What are you doing up here?"

He crossed his arms, content to wait until I figured it out.

"What are you doing up here, *Dominus*?"

"I have found you employment."

"Who's late this time? Is it Kateb? Last time he screamed so loud it woke up his little girl. I had to let him tuck her back in before I sliced his hamstrings."

"The deed is not for me. Word has come trickling through the labyrinth that there be a mystery patrician searching for a person of questionable citizenship and character to do violence for a handsome reward. Very handsome. I thought the prospect might interest you."

"Why me? Why not Kalb?"

"There is no hope for men like Kalb. He owes me more than coin. That Pashtun monkey shall be my slave until he breathes no more. But I am fond of you."

"You are not."

"Jupiter help me, I am." I wondered what the Muslims in Pakitown thought of their peers calling on dead Roman gods for their curses and prayers. It was getting more and more common. "It's always been my hope that you would one day find your windfall and return what is owed. I dread the day I shall have to take your final collection. Perhaps this is our chance to avoid that moment. All I require is my investment paid in its entirety."

That wasn't entirely true, Bijan got off on owning people, but in his own way he was ethical. If you paid him, he left you alone. At least until you came begging again, which most ended up doing eventually.

"What's the job?"

"The details are elusive, but I am told it will assuredly be violent."

"How violent?"

"How does one measure vio—"

"Antonius."

"The deed will be foul. Most foul."

Make dead. The job was a make dead.

"The amount of coin being proffered, Virata. It is not just enough to repay your debt to me. It is enough to *become* me."

I didn't respond. I didn't know how to.

"But you can't be me here. I'm me here."

"I'm not sure I can do that."

"I am offering you a true chance at manumission, release from the chains that bind you to my every whim.

Freedom. From me. Freedom from anyone from this day hence."

"I am not your slave, Bijan."

"In practice, if not in title."

I had killed people in the war. A lot of people. But I had decided to never do it again. Definitely not for country. And not for money.

"It could very well be the end of all your pain."

I could feel my finger throbbing. The ache ran up my arm and made my whole body sore.

One more. One more kill to stop hurting.

"Give me the info."

Bijan pulled out his mobi and tapped the screen a few times. A beat later, mine, still lying on my bed behind me, beeped to indicate a new message.

He turned to go. "You can thank me later."

I headed back into my cube.

"Rata."

I stopped before I closed the door.

"Did Kalb indeed intrude upon your body... your *privacy* this very eve?"

I nodded, said, "Good night, Dominus," and closed the door.

When I woke the next morning, I took another two (*better make it three, for the swelling*) chryo and slipped the packet in my pocket. As I was leaving, I passed Kalb in the hall. When he saw me, he averted his eyes.

His freshly blackened and bruised eyes.

PROXY

‡

III: ASH

I HAD CONVINCED MYSELF AFTER STEWING inside my cube all night that I would do it. Make dead for money. Once. Once to climb out of the hole I had dug. One murder to erase my mistakes and then some.

One last bad thing to disappoint the ghost of my father one more glorious time.

"I need a proxy," the Senator had said.

"I don't understand," I replied because I didn't. Understand. "A proxy?"

"Someone to stand for me and do what I cannot. I'm not a violent man and have no martial skills. When I was in government, peace, to me, was always the first and only answer. I never voted for anything I believed would cause anyone harm. It is just not in my nature; for the last century I have done my best to celebrate life and nullify death. To kill, to be responsible for someone being killed, it's not something I thought I'd ever desire..."

I noticed that his hand was trembling. It hadn't been when I sat down.

"But inside, right now, I am aflame. I've tried to suppress the fire. This burning... Tried to apply the virtues I've espoused my entire life to put it out. Compassion. Reason. Forgiveness. But they haven't helped. I burn hotter and brighter every day I am forced to be without her.

"More so than ever, I am glad there is no afterlife, because the idea of Amelia looking down on me from a fluffy cloud while I think and dream of nothing but doing violence in her name would break her heart. She wouldn't approve of this. 'It is not our way,' she would say. 'Move on, Caden. Live your life.' I can hear the words now in the voice that will never leave me. 'Vengeance solves nothing.' I am betraying her. I truly am. But, you see, I don't care. Not right now. All I can feel is this fucking fire."

He's talking himself out of it, I thought. I could feel the coin slipping through my fingers. And with it, my hope and my chance and my life. Falling back into the hole.

I would belong to Bijan until I was no longer useful.

And then he would kill me.

"But those vocal chords that would sing to me at night are now *ash*. The skin that after eight decades still excited me is now *ash*. The heart that pumped blood, the lungs that drew breath, the brain that loved me, all *ash*. She is as she was before birth: nothing.

"I am alive, though. I want to carry on. But I am being immolated from the inside out. There is only one way to extinguish it."

"I'm still not sure what you want from me," I said. "I can find him, maybe. Kill him, if that's what you want. But as far as your—"

"I'm not looking for justice. My wife met thousands of people in her long life, and she touched them all, but the only one who understands the girth of the hole she's left in the world is me.

"Or someone who thinks like me."

I still had no idea what he was talking about, but I was starting to get the sense I wasn't going to like it.

"I have been recording my memories for sixty years." He turned his head and pulled back the lobe of his right ear. Embedded in the flesh was a black polymer latch smaller than a thumbnail. He flipped it open, revealing a small port. "This is the access point to my memory. Inside is a high-capacity nanochip wired into my brain as a tertiary hippocampus. Everything I experience is etched on it like it would be in my natural brain, without the frustration of cell deterioration and death. It has given me complete and total recall, a memory that would have made me a *Jeopardy* champion for life. I haven't forgotten a thing in six decades."

What the hell is a Jeopardy *champion?*

"I have offered you a great deal of money, Rata, but with it comes a leap of trust on your side. If you take my offer, tonight you will travel to my lab and have your own *meccacampo* installed."

I will? I thought. I said nothing.

"It will not affect the memories you have spent thirty-eight years collecting. But it will add to them. On this piece of cyberware will be my memory of the night Amelia died."

I should have walked out after that. Should have excused myself and ran back to Pakitown and dealt with the life-threatening and oppressive but not bat-fuck insane problems I had there. But instead I sat there and let him keep talking.

Why did I let him keep talking?

"I will share with you my wife's murder and enough of our life together to understand what I have lost. What the world has lost. I need you to feel her dying in your arms. I need you to see her eyes go dark." Emotion made his voice crack. "I want to set a fire in you that will only be quenched when you find and kill the man who took her from me. From us."

He wasn't done:

"And then I want you to bring back that memory to me so I can live it."

I had shown up that morning willing to kill a man to change everything, to save myself. To completely transform the so-called life I had into something worthwhile. But what he was asking was next-level. I had had implants in the past, during the war. A tracking device just under my skin. A biotechnic rangefinder under my left eye. Automated serum injectors to help deal with pain and fatigue. I knew how to handle metagear.

The first thing I did when I left the army was have them removed. Sold them on the black market, where there was always want of hot tech like that.

What he wanted wouldn't work. The tech existed, sure. That idea was solid. Since World War V, militaries had used spies capable of photographic recall through the use of implants. And for a while, there had been a trend of wealthy men buying the memories of others and using them to experience dangerous and salacious things they didn't earn. Which was exactly what Kennedy wanted to do.

But his plan didn't account for the particulars of the user. He was making assumptions about me that I had no interest in correcting. Three million was a lot of cash.

"Five million," he said. "I can sense your doubts. The offer is now five million."

For some reason, I asked, "Why me?"

"I didn't know you existed until this morning."

"But why *me*? I can't be the only hard case you're interviewing."

"My mission to deny the ferryman can, at times, lead me down dark and unsavory paths. Not everything that I do is sanctioned, legal or, for those unenlightened who believe in such concepts, moral. There are closed-minded people who still frown upon cloning and bioengineered augmentations. Amelia and I were forced to fake our deaths in order to escape the whore-hounds of fundamentalism that were biting and slavering at our heels. Out of necessity, I have become well versed in the economics of the black market and underground, and have developed relationships. Not friendships. Even if these people did not disgust me, and they do, I am no longer a man who has need of friends. When I decided what I must do, I reached out to these... contacts and asked them to find the person I was looking for. The perfect weapon to my purpose: someone dangerous and desperate.

"I am told you are both in equal measure."

He wasn't wrong.

Five million.

"*If* I do this," I began, stressing the uncertainty, "do you want it done a certain way or do you just want it done?" I was spinning my wheels while I tried to process what he was asking.

"Lead."

"Lead?"

"I've heard there are ways."

"Ways? I'm sure there are ways, but no one can get to the States anymore, and time machines are bullshit tech-fic stuff. Can you get your hands on some sort of magic lamp?"

"This is serious to me. I need it to be serious to you."

Seriously fucked up, I thought.

"Can it be—"

"I know a guy, well, a girl," I said. "She won't be able to get one, but she'll know a guy. That guy won't either, but he'll know someone else. Eventually I'll get to someone who doesn't know a guy, but who is the guy. Getting caught with a piece like that, though, is big trouble, Senator."

"European weapons are too quiet. Too subtle. I want loud. I want brash. I want messy."

"Dead is dead. I don't know why you'd want to take the risk."

"Call me old-fashioned."

"Let's call you American."

He shrugged, agreeing, but didn't change his mind. "When the deed is done, we will remove the implant. Wipe the slate. Heal the flesh. You will go on as if nothing has happened."

"Except for the money."

"Except for that," he said.

How would I do it? Where would I start?

"Do you know who this guy is? His name?"

He shook his head. "I saw his face. And so shall you."

"Do you know why he did it?"

He picked up the tin of candies, the Bombas Bocas, again, "I have lived long enough to make a hundred enemies, but I care nothing about the why. I'm sure this young man had his reasons. They don't mean anything to me. I just want to see him die."

"You wouldn't rather do it yourself?"

"I am afraid that I would balk at the moment."

"It's not an easy thing to make dead," I said. "Especially if you've never done it before."

The first time I had pulled the trigger and seen someone drop, I had cried. The second time hadn't been much better. By my third day in Saudi, I had stopped counting.

"But I need to experience it so I can move on. I am already the oldest man alive, and I have no plans on lying down anytime soon. I can't go on with these flames consuming my every moment. I have become a slave of vengeance. I want to see, feel, it when you put the gun in his mouth. Please keep your eyes open when you do it. I want to see the look on his face right before he doesn't have one anymore. I need you to set me free."

"When it's done, you'll take it out?"

He nodded. Thinking he had me.

"Wear the chip. Kill the guy."

"That's it."

"And then walk away," I said.

"As far as your legs will carry you."

"Ten million." I didn't remember telling my mouth to say the words, but there they were. He tossed another one of those fucking candies into his mouth.

"Deal."

Before I knew it, I had shaken his feeble old wrist, Orso had come in and escorted me out, and I was back in the foyer with the six armed men. Orso handed me a narrow yellow envelope. I looked inside. Cash chips. Large denominations.

"Expenses," Orso explained. I hadn't had that much money at one time in years. "Will it be enough?"

"The weapon he wants will be more," I guessed. I really had no idea.

"How much more?"

"I'll have to ask around."

"Come back to me when you know."

I nodded.

"I will pick you up this evening at the end of the F Line."

There had been a time when the trains went all the way to the airport, but Fiumicino was now a deserted maze of runways and terminals. The Muratella station was as far southwest as the train would run. Past that, it was gray and empty.

"Half past twenty."

"How do I know I can trust him? Trust you?" I asked.

"You don't. If you are unsure, I believe we can find someone equally dangerous and desperate. Perhaps even more so." He started to reach for the envelope. I gripped it tighter, pulled it into my chest.

"No, no. I'm your guy. This is *my* horrible mistake to make."

"Do you partake of any illicit substances?"

The question took me off guard. I hoped it didn't show on my face.

"Alcohol. Narcotics. Wicked, hypno, ice, junk?" he asked.

"My landlord is a bit of a dazer," I deflected. "Grows green plants on his windowsill."

The man was humorless, "Please do not have anything in your system when I pick you up this evening."

"No problem."

✝

In the past, it would have been a problem. But I wasn't lying. Not this time.

I stepped out of the hotel, past the armed guards, out into the street and popped two (*better make it three, for the buzz*) painkillers. I had fifty thousand yuros in my pocket. For a moment, I thought about being satisfied with the advance and not coming back. But fifty grand was nothing; ten million was everything.

Like it or not, and I surely did not, this was my big play. Nothing like this would ever happen again, of that I was sure. A chance like this. It was reckless and foolish. Maybe suicidal. But if I didn't take the risk, I would be dead anyway.

Ten million.

I messaged Alba with what I wanted her to bring. She said to meet her at our usual spot behind the Cavour Metro-Grav station, just on the edge of The Orphanage. Via Cavour was as far south as Alba would come. Her dislike of Pakitown was absolute.

It was a doable walk. No need to take the grav.

Ten million.

It wasn't war and it wasn't self-defense and it wasn't justice. It was revenge, but more than that, it was murder. Could I swallow that sin and keep it down? It wouldn't be alone, that was for sure. What was another gram or two of poison? It would make me sick, I knew, for a bit, while it rocketed through my system, but it would fade. I had spent six years in uniform building immunity to its long-term effects.

Ten million.

I was having a hard time wrapping my head around what that much coin could and would mean. No more Bijan,

✦

that was obvious. No more cube. No more Kalb. I would never have to borrow another dime or break another bone. I'd buy all new gear. A current-gen sporty e-cart. A house, maybe. A house with hot fucking water. It could be in Roma, but it didn't have to be. I could go anywhere. Paris. London. Even the States, if I could find a good smuggler.

I could go home.

Did I want to go home?

I hadn't wasted any time thinking about it. Kolkata. It had seemed impossible. According to the army, I was dead, my body rotting in a mass grave somewhere in the hills south of Neu Berlin. By now, just bones. My family thought I was gone, and they were better off. It was better than knowing their daughter was a traitor and a coward. What would happen if I walked in my mother's door one day? Would she embrace me? Spit in my face? Recoil in fear at the *bhūta* that had stepped out of the mists and into her home?

There was a not-bad I in Piazza Suburra across from the grav stop, but Alba knew I didn't meet in cafes. Or restaurants. Or snack bars. No coffee, no food. It implied a level of time commitment that I never wanted to make when doing business. Some sort of conversation. I didn't have the patience for that.

I waited across from the I, though, in a small nook next to the portal to the grav station. It was a gross little alley, and I was sure it had been the setting for countless sexual transgressions and probably a few murders.

As much as I didn't want to meet in the I, the fact that I hadn't eaten all day made me consider rethinking my policy.

Alba emerged from the station. She was thirty, tall and slender. Black hair with early streaks of gray. She had two fairly prominent scars—one across each cheek—that

I had always wondered about. But I knew asking would make it sound like I cared and open me up to the whole sad story of Alba's life. I wasn't curious enough to sit through that work of Roman tragedy.

The alley was claustrophobic and trash-strewn. I could hear children playing nearby.

Alba slung the bag off her shoulder and unzipped it. "How you have you been?"

"I honestly don't know." It was not a lie.

"At least you're flush. Bijan know you got enough cash to come calling on me?"

"What he don't know, you know?"

"I do. What happened to your finger?"

The wrap had grown dirty throughout the day; I didn't want to know what it looked like inside. It still hurt like hell. Maybe a few more tabs of chryo would help.

"What *you* don't know, you know?"

She fished into her bag and pulled out a 78-S mobiterm, identical to the one I saw Hala with the day before. I took the device into my hand, feeling its weight. It had mass; its finish was glossy and without flaws. My old rig seemed even more dated and broken in comparison.

"It's good to go?"

Alba nodded, "Just use the same GhostPass you've been logging, unless that one's been giving you trouble. I got a new batch cooked up."

Always trying to sell me one more thing. "No. My Ghost is steady."

The GhostNet was the underground, encrypted, untraceable and highly illegal parallel network running alongside the city's mainstream Ether. It was built by hundreds of privately built and maintained transmitters hidden throughout the city, in some places more than others. It was the only info-channel in all of Pakitown, but in the rest of Roma, the signal could get really spotty. But, unlike the overly policed public Ether, the Ghost was entirely safe to use. *You can't track a ghost*, was the saying. No one who logged on was anyone. You had a contact number, but that number wasn't registered, not assigned a name.

I handed her five thousand-yuro chips. She cocked an eyebrow. "I don't make change."

"I don't want change. It's a finder's fee."

"Have I found something?"

"Not yet."

"What do you need?"

"I need a gun."

"A stinger or a solo?"

"I need something you can't provide."

"There's nothing I can't get my claws on, you know that. You want retail, or you want a hack?"

"I need American steel."

She whistled, shaking her head. "You don't want to be fucking around with that. You need something lethal, I'll get you a nice hacked Spitfire Elite. Antiprint coating. Untraceable."

"Not good enough."

"You get caught with a Yankee piece, you go away for a long time."

I dealt out another chip and handed it to her.

"Can you?"

"I appreciate the coin, but it don't make the idea any less crazy. A good hack will get them just as dead."

"Not the right kind of dead."

"What have you gotten yourself into?"

Something stupid, I thought. "None of your business," I said.

"I don't deal in that type of gear, sexy. You know I'm not that dumb."

"But you know someone who is."

She looked away. Yeah, she did.

"Who?"

Her voice dropped to a whisper, even though we were alone, "I don't know him, but I've heard things."

"Can you get to him?"

"Eventually. Maybe."

"Ask around."

"I've heard he's a little dramatic."

"Please."

"He's a frog."

"I'll manage. Set it up?"

"If I can. No promises." She pocketed the money. "You come here just for a recommendation?"

"And the mobi."

"Anything else?"

I thought about it. I didn't know what it was going to take to find this guy, but chances were it would get rough. "I'll take a hold-out. Retail. Discreet."

She seemed disappointed that I was talking gear and not something else. "Spare batpack?"

Again with one more thing, though in this case, it wasn't a terrible idea. "Two."

She smiled at me, took a step closer. "You want to come by my place to pick it up?"

"No chance."

"You know we'll have fun."

"You'll have fun. I'll have regrets." The memory of her hands on my body aroused me for a moment, but I couldn't entertain the thought. She nodded grimly and took a step back, her eyes on her boots. Sometimes I forgot other people had feelings, even low-life hard cases like Alba. Like me.

I didn't apologize.

"So we'll just meet here tomorrow. Same time." Alba seemed hurt. She was someone who, despite her tough bitch appearance and attitude and reality, got attached quickly. After our last round of adventures, I had decided to cut it off. She had begun to look at me in a way that let me know she cared more about me than I did about her, which was to say she cared at all. It wasn't personal. She was sexy, and I liked her fine. But caring? I didn't do caring.

"Yeah. Thanks," I said.

"Maybe I'll have word on the guy by then."

"That's my girl." It was something I had called her in better times, and I immediately regretted resurrecting it. So did she.

"You want my old mobi?" I asked. "Sell it to the next sucker?"

"That thing? You'd have to be a real idiot to buy a piece of shit like that."

With a forced grin, she went back into the station.

There was no such thing as empathy, at least not for me. My understanding of someone's emotions was always going to be tempered and twisted through my own. It just wasn't part of my default load-out. I felt things but couldn't feel other people's things. And I didn't really want to. Why take on outside pain when I had enough of my own? There wasn't anything to gain by it.

Which was why I doubted Kennedy's entire scheme. I would do the job—wear the chip, kill the guy—if I could. But I was sure he'd be disappointed when I brought the memory back to him. I'd seen the look in his eyes when he talked about Amelia. It was not unlike the looks Alba had given me.

But no cerebral tech-dump was going to change how much I did not give a shit.

By the time the Senator knew that, though, I'd be paid.

Wear the chip.

Kill the guy.

Walk away rich.

That night I took the F to the end of the line. There had been a few hard cases on the train tormenting other passengers, but they ignored me.

Dangerous and desperate. It must show.

Orso was waiting outside the station, leaning on his cane. He led me to a luxury e-cart and held open the door for me. First time that had ever happened in my life. It was a long, black vehicle, with a retro form factor intended to imitate a twentieth-century limousine. I sat down in the cavernous back cabin. I could have stretched all the way out and not touched either wall.

After Orso settled into the driver's seat, the cart hummed to life and we sped forward.

We sped along the road running next to the grav-tracks. It quickly fell into disrepair from that point on. As the rail fell to ruin, so did the communities around it. Hotels, commercial spaces, apartment and office buildings, all lay dormant and crumbling. As the years went on, the sprawling city of Roma had contracted nearly back to its Imperial borders. This region, this desolate area, had once been as much a part of Roma as the City Center. But no longer.

Orso steered the cart up and around a clover-shaped ramp, bringing us onto the old *autostrada.* The six-lane freeway was split down the middle by a median, a low wall

†

with several large gaps that made it a less than effective barrier after all this time.

My finger was throbbing still. I couldn't remember how long it had been since I had taken some chryo. I took two (*better make it three, for a pick-me-up*) more tabs.

The closer we got to the airport, the direr the landscape became. I had never been out that far. The empty expressway, once a major traffic artery, was now bloodless and shriveled. The quiet and the dark made it feel like I was on a path from which there was no return.

Maybe there wasn't.

After ten minutes, we came upon the airport. Driving into Fiumicino was like plunging into a black hole. Darker than dark. An abandoned little city of rubble and junk.

We soared across what was left of the old tarmac, which was even more cratered and pockmarked than the *autostrada,* guided by starlight and the cart's powerful headlamps. I couldn't see anything out of my window in the back; we may as well have been traveling through the middle of the Earth.

We stopped. I waited as Orso got out, came around and opened my door. I stepped out into the dark and cold. The limo had come to a halt outside of a giant steel building, lit up by our headlights. It was bigger than my apartment building. Across the top were large, faded blue letters: E L T A.

Standing in front of the hangar, shielding their eyes from the headlights' glare, were Senator Kennedy and another man. He was a Chinese. Short, but solidly built. Maybe fifty. His head shaved and showing stubble that betrayed his receding hairline. Wearing a white lab coat.

As I approached, Kennedy offered a hand. I shook it. He smiled nervously.

58

PROXY

‡

"A billion pennies for your thoughts."
Oh, brother.
We went inside.

PROXY
‡

IV: MECCACAMPO

KENNEDY TOLD ME THAT THE CHINESE'S NAME WAS JAO and that he'd be doing the cutting. He introduced me as "the patient," but I told him I preferred the title "sinner-for-hire." The 'plantjock himself said nothing, just scanned my body like a tailor sizing for a suit. The pervasive florescence hurt my eyes after the darkness outside. My vision adjusted, and I took in the vast space in which the Senator had built his laboratory. I was disappointed. In my head, I had conjured up a facility straight out of the tech-fic stories my father had loved so much. I wanted walls of interactive living glass, giant cylinders of bubbling red and blue fluids, and artificially intelligent automatons doing the heavy lifting. Instead I got rolling frames of thick white curtains, five meters high, arranged on the floor to create a maze of rooms and hallways. It was quiet except for the hum of appliances and lights, and smelled of chemicals. After the makeshift walls, it was at least forty empty meters up to the roof and skylights. An awful waste of space.

Behind the drapes hid a life's work, they explained to me. Kennedy's slate of projects that he hoped would allow him to live forever. Printers constructing new organs, one layer of tissue at a time. Banks of rodent cages for testing steroids, serums and supplements. Experimental stasis beds. Freezers full of cellular samples and plasma. Two fully geared surgical suites.

"We designed it to be mobile, so we could pick up and stay ahead of the authorities of the unenlightened," Kennedy said in defense of the cursory nature of his lab.

"How many times have you moved it?"

"Since we settled in Roma? Not once. We've been here over thirty years." His voice echoed within the walls of the massive structure.

There were four of us until Orso excused himself and disappeared into the transitory labyrinth. We stood there in awkward silence. The expatriate American Senator, the mysterious Chinese cyberdoc and their Bengali guinea pig, soon-to-be assassin and avenging proxy.

"Shall we begin?" asked the old man.

I let out a long, non-committal sigh, "Yeah…"

They showed me to a small partition near the operating rooms. I pulled back the flap, ducked in and found a green gown folded neatly on a metal table. In the corner stood a portable acoustic shower capsule, the kind the army would haul from bivouac to bivouac. Soldiers and officers tended to care little about hygiene while at the front, but chemical and biological attacks were always possible, and nothing got a man cleaner than an ultrasonic scrubbing, even if it was far less satisfying than steaming water.

"Is this necessary?" I called out loud enough to carry over the walls.

"It is a simple procedure, but Doctor Jao likes to do everything possible to prevent infection. This is your brain we're talking about," Kennedy replied with a hint of patriarchal condescension.

Says the man who is paying to screw around with it.

"Is he really a doctor?"

"In practice, if not in title."

Uh-huh.

"I just showered yesterday. Got a whole three minutes of almost hot water."

"Indulge us."

I pulled off my clothes and draped them over the room's sole chair. I shivered, and bumps emerged and spread in waves across my skin. They kept the place cold. I stepped into the shower and turned it on.

The pulses came at me from all sides of the chamber. My body began to shake and then ramped up to a full vibration. The sensation triggered memories from the service that, for a change, were not entirely unwelcome. Of the times between combat. When things were quiet. Fragments of conversations. Men acting like men and women acting like men. People I would march with into the meat grinder where they'd die beside me.

I was more nervous about the procedure than I thought I would be. Every trooper in the Indian army got a session with the scalpel before being deployed. There was still a scar on the back of my neck from the Analgesic/Stimulant Injector System, and sometimes I could still feel the satellite chip in my right forearm, even though it hadn't been there for years. The rangefinder had been external but still grafted onto my skin and anchored to the bone of my eye socket.

But that had been for my country, and that Virata had been far more trusting than the one currently being pummeled in the acoustic cleanser. The generals, the politicians, they must have known what they were doing, right? *Right.* It turned out they weren't any more trustworthy than a crazy old man and his shady underground meta surgeon.

The dirt rattled off me, grime I didn't know was there until it fell to the capsule floor. I pulled my hair out of its tail and shook it loose. The tension in my muscles slipped away; my pain faded, the broken finger forgotten for a beautiful minute or two.

How long will they let me stay in here? I thought. *I could do this all night.*

Like it had been listening to my thoughts, the power shut off. I considered trying to turn it back on for another go. Part of me expected Kalb to be there when I stepped out, but when I did, I was gratefully alone. I looked at my newly polished body, half expecting my skin to be a shade lighter. It had been a long time since I had been absolutely clean. I felt raw, exposed and, even after I slipped the gown over my head, naked.

When I stepped into the operating room, I had put my jacket on over the gown. It looked stupid, but even a tough girl like me needed a little comfort sometimes. Since I was seven thousand kilometers from my mother, my jump coat would have to do.

Jao saw me and launched into a tirade of Mandarin. The only word I was able to make out was *mhai*, many times, over and over again, "no."

"Mhai mhai mhai!"

Kennedy turned to me. "When was the last time that rag of an overcoat was washed, Miss Das?"

I pulled up my collar and sniffed it. "I don't know. What year did the last war start?"

"Jao would prefer it if you—"

"It's for good luck."

"Luck? You told me you didn't buy into fairy tales."

I shrugged. "It stays."

Jao threw up his hands in frustration. The doctor understood Italian, at least, even if he didn't feel the need to speak it.

"If it gives me an infection and kills me, I promise I won't come back and haunt you."

"I don't believe in ghosts." Kennedy took every opportunity he got to remind you of his complete lack of faith in everything. Like the people that had chased him from the States, he was a zealot. He just preached from the other side of the pulpit.

"Then you've got nothing to worry about."

After a few more angry exchanges, Jao gave up the fight. I was being stupid, I knew, but I was interested in seeing what their relationship was like. It was time to make another demand, "You're not putting me out."

Kennedy cocked an eyebrow, but he did not seem surprised. "Staying awake through the procedure could be most uncomfortable."

"So would my foot up your cunt, but it's up to you."

Kennedy smiled, almost wistfully. "My wife, for all of her delicacies and refinement, had a profanely wicked vocabulary. When angered, her tongue could cleave granite."

"She sounds like kind of a bitch."

"You remind me of her," he said.

"She sounds like a giant bitch."

"You'll know soon enough."

At one end of the operating table was a rig to support a prostrate patient's neck and head. "There will be no need for general anesthesia. As non-intrusive as this will be, a local will suffice. You won't feel a thing. Please. Lie down."

I crawled onto the table and settled onto my stomach. It took a few wiggles to get my breasts in a position where they weren't getting squished. Before I could complain about the cold the open gown was letting up my ass, someone draped a blanket over my lower half. I settled my face into the scaffolding, a rubber bumper supporting my forehead. All I could see was concrete and a few stray shadows.

"You've had implants before?" Kennedy asked.

"Yeah."

"Comm unit? Positioning?"

"An ASIS and a rangefinder unit too. Standard combat suite."

"Standard for a valuable soldier," Kennedy said. "But not for the common fodder."

I could feel a presence standing to my right and slightly behind. Intense cold exploded behind my ear as Jao sprayed on the deadener. A gloved hand came into my line of sight and pushed two quick absorbing tabs towards my mouth.

"For all over." It was the first Italian words I had heard Jao speak. "Take these. Make you dead all over."

Poor choice of words, but I knew what he meant. I opened wide, and he slipped them under my tongue. "Hey, doc," I said. "My left pinky is broken real bad. If you have time, think you can get to that?"

There was no answer. I hadn't expected one.

I heard metal scraping on concrete. Kennedy entered from my periphery dragging a chair. Before he sat, he pressed into my hand a compact Scorp-Tech hold-out stinger. I wrapped my fingers around it.

"I know you do not trust us. If you feel at any moment that your life is in danger, you have my permission to shoot us. But please spare Orso, if you can. He has children back in China."

I looked at the gun. It drifted out of focus and then snapped back to sharp. "You never had any?" I asked.

"Any what?"

"Children."

Now sitting, facing me, he shook his head.

"My dad thought he was going to live forever through his children."

"I'm a more literal type of man than your father."

I had to strain my eyes up to look at him.

"This is not going to be pleasant," he said, changing tones.

"You said I wouldn't feel a thing. I already don't." I really didn't. My whole body felt like it was shutting down. I could feel my fingers already losing their grip on the pistol.

"There will be no physical pain, I promise. But I'm afraid you will feel a great many things. What I'm giving you is a gruesome weight to carry. I need you to be prepared for what is about to happen to you."

"I'll be okay," I said. "I can handle it."

"You will *not* be okay. Not inside. I will *never* be okay. As far as 'handling' it..."

My vision went black for a second, then recovered. Something was wrong. Something was going wrong.

Oh, no.

Kennedy unbuttoned the cuff of his shirt and rolled up his sleeve. On his wrist were three vertical scars. They were pink. Freshly carved and still healing. "Three weeks ago, I tried to take my own life." He ran his middle finger down the raised tracks. "More than a hundred years after I vowed to never die, I cut myself and attempted to lie down for the last time. My major veins and arteries had been replaced with phospholose tubes. It was an effort to open them. They were implanted to prevent that sort of thing."

I was sure what he was saying was important, but I really didn't care. My head was swimming. I felt wrong. "When are we going to start?"

His eyes looked to Jao, then back to me. "The procedure has already begun."

"Oh. That's... disturbing." I really hadn't felt a thing.

Shit. Please tell me I didn't do this. Am I really that stupid?

"I could easily replace the skin on my wrists to erase the damage, but I won't," he said, pulling his sleeve back down. "I will wear these scars to remind me of the time, the one time, I gave up on life.

"That is how *I* handled it. Only time will tell about you." His attention shifted to Jao.

I wanted to fall asleep.

Don't fall asleep.

That Orso guy's going to kick my ass for this.

I tried to catch the Senator's gaze, "What's going on back there?"

He didn't take his eyes off of Jao as he spoke, "Now that the incision has been made, he will guide a telescoping nanowire harmlessly though your gray matter until it finds purchase in the seahorse-shaped segment of your brain called the hippocampus. It is in this place, along with its twin on the other side of your head, where you store and re-access the memories of the things that happen to you. Good times. Bad times. Movies you saw. Books you read. Your tenth birthday. Your first lover."

"Hey, Jao, while you're back there, can you erase the battle of Neu Berlin for me? Or my first lover. Equally horrifying."

Kennedy shook his head. "I'm afraid we can't help you with that. We cannot interpret memories. We can record them, like data, for they are nothing but electrical impulses, but the codec the rest of your brain uses to translate the biological ones and zeros is a mystery to us."

"That's alright. Who would want to forget all that suffering and carnage?"

"Neu Berlin was traumatic for you, was it?"

"You should meet the lover."

I'm giving you an order, soldier: don't fall asleep!

"The device we are implanting, everything it records is time-coded. I know the time at which my Amelia was murdered. Your *meccacampo* will contain a block of time with that moment as its center."

Things began to grow dark. I was falling asleep. His words became a jumble in my head.

"There... other moments... make you... her loss... my archives... cannot... on a term screen... long as I know when... they happened... pass them... you."

"That's... nice..."

Don't fall asleep!

My eyes were drooping. I tried to smile at him, but I'm sure I just let drool run down my chin instead. I concentrated and pushed words past my seemingly bloated tongue, "It may not have been the... uh... smartest move... triple-dose the chryo... on my way here... not mixing... uh... well with... other... but my finger... finger... really... hurts..."

"Jao?" Kennedy stood and vanished from my sight. He seemed genuinely worried.

"Finger... fucking Rida..."

The stinger clattered to the ground. I hadn't felt myself let go of it.

"Stupid. I'm going to... to go... go... go sleep now..."

I was vaguely aware of voices and activity behind me. Kennedy yelled, "What's going on, Jao?"

I tried to hold the doors, Caden old boy, but this gravlev is leaving the station.

I passed out thinking that it would have been funny if, after all this, I had managed to kill myself both by and because of my own hand.

Hysterical.

I could stay in here and die. I want to stay in here and die. If I do nothing, I'll bleed out. Or the smoke will take me. Worst case, I'll starve. I don't want to go back out there. In here it's warm. It's dark. Safe.

Despite deciding to give up, I push up on the wreckage that's pinning me. I strain against the steel and heavy poly. It groans and cracks. I feel my muscles stretch and pull, maybe even tear. The pain is blinding, but I don't need my eyes. I just need my strength.

People are always surprised by my strength.

I keep telling myself that I don't care, that it's okay to rot in here, under the carcass of this burned-out gravtrak. But I push until the debris starts to give, to shift. I shove again, one last big effort, and I'm free. It feels like it takes an hour to get to my feet. A piece of shrapnel has dug into my right thigh, barely missing the artery. I reach up and feel the gash on my forehead. The blood is dry, a sticky sheet of rust coating my skin. The transport, the one I was traveling in just minutes ago, is now a scattered mess of metal and circuitry and bodies.

Bodies.

There were eight of us in the back of this gravtrak. And a driver. We'd been sent on a sortie to knock out a Saudi relay station. We took out the personal, crashed the term, brought down the satellite and were on our way back to Neu Berlin.

And then...

And then?

I don't know what happened then. Something blew us up. Mine. Drone. Ambush. Something. It doesn't matter. It was loud and hot and frightening. Fire ripped through the hull, tearing it apart. I don't remember anyone screaming. There hadn't been time. They were alive, and now they're dead. They don't have to worry anymore. About dying. About killing. They never have to go back. They're all free.

Except for me. I'm not dead.

I have to go back. And they'll make me fight again. My wounds aren't bad enough to get sent home. These days, these desperate dog days, in this conflict of unholy attrition, no one's wounds are that bad.

Only the dead get to leave.

Only the dead get to—

I woke up in a bed somewhere else in the complex. It was dark. I was still in the gown, under a blanket. I didn't see my jacket anywhere. I felt great. No haze. My head didn't hurt. My neck was a little stiff, but from what I could tell, nothing had changed. There weren't any memories in my head that weren't my own. Not that I could find. Had they aborted? Did my absent-minded chryo popping screw everything up?

"Welcome back from the brink."

‡

Kennedy sat on a chair in the corner. Jao stood beside him.

"Did I die?"

"Nearly."

"How long was I out?"

"Sixteen hours."

Chutya!

"What happened after?"

"Jao was prepared for any possible emergency. Once you were stable, we finished the procedure. As well as some other things."

"I better still be a virgin."

"We took the liberty of installing a new ASIS unit in the back of your neck."

It was the last thing they should have done, but I couldn't tell them that. With all this that I had already gone through, I didn't want to let on that they had made a huge mistake.

"And a tracker in me somewhere, no doubt," I guessed. "But you aren't going to tell about that. We didn't agree to—"

"I am investing a lot of money in you. I want you well taken care of. The implant will also monitor your levels in order to avoid incidents such as the one we had last night." The last sentence was spoken with polite hostility.

"I fucked up."

"You fucked up. Best to not do that again while in my employ."

If you wanted someone who wouldn't fuck things up, you shouldn't have hired a fuck-up, I thought. "Yes, sir," I said. "I lost track of how much chryo I was taking, that's all. But in my defense, my finger really—" I held up my left hand. My finger didn't hurt anymore. It was straight. It wasn't purple. I wagged it, cracked the knuckle.

"Jao, you are a miracle worker."

The Chinese smiled. "In practice, if not in title."

"Well, I hate to break it to you guys, for all the work you did and all, but I don't think it stuck. I don't know anything now that I didn't know yesterday, except maybe to stop ignoring recommended dosages."

Jao stepped forward and produced a corked glass vial half-filled with brown and white grains of something. "The most reliable way to access our memories is by stimulating the senses. When you pass a food joint in The Orphanage, does the smell remind you of anything?"

"Home. My mother."

"This," he held up the vial, "is a unique blend of salts and aromatics. Tomorrow, when you are ready to begin, unplug the bottle and inhale deeply. Then, I promise, you will know what 'stuck' and what did not."

I took the vial. Looked at it closely, shaking its contents. "You're a lot more comfortable talking to a woman once you've rooted around in her brain a little, aren't you, Jao?"

"I do not speak idly."

"That makes one of us." I looked at Kennedy. "When do I check in?"

"When it is done. I do not want to see you until then."

"I need money for the gun."

"Have you tracked one down?"

"I'm close," I lied. But I was close-*er*.

"Orso will take care of that. The less contact I have with you the better. I will not live out my last days in prison."

‡

I sat up straighter in the bed. My clothes were stacked neatly on a chair. But something was missing. "Where's my jump jacket?"

"We washed it."

"Gross."

"When you had your ASIS unit before, what was the interface?" Jao asked me.

"Forearm term."

"This one is synapse-controlled. I will teach you the mental commands."

It was much more advanced gear than the chem injector I had been given in the army. Five different commands. Two types of analgesic. Three stimulants. "It won't let you overdose," Jao told me.

"You're never going to let me forget that, are you?"

He handed me back to Orso. The cart ride back to Muratella was quiet. I had been at the lab through night, and the sun was already setting on the next one. I had been worried that my jacket would reek of chemicals and disinfectant. But it was worse: there was no odor at all. I felt behind my ear. Smooth. The synthskin was flawless. I twirled the vial around in my freshly healed hand. My doubts were not gone, but I was curious. I also wasn't tired. I had been asleep, nearly dead, for the better part of a day. I didn't want to wait until morning. I wanted to get started.

Tonight.

Orso dropped me off at the station without a word. Now that the guinea had been pigged, there wasn't any more reason to be polite, I guessed. I didn't blame him. The next gravlev arrived five minutes after I reached the platform. It emptied out, being the end of the line, and I was alone in my car. The train lifted and accelerated. It was going to be a long ride back to The Esquilino.

I uncorked the salts and took a big whiff. The contents smelled of flowers and the sea and...

And...

And...

Amelia. Oh, God, no. My Amelia.

It wasn't like a film. Not like a dream. Things didn't play out in front of me like a story. They rushed at me all at once. No sequence or order. Straight data dump. I experienced. I knew.

I remembered.

On her hundredth birthday, I give her a bicycle. She at first thinks it a joke, but I drag her out into the courtyard. I hold the bars steady while she straddles the seat, grasping onto my shoulder for balance.

"Put your feet on the pedals."

"Caden, honestly."

I look her in the eyes. "I won't let you fall."

I guide her as she pedals. We have both just had hip upgrades, and it is easier than she thought it was going to be. We pick up speed. "Are you ready?" I ask.

"Don't let go. Don't let go!" She pleads like the little girl she once must have been.

And of course, I do. Let go. She yells at me and calls me a cocksucker but keeps pedaling, and soon she has done three laps around the courtyard. I watch with the proud joy of a father. She steers right at me, giggling, and doesn't pull the handbrakes until the last second. The bike slides to a halt, the front tire stopping between my legs. I hold it steady while she climbs off, comes around and kisses me.

✝

I see without seeing, but I know what he looks like. The man. Her killer. Every freckle, crevice and stray whisker.

Our first day in Roma is not my first day in Roma, but it is hers. The wonder in her eyes and the enchantment in her smile as she takes it in fill me with hope. We are no longer nationless fugitives. Not the renegade doctor and disgraced politician. We are simply us, Amelia and Virata. Our love has never been stronger. We are dead and more alive than ever.

Not Virata. Caden.

I hear without hearing, but I know there was a rasp in her final breaths.

She stands above me next to the operating table, my hand in hers, as Jao begins to administer the sedative. I will be asleep in a few moments. When I wake, I will have a new high-filtration liver. If it works, she will be next. We have both had hundreds of procedures, but every time, she stands with me as I'm going out. I always do the same for her. It is the part of the project that we hate the most.

I've battled insomnia my entire life. Falling asleep. It must be what dying feels like. Anesthesia is as close to that as I ever want to get.

As I begin to fade, she sings to me, like she always does. An old British standard. Older than her. Older than me:

"Maybe I just want to fly.
I want to live, I don't want to die.
Maybe I just want to breathe.
Maybe I just don't believe.
Maybe you're the same as me.
We see things they'll never see…"

Before all goes black, I sing the last line of the chorus along with her in my head:

"You and I are going to live forever."

I feel without touching, but I know the pavement on which she died was cold, her skin dry, the blood warm and slick.

I remember the man in white standing in front of me like a ghost in the darkness.

I remember him pointing his weapon at me.

I remember waking up and realizing she was gone.

Amelia.

I remember my Amelia.

"Are you alright?"

The woman's voice startled me. The train was full of people. I had no idea how far up the line we were. Beside me sat a chubby woman in a billowy floral print dress. She looked at me with genuine concern.

"Are you alright? You're crying."

It was only then I felt the dampness on my cheeks.

When I spoke my voice cracked, "No. I'm not alright."

She took my hand. "Has something happened?"

I nodded. More tears were coming.

"My wife has been murdered," I said.

She didn't know what to say to that. How could she?

"And I'm going to find the man who did it."

PROXY
‡

V: THE BLOOD OF ITALY

I WAS AFLAME.

Before I knew her, loved her and lost her, I had never cared for anyone or anything enough to understand. I had said goodbye to family with few tears. Watched scores of compatriots die on the battlefield for reasons that were, to us at least, unknown. But the love I felt for Amelia was so pure and strong and right and true, and her absence painted a viscous coat of dark red over everyone, everything. The anger was nothing new to me, but the magnitude of it was. The burning core that spawned it, coupled with the deep-down certainty of how to make it stop, created in me a rage like nothing I had ever felt. And now that I had, I immediately didn't want to.

Okay, old man, I thought. *I get it. I had no idea. But now I know. I understand.*

Let's go get the chodu.

That night I sat on my bed with my new mobi and the salts. The memories were there, but each whiff from the vial made them stronger. Occasional tears would land on the screen of my term as I worked, and I would wipe them away. As sad as I was, I learned to use the rage to focus me. I tried to isolate the important details:

The gun. I didn't know the model, but I could see it. It was large and seemed even larger when pointed at my face. But it had been shoddily modded. The fact that the Senator was still breathing proved that. It was not easy to find the balance between efficiency and lethality in a weapon that was not built to make dead. Not everyone had skills like Alba.

The nervous, sweaty man. Thanks to the perfect details stored on the *meccacampo*, everything was crystal clear. He wasn't older than twenty-five. White, probably but not necessarily Italian. Clean-shaven but with shaggy blonde hair not entirely contained by the hat. His face was soft with very few strong angles. The nose was a little broader than he probably liked. It had been too dark to see the color of his eyes, but they were light and framed by long pretty lashes.

I used the nail of my thumb to sketch out a rough portrait of the man on my mobi's touch screen. I had shown some aptitude for art as a child but had never developed it. The result of my efforts proved that. I tried several times before getting something that vaguely worked, but the image in my head was so much stronger than the loose portrait that ended up on the screen. I got it as close as I could and hit "store," planning to get back to it.

His clothes. Why would someone committing a crime at night dress mostly in white, from his shoes to his gloves to his scarf and hat? His jacket was blue, but it had been shiny and shimmered in the streetlights. How could he hope to disappear when dressed that? Maybe he was delusional, fancying himself an avenging angel or ghost. Was he making a statement? It could have been unpremeditated. A crime of impulse, and that was just the way he dressed. Or maybe…

Or maybe it was so anyone who saw him would fixate on it. Make the first thing one would notice when looking at him be the thing he could easily change. It was his mask. The whole thing. His way of obscuring his face without instantly making him look like a criminal with a bandana across his face. It was too bad for him he attacked a man with absolute recall. I remembered his face better than I remembered my father's.

The loot. The two mobis had undoubtedly been sold, scrubbed and hacked by now. Untraceable. The cash was spent. But the necklace. Platinum. A unique design with unusual contents. A hockshoppe would only take something that pricey if they knew they could sell it, which probably made the list of places to look shorter. I'd ask the Vulture the next day when I was getting my bike back.

I knew I wasn't going to sleep. I stared up at the ceiling and plunged into my new memories, only coming up for air when the feelings got too intense. Each time the sights, sounds and smells were just as vivid. By morning I had taught myself to tuck them away, at least a little bit. My military-taught mental conditioning serving me well. But it, she, was constantly with me, like Kennedy had planned. The sadness. The anger. The fear. But I had to be able to function. I had a job to do.

I was out of the building early, long before Bijan or Kalb or anyone else was up, and got to the hockshoppe on Via Bonorati just as the automatic shutter lifted. I came into Isra's dark cave of outcast trash.

In the sea of junk that passed for her inventory was the one piece that always stood out to me: a chest of drawers made of a strong synthetic wood, taller than me. It had once been stained black but had faded to an uneven gray. Its golden adornments were in similar disrepair, tarnished and dull. It was an unremarkable piece, or would have been, if not for the carvings. On each side was an image of Ganesh, the elephant-headed god of Indian myth. The carvings were ornate, made with skill and, even though time had chipped away at some of the craftsmanship, beautiful. Every time I walked into Isra's, which had been dozens of times during my years in Roma, it had been there. I found the presence of such an obvious piece of Hindi art being openly displayed in Isra's Pakitown hockshoppe funny and confounding. Who had sold it to her? Who the fuck was ever going to buy it?

The old woman was at the counter, picking at her breakfast of aaloo paratha and coffee. She saw that it was me and grunted, shaking her head. "Not buying today."

"You're always buying."

"Not selling anything so not buying anything. Simple math. Simple math."

"You always were good at math. How much to get my bike back?"

"Which one yours?"

I pointed to my yellow Bowsmith hybrid that hung on the wall with another dozen abandoned two-wheelers.

"Six hundred."

Kuttiya.

"You only gave me two for it."

She shrugged. Went back to her potatoes and bread.

"I'll give you three." I didn't know why I was negotiating when I had ten million coming my way, but years of poverty had made me hate little more than being ripped off.

The Vulture didn't answer. That was how she bartered. Silence.

"Four."

A sip of coffee.

"Five."

She yawned.

"I'll give you a thousand for the bike and some information."

That made her look up from her breakfast. "Fifteen."

"Twelve."

"Fine. Show."

I put two thousand on the counter. "If I like what you tell me, I won't ask for change."

"What would you like to know?" Isra's Italian always got better when there was money in front of her. Her memory and her manners too.

"I'm looking for a necklace." In my head I could see Amelia wearing it, framed by the neckline of her favorite black dress. "A platinum sphere, about this big." I showed her the size with my thumb and forefinger. "With cutouts showing a yellow stone inside. On a platinum figure-8 chain."

She snorted like a bull, "Look around. I look like I deal in shine and sparkle?"

"No, you look like you're a bad week away from buying and selling babies, but I know you carrion-chasers talk to each other. Trade gear. Keep the prices high."

I had guessed on that last part, but she looked away, letting me know it was true.

"Is it yours?" she asked.

No. It was hers. She *was mine.*

"You want me to ask around? Don't know how much I can do. Not a lot of people like Isra."

"Nobody likes Isra," I said. "But Isra likes coin, and if she finds the necklace, or whoever it is that tries to sell it, she will get plenty."

I wrote down my mobi Ghost-ID and told her to message me when she had word. Not bothering to ask if I wanted the extra eight back, she palmed the cash on the counter and slid it into her lockbox.

After getting the bike off the wall, I checked the charger, knowing it had surely gone dry while in secondhand limbo. It would take a few blocks of pedaling to build up some power. When I left the hockshoppe, Isra was already on her hometerm asking around. Nothing like the hope of money to make even the laziest of crones motivated to do good work. I took to the street, and it felt good to be self-propelling again. I didn't engage the motor once the bat was charged; I needed the exercise.

Alba lived north of the train station in a building that used to be the School of Engineering for Sapienza University. A long time ago the college had been free to attend, but now it was only for the wealthy. Fewer students meant that over the years the school had shrunk, and many of the buildings had been either sold or abandoned. Alba liked living away from the criminal hubs of the city like The Esquilino, The Trastavere and *Cinecittà*. She also made a lot of extra coin selling hot gear to students.

I had missed my meet-up with her the day before, which was for the best. She was supposed to have brought me a simple nonlethal, but my needs had changed. I needed fangs. I punched the guest code into the keypad, and it denied me. I tried again, and again no. Trying a third time would trigger an alert. I had to buzz the intercom three times before she answered.

"Store's closed."

"It's Rata."

"The store's closed-closed. Go back to Browntown and bother the hack tramps there."

"But you're my favorite hack tramp."

I waited a long beat, and the lock disengaged. She could never say no, even when she was pissed at me.

Alba answered her door on the second floor stark naked and angry, the two modes of her I had grown the most accustomed to. I looked her up and down and was reminded of why we had been together more than once. Her body was beautiful. Her face, scars aside, delicate and hardened at the same time. Her skin was what drove me crazy, though. Kissing it was like kissing fresh silk.

"You stood me up."

"I slept in."

"You slept in past nineteen?"

"I had a long night."

"I waited at the cafe for an hour."

"I'm here now."

She crossed her arms under her breasts and used her eyes to tell me to kill myself.

"I like what you're wearing." I said, forcing a smile.

She rolled her eyes and turned back into the apartment. I followed. From behind I was reminded that even when Alba was naked, she was never naked. On the backs of her calves, in strong black ink that never seemed to fade, were tattoos of crisscrossing laces, like she was wearing stockings, topped off with red and black bows that always reminded me of butterflies.

Her flat, which had once been a small classroom, was a palace compared to my cube. Plus, she had a sink and had rolled in a portable shower unit, and her bed had legs on it. She grabbed a white tunic from a pile of clothes in the corner and pulled it on.

"How are you?" I asked. Alba paused momentarily on the second button of her shirt, then continued. She seemed to wonder why I cared. Or if I really did.

"Not great. I got woken up four hours early by a graceless, unreliable bitch this morning."

"Did you kick the shit out of her?"

"No, she can take me." She reached under the bed and produced a backpack. She pulled out something wrapped in red checkered cloth and tossed it on the mattress. "One day I'll just shoot her in the head."

She peeled back the bandana to show me a cute black and silver stinger and two extra charging clips. "Two grand. The batpacks are a hundred each."

"I'm going to need something stronger."

She yawned. I had definitely woken her. She sifted through her floordrobe and picked up a pair of panties. "Change your mind about the steel?"

"No. I still need that. Any progress?"

"I'm working on it. Come on."

We went back out into the hallway and entered the stairwell at the far end. Two flights up and two doors down was the other room Alba rented under a different name. She tapped her prints on the inpad in a particular sequence, and it unlocked.

Inside was Alba's inventory. Crates stacked to the ceiling. Boxes of mobis and meta gear. I stepped over an open bin of identical solos, each still in its original retail packaging. The low-powered electroshock sticks were

86

‡

designed for self-defense only, delivering enough sting to get away from whoever was assailing you, but not much more. They only had a range of a meter or so, but in the right hacker's hands, they could be made deadly for one shot and one shot only. They had earned their nickname from an advertising campaign years before: *Don't get caught alone without* one.

Alba knelt down and opened a footlocker full of weapons. Real weapons. Stingers. Designed for law enforcement, sportsmen and military, not for the handbags of old women. She had a belief that if she ever got raided, there was no way they could track the hot tech to her. It seemed to me they could just back-trace the printgear and figure it out. I thought she probably used it because it made her feel clandestine.

"What would cause a piece of hack to make dead on its first shot but not on the second?"

"If it was modded cheaply, quickly or poorly."

"That's what I thought. Would it be possible to figure out who did the work?"

"Do you have the weapon?"

I shook my head. Alba stood and handed me a sleek pistol that fit snugly in my fist. The barrel protruded between my first and second fingers, and it had a thumb-trigger.

"This one," she said, "will kill four grown men before you have to recharge. Or eight kids. Maybe a dozen dogs."

It had heft to it. It was small and well made. Exactly what I needed.

"Do you know what model it is?"

"It's a Sprite 7," I was pretty sure.

"Not this one. The one you're looking for."

I didn't, but I described it to her. Its block frame, low-profile sight and matte finish. The street had been too dark that night to make out any more details like the grip or the trim. "And it was big. Too big. Conspicuous."

"What kind of noise did it make? Was it a crackle, a hiss or a strum?"

I searched around in my memory of the night. When Kennedy fell, he had been out before the sound had reached his ears. As for the shot that killed Amelia, I had been distracted—*he had been distracted*—and the sounds of the piazza were faint but still there. What were the truths just before she convulsed in his arms? What had happened in that final second of happiness and hope? What did it look like, feel like, smell like, sound like—

"Crackle. It was a crackle."

Nodding, Alba started pulling guns from various crates, boxes and lockers and handing them to me one at a time. I studied each one, trying to place it in the killer's hand, lining it alongside the weapon in my mind. Each pistol I dismissed I tossed onto a wrought iron and ceramic table shoved to the side of the room.

After a half dozen stingers, Alba handed me another and froze, seeing the response in my face before it even registered with me.

It was the one.

The squared frame and non-reflective finish. The barely noticeable front and rear sights. I wrapped my hand around the textured grip. It was so big I didn't think I could get to the trigger without spraining my index finger. I knew it wasn't the weapon that had killed my wife, but it was identical, and I hated it. I hated seeing it, holding it. I hated that it existed. It made me quake inside.

"Beretta LPC300," Alba explained. "It's a good gun. Not great, but solid. I would never use it, though. Look how fucking big it is. It's not necessary. It's for show-offs and men with inchworm cocks."

How could he have just stood there and pointed this thing at her? Pulled the trigger, knowing what it would mean. How could he do that? Didn't he know who we—they—were?

"I don't understand how you could fuck up a hack on something like that. The guts on these things are sound. Only one make-dead shot out of that big batpack? Must have made the poor sucker dead-dead with all that juice."

I managed to look away from it for a second. "You know anyone who sells these?"

"Maybe," she said in a way I knew would cost me money. "About two months ago a guy from Napoli came to me trying to sell a case of these. I picked up this one for my collection, but they don't really fit in with my inventory profile."

"Too much coin?"

"None of my clients want to spend like that on something that screams 'Look at me! I'm doing crime!' to anyone who sees it. But three days later, he was back in Free Sicilia and twelve Berettas lighter."

"And you know who bought the rest of them?"

She nodded.

"Five," I offered.

"Oh, it's going to cost you ten, but I need more than that. I need to know what this is about."

"How about eight and it all remains a wonderful mystery?"

She sat on a trunk of who-knows-what kind of smuggled gear. I was going to have to tell her something.

‡

The money I could pay her would only be a fraction of what she'd lose if any of her connections took offense to her letting me behind the curtain. But I really needed her help. Not just for what she knew, but also for what she could do. I'd been in more than one scrape with Alba, and she was a woman who watched your back.

I sat next to her and told her a story about an old woman, her murder and her husband's quest for vengeance, being very careful with my pronouns. *His* wife, not *my* wife. *Their* life, not *our.* I didn't tell her the details. I couldn't.

For her, I made it simple. Kill the man, get paid.

I didn't mention the chip.

"How much?"

"You want ten, it's ten."

"How much is he paying you to do dirty?"

I didn't want to say that, either. "More than you think."

"Hundred grand? Two?"

"Enough to get me paid out and away from Bijan. Enough to get me out of here."

I put my hand on her bare knee. Gently touched her cheek and guided her head so that our eyes met.

A soft spot and a hard-on.

"Maybe enough for *us* to get out of here," I said impulsively. Desperately.

But I didn't mean it. And she probably knew that. But that didn't keep her from smiling.

I had her.

And I fucking hated myself.

I was relieved to find out that the place we were headed to in The Trastavere was just across the river. The old neighborhood on the west bank of the Tiber had become the playground of some of Roma's rougher actors. Behind the quaint bars and cafes were the workings of most of the Roman underworld, not including the Paks and Chinese, because it was also the heart of Roma's nationalist sentiment. Roma for the Romans. Most criminals didn't care what color your skin was as long as your coin wasn't counterfeit, but there was a strain that associated themselves with like-minded miscreants of European history like Caspian, Hitler and Leandro. Anyone not pure-blood Italian, like there really was such a thing, was not welcome. Arabs. Pakistanis. Orientals. Jews. Even the Sicilians with black *moulinyan* blood coursing through their veins.

When Dario Villano went from Senate-appointed emergency dictator to self-proclaimed neo-Caesar, his closed border policies and xenophobic past emboldened them. A series of arsons and murders nearly led to a race war until Villano stepped in and called for peace. Things had been quiet over the last two years, but no one believed it would stay that way.

Once we were over Ponte Giarbaldi, we entered a small park that held a very large statue of a man wearing tails and a top hat, holding a cane. Alba stopped us just behind it, our backs to the water. We peered around the statue and saw, on the other side of the park, across a higher lane, our destination: the bar known as Sangue d'Italia.

She pulled two nubs out of her bag, put one in her ear and handed me the other.

"So you can listen in."

"I'm going in with you."

"No, you're not. That would be bad for both of us. The only way these guys are going to talk to you is if they think they're talking to me."

The Berettas were bought by a small-timer named Ferro Urgola. He ran his racket out of Sangue d'Italia. It was well known as a place where someone who looked like me would not be welcome.

"If he sold the stinger, I'll find out who to," she said. "I've known him a long time, and he owes me a favor or two. Plus, he knows if he's a cunt about it, I'll tell his mother."

Alba pulled out her mobi. "Ping me that shitty sketch you made."

I sent her the image, still wanting to go with her. But she was right. The denizens of Sangue d'Italia would not welcome me warmly. Or at all.

"The transmitters have a short range. Anything more powerful, The Legion scanners might pick it up. But you're close enough here." She left me alone at the base of the statue. I sat on the end closest to the river, to the bridge, to the less brown-hating part of town, on the edge of another dry fountain. Almost immediately, the nubs connected, and I could hear Alba breathing.

"Boys," I heard her say. A door was opened, and then the acoustics changed. Quiet music and a few indistinct conversations. She was inside. It was mid-afternoon, and the bar sounded fairly empty. A chair scraped against the floor.

The man's voice sounded like he had been punched in the thorax enough times to make it stick: "Albalonga Rocco!"

Albalonga?

"Hello, Ferro," Alba managed to get out before things got muffled as he smothered her in a hug. Lips smacked against cheeks, one side, then the other.

"So, have you finally grown out of chasing butterflies and come to find yourself a Roman man?"

"Not chasing, catching," she said. "You should see all the ones I've got pinned to my wall."

He let out a hearty laugh, and then his voice receded as he turned his back and encouraged her to sit.

"This isn't a social call, Little Donkey."

Chairs scraping on the floor again. Rustling as they sat at the table. I heard Alba tapping her fingernails on the wood.

"My own mama doesn't even call me that anymore," he said without an ounce of annoyance. She really had grown up with the guy.

"Ah, but you will always be Little Donkey to me. Your given name is so hard and cold."

They talked some Roman shit for a minute, asking about their mothers, exchanging *cannoli* recipes, planning a murder for the Ides of March, whatever. I spoke the language, but I would never Speak The Language.

I looked up the statue that was shielding me from view. Chiseled on it was the name G.G. Belli, a poet, it said, of the people of Roma. I had never heard of him, but the top hat that rested slightly askew on his head reminded me of Amelia's killer, of that night in the street, and I could feel my skin start to flush.

I wasn't sure what my next step would be if Alba came up short. I'd keep on her, but I really didn't have any faith in Isra. How was I supposed to find one stick-up man in a city full of desperate people? The gun. The necklace. The clothes. The man. Was he just a guy that saw two seniors with money and decided it was the only play he had if he was going to make his *hafta*? But then, why have a hacked stinger on you, especially one too big to properly conceal and too expensive to scrub and chunk?

The clothes were a smoke screen. The necklace probably was as well. The man was hiding somewhere in the fog. But the gun was not a diversion. It was a fact. It had

93

killed her, and it was probably the only thing that could lead me through the smoke and find the son of a bitch who shot it at her and him and me.

"You know a guy looks like this?" Alba broke me out of my thoughts. I assumed she was showing Ferro my sketch.

"Is that supposed to be a person?"

"I know. It looks like a child drew it."

She wasn't wrong.

"He would have been in here buying a Beretta 300," Alba continued.

"Why are you looking for him?"

"That's my business."

"Your business? You mean the business I brought you into? The business you left to start your own? That business?" His voice was calm, so I couldn't tell if this was a gentle scolding or the ramp-up to yelling and punching and calamity.

"The business," she countered, "I left when you started making everyone learn German and burning down mosques? The one I said I couldn't be a part of if it became a job requirement to assault every brown or yellow that I saw in the street? That business? I owe you a lot, Little Donkey, but you told me when I left that from then on, you were you, and I was I, and I should never forget that when we next met."

He laughed. "Did I say that? That is either brilliant or childish, I can't tell."

Alba laughed. "You've always been both."

I heard Ferro shuffling around, playing with his utensils. "You are absolutely correct, my beautiful butterfly. But we are currently at the overlap of my business and your business, it would seem."

Three men came across the bridge from City Center. I shifted, turning my head away from them, hoping they wouldn't see the color of my skin. They passed without even so much as a glance my way.

"He stung an old lady. I'm trying to bring him in," Alba said.

Her name was Amelia. Starr. Kennedy. Sometimes Moreno.

"And by 'in' you don't mean to The Legion."

"No."

I'm going to put a steel cock in his mouth and blow a leaden load out through the back of his fucking skull.

"'In' the ground?"

Her silence said "yes" better than her mouth could have.

"Well, I'd help you if I thought I could or thought I should, but I don't think neither."

"I know you bought that batch of Berettas that come through in July."

"I think you have some wrong information."

Liar. He's lying.

"No, you don't think that. I bought one, and you took the other eleven. All I want is information on one guy, just this one scumbag who bought one."

"Even if I did know, I would never willingly betray a fellow white man."

Not willingly, I thought. I peered around the side of the statue and at the bar. The sun reflected off the large windows, and the glare made it impossible for me to see inside.

"You can't tell if he's white from the picture," Alba said. "He could be Sicilian or a light-skinned Persian."

"But if he was Sicilian or Persian, you wouldn't be in here looking for him because you know I don't deal with Sicilians and Persians, light-skinned or not."

He's stalling, Alba. He knows. Can't you see that he knows?

"If you help me with this, I will owe you."

"You already owe me," he whispered with menace.

I paced back and forth behind the statue of the dead poet. I balled my hands into fists to keep them from shaking. This man knew something. I could just tell. Two more men walked by, and this time I didn't try to hide my face. I didn't care.

I need to get in there.

"Please." I imagined her batting her eyes, maybe even touching his hand.

There was a long pause, and then Ferro exhaled slowly.

"I've never seen him."

Before I knew what was happening, I darted around the statue and towards Sangue d'Italia. I stepped up onto a bench and hopped over, landing and trampling through a patch of red flowers. In my ear, I could hear Alba going back and forth with him, but not getting anywhere. He wasn't going to tell her anything.

Not willingly.

Stumbling out of the flowers, I narrowly avoided crashing into a solid metal trashcan that looked like it had been there forever. I crossed the street, dodging a scooter that whizzed by, and came to the front door of the bar.

There were two large men in black shirts on either side of the door. I slowed to a walk and headed in. The one on my right grabbed my arm. "No Pak—"

I reached up and pulled him towards me with the neck of his shirt and landed a head-butt. As he staggered back, I drove a kick behind me into his buddy's crotch and spun, hammering the guy's face with the bottom of my closed fist. He went down with a grunt.

I burst inside. It was a small place, wider than it was deep. A bar and four tables, the walls decorated with large Italian and Roman flags, Catholic artwork and crooked German pinwheels. Alba was sitting at a table near the wall with a fair-skinned man in a gray suit, his tie loosened and vest undone. When he saw me, he stood, "What is this?"

There were four other men in the place. The bartender and three patrons, all of them with shaved heads. Alba turned and saw me.

"Rata, what are you doing?"

Ferro only had a moment to look at Alba in disgust before I had the Sprite out of my pocket and in my fist. I pointed it at him and used the split second of shock to thrust my off hand into his chest and shove him against the wall.

Even though I was acting like an idiot, even though I was surely screwing her out of future coin and maybe getting her in trouble with her mother, Alba pulled two Spitfire pistols from the small of her back and backed down Ferro's guys before they moved to stop me. It was shit like that that had made me take her to bed in the first place.

And would probably again that night, if I didn't get us killed first.

I pinned Ferro to the wall with my elbow and pressed the barrel of the Sprite up under his chin. "You're lying, Ferro."

"Who the fuck are you, Paki?"

I looked back over my shoulder. I could hear the racing thumps of Alba's heartbeat in my earpiece. I tried to catch her eye, to calm her, but she wasn't happy with me and would be less so if I took a whole lot more time.

"The man in the picture," I said, turning back. "He killed someone very important to me. Killed her with a gun he bought from you."

The blood on her lips. The pain in her eyes.

"I don't plan on stopping until I find him and make him dead. I won't let you get in my way. Anyone who doesn't help me is helping him, and anyone helping him is an enemy. This isn't logic, donkey dick. This is passion. This is lunacy. I will go through you to get what I want, but I will not go around. Do you follow me? Do you know what I'm talking about? A real Roman man like you should understand."

He locked eyes with me. "Vendetta."

Her hand in mine. The smell of her hair.

"You understand how pure it can be."

"I understand you're going to have to dig more than one grave," he said.

I dug the barrel a little deeper into his jaw. "Are you going to help me, or are you going to help him?"

I just want her back. I just want to hold her again.

"You're going to have to kill me, bitch. Because I don't know."

"Why should I believe you?"

"I don't care if you do."

I leaned my forehead against his, almost gently. I could feel tears in my eyes; I could see fear in his. "Let's do this together," I said softly. "Let's see what's on the other side."

Nothing. No heaven. No nirvana. No loved ones. Nothing.

"I can prove it!" he blurted out. I kissed him on the forehead, then pulled back.

"Then prove it."

He yelled something in German to the bartender. He disappeared into a back room, and there was a long minute of tension. I didn't dare lower the gun. If for a moment his guys thought their boss wasn't in danger, things would pop off. If their boss went down, things would pop off. Five of them, two of us. I trusted Alba, but if things turned into a firefight, we'd both end up dead.

The bartender came back carrying a silver metal case. He brought it to us, keeping one eye on Alba and her Spitfires, and set it on the table. "I have to unlock it," Ferro said. I nodded and eased off, keeping the barrel centimeters from his head. If things got ugly, I wanted to make sure the racist son of a bitch was the first one made dead. He pressed his thumb against the lock, and it clicked. Inside the case were stingers identical to the one we were looking for. Each gun had its own slot along the length of the case.

There were twelve berths.

There were eleven Berettas.

"No one wants to buy these fucking things. They've been sitting here collecting dust. A stupid, stupid buy."

Alba walked over to us, not lowering her weapons. Looked down into the case. Frowned. "Shit. I was wrong." She looked around the room. It was still on edge. One twitch would lead to all sorts of bad things.

She looked at her childhood friend. "Honestly, Ferro, I'm hardly ever wrong."

"Get out of here," he said to her. "You and your... whatever this brown thing is. Get out of here, and if I ever see either one of you again, you won't walk away from the moment."

We backed our way towards the door. I had really fucked things up.

"I understand," Alba said. "But do me a favor, Little Donkey, for old times'?"

"What?"

"Don't tell my mother."

VI: BACCHANALIA

I CHASED ALBA ALL THE WAY back to her place. She was furious, and I didn't blame her. I had just put flame to one of her oldest bridges. When we reached her building, she tried to slam the door on me, but I caught it a moment before it closed. I knew there was nothing to say to calm her down. No words. I followed her upstairs and into her flat. I nearly had to force my way in. The door closed, and she turned and looked at me, as mad as I had ever seen her. I didn't want to talk about what had just happened, try to explain it, to her or myself, why I flipped out and blew the whole thing, especially since I wasn't at all comfortable with how my emotions had overridden my brain. So I pushed everything in my head into a corner and decided to do something I could do without emotion and grabbed her and shoved her against the wall and kissed her. She resisted at first, but quickly gave herself over to it. While I slid my

‡

hand up the front of her shirt and bit at her neck, it occurred to me that this was all being recorded, etched in ones and zeroes on the chip implanted behind my ear. That when I finished the job, these memories—the memory of her nipple hardening as I played with the steel stud that pierced it, her hand on my ass, grinding me into her, soft moaning in my ear, the salty taste of her sweat, the quickening moistness between my legs—would get handed over with all of the others for Kennedy to see.

Fuck it, I thought as I undid her pants and pulled them down just far enough to get to what I wanted. *Let the old bastard watch.*

I want you to know why this is happening. Why I am doing this. Why you are beaten, bleeding, and why there is cold steel in your mouth.

I want you to know that in a few seconds, you will be dead, and everything you are and were and were going to be will cease. I am going to fucking erase you. I don't care what you believe, what toxic mythology you have governed your sad little life by.

But I have been to the other side and returned with a message: there is no other side. Just this one. We are both mortal and measurable. So when I pull this trigger, when I drive your brains through the back of your head and deep into the pavement, it will be the end of you. Absorb that. Believe it. Fear it.

Do you remember me?

My name is Robert Caden Kennedy. I have been a juvenile delinquent, a businessman, a politician, a leader, a celebrity, an outcast, a criminal, and have twice been thought dead.

But most importantly, I am the husband of the most remarkable woman in the world.

You killed her.

You remember me now?

You walked up behind her, behind us, and you murdered her. You tried to murder me too, but I don't care. I forgive you for that. I don't want you to think this is about that.

This is because I loved her and you killed her.

I would tell you to say your prayers now, but I promise you, motherfucker, no one is listening.

I woke up feeling like I had betrayed the wife I knew I never had. Alba was still awake. She sat on the edge of the bed, not yet dressed, typing away on her mobi.

"Good evening," she said like she could feel me looking at her. "You've been out for three hours. I'm almost flattered. You're usually out the door before I finish coming."

I sat up. "Are you still mad at me?"

She looked over her shoulder at me. "Extremely. Even after you did that swirly thing with your tongue that you know I like."

"I'm sorry." Apologizes didn't come easily to my lips. Even at that moment, when one was beyond owed, it sounded strange coming out of my mouth.

"For what? For ruining my already-delicate relationship with an old friend and, more importantly, a source of income."

"For that," I said.

"I'm not angry about that. Do you understand what happened there? Never mind you bursting in there, never mind sticking a stinger in Ferro Urgola's throat. Never mind the fact that you seemed content to go down with him, even if it meant I would probably end up dead too. None of that was an offense to those bitches. I'm sure they're not happy about it, but don't think it's the first time someone's threatened to kill Ferro.

"They hated us before we walked in the door. You for being brown and me for not caring that you're brown. That was the end of my relationship with him. Do you think I care if a man like that talks to me anymore? Fuck him."

I was confused. "Then why are you angry?" What did I need to apologize for?

"Because you didn't trust me," she said. "I told you I could handle it. I told you to stay the fuck away. I was wrong about the Beretta. I wasted your time. But I could have found that out on my own without almost getting stung."

"I don't trust anybody." I didn't want to lie. I just didn't.

"Which is why you're not telling me everything." Her eyes grew sad. "You knew her," she half-said, half-asked.

"What?"

"You told Ferro you had lost someone close to you. You knew her. The dead geezer."

"No." *Yes.* "Yes." *No.* "It's hard to explain."

"I've never seen you like that. I was sure the only two emotions you were capable of were annoyed and horny. But that was rage. That was hurt. She must have been remarkable, whoever she was."

She was, I thought.

"I know you didn't mean it this morning," she said. "About us."

"I'm sorry." There it was again.

"I'm not stupid. You didn't play me. I wanted to help."

"Why?"

She shrugged. "We hadn't had an adventure in a while. Sounded like fun."

"Was it?"

"Not as much fun as that time we accidentally stole that shipment of hypnometh from the Black Spinners, but, yeah, it was."

I swung my legs over the edge of the bed. My clothes were in a pile on the floor. I started sorting through them and getting dressed. "I'll get out of here," I said. "Thanks for the lead, even if it didn't pan out. Gives me somewhere to start."

"I'll still help if you want me to."

"I thought you hated me."

"I'm pissed at you. There's a difference. Do you still need me?"

"Yes." I did.

"Then you have to trust me."

"I can try."

I was sure the Sangue d'Italia debacle hadn't been erased, but maybe I had done enough damage control for the time being. I felt genuinely bad about betraying her, about hurting her. I rarely felt genuinely anything about anything. It was disconcerting.

"Can you still find me a gun that shoots bullets?" I asked.

She sighed. "Check your term. You've got a dinner date at twenty-thirty with a Frenchman."

"Dinner? I don't do—"

"Do you think he cares? This is how he does things."

"Thank you." I remembered to say it that time.

"And I'll keep asking around about the Beretta. Hack like that gets noticed."

‡

I stood, and pulled on and fastened my slacks. Swept my hair back into a tail and tied it. "I'll ping you after I talk to him." I pulled on my jacket and reached for the door.

"Was this the last time?" she asked.

"What?"

"You said last time you took me to bed that it was the last time."

"I did. It was. I thought it was."

"Was this the last time?"

"Yes."

"Why don't I believe you?"

"You don't have to. But it is. The last time."

"For now?"

"For now."

"You're a cruel bitch."

I gave a smile I truly meant. "And you, Albalonga, are a forgiving angel."

"For now," she said as I closed the door behind me.

The *trattoria* was tucked at the end of an alley around the corner from the crumbling remains of the Trevi Fountain. When I arrived, he was sitting at a table and already eating. Our meeting had been set for 20:30, and I was only ten minutes late, but he had finished off three plates of *antipasti* and was tearing his way through his first-course clam and squid risotto.

"I see you waited for me," I said.

He smiled with a mouth full of creamy rice and seafood. "You are prettier than I thought you would be." His Italian was proper but affected.

"Based on what?"

"Your name. It is nice, but I don't usually find women of your species to be attractive. Strong, formidable, not to be miscalculated, but generally plain and sometimes hideous. You though, you, you are very fuckable."

I'm what?

"Or would be, if you were ten years younger."

He was probably forty with black wavy-nearly-curly hair. His nose was pointed and his lips thin; there was a light patch of hair between his eyebrows that made them run together if you looked closely. A well-tended and closely kept beard. A gray suit that was custom-fitted and flattered his lean frame.

But it was his eyes that struck me. Even when he was calling me old and insulting my race, they shined in a way that made me forgive him. A vibrant aquamarine with speckles of brown that reminded me of the shallow reefs in the Gulf of Mannar. They weren't eyes so much as they were powerful and priceless jewelry. Genetically issued accessories. They were deadlier weapons than anything he may have had for sale.

He lifted his hand high and cocked his head and snapped and shouted, "Giulia! Two orders of the carbonara—"

"I don't eat meat."

"Make the carbonara synth pork!"

"I don't eat synth."

"You don't eat...*Merde.* No synth!"

"It's not carbonara without the meat!" the waitress yelled back.

He ran his hands through his hair, then called back, "Fine. Bring me a carbonara and her some spaghetti and eggs. Plus whatever your best fish is today, and—" His eyes shifted to look at me. "You like mussels?"

"No," I said. I also didn't like eating with strangers.

"And mussels." He turned back around. "You should like mussels. The mussels here are *très* fuckable." I wasn't sure if it was a language thing or if he really wanted to have sex with a plate of bivalves.

"I didn't come here to eat."

"I know, I know. Business, business, business. But this city, I tell you. It has become a poor, dirty shithole that will die very soon, but the fuckers still know how to cook."

"I'm looking for—"

He waved me off. "I know what you're looking for. You want a big bad American gun. Boom boom boom. But what for?"

"That's not your concern. Why do you care?"

"Because it's not my concern. Other people's private nonsense intrigues me. I'm a curious man." He forked more rice into his mouth and mumbled, "In more ways than one, I've been told." He grabbed an open bottle of vino, one of three on the table, and offered to pour for me. I shook my head. He shrugged and filled a tall water glass to the rim with red.

"Oh!" he exclaimed, wiping his hand on the tablecloth and then offering it to me. "I am furthering the stereotype and being rude. I am Michel."

"I don't care."

He sucked his teeth and took his hand back. "Are you sure you are not French?" His joke made him laugh, loudly and only once.

"I'm not going to tell you why I need the steel," I said quietly. "I don't want to eat with you. I'm sure some people think you're cute and intriguing, but not me. I just want you to tell me if you can get it for me and for you to name the price."

"You," he pointed at me with his fork, "are a blunt and discourteous bitch. That makes you both more and less fuckable at the same time."

I started to get up.

"Sit, sit, sit. Do not try to be more dramatic than me."

I eased back into my chair. He wiped the corners of his mouth with a napkin and looked around to make sure no one was listening, even though we were the only people there that weren't in the kitchen. "Thirty thousand yuros," he said in English. It sounded more comfortable than his Italian did.

"Twenty," I responded in the Queen's own.

He shook his head. "This is not a negotiation. Michel does not barter."

"Twenty-five."

"Maybe it would be easier for you if we switched back to Italian? I do not know any of the brown languages. I talk slower? You are not understanding. The price is thirty, and that is *très raisonnable*. That covers the weapon, a full magazine and the risk to me and my people. Do you know what the penalty for being caught with a gunpowder stinger in Europe is, especially here?"

"I do."

"Once it's in your hands, I care not one shit. The Legion catches you with it, they'll hang you from Trajan's Column or nail you up like in the *vieux-vieux* days, and that's not my problem. But that will not happen to me. Not to this Michel. And making sure of that is not cheap.

"If you like, you can counter me with thirty to make you feel like you set the price."

I smiled despite myself. "Thirty."

He banged his hand on the table and switched back to Italian: "Now we eat!"

As if on cue, the server brought us two plates of pasta, a thick grilled halibut steak and a platter of open half-shells in a yellow sauce. I didn't want to play a game with him, but I had questions and I hadn't eaten since the day before. He grabbed a mussel daintily between his thumb and middle finger, lifted it to his lips and sucked down the meat inside. Before the shell hit the table, he was reaching for another.

"I'm sorry there's no curry in it, but I promise it's still good."

I flaked off a piece of the fish with my fork.

"When?" I asked.

"Several days."

"When exactly?"

"More than five, less than ten. I don't keep my gear within the walls of this city. Villano's thugs have no respect for privacy. But it will be here."

"So you work for the Neapolitans. Maybe the New Town Pirates?" I asked. The city of Napoli, in the nation now known as Free Sicilia, was notorious for its corrupt and porous law enforcement. Most of the things smuggled into and out of Roma came across the border from Napoli.

"I work *for* myself," Michel said. "Who I work *with* is my business. Do you have a preference to the model of gun?"

I knew nothing about American firearms that I hadn't learned secondhand. "It has to be easy to use and clean, and be reliable. Small enough to hide but with plenty of bite."

What would the Senator want?

What do I want?

"And, if possible, I want something old."

"How old?"

"Twentieth, early twenty-first. Something you'd see in old films."

He stopped eating long enough to look at me. "Films? Like old fic-vids? That is fascinating. Curious." He loaded his mouth with noodles and nodded. "I can do that. I have just the thing, I think."

The fish was good; the pasta was better. We sat in silence and ate. Every once in a while, I caught him studying me. Before I knew it, I had finished the pasta and was tempted to try one of the mussels. I pulled out some cash, and he shooed me away.

"Despite everything else about me, I am a gentleman. I will pay. And it will make you much more likely to fuck me next time I see you." He flashed a smile that told me he was kidding, but he wasn't entirely kidding. I gave him my mobi code and left.

Michel was an infuriating and piggish man. I was hopeful that he could get what I needed. Men who operated at that level of nonchalance either knew exactly what they were doing or knew nothing at all.

I was two blocks away from the *trattoria* when I realized that I kind of liked him.

The next nine days were a morass of pedaling, questions, grimy hockshoppes and dead-end bribes. There was nothing worse than deftly sliding a K across a counter only to have the vulture on the other side tell you something utterly useless or completely off-topic. Especially when the expense cash that had once made you feel flush had quickly dwindled to barely enough for grav fare.

After spreading some coin around a few of the more upscale hockshoppes on the west side of town, I walked along the water for a few minutes to clear my head. It was a mistake. I found myself at looking at Castel Sant'Angelo, the circular fortress on the other side of the Tiber. It had been used for several purposes over the years, including housing several Popes, but it was currently the headquarters of The Master of Horse and his Legion. Three poles flew the neo-Roman flag, a golden eagle on a background of red, white and green. Atop the castle's parapets, everyone knew, was a battery of high-capacity scanners searching the city's radio spectrum for undesirable transmissions and traitorous messages. Villano's ears in the sky.

I wasn't worried about walking by; when I went snooping around whiter areas of the city, I went unarmed. It was the bridge that I didn't want to see. It crossed over the river to the fort, and lining it were a dozen five-meter high wooden crosses with people hanging from them.

The bodies were in several states of decay. When more room was needed, the Caesar had the bodies cut down and dumped over the side of the bridge and into the river. The remains of each condemned had a sign hanging around their neck that announced their crime. Murder and treason were the most common, but in the past year, Villano had extended his definition of capital crime. Smuggling. Rape. Grand larceny.

I passed the spectacle as fast as I could, not wanting to dwell on the carnage, but on my end of the bridge, ten meters towards the castle, a small group of people stood around the base of one of the crosses. In black, all. The women in lacy veils. They were crying, praying. One old lady was holding so hard onto her string of prayer beads, her hand was bleeding.

The cross stood next to an old statue of an angel that had long ago been cleaved in half at the waist. The man hanging from it was nude, his hands and legs tied to the cross with rope, not nailed like in Christian myths. Flies buzzed around the shit and piss that had collected below him. His skin was drained of all color.

Soon, his strength would give out entirely, and he would asphyxiate. I didn't know how long he had been up there, but any time was too long. Such a painful and drawn out way to—

He was still breathing. His chest rose and fell, slowly, shallowly, but he was most definitely alive. Careful not to disturb the loved ones who had come to watch him die, I tried to get a look at his crime placard. It read THIEF. Nothing more.

The man didn't have much time left. Hours, at the most.

If stealing could get someone brought to the bridge, getting caught with a piece of Yankee make-dead definitely would. If the Frenchman came through, I would have to be careful not to end up on a crucifix of my own.

I waited in the Imperial lobby cross-legged on a claw-footed divan, silently reveling in having my filthy boots up on a piece of furniture older than the Senator. I had arrived at the St. Regis unannounced to re-up my petty cash. For some reason, I felt more comfortable amongst Kennedy's private soldiers knowing I had the Sprite-7 tucked away in my jacket, which was ridiculous considering the gear they were packing. It was thirty minutes before Orso came out of the suite to greet me. There was a white envelope tucked in the breast pocket of his coat.

"It is lovely to see you, Miss Das," he said with the tone of a man who had been trained his whole life to say things pleasantly whether he felt that way or not.

He handed me to the envelope. "I assume you can account for the initial advance."

"I didn't get receipts, if that's what you're asking. It's considered bad form to ask someone you're bribing to put it in writing."

"That," he said, indicating the new cash, "will go against your final payment."

"Sure," I replied, but what was fifty grand, a hundred grand, to these guys?

"Can I see him?"

"You may not."

"I need some details, things only he would know."

"You are not the Senator's only proxy, Virata. To speak to him, you simply have to speak to me. What is your question?"

He called my bluff. I didn't need anything from Kennedy. I just wanted to talk to him.

"The Senator believes that a recorded memory of you seeing him will be traumatic when he implants and relives your experience."

"The idea of talking to himself creeps him out."

"Correct."

"Okay. I get it. Can I ask you a favor?"

"I am here to serve."

"Tell him that I didn't understand. That I thought he was crazy and sad and stupid. That I thought that as much as he was using me, I was using him more and conning him out of millions. But I want you to tell him I was wrong. I want him to know that I understand. I feel it too. Tell him that I, no, *we* are going to get this done. I promise him that.

"Can you tell him that for me?"

"I can. Anything else?"

"Let him know I miss her too."

PROXY

‡

Isra pinged me during my ride home and said that she had found the necklace. Turning south off Merulana and onto Mecenate, I switched the bike to power and let the engine take over. I was tired and wanted to get there fast.

One more right and one more left brought me to the gates of Chinatown. Back when there wasn't a need for The Orphanage, the Chinese lived on Esquilino Hill along with the Paks and Indians and Persians. But after World War III, the refugees overran the area and the Chinese went a few blocks south and settled.

The first thing I did was stop at the first fruit stand I saw and buy three apples and a pear. I didn't particularly want them, but I needed to be carrying a bag. Visitors were welcome, but only if you had coin. Everyone in Chinatown was selling something, and if you weren't, you had to be shopping, or you weren't welcome.

The hockshoppe Isra sent me to was a microcosm of the whole of Chinatown. It was cramped, insulated, and the man who worked the counter, who looked as old as Kennedy actually was, stubbornly refused to speak Italian until money exchanged hands.

He rooted around under the counter and handed me a gold chain attached to a moonstone the size of a meatball.

I left without a word. It wasn't disappointing to me anymore. Looking for a stolen bauble in a city of thieves, even one as unique as the gleam Kennedy had given his wife, was not going to be easy, if doable at all.

I headed home.

I had padded my request to Orso by twenty thousand yuros. Despite Bijan's supposed affection for me, I still had to deliver my weekly *hafta* on time. Until I finished the job

115

and paid him off, and he granted "manumission," whatever that was, things would keep on as they had been.

In the lobby of my building, I found a man in a white toga with several smears of something brown across the chest, leaning against the wall with his hands laced behind his head. The robe was hiked up over his waist, and a slight and mostly hairless nude man was on his knees, sucking his cock. The recipient's eyelids fluttered with pleasure.

As I passed, he caught my eye and smiled. I followed the tinkling of a harp into Bijan's flat and was greeted by the sight of exposed flesh, the smell of sweat, red wine and marijuana, and the oppressing feel of amassed body heat.

Another fucking bacchanalia.

I stepped over a bald Persian man and a plump white woman aggressively spoon-fucking on the floor, on top of a mosaic portraying a couple engaged in the exact same act. Bijan was reclined on his couch, being fed muscadines by a bare- and large-chested Pak girl, and watching three women pleasure each other in a head-to-crotch triangle on a plush rug.

Bijan's orgies, inspired by the old-old Roma, had started as yearly events but had quickly evolved to monthly and then to what seemed like weekly in the summer months. The indulgent affairs were supposed to celebrate the ancient Roman and Greek gods of wine and ecstasy, but were really just excuses to screw and get tweaked, twisted and dazed. I glanced around the room and could not help but be impressed with the variety of deviants he had managed to assemble. The promise of cock and cunt may have been the only thing that could get a white person to come to The Esquilino after dark.

"By Bacchus!" Bijan yelled when he saw me. "Virata Das has come to join the revels!"

116

None of the building residents ever came to the bacchanalia, even though Bijan had always made it clear that the attractive ones were welcome. I could only see one of his hands. The other was under the toga. I was about to have a conversation with my coin shark while he was stroking his dick.

"Not this time. Not ever." I tried to hand him several yuro chips. He just stared at me. "My *hafta*."

He smiled, "You may keep it if you disrobe and share your beauty with us."

I did a quick inventory of the revelers. There were a few beauties, but most of them were the other thing. There was a skinny Chinese girl playing the harp in the corner. She wore tall black boots and red shoulder pads and nothing else and was no older than fifteen. There were nearly twenty people in the room, and they were all doing something. The ones not drinking were sucking or stroking. The ones not drawing sweet smoke out of the gold and blue hookah were being penetrated, some in more than one hole, some with items not designed for that purpose.

I wasn't about to share anything with anybody there.

"I wouldn't know where to start, Dominus," I said, trying to get away without upsetting him. Bijan was usually fair-tempered, but with all the wine in his blood and all the blood in his prick, he was not himself.

"A bacchanalia is like an organism." He made a face that told me more than I wanted to know about the current state of his organism. "It doesn't start or end or anything so simple. It simply is. It lives. Breathes. Undulates. All you have to do is merge into it and go where it takes you."

A scream came from the back bedroom. The door flew open, and a Pak girl, bare from top to bottom, came running out. She stopped in front of me, her eyes wild.

"Bitch!"

Kalb stood in the doorway with his nose bleeding, his pants around his ankles and his five-centimeter erection standing for all of us to see and be unimpressed by. The girl ducked behind me. Kalb took a few steps forward. Somehow the closer he got, the smaller his throbbing boyhood looked.

He stopped in front of me. "This is much better. Rata can come back with me."

I appealed to Bijan, who had stopped pleasuring himself and looked incredibly angry about it. He sighed, then nodded. Kalb reached for his tiny knob, but before he got there, I punched him in the windpipe and then knocked him out with a spin kick to the head.

No one protested. A man somewhere in the room whispered "thank you" under his breath. I turned around, and the girl had retreated to the arms of another woman, who I was sure didn't have the best of intentions but would probably be much gentler than Kalb.

"I'm going to go merge with my bed," I said, tossing the coin chips to the ground. They landed in a milky puddle at Bijan's feet.

"Fifty denarii fine for that."

"Add it to my tab."

I got to my room wanting a shower, but none of the bathrooms were safe on bacchanalia nights. I had twisted my foot a little when I laid out Kalb. I sent a mental command to my ASIS unit for a light painkiller, and within minutes any ache had faded. I hadn't signed up for that particular gear, and it scared me to have it, it really did, but it was going to prove itself useful.

Only when you need it, I thought. *Only when you need it.*

I collapsed on the bed after triple-checking my security. The best strategy for getting through the sexual siege downstairs was to lock the door and ride out the storm of shit and tears and smoke and blood and pain and come until morning.

It had been a long and unproductive day. Like the eight before it. No one had seen the man, the necklace or the gun.

I had nothing. The Vulture had nothing. Alba had—

My mobi buzzed. There was a message. From Alba.

It read:

I'M LOOKING AT HIM RIGHT NOW

PROXY

‡

VII: ATAVISM

I ALMOST KILLED MYSELF TAKING two, three, four steps at a time as I bolted down the stairs. Two half-naked revelers were late arriving for the bacchanalia. I slashed between them and out the front door. I fumbled with the lock on my bike. I almost panicked and left it and ran, but I managed to steady my hand enough for the print to take. It felt like an eternity, but it only held me back ten, fifteen seconds.

I hoped it wouldn't cost me more than that.

I swung my leg over and got moving before my ass hit the seat. Turning hard onto Via Merulana, I skidded and almost ended the trip before it began. I regained control and gunned it. When I had been still sitting on my bed, processing Alba's news, her next message had brought me a location:

SPANISH STEPS

✦

I knew she had been asking around, going places I couldn't, talking to people that wouldn't talk to me. She had been sure that someone carrying hack that big and showy wouldn't be a quiet and unassuming crook. People hauling gear like that would want people to know they were dangerous. Apparently she had been right and found him. I had told her to tread carefully. I didn't want the guy to suspect that someone was after him.

I hadn't heard one word from Michel since our dinner, which meant I didn't have the gun, the real gun, but I was sure Kennedy would understand. The lead was pageantry, ritual. He just wanted him to fear, to know and to die. It wouldn't be as satisfying, but was satisfaction really what we were after? What was it going to feel like? Exhilaration? Rapture?

I was betting on grim relief.

I got to the top of Via Merulana and veered left at the Maggiore Market. I tried to will my two-wheeler to move faster, but it only had so much juice. I stayed off the cobblestone streets; the sidewalk made for a much smoother ride. The farther north I went, the closer I got to crossing Via Nationale, the more upscale the stores became. They were mostly closed, the occasional late-night snack or wine bar aside.

I crossed Via Virmenale, and my mobi buzzed. Keeping one hand on the bars, I slid it out of my front pocket and checked the new message.

MOVING WEST ON—

My spine tingled, and I looked up just in time to see an e-cart emerge from behind a small wall on my left. The wall ended with a column that made the corner completely blind. The vehicle rushed into the intersection. There was no way I was going to avoid it.

I dove to my right, clearing the bike and landing face down in the street. The impact knocked the wind out of me, but I was able to look up and watch my Bowsmith collide with the much bigger vehicle. The cart slammed to a halt, the bike having drilled directly into the driver's door.

I scrambled to my feet and looked around for my mobi. A few meters from me, on the cobblestones, glowing dimly blue. My shoulder ached in a way that I knew would bloom into full-blown agony in a few hours.

The term was scratched and nicked but functional. A week and I had already managed to scuff it. Pretty soon my new rig would look as beat to shit as my old one.

Alba's message was still on the screen.

MOVING WEST ON CONDOTTI. WILL FOLLOW

That time of night, he was either headed home, to a bar or to a trance hall. There were a dozen of them in the area. The Void. Tech Noir. Atavism. Purple. The Source.

I triggered the ASIS and it released a dose of nitrocodone into my blood to head off the pain that was coming. The driver was struggling to open the door of his cart and was most likely planning on making me dead. My bike, my cheap and speedy bike, less than two weeks out of hock, was done. I had to leave it. I'd have to go on foot. I'd have to run.

Fifteen minutes, maybe. Less if I pushed it. Ten minutes lost.

I hoped it wouldn't cost me more than that.

I took off. The man, still trapped in his cart, yelled something about my mother as I ran past.

I want you to know why this is happening.

I wanted to grab one of the many scooters, bikes and carts parked on the street, but I didn't have any of that kind of gear on me, and I wasn't sure I could remember how to do it the old-fashioned way. It would have cost me more time than running.

I trusted Alba to stay with him. It had become a two-woman operation. Her help was needed, for certain, but she seemed as dedicated as I was and for no real reason.

In a few seconds, you will be dead.

I had tried to exploit her emotions, her feelings for me, to get her to help me, maybe against her best interests, but she had seen straight through that. The idea of taking her with me, of us as any more than occasional bedmates, was one born in a moment of desperation and cruelty on my part.

What if it had stuck? Alba thought she loved me. She didn't. She couldn't. She was confusing my ability to make her climax without touching her above the knee with some sort of deeper connection. She was holding an image, of me and her and us, even as cynically conjured as it had been, in her mind. Not as something that *would* be, but as something that *could* be. A wish. A pipe dream.

A hope.

Shit, I thought. I had lived in the dark long enough to know how dangerous hope could be.

I passed Nationale and kept running. The pain from the crash was coming. This far north, there were more and more people on the street, some of them out for their nighttime strolls. I tried not to bowl them over, smash into them, but some of them got clipped, including an older couple that reminded me of Caden and Amelia on that fateful night.

Everything you are and were and were ever going to be will cease the moment I pull this trigger.

After passing through an intersection with a dry fountain on each corner, the street slanted downhill. I was running so fast, the change in grade made me stumble forward, but I stayed upright.

124

PROXY

‡

I hadn't slept in any way worth counting for over a week, and as I ran, that became more and more apparent. I was starting to slow. I tapped into my injector unit for a small dose of dopadril. My muscles exploded with new energy, the cobwebs in my brain vaporized, and I ran faster. I knew the comedown from the dopa would be annoying, but headaches and jitters were a small price to pay for what I was chasing.

I am going to erase you.

My mobi was still clasped in my left hand, and it hummed again. I eased off my pace a bit and read Alba's incoming missive:

ATAVISM – 20TH CENTURY

The idea of the man who killed her in that retro trance hall, dancing and drinking and tripping, trying to pick up women or men or both, just the idea of him having a good time, stabbed me in the heart.

I was aflame.

To get to Atavism, I would have to change course. I left Via Sistina, and the streets took another steep dive. Ready for it, I used the decline to my advantage and picked up speed. The streets narrowed, lined on both sides by hotels, most of them still in operation. While most of the city was shuttered, the area north of Nationale was still prosperous and booming, or at least gave the impression it was so. The small enclave of Romans who were still flush, who still had time for luxuries, never went south of Nationale, making it the unofficial border between the haves and the have-nots.

Crossing a street, I was nearly crunched by a man and a woman in a cranked-up scooter. I heard them laughing as they sped away. A few turns later, I got to Via Mercede. Down the street several hundred meters, I knew, was my destination. I dodged in and out of the pedestrians, occasionally hopping into the street. When I passed Del Corso, I could see the giant building at the end of the next block.

Atavism was not one of those subtle places that equated obscurity with social relevance. It was bold and loud, with a huge moltobrite display that announced its presence to the neighborhood. The trance hall had been built in an enormous Italian parliament building, a structure abandoned soon after Roma declared itself sovereign. Inside the block-long building were five dance clubs under one roof, each one themed for a different period in history. Atavism was a temple to the icons people chose to remember from the times before their own. It was about nostalgia for things never experienced. There were a lot of togas worn by people like Bijan that harkened back to the old-old days when their city had ruled the known world. Others donned foppish and silly kit from the Renaissance, brightly colored pantaloons, doublets and heavy dresses, many topped off by large, ridiculous puffy hats punctuated with giant feathers. There were jackets and gowns from several different centuries, fashions that had come and gone and come back again and gone again. Native Americans. Twentieth-century military kit. Barbarians. Some even wore tight black shirts with low turtlenecks. This was done by not by people who sympathized with the fascists that briefly but traumatically ruled Italy, but in mockery of them, like devil masks.

I started to feel the thumping of the bass three blocks out; I could hear the music at two.

Another message from Alba:

AT BAR

There were two doors leading into the converted government building, one on each side of the wide staircase that lead to what was once the main entryway. One door for men and one for women. The line leading into the men's entrance moved slowly and, most of the time, not at all. The queue for girls never stopped flowing, but every one of them was scrutinized; women were expected to come dressed to play. In costume or not, they had better be showing something the men wanted to see.

Atavism was a stinger-free zone. The owners had spared no expense when they installed their weapon detection suite and, by all accounts, kept it state-of-the-art. I would have to go in unarmed, but Alba and my quarry would have done the same.

Across the street was one of those green abandoned tourist kiosks. I jogged over to it, ducked behind and took the Sprite out of my jacket. I unbuttoned and stripped off my shirt, bunched it up with my coat and wrapped them both around the gun. I found a loose panel in the structure and pried it open enough to tuck the package inside.

That left me in just my tank top. I let my hair down and shook it out. I felt gross, and I was sure I looked terrible but my best chance to get in fast was to show some skin.

As I approached the club, I slowed down and put a hitch in my step and started blinking too much. As tired as I was, it wasn't too hard to play like I was drunk or spinning. I bumped into the door guy and staggered back a few steps in mock-surprise.

"Whoops! Where did you come from?" I tried to sound the right amount of out of it, but I was sure he couldn't hear me over the music.

I reached out and lifted his chin with my index finger, shifting his eye line from my chest to my face, and leaned into his ear. "I'm up here," I said, with a lilt in my voice, forcing a smile. "Do you have to work all night, or do you get to have fun with the rest of us?"

He reached around with one of his meaty hands and grabbed my ass and pulled me closer to him. I tried not to flinch, resisted the urge to drive his balls up into his body with my knee. I giggled instead. "Is there room for me in there?"

"Will you come find me after?" he shouted.

I wrapped a hand around his arm and squeezed. "Bet on it."

I passed through the contraband detectors and into the lobby. The volume of the music was almost crushing. In my experience, trance-tech was only ever enjoyable when you were riding something beautifully nasty in your bloodstream.

The lobby was packed about five-to-one women-to-men, a ratio that had, on more than one occasion, brought me to the place in the past. A full two-thirds of the patrons were in costume. Two tall and striking Chinese girls walked by me, dressed in floral patterned neck-to-ankle *cheongsams*. The dresses hugged their figures so tightly, it made it both nearly impossible for them to walk and actually impossible for me not to stare at their asses as I passed.

Alba would look great in one of those.

The lobby ran the length of the building, and off it were entrances to the separate clubs. I passed by the Old-Old Roma, Renaissance and Back to the Cave rooms before I came to where Alba had directed me: the Twentieth Century.

Inside was a sea of costumes that, although from two centuries before, were much more similar to modern dress. There were a lot of those black turtlenecks, as well as women in big, flowing skirts and men in leather jackets and denim. One could find something from every decade in the dark and sweat, but certain looks, mostly American ones, were much better represented.

✢

The floor was a mass of flailing limbs and grinding bodies. In the middle of it was the room's only island, a high, circular counter with stools and women in short plaid skirts and tied-up white shirts pouring drinks. I waded towards it. Alba was leaning with her back to the bar. I excused and squirmed and shoved my way through the herd. When I got close enough, she reached out, grabbed my hand, pulled me to her and turned me around.

And there he was.

The first thing I saw in the swarm of dancers was a white top hat. Out of fashion on the street, it wasn't at all out of place amongst the club's costumed customers, but I had seen it one other time, even though it had never actually passed before my eyes.

The man wearing it whipped around in what I assumed he thought was dancing. He was dressed in a checkered gray suit from a bygone age, no gloves, no scarf. The blonde hair that hung down from under the hat swished back and forth as he moved his head, only giving me brief glimpses of the face underneath, but I could make out the shape of it and the outline of his nose, and it was enough.

It. Was. Him.

The sight rocketed a hot chill through my body that for a long second stopped my heart and tunneled my vision, blinding me to everything but that single point in space.

I miss her so much.

Wear the chip.

You took her from me.

Kill the man.

I'm going to—

Get paid.

I'm going to fucking kill you.

Walk. The fuck. Away.

✦

I turned halfway back to Alba, keeping at least one eye on the man in the white hat.

"How?" I mouthed to her, knowing there was no way we would be able to have an audible conversation. She smiled, made a mouth with her left hand and made it talk, flapping the thumb-jaw up and down. It was what she had thought. A man who carried a weapon like that would have to show it off. He'd be a talker.

I read Alba's lips: "What now?"

Even if I had been able to bring in my weapon, it wouldn't have done any good to drop him right there. I needed to talk to him and cause him pain to satisfy the contract. And while there were plenty of places in Roma where the people would scatter when The Legion came for witnesses, Atavism wasn't one of them. It was a safe place, prided itself on being so, and planned on staying that way. It would be hard to enjoy the ten million while locked into a semistasis pod; it would be impossible if I got nailed to one of the Caesar's crosses.

We would have to follow him out of there and track him to a place more conducive to a prolonged retributive murder.

I have been to the other side and returned with a message: there is no other side.

Before I had time to figure out how to communicate my plan, movement erupted in the corner of my eye that was very different from the rhythmic chaos of dancing. A fight had broken out in the space between us and the killer. Two young guys exchanged amateur punches. One was in a toga, having apparently wandered into the wrong room, and the other wore an American black leather jacket and blue jeans, his hair slicked back and unnaturally black. The people around them backed off to give them a pocket of space in which to scrap. My attention shifted to the fracas for a second, a nanosecond, less than that, so briefly that I wasn't aware that it was happening.

But it was enough. It was enough to lose him.

The man was nowhere to be seen.

I felt Alba stiffen next to me and knew she had lost him too. Panic hit. My eyes strained against the flashing lights as they swept the room. Alba tapped me on the shoulder. I didn't turn around. He was out there. I couldn't look away. Not for a moment. A moment could be everything.

W*hen I pull this trigger, when I drive your brains through the back of your head and deep into the pavement, it will be the end of you.*

She grabbed me by the arm and turned me around. She pointed to me, to the right side of the club, and then mimed that she'd take the other half. Alba reached into my front pocket, took out my mobi and slapped it into my hand. I nodded again. She plunged into the crowd. I headed in the other direction, pushing through, looking for the hat, scanning every face. There were hundreds of them. I couldn't let him get away. What were the chances we could find him again?

The few minutes I spent looking felt like hours, wading through the stupid fucking people wearing their stupid fucking costumes pretending to enjoy their stupid fucking lives. I wanted them all to drop dead and leave Amelia's killer the only man standing. They were just obstacles.

I was sweating. My temples were pounding. I gasped for every painful breath that I took and couldn't tell if it was the music and suffocating atmosphere of the room or fear and panic. Every one of them I bumped into jarred my shoulder. It was starting to throb despite the make-numb I had taken.

She was brilliant and beautiful and strong and better than you in every cell of her body.

A pretty young man in a tuxedo tried to grab me and dance. I shoved him away with more force than warranted. He bumped into three people before he finally succumbed to gravity and hit the deck. His eyes showed more shock than anger.

Men were always surprised by my strength.

More minutes passed; more faces blurred by. I could feel the dread rising up through my core. My closed fist vibrated. I pried my eyes away from the crowd to check the message:

MENS ROOM

Alba. My black market beauty.

She's a lot better at this than I am.

But I hit harder.

The bathrooms were on the far side of the club. Between me and Alba and the man with the hat were hundreds of bodies. There was nothing to do but push and shove. I wanted to break into a sprint, but that wasn't going to happen. Working a meter at a time, I moved as fast as I could. I sent three more dancers to the ground before I made it to the stairs.

My mobi hummed:

HURRY

A dozen steps down led me into a long hallway. It was the only place in the club, other than the lobby, where every theme came together. The left side of the corridor was lined with waiting women; the other was empty. I stayed right and rushed past the queue of girls. It was quieter there on the lower level, but the bass still rattled the walls like an artillery barrage.

If he was in the men's room like Alba was saying, things were not going to go as planned. There would be no time for speeches. I didn't have a weapon. If I had to, I could kill him with my hands. I had done it before.

As much as Kennedy wanted to feed the man a meal of steel and lead, maybe he would enjoy slowly choking the life out of him just as much.

I knew I would.

I didn't see Alba. Was she in the bathroom? Had she already confronted him? She didn't know the stakes, the plan. I needed to get there fast. I couldn't let Alba hurt him, not before I could. The door rushed up on me. It was open just a sliver.

I kicked it.

I loved *her and you* killed—

Something came crashing down on my head. Litter rained down as the trash can that had been thrown at me crashed to the ground and rolled towards the bathroom stalls. The blow nearly drove me to my knees, but I managed to stay upright.

Immediately he was on me and had my head locked between his forearms. He pushed forward and pressed me against the wall. I fought to get under his arms and pry them apart, but he had me tight. It became hard to breathe.

Out of the corner of my eye, I saw Alba lying crumpled and unmoving on the tile, her mobi half a meter away on the floor.

His arm was wedged firmly under my chin so I couldn't get my mouth down to bite into his jacket. I crushed my heel down into his foot and his grip loosened, but before I could get away, he tensed up and applied more pressure.

I could feel his breath on my neck.

Shit. My neck.

Dopadril, I thought. *Maximum dose.*
Nicolor, maximum dose.
Adrenaclear, maximum dose.

The stims cranked through my system. Heart rate soared, skin started to burn, head immediately began to hurt. I couldn't imagine what the tweak was going to be like once the drugs faded, but I would deal with the comedown if I lived to see it.

I screamed and summoned what I could and drove both of us backwards across the room. He fought back and tried to stop us, but I kept pumping my legs until we crashed into the bank of sinks on the far wall.

On impact, he let go, and I pushed myself away, stumbling back across the room until I caught myself on the wall we had just come from. Air rushed down into my lungs.

I turned around in a defensive stance and looked at the man who had attacked me.

The man who killed her.

He was on one knee in front of the sinks. He brought up his eyes and leveled them at me.

It wasn't him.

It looked like him. His face was the same shape, but there were differences I hadn't been able to see in the strobing darkness. The nose was thinner, and he was a few years younger. There was a faint scar under his left eye, and he was maybe two fingers taller.

But the hat was the same. The build, the shape of his face, all the same. But it was clear.

It. Wasn't. Him.

It wasn't the man who had killed Amelia, but I had some questions for him. Big questions. He scrambled to his feet just before I got to him, deflecting my first three punches. I dealt with his initial strikes in kind. I ducked under a large right hook and came up under his guard with an open palm to the chin. I drew my hand back, ready to attack again, but had to jump back to avoid a hard kick to the midsection.

Alba hadn't stirred. I didn't know if she was dead or not, but I let myself believe that she was to fuel me. If I wasn't going to avenge one woman that day, I would avenge another.

But if you're not dead, get your ass up and help me.

The man snarled and unleashed a fury of punches, chops and kicks. I was barely able to keep up with them, knock them aside, and whenever I moved to counterstrike, he was already launching another attack. It was impossible to get an opening.

One jab got through my defenses and jacked me right in the nose. Stars erupted, and I staggered back. I groggily knocked away his two follow-ups. I felt blood on my upper lip and was grateful he hadn't managed to drive the stud in my nose all the way back into my brain.

We bashed at each other for another thirty, forty seconds. Fighting a man you don't want to kill who wants to kill you is tricky business. I needed him to talk. Which meant avoiding all the points on his body that, at the moment, I really wanted to destroy.

I grabbed his lapels and sent a knee into his stomach. It hurt him, but he reached up and grabbed my hair. He stepped out of our brace and yanked. I yelled, and it felt like my scalp was going to rip right off. He whipped me around into the wall of one of the stalls.

The cheap metal dented when I slammed into it. I turned and managed to duck out of the way of a round kick that would have taken off my head. I made both of my hands into one fist and from my knees punched up into his crotch.

It landed solidly, but I wasn't able to get a whole lot of power behind it.

He staggered back, holding his groin, then shook it off and advanced. I rolled away in time to avoid being punted, but before I could get up, he followed me and stomped down on my back. I shook off the blinding pain. I flipped over and caught his foot as he brought it down again. Twisted. When it cracked, he screamed and crashed to the floor.

Nitrocodone, maximum dose.

For a long, strange moment, things were calm and still as we both tried to stand. I scooted to the wall and walked myself upright one painful step at a time.

The door swung in, and a man in a blue and white Chinese *cheongsam* dress, mouth agape, stood in the threshold. The tight-fitting fabric was not as kind to him as it had been to the women I saw earlier. He took it all in at once: the dented stall, the cracked sinks, an unconscious woman and two battered brawlers.

He mouthed a swear made inaudible by the music and shuffled away as fast as his costume would let him.

The clock had started. We had to get out of there fast.

My opponent got to his feet, favoring his broken ankle, but ready to go again. I wasn't sure how much I had left in me, but it would have to be enough.

I took a step towards him, and he convulsed and fell to the ground.

"No!" I yelled, but no one could hear me but me.

Alba was awake, still lying on her stomach, her mobi in her outstretched hand. She had somehow hacked it to act as a solo, to get it to emit enough energy to take someone down in a pinch. Leave it to her to find a way to bring a weapon into the most weapon-free place in Roma.

I stumbled to the prone man, hoping Alba hadn't hacked her comm gear to make dead. But he was alive, awake and absolutely stunned.

Alba stood and went to the door, flipped the lock and leaned against it to steady herself. It was a good thought, but once The Legion got there, neither the bolt nor her body would be enough to keep them out.

I sat on his stomach and leaned my face close to his, close enough to be heard.

"WHO ARE YOU?"

He stared up at me, probably hoping to push through the effects of the sting.

"WHO ARE YOU?"

I imagined a unit of heavily armed troopers smashing their way through The Renaissance on their way to us.

"WHY IS THERE ANOTHER MAN WHO LOOKS JUST LIKE YOU?"

I reached behind me and slid my hand down the front of his pants. His eyes went wide. I grabbed his scrotum and twisted. His eyes went wider. He tried to writhe in pain, but I pinned him with my other hand, pressing down on his chest. I looked towards Alba. My chosen form of torture seemed to both impress and amuse her.

"WHO ARE YOU? WHO IS HE?"

I squeezed harder. He tried to bear down and take the pain. When that wasn't enough, he attempted to scream it away, but the louder he got, the more pressure I applied.

"I WILL STOP IF YOU TELL ME!"

Then it happened. An instant before, his eyes had shown me nothing but strength, anger and defiance. But that disappeared, leaving the look of a man ready to give in, give up, roll over. The difference was physically imperceptible, impossible to explain, but very real and very obvious to someone who had seen it before.

His mouth twitched in the initial spasms of speech, but he stopped himself. I eased off on his balls. In my experience, it was often the reprieve that sent them over the cooperative edge.

"I DON'T WANT YOU! I WANT HIM!"

His lips parted. I leaned closer, putting my ear against them. Waited for the words.

His whole body jerked under me. I sat up. His eyes bulged. He grasped at his neck, fighting to breathe, like he was being strangled by a phantom.

I ripped his hands away and felt his throat.

It felt like it was made of steel.

A suicide vice.

There was nothing I could do but watch him die.

The idea was centuries old. Soldiers, spies, zealots, men who would rather die than betray their masters. Falling on knives evolved into hidden cyanide pills, which eventually lead to the invention of the compromise clamp. The constricting metal ring was implanted around the trachea, not always voluntarily, ready to strangle its owner to death before he could hand over any sensitive information.

They could be triggered remotely, but most of them were wired into the bearers' brains, scanning for certain signals that would indicate they had turned the corner on what they were willing to say to save themselves.

I had seen that change in his eyes.

The clamp had felt it in the firing of his synapses.

He couldn't talk and was dying quickly, which made him useless to me. I dug in his pockets for something, anything, that would help me find the real man I was looking for. I found some cash and let it fall to the tile. I wanted an ID, a term, something with information.

Alba yelled something behind me. I couldn't make out what it was.

His body went still. I kept digging.

Alba said something again. I pulled up his shirt. Tucked into the front of his pants was his mobi. I reached for it and then Alba screamed. I still couldn't hear her, but I figured out what she was saying. I pulled a square of red cloth out of his jacket pocket and used it to grab the term. If I had touched it, chances are it would have turned into a rock when it read my bios. I wrapped it up and tossed it into the white hat.

I ripped a lock of hair from his head, taking a little flesh with it.

Alba grabbed my shoulder and pulled me to my feet. I grabbed the hat. We had to go, I knew. But I looked at him, the man who was not the man I needed to kill and yet died all the same. He looked so much like him, like a brother or a sloppy clone, but it wasn't him.

Who was he?

I was still dazed and confused as Alba yanked me out of the restroom and up the stairs into the Old-Old room. It was the biggest room in the building, full of revelers in togas of all sorts of colors. Some of the dancers, I noticed, wore nothing at all. We plowed through them and ran to the exit, into the lobby and out the front door.

We crossed the street to where I had left my jacket and pistol and hid behind the kiosk as two Legion response carts pulled up in front of the Atavism. Men wearing golden polymer armor and wielding sting-rifles pushed their way into the building against the flow of the people being ushered out by the club's security.

I pulled on my jump jacket and slipped the Sprite into the small of my back. The white hat sat on the ground where I had set it to get dressed. It had been crushed in the struggle. I could see specks of red on it. My blood. His blood. I looked at Alba, who was watching the show down the block.

"Shit," she said, shaking her head. "We fucked that up."

"Yeah."

She turned towards me, a giant smile on her face. "But, hey, at least you got your—"

"It wasn't him," I told her. "That wasn't the man I'm looking for."

I sat on Alba's bed while she tinkered with the dead man's mobi. She wore thin gloves and had managed to get the back panel off the term. If any of her DNA touched any part of the outer surface, the thing would shut down and become useless forever. She attached a thin cable somewhere into its inner workings; the other end was hooked up to her Frankenstein of a hometerm. I had never met a hacker who used a retail console.

"I didn't know there was enough juice in one of those things to knock a man down," I said.

Not taking her eyes off of her work, she smiled. "There's nearly as much power in a high-end mobi as there is in those solos they sell to ladies. It just takes a little rewiring and an external replacement antenna that can also work as an emitter."

"That's all it takes?"

"That, and the brains, talent, hands and full-bore fucking sexiness of your favorite hack tramp."

"How many shots do you get with it?"

140

"No shots. *Shot*. Just the one. Hell, I'll be lucky if I didn't fry the thing completely. I haven't checked yet."

"Can you rig mine up to do that?" I asked.

"One thing at a time, Das."

It had taken me the entire walk back to Alba's to explain to her that the man we sort of killed hadn't been the right one. I told her what she had done was incredible, but that it wasn't him. That I thought he was related or something.

"Across the room, I was sure," I had said. "But when I saw him face-to-face, it just wasn't him."

She had closed her eyes and inhaled deeply and gingerly touched the top of her head and brought back down two fingertips slicked with crimson. She rubbed the blood with her fingers.

"Then we keep looking," she had said then.

"I got a number," she said now.

I stood and came to the table to look. "Just one?"

"And nothing else. No personal information, records. Just one Ghost code."

There was no way of finding out whose number it was. They called it the Ghost for a reason.

"Does the thing have voice?" I asked.

"Sure." She sounded reluctant.

"I want to call it."

She shook her head. "We don't talk on the Ghost. You know that."

While it was rare on the mainline Ether to communicate voice-to-voice, it did happen. But it was forbidden on its illegal shadow. The bandwidth on it was so narrow, it was precious. There was no upstream or downstream for data. It was one narrow and intermittent brook, not nearly wide enough for two ships to pass each other on it. Chunky data, like a voice call, could clog up the flow for anyone in the area.

"I only need one minute," I said.

I could tell Alba was torn between her desire to help me and whatever self-imposed "code" her and her gear-hound cohorts held themselves to. "We won't be able to track it. Whoever is on the other end will immediately toss their pass, if they haven't already."

"I know. I just want to ask one question."

She sighed in a way that let me know she would relent. "One minute."

"Probably less," I promised.

With a few keystrokes on her hometerm, Alba managed to turn off the mobi's bio-security. She unplugged it and handed it to me. I sat back down on the edge of the bed. On the touch screen, there was one number. I took a deep breath and tapped it.

I put the mobi up to my ear. I heard a buzzing noise. Once, twice. The third ring cut off mid-buzz, and a man's voice said:

"The balls you must have, girl."

"Who is this?" I asked.

"You'll know soon enough. You've made it a certainty that we will meet very, very soon."

"Do you know who I am?"

"You're the Paki cunt who killed our friend."

Our friend?

The man in the bathroom, Not Him, had apparently been wearing some sort of vid 'plant. The man on the other end of the line had seen my face. Alba was sitting beside me on the bed, trying to hear the man on the other end, but he spoke quietly and softly, despite the malice in his words.

It had to be him. The man who killed her.

"There are a lot of brown bitches in this city, but we will find you, I promise that, and when we do, the shit we'll do to you will have you begging to die. You, and that white girl with the fucked-up face you brought with you."

Alba heard that. She smiled grimly and put her hand on my knee.

"You saw the fight, I take it?" I asked.

"Yes."

"You saw what I can do?"

"I did."

"What makes you think you'll fare better than your friend?"

"I won't be alone," he said and severed the connection.

I stared at the mobi for a few hard seconds, then threw it across the room. It hit Alba's wall and cracked into three pieces. I expected her to yell at me for it, but she just squeezed my knee harder.

"Was that the guy?" she asked.

I looked at her.

Then we keep looking.

"I don't need your help anymore," I told her.

She took her hand back.

"Like hell you don't need my help."

"I don't *want* your help anymore. You almost got made dead tonight, and now we know they've seen your face."

"I knew what I was in for. The game is dangerous."

I stood and started to gather my things.

"I appreciate the sentiment, Rata, but I can take care of—"

"This is not a game," I said in a way to let her know I was serious. "You are in this because you have taken a lie I told you, and you're trying to make it come true. Holding onto some idiotic vision of us running away, even though you know it was bullshit. It's not going to happen. When this job is done, and the ten million yuros are in my hand, I am going to disappear, and you are not going to be with me."

Her voice quivered a little, "Then why do you care if I get hurt?"

"Because I like you. More than I should or want to."

I hadn't known that until I said it. Was it true? A week before, it would have been another lie. But on this night, I cared. When had that happened?

It felt strange.

It felt stranger to see Alba trying to hide her smile.

Shit. I may as well have proposed.

"You don't like me. You hate everybody."

I turned around to face her.

"And I hate you the very least. Which means I don't want you to get killed chasing something that's not going to happen. Because 'like' is as far as I go. To give you that thing your pretty head can't let go of, that would have to be the other thing. I don't do the other thing."

Except for Amelia. I love Amelia.

"How about this?" she began, the wheels in her head turning. I had given her an opening. No, not an opening. I had taken down the entire wall. I had handed her more hope. "My help, in exchange for two things. One, that you will keep an open mind about you and me and us and where we are going. I'm not asking for babies, just don't write it off until the dust settles.

"And two, you pay me two million yuros for helping you find and kill this man. That way, if my heart gets broken, I can go home and cry in a bathtub filled with coin. I don't even know what this is all really about. How you knew this woman, why care so much. You told me what you told me, but it doesn't add up, and I haven't pushed. But it means a lot to you, that's clear, and you, against every bit of reason and sanity I possess, mean a lot to me."

"I don't—"

"I'm not asking you to return the sentiment. Give me some credit. 'Hate the least' is the sweetest thing you've ever said to me, in or out of bed. Without me, I'm not sure you can do this. That man on the phone, he's coming for you. For us. You need someone standing back-to-back with you. Think of me as an employee and leave what I'm feeling and hoping for me to handle. Because you're a fucking sexy piece of hack, but you're not anything two million yuros can't help me forget.

"Deal?"

I didn't believe her, but she wasn't going away.

"Half-million," I offered. She smiled. She was as uncomfortable talking about her feelings as I was. The return to a business state of mind put us both at ease.

"One," she countered.

"Deal. One million."

"Good. Let's celebrate."

She took my hand and yanked and pulled me down on top of her. Her hands quickly reached around and grabbed my ass, pinning me to her. The heat of her body against mine, despite being in utter pain from the fight just hours before, got to me. She raised her head off the bed just enough to kiss me. Her tongue slipped past my teeth and found mine. She wrapped her legs around my body, and I began to grind into her. I heard her moan into my mouth.

We came up for air, our lips separating. She smiled.

"Your face looks terrible," she said.

My eye was already half-swollen shut. I'm sure I had started to bruise. My upper lip was split and throbbing, and it had hurt to kiss her, but I didn't mind.

"You're one to talk." I traced a finger along the scar that ran across her right cheek. I found I truly did want to know how she got them, but I was sure the story had to be sad and violent and would have ruined the current mood, and my body was beyond the point where I could switch gears. I sat up, straddling her, and pulled off my shirt. Almost immediately, she was up, and her face was between my breasts. I gasped when I felt her mouth engulf my left nipple.

"Is this part of the—" She pinched the erect nub between her teeth, gently but hard enough to make my whole body vibrate. "Oh, God," I managed to whisper.

She took her mouth off me.

"No, don't—"

"You were asking me a question," she said, lying back down onto the bed.

"Is this part of the deal?" I asked.

She started unbuttoning her shirt. "It can be."

"Always trying to sell me something else."

"That's what I do."

I leaned down, and our mouths met again.

One million yuros for her help and a little bit of this.

I hoped it wouldn't cost me more than that.

PROXY

‡

VIII: ĒPSILŎNA ERIDANI KĪ RĀJKUMĀRĪ

THE BARE-CHESTED MAN STOOD SURROUNDED by a dozen three-meter tall armed and armored alien humanoids. They had four muscular arms, long, tapered necks, flat faces without noses and cutlass-like tusks. Their skin was black. Not black like Africans. Not brown or tan or caramel like me. Black. Like onyx or the space between the stars. The soil beneath their feet shimmered like lavender glass; the sky was green with streaks of pink and looming dark clouds. It was a world unlike Earth in nearly every aspect, with impossibly formed mountains and fauna torn from a botanist's nightmares.

War veteran and accidental extraterrestrial explorer Arjuna Sen held his ground as the tallest and strongest and meanest of the alien tribesmen stepped towards him, his long and wickedly barbed spear held out before him.

✦

The look in the chieftain's crackling red eyes frightened me every time. I reached over in the dark and groped for my father. He took my small hand in his and held it tight, but not for a moment did he take his eyes off the screen. We were coming up on his favorite part.

Two years after the possible discovery of intelligent life outside of the solar system and fifty years before I was born, six Chinese astronauts landed and walked and drove around on the red sands of Mars. Their historic accomplishment was met on Earth with a collective shrug.

Despite the speculation for centuries about little green men and ancient underground rivers, it was common knowledge amongst scientists, lay people and even starry-eyed dreamers that Mars was a desolate and lifeless desert. It had once had water. It had once had life, but it was microscopic, and only fossils remained. People were only excited by aliens with faces. It was of little interest to everyday people, only to scientists, and in a world exhausted by war and steeped in failure and collapse, there was only enough room in the public imagination for one otherworldly fantasy.

That fantasy was now called Epsilon Eridani.

Like the men who had traveled to the Moon a hundred years before, the Martian voyagers brought back stories, rocks and breathtakingly beautiful and humbling images and vids. They were not greeted by warring tribesmen chasing a runaway princess, nor were they abducted and prodded, brainwashed or turned into hosts for sticky amorphous parasites. In two weeks on the surface, they did not see any crumbled ruins or excavate any monstrous, six-limbed fossils.

It was interesting and monumental and mankind's grandest achievement, but compared to sending unreadable messages back and forth with intelligent life-forms eleven light-years away, it was boring.

There had been parades. They were made Admirals, Saints and Knights. The great men of the trade were well known, at least in my home, at least with my father. Yuri Gagarin, the first man in space. Neil Armstrong and Buzz Aldrin, the first men on the Moon. Justin Scott, the man who saved the world the one time it was in actual danger and not just paralyzed in fear by the lies of presidents and scientists. John Glen. Valentina Tereshkova. Alan Shepard. Guy Bluford. Madhu Bhatti. Sally Ride. Yang Liwei. Caroline Lamè.

The crew of the *Wángcháo-Sān* (Chinese records were lacking any information about the fates of the first two craft) took its place amongst those ranks. But after a few months, the present became the past, and the past became history, and the general populace, who knew very little about the actual nuts and bolts of interplanetary travel, never mind intersystem travel, had but one question:

"Great. Now when are we going to Epsilon Eridani?"

The scientific community knew that it would never happen. It had taken three and a half millennia to go from noticing Mars in the night sky to walking on its surface, and the red planet was just down the block compared to Xian Hao's friends a hundred trillion kilometers away. The fact didn't stop the imaginations of both the creatives and the crazies from postulating on what this alien world and peoples could and would and should look like.

I felt Father's hand bear down on mine a little tighter. He was a serious and dower man, but in the darkness of this old-world style *vīḍiyō-ghara*, one of only three in all of Kolkata, he became more childlike than his thirteen-year-old daughter. It was the third time he had taken me to see

Epsilŏna Eridani kī Rājkumārī. It was his favorite fic-vid of all time, and by extension, mine as well.

In the old days, he had told me, before he was born, there had been thousands of theaters across the world that showed vids on screens as tall as two houses. I was the only kid I had ever known who had been to one. Entertainment was a luxury, and nearly all of it was served at home on full-wall terms or VR lenses that co-opted your vision and played the stories across your eyes and immersed you in the experience. My father insisted on calling the old vids "films." *Sinēmā.* "It is very important in the bad times," he would often say, "to allow ourselves to escape into our imaginations and the imaginations of others to visit places and do things the material world can never allow, even for just two hours, then return to our real lives bearing the lessons and visions the films have given us."

"But why do we have to travel two hours to do something we can do at home?" I once asked.

"Because there is nothing like sitting with two hundred people in the dark and laughing or crying as one."

In the two years he had been bringing me to his favorite *ghara*, there had never once been two hundred people. Twenty was a good night. There were times when it had been just me and him, but the joy for him was never once diminished.

On the screen, in a two-dimensional image that simulated the existence of a third, Arjuna Sen stared down the Eridani tribe's lord and master. They circled each other, slowly, each waiting for the other to make the first move.

Arjuna crouched, smiled, almost right at the audience, and then he leaped.

Not leaped. Soared.

150

Ten, fifteen meters straight into the air. The savages craned their necks and watched him go end over end once, twice. He landed behind them in a stance that said he was ready and expecting to fight. After a beat, the ebony chief raised his arms to the sky and pulled the corners of his mouth up into a very human smile.

"Ha!" My father clapped his hands together. It was a simple moment, but it made him so happy.

He loved those vids.

Future- and tech-fic were his favorites. When he was young, he had found a picture book chronicling the voyage of the *Wángcháo-Sān* and became obsessed with it. The images of men standing on the surface of a distant planet lit a passion for the subject that informed his entire education and that he tried to imprint on his oldest daughter. He was successful, for a while, but when I got older and started getting into a little trouble, then into very big trouble, I stopped caring, and we both stopped trying.

The thirty-year-old *Princess of Epsilon Eridani* was based on an older folk tale, told a hundred ways throughout the years. It was about a solider, a veteran of The V, named Arjuna Sen. He was apparently known by other names in other countries. Arjuna was somehow magically transported across space and time to the surface of Epsilon Eridani.

There he was used as a pawn by warring tribes struggling for control of the planet, found himself with super-powers, was eventually accepted, due to his martial skills, as one of the four-armed Eridani, and met, fell in love with and rescued, multiple times, a beautiful warrior-princess.

That was about all I understood. The story was mostly an excuse for thrilling adventure, cheesy romance, large, nonsensical musical numbers and giant scenes of spectacle.

It was a glorification of mankind's new Mars.

Xian Hao had discovered the proof of intelligent life outside of our system, but that was all. Epsilon Eridani was actually the name of the star, but, after Hao's announcement, it became a placeholder for whichever planet turned out to be the inhabited one. There had been no actual communication taking place, just a series of speed-of-light grunts and mumbles neither side could understand.

The residents of that far-off world were known, but they were utterly unknowable. Which, of course, made them the subjects of rampant prediction, speculation and claimed interpretation.

"Noble warriors of Barsoom," Arjuna Sen bellowed, using the natives' name for their planet rather than what he had called it on Earth. He stood between two opposing armies of Eridani soldiers, both frothing to wage war and spill green blood. "The people of my planet, of Earth, a blue and green globe so far away from here that a man could live a thousand lives and still not traverse the cosmos in time to see it, once lived under the black cloud of total annihilation like you do now. Every religion and culture on my planet, and on your planet, I have learned, have a name for it. Apocalypse. *Yawm ad-Din.* Armageddon. *Ragnorok.* Holocaust. For seventy-five years the humans of Earth lived under the belief that we had found a way to bring about the End Times by our own hand. That we had somehow found a magical way to harness the power of the Sun," he pointed to the red burning red sphere in the Eridani sky, "our *Kel-ta*, to create weapons capable of laying waste to everything we had built. Our leaders wanted us to fear, to cower. They wanted us to believe that the next war we fought would be the last war. That with one command, one man could nullify our entire history. They staged fraudulent demonstrations of this magical weapon. Leveled entire cites to exemplify its power.

"But it was all a lie. A myth woven to end one war and to prevent any wars to come. But their bluff was called by the aggression and violence of men willing to kill millions over a small patch of dusty land. The truth was brought to light. We had not bottled fire.

"Here, on Barsoom, your elders are telling you the same thing ours once did. That they have developed world-breaking doomsday weapons. That if the wars between your tribes spill into the fertile lands they keep for themselves, they will be forced to vaporize everything that roams across the surface of this beautiful world. This world I was reluctant to come to and which I will one day be reluctant to leave." Arjuna turned in circles as he talked, trying to make sure all heard his words. "Do not believe them. They say these things because they know if you stopped fearing, if you stopped fighting each other, they would be helpless to stop you from taking back control of Barsoom. Your world will end when it wants to end. Not one second before. But their reign will end. Let me lead you, and we will see it end this very day.

"For Barsoom!" he screamed, raising his spear above his head.

"For Barsoom!" the warriors called in unison.

"For Barsoom!" my father and I yelled. He took a handful of ricepops from the bag we were sharing and tossed them into the air; they rained down on us like salty confetti.

We were shushed by a voice coming from somewhere in the dark, but not before Father slipped one more "For Barsoom" in my ear before we settled in to watch the climactic battle.

CHAD J. SHONK

Aside from works of fiction like *Rājakumārī* and the famous Chinese opera *Yuǎn de Lǐngyù* and the theories posited by every leading scientist of the day, the mysteries of Epsilon Eridani became prime fodder for the believers.

Some already established religions decided that the signals were not from an alien race, but messages from their God or gods. Messages that, of course, only they could interpret and that, of course, reinforced their own terrestrial dogmas. It also spawned dozens of new faiths, the most famous being the Children of Eridani, a cult who believed the far-off beings were undoubtedly our Creators who had traveled to Earth eons ago, built us, then left us to our own devices. Well, they *were* a cult, once. By the time I was born, they were the fourth-largest religion in the world.

It was all just as much nonsense as Krishna or Jesus or the old-old gods that looked like dogs and cats. No one knew what was out there. No one would ever know.

When the film was over and Arjuna Sen had returned to Mumbai after uniting and saving the peoples of Eridani, Father kept hold of my hand and led me out of the theater. He didn't let go for the entire short walk to the train station.

I enjoyed the films, usually, but it was the gravlev trip home that I really looked forward to. I knew I had an hour of post-adventure bliss before my father reverted to his stern and defeated self. We would laugh, try to sing songs we had just heard without any clue of the lyrics, act out our favorite scenes and complain about the worst.

There was a light in his eyes that was absent when he was at home or at work at the factory. He was a smart and educated man working a job that required neither intellect nor knowledge. Even looking at my mother, my sister, me, did not bring that vibrancy out of him. I wasn't old enough

154

to remember my brother, Dev, but it was clear his death had hollowed Father like fire through the husk of a dead tree.

The train pulled into the station, and we found seats facing backwards. A few more people filtered in before the doors closed. It wasn't until we were on our way that he released my hand. I looked at him, waiting for the question.

"Thoughts?"

I knew what he wanted, but I still asked, "About what?"

"About the film. What did you think?"

"We've seen it here three times. And a million times at home."

"But what did you see differently?"

"It's the same every time."

"But you are not the same. Every time you see *Eka Rājakumārī*, you are older than the last time, wiser. Many more things have happened to you. The Virata you are now is not the Virata that saw the adventures of Arjuna Sen for the first time. When a piece of art stops surprising you, it is no longer worth returning to."

I thought for a long few seconds. I knew that no matter what I answered, we would still go see it the next time it screened. But I also didn't want to disappoint him. The longer I could keep the conversation going, the more time I had with the Father I liked and not the one I feared.

"The princess," I said.

"Dejah."

"Dejah Thoris."

"What about her?"

"She is beautiful."

"She is."

"And smart and strong and smart."

"She is very capable."

"Then why is she always in trouble?"

"Is she?"

"Arjuna had to rescue her three times. I counted."

"You did?"

I nodded.

"Why do you think that is?"

"Because she's stupid."

"You just said that she was smart."

"She does dumb things."

"Why does she do dumb things?"

"I don't know."

"Does Arjuna?"

I ran the story through my head at high speed.

"No."

"So why is Princess Dejah always getting into trouble?"

"Because it is a story written by men."

He smiled.

"And men," I continued, "want to feel like women need them to protect them."

"And do they?"

I crossed my arms. "No."

He put his arm around my shoulders.

"When you grow up and get married, you are going to make your husband miserable and humble, and he will thank you for it."

"I don't want a husband."

"You will."

I won't, I thought. "Yes, Father," I said.

I pouted for a minute. I never wanted to get married. Have children. My parents were so boring and dead. My sisters were like Dejah Thoris at her stupidest: all *rājkumārī*, no *yōd'dhā*. No warrior. A life of adventure and excitement was waiting for me.

I wasn't entirely wrong.

Father squeezed my shoulder and leaned into my ear. "But Ūna was still pretty cute, was he not?" Ūna was Arjuna's Eridani pet, a big, slobbering, loyal alien dog. He was my favorite part.

"He was adorable!" I broke, my pout vanishing. The rest of the trip we recounted Ūna's hijinks over and over until our sides hurt from the laughter. By the time we arrived home, his smile had faded, his shoulders had hunched, and the serious taskmaster had returned. My friend was gone.

I wouldn't see him again until the next trip to the *vīḍiyō-gharato*.

It was always worth the wait.

Until it wasn't.

IX: PRACTICAL

"THIS FUCKABLE LITTLE TART is a 1990 Browning Hi-Power Practical. *Neuf millimètres.* Is one of the most solid handguns of the lead and steel old times. Designed for the French by an American and a smelly Belgian. Have you ever met a Belgian? The Browning was used all over by soldiers and pigs until the Pact swept in and took them all away. Fucking stupid law, but it has made me a lot of *l'argent*, so I should not bitch. But I will always bitch. I am known for it. They call this model the 'Practical,' but it is no more useful, just much more sexier. Beautiful blued slide. Smooth nickel-plated body. Diamond-pattern textured grip. It is a sleek and impressive looking little thing. I would wrap my lips around it and suck it if I thought it would give it pleasure. But you don't care one shit, I know, I know. You just want to load and point and bang and kill. Michel will show you how. The magazine, this one here, holds thirteen rounds. You can

159

squeeze in one more if you want, but you don't want. You might get away with it, but it will more likely jam up on you and then where would you be? I don't give refunds for customer fuck-ups. I don't give any refunds. I told you that, right? No refunds. Well, yes, if it is *merde*, I will replace it, but only if I deem it to be *merde*, and this weapon is not *merde*. You just slide the clip up the pistol's ass like this. Fits tight. This little round button here makes it unclench and let it go. You see? Like this. Slide it in. Pop it out. Safeties on both sides. Slide it back like so, then pull back the hammer. See? It has only a single action, so you have to cock it before you fire the first shot, but after that, you can just pull and pull and pull until it goes click. It has enough balls to kill any man or beast on Earth and probably take down a Martian from Epsilon, whatever those assholes turn out be. I like to imagine they have heads like wolves and bodies like penguins. But that's just me. I doubt we'll ever see them, so might as well envision them as something amusing. I call them Lupguins. Pengwolves? The Lupguins of Epsilon. Anyway. Then you just aim it and shoot. The trigger on this one is tight like a schoolgirl, but it's smooth, and once you get it going, it should loosen up. Like a schoolgirl. This little asshole of a hammer will reach back and bite you in the web of your hand between shots. But a little soreness is the price you pay for your sins. Also like a schoolgirl. Here, take it. It should feel good when you hold it. How does it feel?"

The pistol fit in my hand like it had been forged just for me. I had never held a classic American make-dead. It was light but solid and substantial. It really was kind of sexy. It felt like death. It felt like power. In my mind's eye, I jammed it between the murderer's teeth and squeezed.

It felt right.

Bijan ignored an outstretched hand, knowing it was offered insincerely. He peered around the taller man. "Once you have cast off this plebeian, I have need of you in my chambers."

"You are a preposterous looking little man, but you know this," Michel said with a sense of wonder. "You have to know this. How could you not? I just..." He scanned Bijan from his sandals to his white robes to his unnaturally white hair. "How could you not?" He read the rage building in Bijan's eyes. "Oh. I see. You did not know, and I have broken the news to you rather ungracefully. Apologies, *Monsieur* Dominus."

"Are you feeble, or have you a desire for me to deliver you into the maw of Cerberus?" Bijan asked, his tongue tripping over the awkward phrasing. Always trying to stay in character.

"Italian is my fourth, perhaps fifth, language. I'm afraid you will have to speak slower and less ridiculously if you want me to understand."

Bijan spoke slowly, "Are you stupid, or do you just want me to kill you?"

"I am not, and I do not. Is there a third choice?"

The toga-clad idiot reached behind him and whipped out his pistol and leveled the gold and chrome hack at Michel's face. "No."

"*Tellement bête*," Michel said quietly.

I wasn't worried nearly as much as I was annoyed. "Boys, as much as you two killing each other would solve many of my problems, it would create a whole lot more. Can we just agree that you're both tough and weird and get on with our nights?"

After a beat of masculine staring, a smile crept across Michel's face. "Ha!" he yelled and gently nudged the gun

165

‡

aside. He grabbed Bijan by both sides of his head, pulled him close and planted a solid and audible kiss square on his lips.

"It was nice meeting you, *Monsieur* Dominus."

He took my arm, and we stepped away, leaving Bijan standing dumbstruck and seething in the hall.

"I believe I am passionately in love with that little man," he joked once we were outside and away from the building. "He is your lover?"

"Gross."

"But he has been in the past."

"Gross."

"He would like to be."

"He's not my type."

"Because he is a man."

"You give him too much credit."

"But it is because he is *anatomically* a man."

"It doesn't help."

"You owe him a lot of money."

"Yes."

"How much?"

"More than none."

"You are his slave."

"I'm nobody's slave."

"Everybody is somebody's slave. Even Michel. May I ask you something that has nothing to do the sexual energy flowing between us and that *très peu* man I just met?" I didn't say no in time.

"I ask not because it is my business but because it very much is not. What you going to do with the erotic piece of alloy I have sold to you tonight?" It wasn't his business. I tried to convey that with silence, but he blew through the sign and kept talking. "You have a hundred different ways around you to make someone dead, why do you want the only one you cannot have? A way that can get you nails through your wrists before you even get a chance to use it?"

They don't use nails. They tie you.

"I admire the weapon very much, but the dead it makes is no deader than any other hacked-up stun-gun you can buy on the street."

"It's not the right kind of dead."

"You do not make one sense to me. Who is this man you're going to kill?"

"How do you know it's a man?" I asked.

"I've never met a woman who deserved to die. It is a shame that they all must at one time or another. But men? There is always reason to kill a man."

"You've been paid. Go home before you give me a reason to kill you."

"Surely," he said. "I am on my way. But..." The longer I stood out in the street with Michel, the angrier Bijan would be when I got back inside. And drunker. "It's just that I have never sold American steel to someone who I knew actually wanted to use it."

It took a full beat for the sentence to register.

"What?"

"I sell to collectors. I sell these things to rich old men who want to display them in their offices. Perhaps some of them were intending on using my wares for nefarious purposes, but I have never been *absolument* aware that I would be causing the death of another human person. I find the situation frightening and exciting, but mostly, I am feeling sad."

I wasn't sure I understood. "You're not a gunrunner?"

"Technically, yes, I guess I am. I run guns, but I also sell art. Exotic spices and textiles and pets. Smuggled more than one illicit animal. The first time I was ever in Roma, I was delivering two albino Bengal tiger cubs, perhaps from your parents' back yard, to your current Caesar."

"Romulus and Remus."

"Oh, lovely. They are famous. I would very much like to look in on them."

"Why didn't he get wolves? With the names, they should have been wolves."

"The August One is afraid of dogs," he said as if it was common knowledge.

"And not of tigers?"

"Tigers are not dogs. They are just giant pussies."

I ran my hands down my face. I was surprised by his revelation, but it didn't mean anything to me. "I don't care. About you, about what you do. It doesn't matter. I have what I want. You have what you want. Too much of what you want, but it's the price I agreed to. I just want you to go away."

He nodded along with every point I made, but when I was finished, he said, "But you are not a collector. Not an old rich man. You plan to do violence. I've known this since the moment you walked in the door and lied that you didn't like mussels."

"I don't like mussels."

"The lies continue."

"But you sold it to me anyway. Why?"

"The mussels?"

"Why?"

"Why does anyone do anything?"

"Why?" I asked again.

"*Je ne sais pas.* Curiosity will one day kill this frog."

"And it's a lot of coin."

"It doesn't hurt." Michel pulled the lapels of his coat tighter. He gazed down the street. "You do not have to tell me anything. I only ask because I have no intention of ever speaking to you again. I have provided my service, as you have said, but I will have nothing to do with what you are planning."

"I'm not asking you to."

"Please lose my mobi number."

"It's already lost."

He looked at me and shook his head. "*Il n'y a pas une seule chose à propos de toi qui n'est pas honteuse.*"

"My French isn't very—"

"There isn't one thing about you that is not a shame," he said.

"You're not wrong."

He forced a big smile on his face and bowed. "*Mademoiselle* Vas."

Michel turned and walked away into the night like the dramatic caricature he claimed to be.

Bijan was waiting for me on his couch.

"Who was that intolerable Gaul?" he asked.

"A friend."

He snorted incredulously. "You have not friends. On not one occasion have I beheld a person or persons in this domicile with the purpose of calling upon you."

"I don't want anyone to see the luxury I live in. It would just make them feel bad."

"He was fortunate I did not smite him."

"He most definitely did not want to be smoten."

"He is your lover?"

"If one more person asks me that..."

"Is he?"

169

"No more than you or Kalb."

"I see."

I wasn't in the mood for this. All the men I knew were acting like sulking children.

There is always a reason to kill a man.

"You had something you wanted to talk to me about."

He pointed at me. "He do that to you?"

"Who do what to me?"

"Your face. Did that motherfucker— Did that ghastly man lay his hands upon your visage?"

"Is that what you wanted? To talk about how fucked up my face is?"

He shook his head. "The tribute you paid to me upon the last bacchanalia was short."

"Fuck you, it was short."

"Watch how you speak to me. My affection for you does not provide as much tolerance as you suppose. That's another hundred denarii."

I didn't apologize, but I changed my tone. "I'm never short on my *hafta*. You know that."

"And yet, on this occasion, you were. By two thousand talons."

"Maybe one of your playthings thought it was something else and swallowed or snorted or shoved it."

"Two thousand."

"I gave you the same coin I always do."

"And you owe me a great deal more, now that you have stepped away from the rank of my soldiers." Since taking the job for Kennedy, I hadn't collected any overdue gambling losses or broken the legs of any store keepers. That extra bit of violence had been keeping the interest at bay.

I hadn't considered that.

He was right. I was behind.

"Do you have it?" he asked.

The last of my coin just walked out of here with that intolerable Gaul, I thought.

He was exhausted, I could see. It didn't look like he wanted to dive into this, the most common of lender-lendee waltzes. The question was the first step in a very familiar dance.

"I don't."

"I have given you a wide berth for your adventures, Rata, but you *will* pay me, and you *will* pay me on time from here on out. You may pay this week's difference, plus a fine of five-hundred for your tardiness, on top of your next *hafta.*"

"I'll have it tomorrow," I said. And I would. Which made the entire conversation boring.

"How?"

"I'll have it. Tomorrow afternoon."

"You promise?"

"Absolutely."

"Tomorrow afternoon, or we are going to have a conversation of an entirely different sort."

"You have my word, Dominus." I went back upstairs and into my room and fell on the mattress. The next day was going to be busy. I needed to get more money from Orso, which would take care of Little Antony down there, maybe get enough to pay up for a few weeks ahead. I also needed to ask Jao if he could take the lock of Not Him's hair I had pulled off of his deceased head and run it for DNA. Then I wanted to talk to Kennedy himself. This was not a random criminal gunning down a random woman. There were others involved. I had spoken to one of them. He wasn't telling me everything.

‡

As I drifted off to sleep, Bijan's last words rattled around in my head:

"A conversation of an entirely different sort."

PROXY

✠

X: KADIRA

THAT WARM MAY AFTERNOON, I REACHED *Piazza della Repubblica* having no idea everything was about to come crashing down to bury me like the ashes of Pompeii.

I took long, quick strides. Three messages to Orso had gone unanswered, so I would be showing up at the St. Regis unannounced and unhappy. "Listen, Orso," I was going to say. "I need to talk to your boss, and don't give me the nonsense about not being able to handle 'meeting himself' or feeling weird about it. I don't care about feeling weird. I'm the one out there. I'm the one getting my face knocked around. You see my eye? Here? Do these look like the bruises of a woman who cares if some old man feels weird?"

Orso would remain calm and stoic and try to deflect me.

"Miss Das, The Senator believes—"

"I don't care what he believes. There is more to this. He's not telling me everything. He wants this done. I want

173

this done. But there's no way I can do that with only half the story."

"Miss Das—"

Maybe I would grab him by the collar, send his cane clattering to the floor, and growl, "If you call me 'Miss Das' one more time, I will break your head. Stop it with the unflappable manservant thing. I've had enough of men playing characters. I'm tired of fronts. Go in there, tell the ancient fuck what I said and don't come back out until you've convinced him that talking to me, face-to-face, right now, is the best idea in history."

And then I would beg him for another advance on my allowance.

The math had been done. I needed coin to keep Bijan off me for several weeks, a month if possible, plus enough to keep the job moving forward. I also had a lock of Not Him's hair in my pocket. I didn't have the resources to run it, but Kennedy did. If they were serious about finding the real killer, they would have to help me find out who the fake one was. Alba had the rest of the hair. She thought she had someone who could read it for us, but we had decided to split the sample and see what each of us could come up with.

Reaching the hotel, I cut down the shady path towards the diplomatic entrance. It took a full beat for it to hit me, but something was definitely wrong.

No guards.

Nobody at all.

I got to the green double doors and tried to push them open, knowing they would be locked, then punched the call button on the pad. The command registered, the screen blinked and then reset, not even attempting to ping through. Two more tries fell flat, and I headed towards the front of the building. When I hit the corner and turned right, I fought the urge to run. I wanted to keep calm. It was probably nothing. The dolts that usually watched the door were probably getting lunch or had sneaked away to sodomize each other. Maybe the Senator was out somewhere, and his gunmen were traveling with him. I was just annoyed that Orso hadn't messaged me back and that the trip could turn out to be a waste of time.

I really needed the money. Right then. I had been very clear with Bijan and couldn't come back to him that afternoon with empty pockets.

I reached the front entrance, between the columns that framed the portico, and, when the doorman had his back turned, rushed inside. The lobby was overpoweringly gold. All shades of it covered the ceiling, the walls, the molding, punctuated occasionally with a red leather chair or wrought iron handrail. It was a place with no concern for or notion of the state of things elsewhere. The same as the people who frequented it. Many of the richest people in Roma, people like Kennedy, had made their stays at the St. Regis permanent, preferring the insulated and pampered living it provided over the harsher realities of the true Roma.

Immediately to my right was a narrow chamber with three check-in desks. Only one was manned. The clerk at the desk wore a red blazer and a loosely knotted necktie, and stiffened when he saw me coming. I tried to make my face neutral, keep down any signs of agitation or anger. I just wanted to get up to see Kennedy.

"I'm sorry," he said to me. "The custodial entrance is on the northern side of the building."

The only people who looked like me who got to frequent the St. Regis were the maids and sweepers and cooks and servants employed there.

"I need to get up to the Imperial Suite."

"The Imperial Suite?"

I nodded. "I usually go up the private lift, but the men who let me in before are gone. I need to get up there or at least take a message to the room."

"That's not going to happen, but for my own sense of curiosity, why?"

"I have business with the man staying there."

"Business?"

"Yes. With Senat— With Admiral Moreno."

He cocked an eye. "We don't allow that type of business on these premises."

"I'm not a whore. I have real business."

"Whoring is a real business," he said, like he had experience with it. He swiped around on his datascreen, paying attention to it instead of looking me in the eyes.

"I wish I could help you, but—"

"No, you don't."

"I truly do. It is my job to help, and I take pride in my job. I like to do it well. But I cannot allow you up to the Imperial Suite. For many reasons, to be sure, but mostly because there is no one staying in the Imperial Suite."

What? I thought. "What?" I said.

"There is no one in the Imperial Suite."

"Since the fuck when?"

"I'm sorry."

"What about Kennedy? Moreno?"

"I'm sorry." He looked at my hands, a stark contrast against the white marble counter. "Are you related in any way to the former tenant?"

"You know I'm not."

"Then I cannot help you. If you would like to rent the suite, I can tell you that there is a four-year waiting list, and with a deposit of five hundred thousand yuros, I can put you on it."

"Where is he?"

Disdain flashed in his eyes. "Get the fuck out of my hotel before my friends behind you throw you out on your Paki cunt."

I backed away from the desk and turned around. Two large security guards were walking quickly towards me from the lobby. I put my arms up. They slowed, but just a bit. It looked like they really did prefer I left on my own. "Okay, okay. I'm going."

I walked backwards towards the doors, not wanting to turn away from them. Every eye in the lobby was on me; it was probably the most excitement the sequestered rich had seen in some time. I couldn't tell if the clerk was a born motherfucker, or if I had stumbled onto something else. The guards kept pace with me, staring me down, but never moving towards the stun batons hanging from their belts. They just wanted me gone.

I obliged.

I turned and ran, slamming into and pushing my way through the doors and back into the street. Out on the sidewalk, I stumbled into two men, sending them staggering away. I lost my balance, tripped and fell ass-first into the street.

In the gutter. With the rest of the...

Northern entrance.

I stood back up, checked to make sure that no one from the hotel had come out to watch me and then walked north along the length of the building.

Before the corner, I passed the Whistling Lions, an old fountain, with an image of an even older god looking down on four resting great cats. When it was built, water poured from the rounded mouths of the beasts, but now, they looked like they were whistling. There were hundreds of whistling animals all over Roma.

No one in the suite? What the fuck did that mean? I pulled out my mobi and sent another message to Orso. And got no response. Again. A rush shot through me like someone had replaced the stims and painkillers in my ASIS with fear and anger and nausea. What were the chances of the room being empty and Orso's mobi going silent at the same time being a coincidence? Something was going on, going wrong, going to shit.

I got around the corner and found the service entrance, but it wasn't what I was looking for. There would be security, bag checks and people who saw each other day after day and would notice a strange face. Across the street, though, was a lunch truck, parked in an alley next to an old church. A queue of hotel workers led up to its window. Most of the waiting were brown-skinned and wearing the uniforms of cooks, cleaners and carriers.

I got in line behind an old Pak man wearing a crimson and gold bellman's suit made of material so cheap I was afraid another few moments of sunlight would send it up in flames. He turned around and gave me the once-over, then turned back around. I fished into my pocket and pulled out a few hundred-yuro chips. There was another thousand stashed in my cube, but after that, I was done.

"Old timer," I leaned in and whispered to him. "Can I ask you a question?"

When he turned back around, I had a hundred yuros between my fingers and was holding it up for him to see. His eyes flicked to it. He said nothing, but he didn't look away.

"Did something happen in the Imperial Suite this week?"

His eyes shifted from the money to me. "You don't work here."

"There's been an old American living on the top floor. I want to know when he left, where he went, anything. I've got more coin to move around if you know anyone who can help me."

Not that much more, though.

"You should talk to Kadira." He nodded towards the stairs of the church, where a majority of the workers had chosen to eat their lunches. "Kadira can help you."

"Which one is Kadira?"

"The cleaner, there, that one. Sitting on the bottom step. The tall one with the long braid down to her ass."

"And why should I talk to her?"

"Because she saw the body."

He plucked the chip from between my fingers and turned back around to wait for his lunch.

We were three grav stations away from the end of the line, and the man across from me was still asleep. His bike was leaned against the wall of the train, a meter out of his reach. He was snoring softly and may have been on something or coming to the end of a long day, but either way, I was going to be cruel to him when we stopped at Muratella.

"No one was allowed in the suite," the cleaner named Kadira had told me. She was a beautiful woman with damaged eyes earned through three decades of serving others without gratitude. "Not since the old American got here. Food carts went into the lift by themselves and came back down empty and piled high with dirty linens and clothes. People talk. Make up stories. They say that the man was older than a man should be. An ancient one, or a sorcerer. You know the man? You do, huh?"

I tapped the chips I had placed on the step in front of her to remind her that I was the one asking the questions.

"Anyway," she continued, "three days ago, I was walking to work and saw the guards were gone. I got around to here, and everyone was mumbling and grumbling, and my shift boss grabbed me and Jena and told us to grab our gear and took us to the lift. When we got up to the suite, I was surprised it looked just like it had before. I had a picture in my mind that he had made it into some sort of crazy person cave."

"Kadira," I said impatiently. "The body."

She nodded. "There were two Legionnaires standing over him with scanners in their hands. He was on his back, wearing one of our robes. It had spread out under him like a cape. He looked very old but also not so old. Frail and worn but a full head of hair and not so wrinkly skin. Very strange."

After the cleaner's brief but accurate description of Kennedy's contradictory traits, I stopped paying attention to what she was saying. My head was spinning. How could he be dead? He was supposed to live forever. He had spent billions to make sure he would live forever.

How could he be dead?

"What happened?" I managed to ask.

"What?"

"How did he die?"

"Don't know. My boss shoved me and Jena into the bathroom and told us to start cleaning and closed the door. By the time we got out, the body was in a bag."

"Was there anyone else there? A bald man, maybe fifty years old. An Italian?"

She shook her head.

I had thanked her and left her with my last three hundred yuros.

The train slowed as we approached the end of the line, and the slumbering man started to come around. The lights of the station came towards us. He yawned and stretched. I would have to time it just right. We stopped, and as the doors began to open, I darted over, grabbed the bike and slid between the doors before the man got to his feet.

I had gambled on it having some charge in it, and it did. When I hit the platform, I threw my leg over the seat and punched it all-forward, careening down the six concrete steps that led to the street. Behind me, I heard the rightful owner calling me a bitch at the top of his lungs.

He wasn't wrong.

I guided the bike along the same route Orso had taken me the night I had let them play around with my brain. The long ride was spent combating my natural tendency to assume and expect and embrace the worst. I had no reason to doubt what Kadira had told me, but I had to.

Had to.

The dead and rotten roads leading to the ruins of Fiumicino didn't seem as frightening in the afternoon sun as they had in the black of night. I had to keep the charge in the bike up by pedaling when I could. My calves were screaming by the time I arrived at the perimeter of the abandoned airport, but I couldn't listen to them. I sent a dash of chryo into my stream to shut them up.

I couldn't wrap my head around it. I had to find Orso. If Kennedy was dead, I was still owed money. The full ten million would be too much to hope for, but he would have to give me something. Something for the time and the effort and the pain. Something for carrying around his boss's memories and heartache in my brain.

Something for having dangled hope in front of me like Hala's gold watch only to snatch it away when the immortal man who offered it turned out to be very mortal.

I was carrying the thoughts and memories of a dead man in my head. At the very least, I had to find Jao, the Senator's scalpelpunk, and have him rip the *meccacampo* out of my head and erase the entire thing so I could forget all about Caden and Amelia Kennedy. I was facing enough problems. The nightmares and flashbacks had to go.

I pulled onto the Fiumicino tarmac and headed in the general direction of Kennedy's laboratory. I could hear a gentle wind, the whirring of the stolen bike's tiny motor and my heart thumping furiously in my breast. The rest was desolate silence. I dodged and wobbled between the craters and piles of rubble that Kennedy's limo had handled easily. I passed a dozen empty hangars before I came upon the one with the blue E L T A printed on it.

Kennedy and his lackey were not waiting for me out front. I was not greeted with a quip. The hulking structure stood cold and quiet like all the others. To no surprise, the front door was locked. I couldn't kick it in; it was steel and not going anywhere.

How am I going to—

"Skylights."

There had been skylights.

I found a manageable-looking pipe and began to climb. The act reminded me of basic training, a time in my life when I had actually been good at things, when I had felt like I was making right decisions and that maybe I had a future worth getting to, despite knowing I soon would be launching myself out of a Stealth Insertion MagJet and into a war. In camp, I was a star. Stronger, faster and smarter than the rest of the recruits. Even when I joined the jumpers, who were considered elite, I stood out. Superlative in hand-to-hand classes, the woman you needed to knock down if you wanted to be seen as the new big dick. No one ever did.

By the time we hit the sky, I had been promoted to *Subedar-Major* and given my own squad. I was very good at being a cadet, but, turned out, shit at actual soldiering and a fucking tragedy at being a leader of men.

I reached the top and pulled myself onto the roof. There were four large skylights on the roof that looked down into the massive structure. I knelt next to one and peered into the building below. The lab had been trashed. The makeshift walls, pulled down. Equipment bashed into components and scrap. Tanks shattered, their fluids collected in pools that had run together to make a web of chemical solvents on the floor, the organs in them most likely shriveled and dead. I was too far away to tell for sure. They could have been taken. Either way, the new insides Kennedy had been growing for himself were gone.

Tables had been overturned. Papers torched. Freezers had been unplugged, and terms had been smashed. The Senator's entire operation had been murdered and left to rot on the cold hangar floor.

And so had his right-hand man.

The body lay face-up in what used to be one of the surgical suites, its left leg twisted underneath its torso, the arms splayed. Blood pulp and tissue where the face used to be. A pool of dark and dry blood framed a shattered head. It was dressed in a suit. A suit I knew well.

On the floor a half-meter from the corpse's outstretched hand was a simple black cane. I couldn't see from that height, but I knew it had a bronze sphere at one end of it.

Orso was dead.

And Kennedy was dead.

‡

Virata wasn't far behind.

I stood up and walked back towards my drainpipe. My vision was blurry, my whole body humming. I reached the edge and stopped. Fifty meters to the ground. It would probably be enough to get it done.

To get me done.

There was no doubt the Senator had been murdered. Kadira hadn't seen anything to hint either way, but the destruction below me was solid evidence. It must have been the same guys that killed Amelia, either coming back to finish the job or getting wind of Kennedy's quest, my quest, for vengeance and deciding to take preventive measures. They wanted me. The man on the phone had told me so. I was the one who had killed their man. If I hadn't been standing on the precipice of the end of my life, I would have thought it funny that *they* were seeking revenge on *us*.

It dawned on me I was probably being watched, but I was beyond caring. I had banked on this job as the final solution to the all-over problem that was my life. I was either going to get out or go down trying, and it had turned out to be the latter.

I couldn't say I was surprised.

I inched closer to the edge.

I couldn't run. The train out of Roma only left once every two weeks, sometimes not even then, and to get on, you needed proof you were a real, legal person. Solid, airtight documentation in the form of an ID pass and a passable fingerprint check. Because once you left the borders of the city-state, you were in foreign lands and, even in a kleptocracy like Napoli, needed to prove who you were to get off the train.

I had spent the money I was advanced frivolously. No one who could make an ID that would pass scrutiny would do it for free. The only person who maybe could have, Michel, I had driven off. He had walked away from me, frightened. There were other smugglers, men who could get me out under the cover of darkness, hidden in the backs of cargo haulers or under the floorboards of gravtraks. But again, that would cost coin, and at the other end of the trip, no matter where they dropped you off, you had to prove you were allowed to be there.

And if they found out I wasn't, I'd be printed, cross-checked and sent back to India, exposed and tried as the deserter and traitor I was.

If I came down from the hangar any other way than plummeting, I would be going back to a life in which I was cripplingly indebted to The Sindeketa and possibly sought by an unknown group that had managed to kill an immortal man. It was a life in which I had made enemies, spurned friends, burned bridges to cinders.

I hoped someone was watching me. Begged for a silent shot from an unseen sniper to take the decision out of my hands, but it didn't come.

Maybe the old man had been wrong. Maybe my father had been right. Maybe I would hit the ground and be instantly tossed back into the painful fray. Or cradled to the bosom of my creator, reunited with those I loved. Merged into some sort of collective to live forever as glorious light.

Maybe I would wake up on Epsilon Eridani at the beginning of a new adventure.

I didn't want any of those things.

I just wanted it to be over.

I closed my eyes and spread my arms. I willed my foot to move, but it wouldn't. Paralysis took me. My mind wanted to die, but the rest of me refused. Retreating from the

✝

edge would bring me nothing but pain and struggle. For the rest of my life, however long I was able to hold on to it.

Continuing forward, though, would bring nothing but peace.

I took two large strides backwards.

Kāyara, I silently screamed at myself. *Coward.*

I had proven at home, on the battlefield and now, once again, on top of an abandoned airline hangar, I was scared. Scared that there wasn't any more to death than darkness.

And even more scared that there was.

XI: THE BLACK, THE DARK, THE VOID

THE NEXT TWELVE HOURS blurred past in a brew of desperation, fear and hourly doses of chryocane and nitrocodone. I had sworn to never go that way again, to never medicate myself to get through, but they had given me a 'plant that let me make-numb with a thought, and I didn't want to feel a thing I didn't have to.

I tore my way through Chinatown asking about the 'plantjock I only knew as Jao, threatening and charming and promising phantom bribes and being met with empty stares and colorful suggestions in both Italian and Mandarin that I go away and pleasure myself if I didn't have any actual coin to put on the table. And I didn't. Have any actual coin. I had spent the last of it paying a maid to tell me my life was over. After a few hours, I started to attract attention, and the local enforcers started to tail me. I wanted to start something. I wanted to fight them. To fight anybody.

I didn't even know if Jao was alive. The odds were against it. He could have been sharing the same grave as Orso, and I just hadn't seen him, his corpse hidden under a toppled wall or table. But he was my only chance for answers. Someone had to be accountable for what I was owed. Explain to me what had happened. Someone needed to help me, because even though the reward wasn't going to happen, I still wanted to find the man who killed Amelia. And that was unacceptable. If I wasn't going to walk away rich, I wasn't going to wear the chip, and I wasn't going to kill the guy.

No matter how much I wanted to.

I needed Jao to rip the dead American out of my head.

My head was fuzzy, a mess, so I started streaming Adrenaclear to give me some pep. Sleep wasn't an option. I had more to do. No time to waste.

It's not enough you're devolving back into a fucking chryo-freak, now you're going to start spinning? What are you doing? You swore.

Halfway back to The Orphanage from Chinatown, my mobi buzzed for the twentieth time, with the twentieth message from Alba. I hadn't responded to any of them, but she wasn't going to stop. I needed her to stay away from me:

JOB IS DONE. SO ARE WE. FUCK OFF

I didn't bother waiting for a reply. I powered down the term and put it away. There was no need for further conversation. The job was done.

Whatever she felt for me, whatever I deluded myself into thinking I felt for her, it no longer mattered. I had to look out for myself. The decision I had made, the last play I thought I had to make, it couldn't involve her. She was going to have to fend for herself. She was tough. Strong. She could handle it. She needed to forget about me.

She needed to fuck off, for her own good.

And for mine.

I lay on my stomach as the odorous and rude man ran a humming wand up and down my body. The stench of booze, smoke and sweat made me miss the antiseptic aroma of Kennedy's operating theater. "I don't see anything," he said.

"Keeping looking."

"I've scanned you top to bottom twice. No homing gear. None. You're clean."

I rolled over to look at him. I had dealt with the cutter known as Grease before, but never as a patient. The wilderness he had grown on his face and neck was probably there to cover up a monstrous face. It for sure didn't make things feel any more sanitary.

"Then just take the chip."

"It's not worth anything, kid. Pennies' worth of material. But the wiring, the rig itself, it's well done. Deft as fuck. If you can sell me the hands and brain of the chink who planted it, I'd pay you very nice."

"He's a ghost."

"Aren't we all? I can give you a little cash for the ASIS. What shape is it in?"

I touched the back of my neck. I could feel the polyplast unit under my skin.

"New-new," I said, then asked, "How much?"

"I'll give you a thousand."

That wasn't enough to get me anywhere. Not on the street, in the world, not with Bijan. Grease was low-balling me, but you didn't run a business like his by playing fair. I still could have used the coin. It would have been something.

But the deadeners and stims I was getting out of the unit were the only things keeping me going. I couldn't move on without them. The road ahead was going to be rocky, and I would need them to make the ride a little smoother.

I needed them.

You promised, bitch. You promised.

"Leave it."

"Fine. And the chip?"

I thought about Amelia and love and loss and her dead in my arms. I thought about the man in the top hat and shiny suit, the rage and the fire. About Not Him dying on the bathroom floor, his words smothered and aborted in his throat. I thought about Alba and Michel and Bijan and the man on the other end of the mobi call. The dead butler. A murdered old man. A top hat. Suicide vice. A necklace of amber. Ink stockings on a perfect leg. Mysteries. Lies.

I thought about the hole in me that wasn't there before Doctor Amelia Lynn Starr-Kennedy-sometimes-Moreno came into my life. A space that had before been filled with dull and inert matter. I missed that matter, the gray null. The cold stuffing of this dangerous and desperate doll. It had been useless, but it hadn't hurt. It hadn't anything.

But the dark, the black, the void, the hole that had been ripped right through my core since meeting and losing Amelia, that gaping wound, it—

"Take it out," I said.

"And grind it to dust."

I came to Bijan with empty hands and pockets. I didn't have his money. I never would. It wasn't coming. My miracle had been a mirage.

PROXY
‡

I could have gone back to the Circus and hidden amongst the other hard cases and addicts, and waited for the chryo to get the best of me. I could have stolen, cadged or sold my body. I could have joined the dregs and become invisible, like the Untouchables of old-old India.

But instead, I came to Bijan Antonius, knowing he would find me if I didn't.

I wanted him to be angry. But he wasn't.

I wanted him to be cruel, but he was calm and kind.

I wanted him to tell me I was done. That he had no choice. That he had floated me as long as he could, but eventually The Sindeketa collected on its debts, one way or the other.

I wanted him to kill me.

Instead, he took me by the hand and sat me on his couch.

Instead, he told me it would all be okay.

Instead, he told me there was a solution to all my problems.

Instead, he smiled.

Because he knew he now had what he wanted.

He knew he had me.

PROXY

✝

XII: DOMINUS

EVERY TIME I WOKE UP IN BIJAN'S BED, it took a long moment of luxuriating in the silk sheets that smelled of flowered oils and sweat to remember where I was. When I did, the tsunami of hate and despair and *gross* crashed into me, and I had to get up and out before it pulled me under and out to sea.

Bumps erupted over my bare skin when it hit air. My dress was on the floor; I stepped into it, pulled it up and hung it on my shoulders. I wanted my jacket, but it was in my chest in my cube with my mobi and the other gear I wasn't supposed to have on me while I was serving my Dominus. I could hear the shower in the other room, which meant I couldn't leave. Not until he came out and gave me permission. I slid into my sandals, put on my serpentine jewelry, tied up my hair and, to complete my morning ritual, jacked a good-size dose of nitrocodone by way of the unit in my neck.

"Good morn, my flower." Bijan stood in the doorway, his body still glistening, his omnipresent hair matted and dark. I hadn't heard the water stop running.

"Good morn, Antonius."

"How did you slumber?"

I hadn't managed to put together one night of unbroken sleep since I had come to Bijan to beg for leniency on my debts. *How do you think I slumbered? I was lying next to you. Every time you touch me, I want to carve the offended skin out with a scalpel*, I thought. "Just fine," I said. "Dominus."

"You've already donned your gown."

"Should I not have?"

"I believe you should never be engarmented. You possess a body that surely drives Venus herself into fits of envious rage and fevered Sapphic madness." Bijan had spent the first week trying to get me to talk like him, but I was willfully inept at it, and he stopped. "It is spitting in the face of the gods to cover it. But the everyday Muslims amongst whom we live still cling to their ancient mores and a ridiculous sense of shame."

When he mentioned my body, I couldn't help casting a brief glance down across the landscape. I had lost three or four kilos during my month of bondage. I couldn't see my ribs, but I knew they had begun to show. Bijan had more food around than anyone I knew, but I had no appetite. I ate only what I needed to sustain me, and sometimes less than that, and it all tasted like dirt. I was sure the stimulants hadn't helped, either.

Bijan made no move for a towel and instead swaggered across the room towards me, drizzling water along the tiles.

He had had so much to drink the night before, it was surprising to me that he could put one foot in front of the other.

"You're expected in twenty minutes," I said, hoping to get his mind on the business of the day.

He placed a hand on either side of my face and pulled me to him, and when he put his lips to mine, his breath still stunk of wine. The tongue he slipped into my mouth was dry and rough. His hands left my cheeks and slid down to my neck as he continued to maul me with his kisses. He hooked his index fingers through the straps of the toga and pulled them off my shoulders. He stepped away from me just enough to give the dress room and time to drop. I felt it pile up around my feet as he stepped back into position.

His cock stiffened against my inner thigh, and I braced myself for one more dip into Hell.

Bijan and I parted the weekend crowd arm-in-arm, slowly, through the Maggiore Market. His hands locked behind his back, and his gait consciously slow. He nodded to every man he passed. Subtly bowed to the women. Most of them smiled back. Some respected him, some feared him, hated him, thought him a joke, and a few females, unbelievably, seemed to covet him. He was a known man. Known to have money, to have power, to be the only cousin of Sarkis Wur. Several times, in the privacy of his flat, I had seen Bijan break the character he had created for himself, but out in public, amongst his people, or who he thought were his people, he was always on. He was a Roman citizen of the old-old times. A gangster. A leader. A soldier. A benevolent prince of Pakitown.

He was, in the narrative he held in his bleached head, Marc Antony. Not the Caesar but the Caesar's man.

✝

And he had found his Cleopatra.

Two days after I had agreed to act as his consort, he brought me the sleeveless white toga-like dress and a pair of matching gold armbands formed to look like entwined snakes. Wearing them was not optional in his presence.

"You will be my valet, my bodily security and, to the eyes of others, my companion," he had said to me twelve hours after I stupidly had chosen not to jump off the hangar roof. "I will not force you into my bed. I am a rich man and have my pick of any hole in The Esquilino. I will not force you, but you are, of course, welcome at any time. And if you ever want to bring along that cut-up street bitch I see you with, you will be doubly so."

But after a week, Bijan's chivalrous attitude gave way to his lust, and it became obvious that me coming to him was what he wanted. Soon it became what he expected. Then required.

So I did. Go to him.

I needed him to feel like I was his, that he owned me. He was a territorial and jealous little creep who demanded people respect the things on which he had pissed. I needed to be his property. No one would touch me when I was with him. They, the white hats, whoever the they were, wouldn't want to start a war with The Sindeketa. If it meant an occasional two and a half minutes of soul-smothering unpleasantness to keep them away, I had endured worse.

It would buy me enough time to find a way out or enough courage to throw myself in front of a speeding gravlev. Until then, the hydro and nitro would keep me fuzzed-out and disinterested and largely pain-free. I never went long enough without to get the shakes and trusted the ASIS to keep me from dosing myself to death, even though part of me, a lot of me, wished that it would.

PROXY
‡

Bijan stopped and casually picked an apricot off a cart. He smiled at the vendor, an old man who had seen enough in his life to know he didn't have to smile back. Bijan turned the fruit in his hand, then bit into it. The juice ran down his chin. He chewed and swallowed, then tossed the remaining majority of it into the street.

"You wares are most tastyful," he said, then turned to go. The vendor scowled and caught my eye as we passed. I wanted to give him some coin, but my dress didn't have pockets. I tried to give him an apologetic smile, but it was returned only with contempt.

At that moment, he and I had the exact same feelings about the woman named Virata Das.

The make-numbs were doing something more important than making it easier to be a disgusting man's slave and whore. That was pain I probably could have handled on my own. Pushed through. There was something else in my head that I was trying to drown in the chems, but the results had been spotty. It was a buoyant thing and a good swimmer and managed to get its head above water just often enough to keep breathing:

I remembered Amelia Starr.

The memories were still there, as bright as before. Beautiful, hideous and burning.

And the hole. The void.

Thirty days. Still there.

The chip had been removed and destroyed, the nanofiber connecting it to my brain severed, and the man who had birthed the memories was a month dead and gone and probably now a pile of ash, but everything he had given me was still there, metastasizing from the *meccacampo* to my natural gray matter.

I missed her. I mourned her. I needed her.

‡

I still wanted to find the man who ended her and take the Browning and paint the cobblestones red and gray.

And maybe do the same to Bijan while I'm at it.

But it wouldn't help me.

It was a job that got shit-canned mid-shift, a night-cover drop sortie aborted after I had already jumped from the SIM and into the enemy dark. There was no material motivation for me to continue with the search, and I really had no means with which to do so. Nor did I want to. Amelia's death hadn't just killed her; it killed the Senator, Orso, the guy in the bathroom and who knows how many others. It had nothing to do with me. Whatever had happened, whatever web had been spun and whatever dominoes had fallen, I didn't want to care.

But I did.

I wasn't going to pursue it any longer.

But I needed to.

I was still aflame.

And I would drug myself for the rest of my life if it would help me forget the woman I had never met but loved with all of my heart.

My Amelia...

We continued north towards Santa Maria Maggiore. The thugs watching the door patted both me and Bijan down for weapons, then, satisfied, held the door open for us. We stepped inside, and it immediately grew several degrees colder and uglier.

The inside, due to its art being handed back to the Church in return for ceding the building, was a flavorless and dull cavernous husk with only the marble columns and some of the stained glass remaining. The enormous basilica was used mostly by the Paks as a warehouse. Pallets and pallets of crates, stacked four and five high, filled the main chamber. The towers and avenues between them looked like a miniature city. There was a live animal pen with chickens and hogs. A nice-looking e-cart, no doubt freshly stolen, was parked near the entrance, half-covered with a tarp.

I let go of Bijan's arm and paused for a step to allow him to take a small lead. In this place, I was his servant and bodyguard, seen, not heard, over his shoulder but always close enough to throw myself between him and danger.

Just inside the church, on the far right wall, was a small chamber. It had once been, from what I could tell by what was left of the markings, the tomb of a long-dead Pope. The round chamber had high ceilings, and everything ornamental had been stripped from the walls. In the middle of the room was a circular recess, surrounded by a small wall of red and white marble. In the recess, which was only two steps down, was a large round table.

This was the meeting hall for the *Yatiim* Senate.

The men and women stood around the table. Zita Mira, who was a dwarf, stood on a stool to see her peers eye-to-eye. Safia Gondal, a thin bird of a woman, stood next to her. There were two men, Imam Harb Niazi, sixty years old and always wearing his clergy clothes, and Amir Campisano, who looked as Pak as the others but had elected to keep his father's Italian name.

They called themselves a senate, but they weren't elected, nor did they pass laws or conduct their affairs in a public forum. They were a cabal, a quintumvirate of two women and three men who decided what was best for everyone.

But mostly what was best for them.

Bijan wasn't a member; he acted on behalf of his younger cousin, Sarkis, who was a real boss and not a pretender, but who also hadn't bothered to show up to a session in over a year. Which left my master the effective representative of The Sindeketa in Pakitown.

"Fellow legislators! We once again meet in The Curia!" Bijan called as we approached the meeting. His voice echoed upwards. They all looked at him with expressions that clearly read, *Great. The maniac is here.* I nodded to the other aides and guards and, like them, sat on the marble floor with my back to the rounded outer wall.

The first thirty minutes of the meeting were boring to me and even more so for Bijan. It wasn't long before he was nodding off, or at least pretending to, although I was sure the giant green cigarette he had smoked before we left the flat wasn't helping. They talked about the possible taxation of The Orphanage, which of course was shot down for the thousandth time, and leveled accusations of price-fixing at Zita Mira, who represented the *Yatiim* merchants.

I zoned out, still listening and picking up key words, but not bothering to follow the conversation. The imam was talking, and I had no desire to listen to yet another diatribe about how he would like to roll the community back to the time of *burqas* and veils and throwing stones. He ran three mosques, all of them in abandoned white churches, the closest of which was just south of Maggiore.

The religion is, of course, nothing more than a toxic mythology, but aren't they all? Kennedy's voice echoed in my head. I couldn't disagree. Every institution of faith was as gutted and rotten as the church we were in. Islam. Christianity. Hinduism. Roman Paganism. The Children of Epsilon. All empty and without answers, because there were no answers to be had.

Learned men do not grieve for the Dead or the Living.

Safia Gondal did most of the talking. She had been appointed the year before by the other Senators to represent the people and, much to their frustration, took the job seriously. She was popular, and what she wanted and thought held sway. She was also a brutal and cold bitch when she went after what she wanted.

I liked her.

"Which brings us to the subject of crime," she said. I looked back over my shoulder. Bijan's eyes were closed, his chin resting on his chest.

"Antonius," she said sternly. The Senate was the only place where anyone called Bijan by his preferred name with any sense of consistency and with a limited amount of ridicule. "Antonius!"

He opened an eye at her. He hadn't been sleeping; he had been making a point.

"Yes, Safia?"

"Have you been enjoying yourself so far?"

He stretched. "By the balls of Sulla, I have not, but do not let that impede your progress."

"My contact in The Legion has informed me that there has been a rapid increase in theft and violence in Roma proper being perpetrated by people who look like us."

"No one looks like me."

"*Ḍakait* from The Orphanage."

"Hath there been? Of this I am ignorant."

"And of many other things," Campisano chimed in.

Bijan ignored him. "I am certain this bodes well for Miss Mira. With the criminals going outside to feed, it leaves her traders alone and able to carry on with their more subtle version of thievery."

The little woman shrugged.

"I am not sure why this is a topic you have deemed worthy of rhetoric," Bijan said.

"We have provided every Orphan in the city assistance and asylum, no matter what they're accused of," Gondal continued.

Bijan nodded. "As well we should."

"I propose today that we stop doing that."

Her words caused all of the others to bristle.

"And why is that?" the holy man asked.

"Because I want them to stop leaving The Esquilino and victimizing the Romans."

"You would rather we prey on our own?" Bijan asked.

"I would rather there be no crime at all, but since that would offend twenty percent of this body—"

"Forty." Bijan pointed at Zita, who again shrugged.

"The Orphanage is not just our neighborhood. It is our nation. These are our homes, our streets, our business and families. If we want it to stay that way, if we want the Caesar to ignore our sovereign city in the middle of his sovereign city, then it needs to stay our crime, as well."

Campisano shook his head. "I don't understand."

Bijan began to pace like a trapped jungle cat. "Carry on, woman. Speak your nonsensitudes so you may clear your enfeebled mind of it. And be concise, for thus far your position smells of perfidy."

She sighed. "Just for once, I wish you would stop speaking like a brainsick street performer."

"Just as I wish you would stop acting like a petulant sow, my lady. But the chances of that seem to be desperately slim."

The others watched without speaking.

"What do you do when a white Roman steps foot onto Esquiline Hill?" she asked.

"We observe him until he departs."

"What do they do when one of us is seen walking in the Trastavere or socializing on the Steps or going anywhere north of Nationale?"

"The same."

"The same."

"But they don't come here."

"And why is that?"

"Because they are afraid of us."

"Do you know what will make them more afraid? When we are pulling stick-ups, selling hypnometh and running whores in their neighborhoods."

"Let them be afraid."

"Your defiance is stirring until they decide to send The Legion."

"No Legionnaire would dare set foot in The Esquilino."

"Not one. But if all of them did, side-by-side, if a wall of Villano's shocktroops marched across the river and up Via Merulana and pounded on the doors of this building, what could we do? What could you do, Bij— Antonius? You and your pack of ignorant *ḍakait*?"

Bijan looked to the others and got blank stares in return.

"We would fight them. We would place our most deadliest of carbineers atop the tower of this ruin and repel them. Make this decrepit Christian relic to us as Vesuvius was to the host of Spartacus. We would smite them like Jupiter smote Hiroshima."

"And we would die," Gondal said. "We would lose everything. They are frustrated. They will not tolerate another dead Roman."

"And you know this how?" Bijan asked. "Your contact in The Legion?"

"Yes."

✝

Bijan let out a long sigh. "I cannot give my consent to abandoning citizens of Pakitown—"

"The Orphanage," the imam corrected.

"You call it by whatever fucking name you desire, Holy Man, but so will I. You may don yourself in orphan's rags in an attempt to draw the world's sympathy, but you are just a dirty Paki like me, like all of us."

He turned his attention back to Gondal. "I will not abandon brothers in times of strife."

"Strife they bring upon themselves," she said.

"I care not its origin."

"I spoke to your cousin yesterday. He agrees with me."

Bijan pounded his fist on the table so hard Zita Mira almost toppled backwards off her stool.

"You had no right!"

"He agrees with me."

He looked over to me. He wanted to make sure I was close in case he did something impetuous or violent or stupid. I stood, slowly, trying not to garner any attention, but all of the other valets were doing the same. There wasn't a man amongst them I couldn't have beaten one-on-one, but all four of them at the same time would have been dicey.

Bijan lowered his voice and spoke through gritted teeth. "I am not Sarkis, you cunt, and until that *kutee ka ghanta* stands in this Curia and speaks for his own fucking self, it is my vote to cast."

"Then cast your vote," she said with a smile. "And then the rest of us will cast ours."

Situations like that were why weapons weren't allowed in Senate sessions. After the votes were counted, I had expected Bijan to fly into a rage and either defiantly storm out of the building or start a brawl. But he didn't. Gondal had cast the tie-breaker, making it the new policy to stop protecting Pak *ḍakait*, bandits. Bijan just shook hands, issued his goodbyes, and left as he had arrived, with me a step behind.

When we came outside, his reached back and drew me to him. I looped my arm in his. Our pace through the market was markedly faster than it had been when we were heading towards the church. For a long time he was silent, just smiled his idiot's smile and guided us through the crowd. After we broke out of the market area and into the open street, still several blocks from home, he looked at me.

"Have you thoughts?" he asked.

I try not to these days, I thought. "She is not entirely wrong," I said.

"No, she is not altogether erroneous. She may, in fact, be correct. The position she posits is the best course of action for her community."

"So you'll do as they say?"

He shot me a sideways glance. "I have many a great endeavor all across this grand city, not just within the imaginary borders we have confined ourselves to. It will be substantially more difficult to convince worthenwhile men to operate them if they are not guaranteed a safe haven to which to return to. I give not one twat about the welfare of this ghetto. The riches are north of Cavour. North of Nationale. Pakis have nothing to steal. I am growing unfond of fucking Pakis."

Aren't you a Paki? I thought. *No, you think you're a Roman.*

"Antonius works for the betterment of Antonius first, The Sindeketa second. I have no tertiary concern. I will do business and steal from whom the fuck I desire."

"They won't like that."

205

"That repellent harpy won't like it. The others care not."

"And if she finds out?"

"As you hath said, she is not *not* correct. Not from her perch. If she was wrong or unpopular, it wouldn't be considered a crime for me to kill her. But she is neither, so it would indeed be considered thus. Which is why I am tasking you to kill her for me."

"I won't," I replied without thinking.

Bijan grabbed the front of my dress, dragged me into an alley and slammed me against a building. Even through the haze of the chryo, I knew I could have grabbed his arm and snapped it in half, but I didn't.

I was tired of being strong.

"Do you think I am under the illusion that you fuck me because it is the desire of your loins?" he spat. "That it does not repulse you? Every time I enter you the hatred you feel for me swells. Do you believe me to be daft? If I tell you to fellate me, you will drop to your knees. If I tell you lay down across a puddle, you will smile as I walk across your back. If I tell you to end someone, they will die by your fucking hand."

His hands had drifted up to my neck, his fingers twitching with the desire to clamp down and choke. "That woman went behind my back to my cousin and had the gall to tell me of it? She did not do that to change my mind. That was not her purpose. It was to remind me and all who were present that I am a placeholder, a pretender. That despite everything I have accomplished, there is still another I must answer to."

Not the Caesar but the Caesar's man.

"Her disrespect, not her agenda, has predicated her demise. It matters not to me how it is done, but she will be cold by the end of the week."

✝

"That wasn't the deal," I said.

"Deal? There is no deal. You have no voice in this. You belong to me. Every piece of you. Your life is mine."

His grip on my neck tightened.

"If you'd like, I could just end it now."

Yes. Please. I thought.

"No. I'll do it. I'll kill her."

"I know you will. And after that, you're going to kill my baby cousin."

That night, after Bijan was satisfied and asleep, I dressed and slipped out and up to my old room to grab my jump jacket. I pulled it on and went outside to escape the smell of sweet smoke that filled his, our, flat. The night was warm, but I still held it tight around my body. I started walking, in no direction in particular, not intending to go far. I just needed to move or I was going to cry. I felt the tears lingering like an unspoken word on the tip of my tongue. They should have come, but they didn't.

I took two rights, headed towards Dante Park.

Just weeks before, I had been committed to murdering a man for money and freedom and secondhand vengeance. Even before I had met Amelia Starr, I had convinced myself to do it, rationalized it as a dirty means to a desired end.

Why couldn't I do the same thing about killing Safia Gondal?

I crossed the street and climbed two stairs to a small park closed off by a rusting iron fence. It was, as always, deserted. The grass was overgrown with weeds, and all that was left of the grounds' former life were the remains of a children's slide made of faded blue and red plastic.

No one came to Dante Park because decades before a woman had been murdered there, horribly, and many still

78971813183

believed her ghost haunted the place. People swore they heard noises, moaning, coming from the park at night.

I didn't mind it so much.

I had given everything I had in my efforts to preserve my miserable little life, a life I didn't want but was too afraid to leave. I had handed over my body, my spirit, my talents and my hope. I had known the day would come when Bijan would command me to take a life. Despite the illusion of me being his woman, he saw me first and foremost as a tool, a weapon, and if I couldn't be that, I was useless to him.

I am a rich man and have my pick of any hole in The Esquilino.

If I wanted to live, I was going to have to kill a good woman because she insulted an evil man who deserved insulting.

I took a few more steps into the park. Glass crunched beneath my feet. I decided that when I finally worked up the courage to take my life, I would do it in Dante Park. Maybe the ghost would like the company.

If I hadn't been spaced out on nitro and chryo, and wallowing in my darker thoughts, the person wouldn't have been able to sneak up behind me, but I didn't notice until it was too late. A split second before I was grabbed, I knew who it was. I knew her scent. She locked an arm around my neck. I knew her touch. I felt the emitting end of a solo pressed into my back.

Alba tapped the switch, and all went black.

XIII: SUBJUGATION AND MANUMISSION

I HAD BEEN BOUND BY BOTH WRISTS IN ALBA'S BED once before, but that moment had been far sexier than the one into which I awoke. I tugged weakly, but my arms felt like boiled linguine, and the belts she had used may as well have been fabrosteel chains.

Alba stood next to the bed, her arms crossed.

"When you told me to fuck off, I told myself, 'Hey, it's Rata. This is what she does. She has moods. You know she has moods. You like her moods.' But I messaged you a hundred times, tried to come by but could never get into the building."

"It's almost as if I told you to fuck off. How did you get me here?"

"I boosted a cart parked outside of your building. Some unlucky Paki will be taking the grav tomorrow."

"What is this?" I asked, trying the restraints again.

"I heard things, but it wasn't until I watched you with him today that I could believe—"

"You were following me?"

"Out in public for everyone to see. With that man. *That* man. That *man*."

"I've never seen you jealous," I lied.

"I'm not jealous. Worried. Disgusted."

"And jealous."

"I'm Italian. I'm always jealous."

"Untie me."

"Fuck you."

"If I tell him about this, he'll kill you. He's very protective of his things."

"Things? His things? He doesn't own you."

"He does now."

"You are not property."

"I am."

"Why, because you owe him money? There are ways to make money."

"Not enough."

"I don't under—"

"It was the only way," I said.

"The only way what?"

"The only way to save my life, to fix things."

She cocked an eyebrow. "This is fixed?"

"I don't owe Bijan. I owe The Sindeketa. And they're everywhere."

"I don't care if you owe Trishnu herself—"

"That's not a real—"

"This isn't how it's supposed to be. What the fuck do you think you're doing?"

"I'm staying alive," I told her. "The man on the phone said they're coming for me, and they did. They killed the old man, the one that hired me. I was next. I am next. But if I'm standing next to Bij—"

"What about me?" she asked. "I was there. If they're after you, they're after me. Did you think of that?"

"No," I answered, but I had thought of that. And I had chosen to abandon her.

"You wouldn't be you if you had. For a little while, I tried to write you off like anyone with brains, but there's a stupid part of me that won't let you go so easy. I hate that part of me. It makes me do all kinds of stupid shit. Shit like..." She waved a hand to indicate me, the bed, the whole setup.

Alba climbed on top of me, straddling my chest. She leaned in close and examined my right eye. I tugged again at my wrist. No give at all.

"I was going to ask you if you were stupid or high," she said, "but from the webs of pink across your whites, I think I know the answer. How much are you on?"

"Not enough."

She sat up, looked around, avoiding eye contact. "Numb all over, huh? Inside and out."

I nodded.

She struck me, across the face, with the back of her hand. Stars lit up my sight for a flash, but it barely hurt. "Did you feel that?"

"No," I said.

She gnashed her teeth and, with fury in her beautiful Latin eyes, pulled back her hand and smacked me again, harder. There was more pain, but still very little.

"How about that?"

"No."

"So this is what you want to be? Lifeless and pain-free. You're one of the strongest people I've ever met and— And

211

now— Is this what you want? To be his whore? You could rip his throat out so fast you wouldn't even get blood on your hands. Instead you let him touch you. You don't need to do that. What is it you want, Rata?"

"I want you to leave me alone."

"Not going to happen. What else do you want? Fight past the chems. If you could have anything in the world, what would it be?"

The answer roared out of me. "I want my wife back!"

I pulled my hands forward; the belts unraveled like birthday ribbons. The knots had been poorly tied, but until that moment had felt ironclad. Alba tried to crab back away from me, but I dove at her, slammed my hands into her chest and drove her all the way onto her back. She grunted as her legs were pinned beneath her.

I could feel the fabric of Alba's shirt in my hands, the rapid thump in my chest, anger and sorrow and shame and guilt and regret in my heart, as if the rage had flushed the chryo and nitro out of me, if just for a moment. I stared down at her, like she had done to me, and she wasn't scared or angry.

She was happy. Smiling.

"That's my girl," she said.

I pushed off her and stood. My legs wobbled. How long had I been there? I leaned against the wall. Alba sat up, wincing in pain. I had hit her pretty hard.

"You keep calling her that."

"What?"

"The dead lady. She wasn't your wife. Why do you keep calling her that?"

"It's impossible to explain."

Alba closed her eyes, in pain or confusion or both. "She's not coming back," she whispered. "She's dead, whoever she was. What else do you want?"

"I don't—"

"What do you want?"

"I want to kill the man who took her."

"We can do that."

"There's no point."

"I know how we can do that. While you've been high and debasing yourself, I've kept digging."

"Why would you do that?"

"Because we had a deal."

"There's no money. Not anymore."

"I'm not talking about the money."

I looked at her. Any anger I felt towards her was gone and redirected at almost every other person alive, including myself.

Especially myself.

"I tore through a lot of favors and scorched a little earth. Cost me some coin. But I found them."

"Them?" I asked.

"They call themselves the Kings of Roma. There are seven of them. Or, were. They put themselves out there as a pack of high-end murder pros, but from what I can suss out, there's not a whole lot to back that up. They dress alike, talk a lot, act like hard cases who think they're hard-asses and are known to wear their stingers, matching Beretta 300s, out in the open on their hips like old-time American horseboys—"

"Cowboys," I corrected, a decade of being dragged to the *Sinēmā* by Father paying off.

"—which means they are either stupid or not afraid of The Legion, which of course makes them even stupider. They're pretty social; they like trance halls and bars and

213

anywhere where people gather to make bad decisions. But no one's seen them out or anywhere in over a month."

"We had something to do with that."

"Maybe a little," she smiled. "From what I can tell, they made their bones a year ago with a sequence of ambushes in the Trastavere that wiped out one generation of mid-bosses to make way for a new one. They've been coasting on those kills since."

"Make-dead artists," I said. "The guy we fought. He looked so much like— Are they all related?"

"Brothers or cousins, maybe, but nobody really knows who they are. They use aliases. Numa, Tullus, Tarquin, stupid old-old shit like that."

"The Roman kings. Which one did we kill?"

"No way of knowing."

"And the man I talked to on the mobi?"

"One of them, I guess."

"How do we find them?" I asked.

"I'm working on it."

She was working on it. While I was wallowing and dosing myself dumb and giving up and letting Bijan... She had been working on it, and I had done nothing. Alba, my black market beauty, taking risks, spending coin, wasting her time pursuing a job that didn't exist for a reward she would never get.

All for me.

And here she was, trying to save me.

For a fleeting moment, I loved her. Not for long, but I did. It worried me.

She couldn't save me, but at least she was trying.

She couldn't save me.

But *I* could.

"The guy killed the old lady—Amelia. Amelia, right?"

I nodded, already forming a course of action in my head.

"He killed her, but he didn't kill her. You understand that, right?"

"He pulled the trigger," I said.

"He was doing a job, just like you and me would. The man you want is not the man you want. He was doing dirty for some twat who was too much of a coward to do it himself."

"So I'll kill him too."

"Leave the shootout to the men with the money and the real grudges. You and him, you're just pawns. You're the same."

"Maybe, but there's a difference."

"What is that?"

"He. Killed. *Her*. I will make my way up the ladder all the way to the Caesar if that's where it goes, but the first rung will be the man who pulled the trigger. This isn't about who deserves what. Nobody deserves anything. But it's what I'm doing. If I'm going to do this, this is how it has to be. There are going to be bodies. One of them might even end up being mine. And if you help me, yours. I need you to know that's how it's going to be."

"How much blood are we talking?"

"I want to spill all of it."

Without asking, I went to Alba's closet and grabbed a pair of olive pants and a white tank top and a pair of brown boots that were a little too small but fit enough. I wasn't going to wear Bijan's costume any longer. Fuck his sandals. Fuck his toga. I tossed the gold snake armlets onto the bed.

Fuck Cleopatra.

"Sell those. I'm sure they're expensive."

215

She picked one up and turned it over in her hands. "They're kind of sexy on you."

"Get rid of them," I said, not willing to joke and flirt about something that meant what that jewelry meant. She noticed and tossed the serpent back onto the mattress.

"Sorry," she mumbled.

I got dressed and noticed Alba had hung my jump jacket carefully amongst her wardrobe. I grabbed it. "I'll be back in a couple hours," I said as I tied up my hair.

"What are you going to do?"

"Something desperate and dangerous."

"What should I be doing while you're gone?"

"Arrange a meeting. I want an audience with the Kings."

"We'll have to pretend to hire them."

"That's fine."

"There's a deposit just to talk to them."

I tucked my coat under my arm and went for the door. "I'll be coming back halfway to flush."

"Anything else?"

"Find me an underground Chinese 'plantjock named Jao."

"Are there any above-ground Chinese 'plantjocks?"

"I don't care how you find him, how you get him here. His mouth and his hands need to be working. Every other part of him can be broken and missing, but I need the part that does actual stuff. Pay whatever you can. If you don't have enough, promise more. But I need to speak to him. We need to."

"Jao. Got it. That it?"

"We're going to need guns."

"Guns I got."

I looked at her. Guns she had. And a lot of other things, some things I was just beginning to see. "You came south of Cavour for me."

"Like I said, you make me stupid."

"My place is about to get unfriendly, so I'll probably have to crash here with you tonight, and for several nights after, if that's okay."

She smiled. "Yeah. That's okay."

Outside I found the cart Alba had stolen, a decade-old red Fiat Electron 714. It was parked slanted, half-on, half-off the sidewalk. I got in and saw where she had ripped the guts out of the dash and snapped them into a pirate starter. Flipping the switch made the motor whirr to life. The cart bucked as I pulled it over the curb and out onto the street.

I had known that in order to fix my life I was going to have to kill someone.

For Virata Das to live, another would have to be sacrificed. It was supposed to have been the murderer of an old woman, but that path had become impassable. Then it was going to be the Senator, a woman who had never done anything wrong other than insult a maniac.

Neither death was the answer.

I was still going to kill the murderer, but that wasn't going to save my life. It would probably take my life from me. I had heard and understood what Alba had said about assassins and kings, but I had no idea what it meant. Only that I was very likely to die. But that was okay. I had no problem dying while avenging my wife. I wasn't afraid of that.

But in order to risk my life, I needed one to wager.

✝

I had known that in order to fix my life I was going to have to kill someone. By the time I parked the jacked e-cart in front of 13 Via Machiavelli, I was ready to do just that.

Anytime a tenant swiped their print to enter the front door, Bijan got a notification on his system telling him who was coming home, so I needed to be quick getting up to my cube. I got through the door and rushed to the stairs. My legs felt heavy. I had gone up those stairs a million times, but they felt like a chore. I resisted the urge to tap into my ASIS for some stimulation. I wanted to forget the thing was there.

When I got to my room, I grabbed a satchel and threw in three handfuls of clothes and my boots. Opened the trunk. Grabbed my mobi, weeks unused and completely drained of charge, the Sprite 7 and a few yuro coins that had spilled into the bottom.

I left behind some unwashed underthings and a packet of retail-grade chryo tabs.

Lastly I pulled out the Browning, wrapped in a dirty piece of cloth. I took the magazine and slapped it up into the butt of the gun. There was an audible click as it locked in.

Snap, unlock, cock and shoot.

I placed the pistol in my jacket pocket and left my cube for what I hoped would be the last time. Into the stairwell, hoping I wouldn't run into Bijan on the way down.

I didn't.

I ran into Kalb.

I turned the corner at the end of one flight of stairs just as he did the same coming up the other way. We both froze.

Fuck it, I thought. *Two birds.*

Before he could register that it was me, I jumped down four steps and landed a flying boot square into his chest. The impact knocked me back, and my ass crashed into a step; Kalb went tumbling down a flight and a half. I'd hoped the

"Not as long as you think."

"I fucked up your clothes."

"Shit," Alba said as I came through the door, using the frame to keep myself upright. She took the satchel from my hand, guided me to the edge of the bed, peeled off my jacket and pulled the shirt over my head. She tried to use it to wipe the blood off my face, but it had already dried. I had apparently left my bra at Grease's. Who knew what he was doing with it.

"He's dead," I told her. We hadn't spoken his name out loud, but we had both known what I had left to go do. "I put a bullet in his face and blew his fucking head off."

"A bullet?"

"1990 Browning Hi-Power Practical," I said, hearing Michel's voice in my head. "*Neuf millimètres*. Beautiful blued slide. Smooth nickel-plated body. Sleek and impressive and very fuckable."

"Lie down." I reclined back onto the bed, my legs still touching the floor, and stared at the ceiling. Alba unlaced my boots and pulled them off, then undid my belt and gently worked me out of the slacks.

"The Pakis won't forget this," she said.

"Won't take them long to figure out who did it. I had to use my print to get in the building, then into my cube. They'll figure it out. Bijan was a pest to them, but they'll still come. Some Hindi bitch killed Sarkis's bug-fuck crazy cousin? No. Won't forget. Won't forgive."

"You'll have to run."

"Not yet. Not until it's done."

"What happened to your neck?" she asked, brushing aside my hair.

"I stopped by Grease's on the way back."

"That was probably a good move."

"That's me. The queen of good moves."

"Grease don't do charity."

I pointed to the bag. "I took some gleam and gear before I left."

Every part of me was shaking. She covered me with a rough blanket, sweetly tucking it in at the sides. "You need to sleep for about twelve hours."

"I'm going to need more than that. I have to get this junk out of my system. It's going to take a week, at least, and even then I won't be all the way back for a long time."

"You've gone through this before." It wasn't a question.

I nodded. "I'm going to become very unpleasant and difficult to be around very soon."

She smiled. "So it'll be just like every other day. What should I do?"

"Leave me alone. Let me scream, cry and pound holes in the walls."

"Not in my walls."

"Can you clear out enough space in your storage room for me to curl up on the floor?" I asked.

"No. I'll find a place to flop. You stay here. Get well."

"You don't—"

"Shut up. I can sleep anywhere. I was going to get started tonight. Is it okay if I leave?"

"I won't notice you're gone."

"So very sweet."

"After I get through this, I'll start living my real life even if it kills me," I said.

"Good. I'm tired of doing all your work for you."

She went for the door.

"Every once in a while, if you can, check in on me to make sure I'm not dead."

PROXY

‡

"Sure, but if you puke or shit in my bed, I'll hate you forever," she said.

"No promises."

I'm waiting for the doors to open and for me to jump and fall and fight and fall and kill and fall and die, and I've forgotten something. I don't know what. I can almost see it in the corner of my eye but whenever I turn to get a good look at it, it's not there. What did I forget? I look around at the others and their faces are stone. They aren't worrying about anything, not praying, certainly not feeling like they're forgetting something like I am. My rifle is strapped across my chest and my boots are on and my helmet is on... The light is going to turn red any second and I'll have to jump but what have I forgotten? My boots are on and my helmet is on. My pack is on my back and my— The light pops and I'm third in line to jump. The SIM doors open and the first trooper goes and Bijan turns around to me and says, "Are you ready for this, Cleopatra?" and I say, "No. I forgot something." And he says, "Doesn't matter now," and then leaps out into the sky and that makes me next and something sharp pokes me in the back. "Jump," he says, and I look behind me and Arjuna Sen points at me with his old-old looking Epsiloni spear. Where is his grav-suit? Where is his rifle? "Jump," he commands again, jabbing forward and backing me up towards the portal. "I forgot something," I try to say but before I can he says, "Doesn't matter now" and jabs again. My heel slips over the edge and I windmill my arms to keep my balance but it doesn't work and I fall backwards out into the sky in a whoosh and tumble end over end through the darkness. It feels like the spinning will never end and I manage to flip up the visor of my helmet before I heave and offer the contents of my stomach up to the winds.

229

‡

The vomit rips my throat raw and won't stop coming. When the tumbling stops, I find myself facing the ground, my arms and legs akimbo, free-falling, the lights of Kolkata below me. Explosions rock the city of my birth, fires rage, buildings collapse. From kilometers away, I can hear screams, cries and quiet prayers. I reach to my forearm unit to activate the grav-suit's decel banks and it's not there. Nothing is there. Not my boots, not my rifle, not my helmet. I am naked and defenseless and, even though I know I am falling to my death through the freezing air, I am not cold but burning up and the ground and dying city below aren't getting any closer. Falling but not falling. Suspended. The last moments of my life slowing down to a— The world rumbles and shakes, and a wave of pressure passes through me that feels like it rearranges my entire insides into a completely different woman and an impossibly bright flash of white blinds all of existence and is gone as quickly as it came and on the horizon erupts a cloud. Kilometers into the sky, an upward cylindrical rush of dust and smoke. At its apex, the pillar of purple fire slows and spreads. The whole thing looks like a flower or a toadstool and reminds me of how religious fic-vids portray the gods' mythical destruction of old Nippon. It is massive and terrifying and, while moving and fluid and alive, seems like it will remain there forever. Another blast, rumble and flash, and another cloud appears, to the east, and then another southward. And then below me. The heat engulfs me and I look down and I can't see the city, just the angry red cloud billowing upward and then I'm falling towards it. I brace myself for the end and then— My foot taps impatiently, and I check the time on my cell. Amelia is always late. She is a woman that defies stereotypes in every single way but one. When we are due somewhere, when we are running behind, when I am dressed and ready, she will always be another twenty minutes. *I always tell her she's already beautiful and doesn't need to change a thing, and while I'm always telling the truth she still comes down looking sexier than she did when she went up. In over a hundred and fifty years of desiring the fairer sex, I have probably spent at least three of them waiting for beautiful women while they attempt to make themselves more beautiful. There was only one who had never truly bothered. With most it had not always been worth it; they arrived painted like clowns or whores with their hair in formations less attractive than their natural states and wearing high heels that were nice to look at but made them walk like zombies. But Amelia always does just enough: just enough color added to her cheeks, just enough accent in her hair, just enough dress, just enough heel. But nearly everything in Roma starts late* except *for the opera, and if she doesn't get her ass down here we're going to miss the first act. She finally comes down the central staircase and looks amazing. I am an exceptionally lucky old man. Without a word she takes my arm and we cross through the foyer, out the front door and to the roundabout, where the car is waiting. Alba, dressed in a shiny, scaled suit with white gloves and a white hat, holds the door open for us and takes my hand to help me climb inside. My bones creak but they hold strong. Amelia gets in after me and Alba is already in the driver's seat when our door closes and without pause the limo is moving. "Alba, slow down," I command because it feels like we're going three hundred miles an hour, but she says "It's okay, Caden, we're safe." in a voice that isn't hers. "Caden, we're safe," Amelia parrots, holding my wrinkled hand in hers. But we're not safe. We're not. We're going too fast. The city blurs by the window. You can't drive like this in Phoenix. The cops are hard-asses, and dad says if I get into any more trouble he's going to send me to military school or boarding school or "kick my fucking slacker ass out onto the street" so I can see how much I really like trouble. "Jacob, slow down," I say but we are playing The White Stripes so loud he can't hear me. I turn down the volume and say it again. Every part of his Honda Civic is rattling. "Jacob," I say for the third time, "Slow down." He smiles and says, "Caden, it's okay. We're safe." He laughs and is still laughing when the headlights of the oncoming tractor-trailer flood the car and all I can hear is squealing rubber and Jack's guitar and the car horn and Meg's drums and crunching metal...*

Sometime, during some night, what night was unclear, Alba returned to check on me. I looked at her through blurred and blighted eyes.

"You look terrible," she said.

"Fuck you," I mumbled back.

"Not looking like that you won't." She came into the room and knelt down to unzip the satchel. I tried to sit up. My heart was trying to beat its way out of my chest. My whole body was sore from vomiting.

"Don't. I'm just doing what you asked, and from what I can tell, you're not all the way dead." She took out a stack of yuro chips and slid them into her pocket. "I'll be back when you're less, you know, scary and sad."

She left. I faded away again...

Bijan is on top of me and inside of me and my hands are feeling around in the sheets for a weapon. A stinger, a knife, a brick, a bit of cord, a hunk of pipe, anything to shoot, club, gash or choke the disgusting man I am letting fuck me. There is nothing. The bed seems to be infinite but I find nothing that will chop, crush, suffocate or do anything to make dead.

PROXY
‡

His breath is on my neck and his hands are wrapped up in the back of my hair and every time he thrusts he pulls a little harder. I look around the room for help but there is nothing but seamless white where the walls and floor should be— The murderer is eight, nine, twelve feet tall. I sit in the street with Amelia dead in my arms. The giant is dressed in white and stands over me, his monstrous fists wrapped around the grip of a shining chrome handgun half his size. "Why are you doing this?" I ask him, my voice thin and hoarse. "We're not supposed to die." His lips, as thick as rope, pull back in a smile. "We're all supposed to die." He levels the weapon at me and— Father and I come out of the void of the vīḍiyō-ghara. He didn't like the film and it made him angry. He drags me by my hand through the crowded streets. The people pay me no mind, bumping into me and nearly knocking me down more than once. I call to him but he doesn't turn around, just yanks me on like a pack animal. We cross paths with a school of bicycles and he doesn't break stride. One of them clips me and I let go of his hand and I drop to my knees and the wheels whiz by my head and I scream but he doesn't come back. He doesn't come b— "What do you want to do with Mrs. Kennedy's remains, sir?" Orso asks me. He and Jao stand at the foot of my bed. I haven't left it in days. Maybe weeks. Jao has his head down. He hasn't looked at me once since it happened. I don't want to look at him either. "You swept her?" I ask. He nods and says, "We have found nothing to point us to her killer." I had hoped the man's fatal mistake would be taking Amelia's necklace and leaving behind something to track him by. But he had been careful, apparently. But not careful enough. He had forgotten one thing: to make sure the old man was actually dead. "Burn her," I say. "Is that what the doctor would want, Senator?" Orso asks. "My wife doesn't want anything, Orso. She is gone. We leave behind no will or last wishes. Burn her. Make her ash." My manservant swallows hard. "But, sir, there will be nothing left of her." "That's not entirely true, is it Jao?" I ask. The man finally pulls his eyes away from the floor and looks at me. No, it's not. It's not true at all— I am moving but not walking. Out of my cube, down the stairs and into Bijan's room. The bacchanalia has begun without me. No one notices me enter. Everyone is fucking. The floor is wall-to-wall-to-ceiling occupied by naked flesh. Men, women, children. I can't tell where each one ends and the next begins. I try to step over them, but I have no legs. They pass under me without friction. It is silent. The harpist plucks with vigor. Skin slaps rhythmically against skin. Mouths are agape with pleasure and pain. But I hear nothing. Not even my own breathing, the beating of my heart, the ringing in my ears that has been there since the war. It is a vacuum. Bijan sits on a golden throne watching the activities. He is nude, his erection on display. He points at me. I do not want to go to him, but I do. My agency is not my own. I am pulled through space towards my master. Skimming the surface of the sea of fuck. It seems like there are hundreds of them. As I get closer, Bijan stops looking at me. His gaze snaps to something behind me. His eyes widen. I turn. The orgy is gone. The bodies vanished, leaving pools of blood, sweat and come as the only evidence they were ever there. At the front of the room where the door should be is a large wooden crucifix. On it hangs a man, spikes driven through his wrists and his crossed ankles, like in Christian myth. It's not right. They don't nail. They bind. Michel is still and limp. He wears no placard but written across his chest in dried blood is the word SMUGGLER. I fly to him, wanting him to say something to me, but he is lifeless. I will his eyes to open, his mouth to part. Any sign that he— I'm waiting for the doors to open and for me to jump and fall and fight, and I still can't remember what I've forgotten. I look around the gravjet cabin and I'm alone. No troopers, no jump director. No one. I undo my straps and stand and walk towards the front of the SIM. Smooth flight. No bumping. No swaying. Like walking on firm ground. I reach the cockpit and swing open the door and Kalb is behind the controls. The nav-term is unmanned. I start to say something but he points towards the windshield and I see it on the horizon. Another cloud. The towering, terrifying mushroom—

The gun!

I woke up drenched in sweat and other less desirable fluids, and realized I had left the Browning in the stolen e-cart.

"Alba?" I called but knew she wasn't there. I didn't know how long it had been. She didn't have any windows, so I checked my mobi: just past midnight. Five days since I had killed Bijan. I searched around in the dark for my clothes, all of which I had managed to remove. I was soaked with sweat. The room smelled of it, along with shit and vomit and spoiled food. Head pounding, I got dressed and, forgetting my boots, went to the door. With each step I struggled to stay upright, but I had to get downstairs.

The pistol, the very expensive and very rare pistol, my Schoolgirl, had been sitting in a jacked and abandoned cart parked in front of Alba's building. There for the stealing.

I needed it.

Kennedy had needed it. It had been his fetishistic request, and he was gone. I was going to find the killer, but I was no longer obligated to finish the ritual. I wasn't bringing the memory back for the old man to relive. How I executed my revenge was up to me.

And I needed the gun.

I needed her.

Before I let Alba's door close behind me, I realized I had no way to get back in. On a hunch, I pressed my thumb to her lockpad, and it recognized me. I heard the lock disengage. She had added my print to her entry list. I was pretty sure she had never done that for anyone else.

Outside I didn't have to wait for my eyes to adjust to the night. I had been living in nothing but darkness. At first my heart skipped because the cart wasn't there, but then I saw it parked on the other side of the street. Alba must have been using it while I was out. I knew she had come and gone a few times, checked in on me, and I had a hazy memory of her trying to give me some information but stopping when she realized I wasn't retaining any of it. Something about the Kings, maybe about Jao. I had no clue.

The Fiat was unlocked and full of trash and clothes. Had Alba been living in it? I had run her out of her room and bed. She had volunteered, but that didn't make me feel any less guilty.

Great, I thought. *I'm a person who feels guilt now.*

On the road between killing Bijan and showing up at Grease's shop I had grown nervous about the gun. Driving a stolen vehicle with blood literally on my hands and everywhere else. And I wasn't in Pakitown, which meant there was a chance of running into a patrolling Legionnaire. So I had done what every queen of good moves would have done: I stashed the steel under the seat. And it was still there, sticky with the blood of a coward. The metal was cold to the touch, having spent several nights outside. When I held it, I relived the rush of the night I had both set myself free and, most likely, condemned myself to death with one brutal action.

Closing the door of the Electron, I—
What was that?

Something, someone, up the street. A moving shadow in the street lights. I grasped the Browning and let my finger slide around the trigger. I walked slowly, my bare feet virtually silent. For a few long moments, I saw nothing, but then something stirred in an alley, and I ran towards it, taking the safety off the Hi-Power and bringing her to bear. Several strides sent my feet down onto painful gravel or maybe glass. I reached the mouth of the alley.

Nothing.

Had I really expected something?

"Hey!" I yelled. It could have been the Kings. It could have been The Sindeketa. I hoped it was the Kings or The Sindeketa. We were headed into a three-way scramble, and I was anxious to get started. "Are you down there? Are you here for me?"

No answer came from the darkness.

It could have been anyone.

It could have been no one.

They could have been waiting in the shadows, watching.

Shit. It could be the Kings.

It could be the Paks.

I was bare-foot, alone, weak and confused. I didn't want a fight. Not yet.

The alley remained silent. I backed away slowly. Dropped Schoolgirl to my side. If there had been anyone, they would have already struck. I was overreacting. I was paranoid. I was not thinking clearly.

I was not ready to be outside.

I couldn't get back to Alba's room fast enough. I threw myself onto the putrid bed and burrowed into the sheets and hoped sleep could take me for a little while longer.

When I next opened my eyes, two people were standing over me. One was Alba, the other a man.

"You are looking less than fuckable, if you do not mind me saying so."

"Why are you here?" was all I could muster through my shock of seeing Michel in Alba's flat.

"You messaged him," Alba said.

"The fuck I did."

"The fuck you did indeed," Michel said. "Two nights ago. The words you used were very confusing, some were not even in Italian, or French or English or any other decent human tongue."

"I don't remember doing that."

"You promised you would delete my number."

"I lied. How did you know it was from me?"

"I lied as well."

"Why did you come?"

"Two reasons. One: you mentioned something about Michel and a crucifix. I was very curious to see where that was going. And two: you sounded like you were in trouble."

"Why does that matter to you?"

"Because I believe one day you will be the mother of my children."

"Gross," I said. And at the moment, I knew gross.

He turned to Alba with a smile, "She is very much quite in love with me."

"I can see that." There was a lightness in Alba's voice that let me know she had quickly warmed to the outlandish Frenchman.

"Your lady-husband has not given me many details, but you look to be such a mess I cannot help but offer Michel's services."

"I feel better than I look." I meant it.

"Then get your disgusting ass out of my bed," Alba said. "We have things to do."

XV: TULLUS

ALBA'S SHOWER RAINED DOWN water that was a few degrees short of freezing, and I welcomed it. After being locked in an airless room for nearly a week, sweating through the bedding, the cold was an energizing respite. It was the third time I had bathed since beating the come-down, and the water that ran off my body and swirled in the drain was still a murky, grainy, and sometimes bloody, brown.

My body was less bruised than it had been in years; a month as a kept woman had given me plenty of time to heal, at least on the outside. Any scars showing had been there before, most notably the craggy one on my upper right thigh where the shrapnel had missed my femoral by less than a centimeter. The field-med came to me with a look on his face that said, "This bitch is dead." But he did his job, saved my life and then took a lethal blast from a Saudi sniper three days later.

I had showered plenty at Bijan's, both with and without him, in water so hot it sometimes scalded, but I had never once stepped out feeling clean.

"You may finally be clean enough to sleep in my bed again," Alba cooed in my ear. She was supposed to be washing my back, but her hands weren't scrubbing my skin as much as they were caressing and savoring. Every once in a while I could feel her breasts brush against my bare back.

"Who says I want to?" I asked.

It had been two days since I emerged from the comedown. Alba was still angry at me for walking away from her. For how I had tried to end it. We had barely spoken. But that morning she had woken in a different state. Perhaps she had forgiven me or come to understand my point of view. I had apologized more than once. Maybe she realized it was time to move forward, and that dwelling on what had happened before wasn't going to help anything.

Or maybe she was just horny.

She slowly ran her hands over the curves of my hips. I tried not to react, but the change in my breathing gave me away. The chill from the water gave way to a warmth inside. "You just managed to air out the sheets, and you want to get them dirty again?"

"Only the..." A kiss to the back of my neck. "...right kind..." A teasing nibble. "...of dirty." She slid her hands up and around to cup my breasts, massaging them. After she felt I was properly aroused, her right hand wandered south of my waist.

Even with how insistent and effective she was being, her touch was tentative. Not her normal aggressive self. I silently thanked her for it. It was the first time she had touched me, really touched me, since Bijan. I had submitted myself to him, in my weakness, in my fear, in a misguided attempt to keep myself safe, but that hadn't made it feel any less violating. He was still all over me. Inside me.

I didn't want Alba to think about him, about what he had done to me, but she must have been. She stroked me gently, probed lightly. I focused my energy on her hand between my legs. On her body pressed against mine. The water cascading over both of us. The feel of her mouth on the back of my neck, my shoulders.

It hadn't been like that with Bijan. With him it had been business. Dirty, painful and quickly resolved. His only goal had been his own satisfaction.

Every time I enter you, the hatred you feel for me swells, he had said, but had done it anyway.

Remembering that made it easier to distinguish between what had happened then and what was happening in the shower. I felt myself let go and so did Alba. She grew bolder, more assertive and began to make love like the Albalonga Rocco I knew, not the timid first-timer she had been pretending to be.

"You're not mad at me anymore?" I whispered.

"I'm furious," she cooed.

A wave of ecstasy hit me, and my thighs tensed and held Alba's hand right where it was until it passed. After my last shudder, I turned around and met her mouth and tongue with my own. Our lips locked, and it wasn't until after we had climbed out of the shower, the water still running, dribbled a trail of wetness on her floor and collapsed onto the bed that they parted.

I turned her over onto her stomach. I kissed one of her tattoos, her sexy permanent stockings with the butterfly bows, and then up the back of her leg. She shivered and moaned when I reached the backside of her knee, then took in a sharp breath when I arrived at the treasure between her legs and put my mouth to it.

Every time I put my hands or lips or any part of me on or in Alba, though, I still felt guilty. Amelia Starr was very much alive in my thoughts and heart. I had no memories of sex with her; even with all of Kennedy's enhancements, it had been decades since they had attempted it. But that hadn't diminished his love and devotion to her at all.

Burying my feelings under a fistfuck of chems hadn't worked, and now that my system was clean again, it was going to get harder. As I tasted Alba, devoured her, pushed her closer to the edge, part of me felt that I was being unfaithful. Virata had never cared about being true to any one woman, but apparently Caden Kennedy had.

Alba loved me, or thought she did, but I couldn't love her back.

I just couldn't.

Amelia climaxed—

Alba. Fuck. Alba, I scolded myself.

Alba climaxed with a silent scream that had her clawing into the mattress. She reached back and grabbed me by the hair and pulled me up to her as she rolled over onto her backside and leveled a look at me that let me know we weren't done. She beckoned to me.

I went.

In my fevered nightmares and jumbled memories, I had remembered and seen a house. A rich person house. I had seen the foyer, the stairs, the bedrooms. Outside, the driveway, white columns, a grove of pines. And inside the mansion, I had seen Jao. The second-most sought after man in my life. The man who had cut into my brain and changed me forever. The only person that I knew had answers. Maybe not all of them, but some, and for sure more than me. Grease had never heard of him. Neither had any of the other 'plantjocks Alba had talked to. And walking into Chinatown and looking for a man named Jao was as fruitful as going down to the Trastavere and asking if anyone had seen that guy Mario.

I had seen him, Jao, in the memories he had given me, memories that stuck even though I had tried to rip them out and crush them. I had seen him at the foot of my, his, bed, standing next to a dead man. He had been effusive, stunned and seemingly heartbroken. The man I had met, real-life met, was a man of few words, but he had a sly smile showing at all times, and a twinkle in his eyes. The moment in the bedroom must have taken place no more than few days after Amelia's murder. It fell in the two-week swath of memories they had given me. What they had told me was only two weeks. But I had also seen a boy. A teenaged boy. White. Driving an old-time cart. The music had sounded ancient. What was a White Stripe? Was it a glimpse into Kennedy's youth? It surely wasn't from mine. And if it was his, why was it in my head? I was only supposed to have gotten the necessary amount of data. Why was I stuck with his childhood memories too?

All the more reason to find Jao.

The house was a detail I had overlooked, passed over for what I thought were the more promising leads and images. Orso told me the Senator had been in Roma since before I was born. The hotel was his escape. The ghosts of his wife were probably too omnipresent for him to walk the halls without bursting into tears.

But there was a house somewhere. I could see it in my head, to the detail. I had effectively lived in it for two weeks. I just didn't know where it was.

After hours of intense physical give and take, I mentioned the house to Alba. "I would have to tap into a mainstream term to get access to those types of records," she said, panting, sweating. "It won't be easy. You have to know your exact search parameters and run them fast, because any hacking will be spotted by The Legion's Ether fascists, and they'll pinpoint the location in seconds."

"Can you do it?" I asked.

"This guy that important to find?"

"Yes."

"Was this your plan? Make me come, then put me to work?"

"You started it."

She turned her head to look at me. "You know why I'm here, right?"

I nodded.

"The money never mattered," she said.

"Yes, it did."

She smiled. "It did. It really did. I'm a criminal. Money always matters. But that wasn't the why. It wasn't the why at all."

"I know."

"Good. Now get dressed and write down the data you need me to mine for. I need specific parameters, and as few of them as possible. I'll need to get in and out fast if I don't want to get arrested. I've been by Sant'Angelo and seen how Villano deals with people like us."

"Come and eat lunch with Michel," he said. I had found him sitting on the front steps to Alba's building, staring off into space. I slipped my hand into my jacket pocket to make sure the Sprite was there. Before all of this started, I never carried a weapon. It was never worth the hassle, the risk of a random Legion pat down. My hands, knees, feet and forehead, with my training, were capable defensive tools. But now I never stepped outside without some sort of piece. It had taken both Alba and Michel to convince me not to carry the Browning with me at all times.

Michel seemed to know a restaurant in every neighborhood. Then again, I didn't know where he lived. His apartment could have been around the corner from Alba's. The small and noisy *osteria* was filled with students from what was left of the nearby university. Even in dire times, times when things kept getting darker and it looked like the end was surely near, there were still young people, and some old ones, who wanted to learn, better themselves, probably thinking they would be the ones to swing the pendulum back the other way.

I always thought of them as suckers.

We took the only empty table for two. The menu was digitally laid into the tabletop. I was starving. My last meal was a fuzzy memory.

"I know it is loud in here," Michel said. Our conversation was going to have to be a hybrid of strained hearing, lip-reading and, at least on Michel's part, wild gesticulation. "The kids, they talk and talk and talk and say not but horseshit, but I swear by the entire menu."

"How are the mussels?" I asked, feeling a smile.

"Except for the mussels. The mussels are like eating shit dipped in man milk. Do not get the fucking mussels."

"That's okay. I don't like mussels."

The server came over, and as Michel ordered too much food, I hurriedly scanned for something I wanted. My eyes settled on something that made my mouth water but also confused the shit out of me.

"I'll take the beef stew," I said.

Michel cocked an eyebrow and turned to the server. "Give us a minute, woman, please. My friend is not feeling well."

She rolled her eyes and waited. He leaned across the table to me. "They have real beef here. Not synth shit. You do not eat meat."

"I do now." Apparently. I wasn't sure where it had come from.

He shrugged. "The beef stew for the *bella femme*." The waitress left.

"Beef. You are a terrible Hindu-type person."

"In the past week, I've stolen, lied, killed two men, half-dosed myself into a zombie and had sex with someone I wasn't married to and who wasn't a man. Yeah. I'm a fucking terrible Hindu-type person."

"I am now going to change the subject without grace or wit," he said. "I told you before I would stop asking, but I must one more time now that I have been pulled into this. What in the fuck is going on?"

My first instinct was to lie to him, to keep the strange details to myself, but why? What did it matter? So I told him. About that first day at the St. Regis. The Senator. Amelia. The money. The implant. The memories. About Atavism. About Not Him. Kennedy's murder. Orso's body on the floor of the destroyed laboratory. I told him about the Kings of Roma.

As I explained everything, he listened quietly, his default smirk and good humor absent altogether. It felt good to tell him. I hadn't told anyone. Alba knew pieces, but the only living people who knew the whole story were me and the elusive Jao.

And now the French smuggler.

I hadn't planned on telling him, but when I was done, I was glad I did.

We sat in silence. The waitress came with our food. Neither of us thanked her. He picked up his fork and spoon and began to twirl his pasta, but then stopped. Dropped his utensils. Looked at me.

"That is much fucked, Virata. *Very* much fucked."

He wasn't wrong.

I took up a spoonful of my stew, making sure to get a large chunk of brown meat. The beef fell apart in my mouth. It felt like murder and was the best thing I had ever eaten. "I think I may have inherited his American taste buds." I shoveled in more.

"You want to continue with this?" he said, ignoring my newfound love of bovine flesh and fat. "You have already angered so many. There is no longer an award, only danger. There is no sense in being the assassin for a dead man. It is not your fight."

"Yes, it is."

"But you are just an assassin. Muscle for hire."

The swirl of images and memories and emotions that hijacked both my waking and sleeping hours said otherwise. The old man had been right: his pain had become my pain. His grief had become my grief. His wrath had become my wrath.

There was no going back. Until I drove a bullet into the murderer's face, I was the tool of vengeance of Senator R. Caden Kennedy. I thought then, hopefully, if I could satiate the rage and find some sort of closure, both he and I could rest.

"I'm more than that," I answered after a long pause. "But I have to do this. This man killed my wife. We were never married; I never met her. But it doesn't feel that way. She is part of me now. I will avenge her, or I will join her."

Michel sighed. He had heard every word but still wanted to dissuade me. "What if a certain handsome and sexually vigorous *contrebandier* you know could arrange transport for you? To Paris, perhaps."

"You're not welcome in Paris."

"Sadly, I step one foot into my home country, and I will either be thrown into a cell by the police or have my nuts cut off and fed to me by my former colleagues. But I am not without friends there. You can forget all of this. The Paks. This bizarre hunt. Move on. I could maybe even sneak in your special friend."

The image of Alba and I holding hands while perusing the boutiques of Paris's famous Upper City was comical and inconceivable.

"She is yours now, is she not?"

"I don't know."

"But she is yours," he said again, this time not a question. "If you want her to be."

"Yes. I think so. For now." I directed the conversation back. "There are Paks in France."

He nodded. "When a whole nation of people has no home, they show up in everybody else's. But you would be a step ahead of them."

I shook my head. "I appreciate it, my friend." *Friend? He's my friend now? I guess he is. Girlfriend, friend, emotions. Seems I got more from Kennedy than just grief and carnivorousness.* "But I'm not leaving. I could use your help. Any help, but this isn't what you do. I understand that. No hard feelings if you walk away."

"Some hard feelings," he said.

"Some. But not a lot. Honestly."

He broke off a large hunk of bread and shoved it in his mouth. Chewing loudly, he looked lost in thought. He swallowed. "I will help you. On one condition."

"Me, you and Alba are *never* going to—"

"No, no. I will save that scenario for my lonely moments, but no. Give Michel more credit. I will help you if you promise to consider my offer to make you disappear."

If I'm still alive, I thought.

"Okay," I said.

I felt a presence beside me, and suddenly I was sharing my chair. Alba grabbed a hunk of bread and bit into it. "How did you know we'd be here?" I asked her.

"Froggy and I ate here a few times while you were sleeping. And this guy could be on fire and still wouldn't skip a meal."

Alba looked down at the menu. "Don't get the mussels. I think they grow them in the toilet."

"Froggy has already advised her of that," Michel said.

"Good. Has he told you about the pengwolves?"

"Lupguins," Michel and I corrected in unison.

After a casual beat, Alba said, "I found them."

"Found them?"

She smiled. "Who's the queen now?"

"You found the Kings?"

"A colleague of a friend of a rival of a business partner of a second cousin of a friend, a dozen favors owed, probably a few bridges turned to cinders, but I finally got word back that they're entertaining new contracts. They're waiting to hear back from us." She looked at me. "What do you want to do?"

251

"If we set up a meeting, there is a one in seven chance—"

"One in six," she reminded me. We had already crossed one off the list.

"One in six chance that the guy that shows up is our guy."

"If they do it face to face," Michel said. "They could send someone to talk for them."

"Either way, whoever shows up will be a direct link to the Kings. We'll grab whoever comes, and we'll get him to answer some very serious questions."

"Last time we tried that, the guy clammed up in a fatal fuck way."

"I've got an idea about that too," I said.

"And what if the man who walks through the door is the one you are looking for?" Michel asked.

"I shoot him. More than once."

"How very American.".

"Either way," I continued, "we're going to need a meet-up. To offer a contract, talk coin. In person."

"Problem is they know us. You and me."

"Tell them," Michel said, "that they shall be meeting with a curious yet wealthy Frenchman who has been cuckolded by his whorish betrothed and needs someone to extract lustful retribution on his behalf."

"Are you sure your ego can handle playing a cuckold?" I asked, glad Michel was on board.

"With a sense of self as large as Michel's, pretend slings and arrows are barely noticed. I will have to downplay my supernatural charms in order to sell the fact that a woman of mine would dare look at another man, but I am a master thespian. At least, I'm sure I could be."

"Then do it," I said. "Send word through the chain of friends and cousins and colleagues and whatever the fuck that a man with big coin needs a job done, and he only wants the best in Roma to do it."

Alba nodded.

"Now get the waitress's attention. I need more meat."

While we were waiting to hear from the Kings, a curious message arrived on my mobi:

HAVE NECKLACE COME GET BRING COIN

I had all but forgotten about Amelia's necklace. The platinum sphere, suspending a sample of her DNA in amber. It had been months since I had offered Isra many yuros to find the precious bauble. And the Vulture claimed she had it.

Except she didn't.

Isra's shop was firmly in the borders of The Esquilino. By now what I had done had gotten around, I was sure. The price on my head would be far more lucrative than the paltry sum I had offered the hockshoppe matron. And the odds of the killer, a white man, walking into Pakitown this long after the killing to sell the trinket were more than slim.

I showed the missive to Alba. She smiled.

"That, my dear, is a trap."

I nodded. "I show up, and there will be ten of Sarkis's men waiting. Maybe even the man himself. I've heard he likes to get his hands dirty."

"What are you going to do?" she asked.

"Nothing. I'm not doing The Sindeteka's job for them. They're going to have to get more creative."

"It doesn't worry you?"

"Being hunted by the Pak mob? No."

"It probably should."

"It will, later, maybe. But right now I've got other things on my mind."

The word came three days later. A meeting in an outdoor cafe, early afternoon, a public space. We were told under no circumstances was the client to be armed, nor to make any literal references to the job at hand.

"I am a smuggler," Michel had said. "I am better speaking in generalities and codes than I am in actual tongues. Besides, my wits are weapon enough." I was sure he just didn't like or want to fight and was relieved he wouldn't be asked to. We raided Alba's storeroom to make sure we were properly armed and connected. Earpieces for all of us and a make-vid contact lens for Michel, linked to Alba's mobi.

Alba and I sat parked in the Fiat around the corner from the cafe. Michel was running late in a fitting tribute to his ancestors, but we could hear him breathing in our ears. The camera jostled with each step as he hurried up the street towards us.

"I think I found the house," Alba said.

"Kennedy's house? You're sure?"

"No. That's why I said 'I think.' I bridged over from a transmitter on the outskirts of Chinatown. Ran your names and keys as fast as I could and got out. Got a few hits, mostly fragments, grabbed them and ran. The Legion was there before I got down the block. Going to be a lot of angry yellows trying to figure out why their mobis aren't connecting. Hopefully we won't need him after tonight."

"Talking to Jao has everything and nothing to do with what happens tonight. No matter how this goes, I need him. Do you really think you've found it?"

"On the books for thirty years as the property of a Jonah Moreno."

If Jao wasn't there, I would have to give up looking for him. He was either dead or halfway back to China.

Michel hit the patio of the cafe and began to scan the tables. I leaned in to look at the mobi screen. "There," I said, my voice echoing in his ear. "Back corner."

A man dressed like the other Kings we had seen sat alone with two espresso cups, a half-eaten sandwich and his top hat on the table in front of him. Michel walked towards him. The man looked up, directly at us through the vid-lens.

It wasn't him.

Again, he looked like the killer. Similar facial structures. The same color hair. The same uniform. But this man wasn't even a man. He was fifteen, sixteen. His face peppered with not-yet-shaven stubble.

Michel sat. Tried to offer the kid a hand, but it was not taken. Tried to get a name, but was not given one in return.

"You don't need to know who I am, and I don't need to know who you are. You understand me?" he said. His voice was not that of a boy, but certainly not of a man, either.

"I do. Straight to business. *Parfait.*"

"I understand you need someone tended to."

"'Tended to?' I— Oh, yes. Tended to. Correct." Michel was playing befuddled first-timer well. "You see, this man, this horrible man, he fucked my wife. Fucked her many times, you see, fucked her in the—"

"Stop. I don't give a shit," he said. "Your reasons are your own."

I switched off my mic for a moment and turned to Alba and finally said, "It's not him."

"Are you sure?"

"Yeah. It's another one of the brothers or cousins or clones. This one's a child."

"He's a baby. Plan B then?"

I sent my voice back into Michel's ear: "It's not him. Keep talking, get some more out of him, then get him outside."

"I understand." He was talking to me and the boy assassin sitting across from him. "The man I speak of is nothing special, just a man with no tact and an overambitious cock. But there is a part that is a bit of tricky, though. The man I need *tended* to is an Italian. A *real* Italian, you understand."

"This from a French?"

"Yes, I know. But that is what I mean. I am not like this man, these men, you men. This man, he has a boy. Eight or nine years old. Blonde little fuck with a bit of a hair-lip, which will probably make him a mean and unfuckable adult man. This man's son is always with him. Always. I hold nothing against the tiny monster, his genes are not his fault, but I cannot have him grow up and come back to settle his vendetta. So very Italian. All men die, but I surely do not want to be murdered at the hands of a sixteen-year-old guinea twerp I could have taken care of well before his balls dropped."

"You want the boy tended to as well."

"I know it is a ghastly thing to ask. Hearing myself say it out loud makes me doubt my sanity and devotion to Christ. If this is not something your org—"

"It won't be a problem."

"It won't?"

Alba pulled the cart closer to the cafe. We could see Michel and the boy at their table.

"I'm a real Italian. And a real guinea twerp. I understand. The biggest mistake you can make when deleting a Roman is leaving his sons alive."

"So you would be willing to—"

"Of course. That is not a problem for us."

"That is a relief. The idea makes me ill, but I must look out for *moi* and only *moi*."

"Get him out of there, Michel. We're ready," I whispered into his earpiece.

"That is the way of things," the young man said, stroking the embarrassingly thin upper lip hair that he probably considered a mustache. "You are the only thing that matters to you, and I am the only thing that matters to me. Which leads us to—"

"Of course. The money. Well. I am pleased that I can offer you a very generous payment of..." He paused for what I assumed was dramatic effect:

"Five hundred denarii."

I heard Alba stifle a laugh. We didn't need the camera to register the change in posture and utter disgust the figure created in the boy. "Five hundred denarii?" he asked, stunned.

"I know. So much coin. It is probably too much, but I am desperate."

It's my first time purchasing mortal retribution. I'm afraid I don't know the market value, the Senator had said. I felt like a lifetime ago.

"You want us to kill a man—"

"Tend to—"

"To kill a man and a child for five-hundred denarii?"

"That, of course, also includes the gratuity."

"Who do you think you are dealing with?" He pushed away from the table and stood up. "We were told you were a serious man."

"Oh, I am very serious. It is every bit of coin I have in the world."

"You're lucky I don't sting you dead right here and now for wasting my time."

"I certainly didn't mean to—"

"Fuck off, old man."

The boy stormed away, out of the patio area and into the street.

"Old man? Little guinea twerp..." Michel mumbled in my ear. Alba kept the cart at a crawl, keeping as much distance from the kid as we could without losing sight of him. From our experience in Atavism, we knew we had to catch him unawares. I took out a cherry stinger and held it across my lap. There were plenty of people on the street, and I was waiting for him to wander into a less-populated area.

The boy was mumbling to himself, still fuming from Michel's insulting offer.

"Shit," Alba said. The traffic was stopped in front of us. Bicycles and carts congested at an intersection. Our target began to increase his lead on us, and we had no idea where he was going.

"Catch up as soon as you can." I hopped out of the Fiat. I left the Sprite in the cart. I needed the guy alive. He turned right around the corner. I waited a beat before I did the same. I came around and saw him mounting a scooter. With me on foot and Alba around the block in the cart, if he got moving we would lose him.

"Hey!" I yelled, hoping to delay him just enough for me to get in range. "Hey, you, the little boy in the hat!" He turned. I wanted to get a meter or so closer, but as soon as he laid eyes on me, he recognized me. He quickly drew his pistol, an identical weapon to the one that had killed Amelia.

I fired twice, the unhacked stinger hissing quietly with each shot, but I was on the move and too far away. I heard the crackle of his gun and dove behind a parked cart. An energy weapon battle wasn't like the gunfights in old films. There were no visual indicators of where a shot missed. No red laser bolts. No bullet holes. If your opponent kept moving, you had missed. If she fell down, she was dead.

I wasn't dead.

I didn't want things to devolve into chaos. While I was firing nonlethal blasts, he wasn't, and anyone who caught one of his strays would stay down forever. He fired twice more. The distinctive report of his pistol brought memories of Amelia's death to the fore, and those brought with them a surge of anger.

I came around the end of the cart and, without any cover, fired two, three, four times at him, but nothing landed. I found myself missing my old *Śikārī*-6.

I can knock down a bird at a hundred meters with a rifle. But with these cheap street pieces, you just have to keep firing and hope the other guy falls down.

The King dove and crawled, trying to get his bicycle between us. He sent a few blind shots my way, but I advanced without flinching.

She sang to me. An old British standard. Older than her. Older than me:

"Maybe I just want to breathe.

"Maybe I just don't believe."

The batpack in my stinger was running low, and taking time to load my spare batpack would have been a deadly delay, but I couldn't go to Schoolgirl.

"Maybe you're the same as me.

"We see things they'll never see..."

"Alba, fucking now."

"Coming," came her voice in my ear.

He popped up from behind the two-wheeler, firing, his weapon crackling over and over. I took a deep breath, knowing it could be my last if any of his shots landed true, and squeezed my trigger as many times as I could. One of us was going to go down.

"You and I are going to live forever."

I stayed upright.

He didn't.

The boy shuddered and collapsed forward, toppling and landing on top of his scooter. I looked around. At least a dozen people on the street, more coming, staring at me. I got to the unconscious man and took out the gear Grease had given me, a round disc of poly with three prongs coming out the bottom. I slapped it onto the back of his neck, driving the spikes into his skin, and hoped it would do what the 'plantjock told me it would. Any signals coming from his implants needed to be cut off; I couldn't have the Kings tracking him.

"I got him," I told Alba and Michel.

"I see you," Alba said. "Be there in five seconds."

The baby assassin's eyes flickered and then snapped open. He tried to sit up, but that wasn't going to happen. He was strapped to the operating chair by his neck, chest and legs.

"I know it's uncomfortable," I said to him. "But we didn't want you coming to and struggling while my friend was working on you. Safety thing."

There were two wires coming out of his neck, just below the jaw. They ran to a small touchpad that Grease had resting on the table. "What the fuck did you do to me?"

"Last time I met one of your buddies, our conversation got cut short by that nasty little gear you've got wrapped around your throat. My friend here is keeping it from triggering before you and I finish our chat."

"I don't know what you're talking about." He was trying to keep his voice tough, but it was wavering and scared.

"The clamp that all of you wear. A LightningCorp Compromise Prevention System, they call it in the catalog. It's there to keep you from saying too much, but too much is exactly what I need."

"You stupid bitch. I don't have any—"

"Show him," I said.

Grease tapped the screen. The boy seized, choking, desperately trying to get his hands free to claw at his neck. His eyes bulged. His face began to change color. I motioned to the 'jock. The clamp released, and air flowed into our prisoner's lungs. He coughed violently.

"That clamp," I said.

"I didn't... was... I didn't..." he squeaked out.

"What was that?"

"I didn't know that was there." The fear and anger in his eyes confirmed the story.

"All of you have them. All of you Kings of Roma. It's so you don't spill. It reads your brain, and when it feels like you've been broken, it makes sure you'll never talk again. They didn't tell you about it?"

He shook his head. I had initially been frustrated that we were stuck with such a young one but was starting to feel like he'd be easier to crack. "They must have put it in when they did your other 'plants," Grease explained. "The comm. The stim-kit."

"The good news," I said, "is that we've turned it all off. For now. We can take it out for good, but before that happens, you and me are going to have a talk."

"I'm cammed and tracked. They're probably coming for me right now. And you'll regret messing with—"

"We turned that off too. No one knows where you are, boy. Nobody but us, and we're not telling."

I pulled up a chair and leaned in close to his face.

"You're going to feel something cold running through your veins. That's just a little syrup that's going to let you relax. Help you open up to me."

"It won't work on me," he said, trying to stay defiant.

"We'll see. Do you know who I am?"

"You're the Paki bitch who killed Numa."

"I didn't kill him." I tapped his neck. "This did. But that doesn't matter. Do you know why I killed... what was his name?"

"Numa."

"Numa. What do they call you?"

"Tullus. I am Tullus."

"That's your pretend name. What did your mama call you?"

"We are the Kings of Roma," he said. "We take the names of the Kings of old-old times and renounce our modern—"

I cut him off. "I don't care what your fucking name is. Are you all brothers? Cousins?"

"No."

"You get cut to look like this?"

He nodded. Grease had guessed as much. He had found some evidence of cosmetic work. His services were costing me half my purse, but so far he had been worth it. "You get modded to look like who?"

"Like Rom."

"Who's Rom? Your boss?"

Romulus. The founder and first king of Roma.

He nodded again, annoyed at himself for doing so. The serum in his blood was starting to get to him, make his head fuzzy. Making him talk before he could think.

"I have to ask, what's up with the costumes you guys wear? Also Rom's idea?"

"Rom says it's from an old song." He half-sung a little bit of it, his voice weak and strained: *"All the early Roman kings, in their sharkskin suits. Bow ties and buttons. High-top boots."*

"And the hats?" I asked.

"They're in the next verse."

Everything I learned about the guys made me hate them more.

"Do you know why I killed Numa?"

"Never told us. Just showed us your picture."

"Several months ago, you guys took a contract to kill an old lady. You shot her dead outside of Piazza Navona. Do you remember this?"

"No."

I leaned in closer. I could feel his breath on my face.

"Do you remember this?"

"Yes," he said.

"This is simple, Tullus. I don't care about you. I don't want to hurt you. I don't want to hurt Rom or any of you other idiots with play-names. I just want the man who made the old lady dead. That's it. Give me him, and you leave here on two legs."

He smiled. Then chuckled. Then began to laugh.

I looked back at Grease. Had we given him too much of the chem? He shrugged.

"Why are you laughing?"

"Servius. You're looking for Servius."

Servius. I had a name. A stupid name. A fake name. The alias of a court jester pretending to be a king.

But it was a name. A point in space on which to focus my efforts and hate.

Servius.

"If you can find Servius," Tullus continued, smile still on his lips, "you can have him. Rip his fucking heart out. The Kings will be grateful."

"You don't know where he is?"

"Haven't seen him for months. He's not a King anymore. He's not even Servius anymore. We'll give that name to whoever we find to replace him."

"Where did he go?"

His eyes started to wander a bit, looking around the room. The serum we were pumping into him was making him groggy. I hoped Grease had been careful on the dose. "Where did he go, Tullus?" I asked again.

"Who the fuck knows?" he replied. "Serv's a spinner. He'll take anything for a tweak or a twist, but he loves the hypno. Blows all of his coin on it. Rom told him to get clean or leave. He left. Got all of his on-board removed so we couldn't find him. He's probably sleeping in the mud at the Circus or sucking dick for coin or dead. Probably dead."

"He's not dead."

"How do you know?"

"Because I'm the one who's going to kill him, and I haven't done that yet."

"You're not going to hurt me, are you?"

"Who took out the contract? Who paid for the old lady to get made dead?"

"Oh. That one's easy."

"Why's that one easy?"

"I take all the meetings. That's all I do... did. That's what new brothers do. Take the orders. The last Tullus's mama found out what he was doing and made him quit. I wasn't a real King yet. Low man. Contract boy. That way if I got busted, Rom wasn't losing anything worth anything... Wasn't a real King yet."

"Who, Tullus? Who did you talk to?"

"He was Italian."

"Going to need more than that."

"Bald guy. Nice suit. Real... real attitude, now that I... fucker. Attitude. Bald as shit. Look down on me when you don't have any hair? Fucker. Bald shit."

A bald man. A Roman. It wasn't a lot to go on.

"A name. I need a name."

"I never ask their name."

"Did you ever see him again?"

"Once more," he said, his voice starting to fade.

"When? When did you see him again?"

"At a... my first job."

"Your first job?"

"Was supposed to be Numa. But Numa didn't come home and... some Paki cunt, he said, Rom said. And with Serv gone, Rom told me it was my turn to... be a King... pull the trigger."

"And you killed this man? The bald man?"

"No. Not him. Some old guy. Real old guy. Fancy hotel downtown. Felt... bad. Killing old guy. But I did it. Pulled the trigger. Made dead. Made me... real King."

"And what about the bald man, Tullus? What was he doing there?"

"He opened the door and let me in."

Stunned, I stood up.

✝

He opened the door and let me in.

"Grease," I ordered. "Choke this bastard out."

"Wait," Tullus pleaded. "You said... didn't want to hurt me."

"Did you really kill that old man, Tullus?"

He nodded.

"How did he take it? What did he do?"

"He begged, cried. I told him it was okay, it was his time, but he said he didn't have a time. I just... pop, crack... hit the floor... you know? Killed him... killed him dead as fuck."

I nodded to Grease. He turned the clamp back on.

I walked away.

XVI: LOVE LIES A'BLEEDING

ALBA HAD INDEED FOUND THE HOUSE. Ottavo Colle was an upscale neighborhood that wasn't just north of Nationale, it was north of everything. It was a very green piece of land that had once been a public city park known by another name. The closer I got to it, the more things came back to me. At first, every memory from Kennedy had been crystal clear and detailed, but ever since Grease removed the chip, things had gotten fuzzier. I wanted them to go away altogether, but for some reason it hadn't happened.

But when I made a familiar turn, passed a forgotten tree stump, saw a broken bit of wall or caught whiff of a blooming tree, I remembered. I knew exactly where I was. And by the time I reached the front gate, I was no longer looking for the house. I was going home.

There had been a few close calls on the way. Wealthy neighborhoods always had more Legionnaires on patrol. I had seen three pairs of them on the road leading into the posh community. I had to jump in the bushes twice for cover. I had eventually found enough of a gap in the patrols to make my way into the neighborhood proper.

The lot was framed on all sides by a three-meter stone wall topped with sprawling bougainvillea vines, their pink and purple explosions of bloom hiding thousands of spiky thorns. *Bougainvillea.* The word came to me in Amelia's voice, not my own, from Caden's memory, also not my own. What other useless shit had they given me?

Getting over the floral barricades might have been a difficult, painful and impossible process, so I was relieved that the wrought iron gate was swung all the way open, giving way to the driveway, which was lined on both sides by tall shrubs. The pea gravel crunched under my feet with each step. The drive split to the right towards the garage. I couldn't see it though, not through the trees and bushes. There was an apartment above the garage. It had been Orso's.

Orso.

The driveway turned left and morphed into a roundabout that circled an island ringed with azaleas and featuring a neglected multitiered marble fountain. At the top of the circle was the house. It was large and classical-looking, not quite a palace, but close enough. Two stories, with a green-glass arboretum attached to the south wall. Impressively large windows. Old-old style marble columns, like the ones in Bijan's flat but larger and not made of cheap poly, framed the front porch while also supporting the veranda above it.

It was four marble steps to the porch, into the shade of the second floor terrace, and to the double doors, both twice as tall as a man. Each was monogrammed with a large M, which I found both narcissistic and funny, since Moreno hadn't really been their name. Considering the state of the front gate, it didn't surprise me that the doors opened with just a push.

I had three weapons on me. I pulled out the only nonlethal one, the retail piece I had used to take down Tullus, and pushed the right door a little further open and stepped inside. The double-high foyer was sunlit by the large charge-glass skylights two stories above. Two grand curved staircases met a landing, which then led to the second-story hallways, which had wrought iron rails along them to keep one from falling to the foyer below. In the center of the rotunda, flanked by the stairs, was a statue of a winged woman. Not a woman. Panacea. The healer goddess of old-old Greece.

Alba had indeed found the house.

So had someone else. The entire placed had been tossed and wrecked. Stinger at the ready, I moved from the parlor into the living room, past Caden's study, through the dining room and into the kitchen.

Every drawer had been opened. Every book ripped from its shelf. Not once piece of furniture had intact upholstery. Mirrors were shattered. Vases and lamps dashed on the hardwood floors. Paintings torn from their hangings in an attempt to reveal things hidden behind them, the expensive-looking artwork left torn and stepped on. In the kitchen, the cutlery was scattered on the tile. The contents of the cooler pulled out and left to rot and melt.

I opened the door from the kitchen that lead to the arboretum, the greenhouse that had been Amelia's favorite feature of the house. It had not survived either. All of the shelving had been torn down. The plants smashed on the ground. A bloodbath of soil and dried roots.

Returning to the foyer, I ascended the left staircase, and took the hallway to my right, passing by the small private lift in the back. I nudged each door open with my left hand while keeping the stinger up. Amelia's office. The guest bedrooms. The bathrooms. All trashed but devoid of life. I looked down over the railing to the parlor below, then kept moving forward, all the way to the front of the house. A door took me out onto the terrace, from which I had a view of the front yard I had just come through. How many times had Caden and Amelia stood there, watching the sun come up, searching for constellations in the sky?

There was a door at the other end of the balcony. I went back inside, into the hall opposite the one I had come down, took a left and was in the master suite.

Their room. Our room.

The bed they had slept in, the bed he had wallowed in for weeks after her death. It had been tossed and trashed just like the rest of the place, but seeing the destruction in such a private place, made me furious. I crossed the room, stepped onto the raised second level, and regarded the four-post bed. The blankets and sheets had been ripped off, and the mattress had been sliced open and gutted right down the middle. I wrapped my hand around one of the posts.

"Yeah..." I exhaled. I wasn't sure what I had expected. They had known about the hotel and the laboratory. Of course they knew about the house. It was not a secret place, not a mystery. This had been their home. The St. Regis had been an escape for Kennedy, from physical danger and perhaps from the shadows on the walls at home. The whispers of their life together were overwhelming to me. I could only imagine what decades there, decades there *with her*, had left behind for him.

In the shadows, I also saw traces of Orso.

Orso. The turncoat. The traitor. The manservant turned executioner.

That Orso had ordered the murder of Amelia, and then of her husband, was shocking but not surprising, only because I knew nothing of the man. I had assumed loyalty but had never really seen any proof of it. From the pieces of Kennedy still swirling around in my head, I felt faith in the man's abilities, maybe even some fondness, but surely no warmth or trust. He had been an employee, a good one, but he had not been a friend, and why Kennedy had allowed him to witness so many of his secrets was beyond me.

But Orso had ordered Amelia's murder and, at the very least, assisted with the Senator's. If the frightened and drugged young man, the man whose body Grease had no doubt tossed into the Tiber by now, was to be believed. I was feeling a twinge of guilt about killing the most junior member of the Kings of Roma. He was willing to take a contract that would have involved the murder of a small child. Worse, had encouraged it. He had pulled the trigger on Caden Kennedy. Admitted it, even though the chemical haze we subjected him to, with pride. He deserved what he got.

But he had been young and had just done what he had been told. I knew what that felt like. He was as innocent a murderer as I had come across since the war, but that did not make him innocent; it did not make him less of a murderer. He killed Kennedy, the man who was now part of me. How often did one get a chance to avenge their own murder?

Orso had ended up just as dead as his bosses, on the floor of an abandoned airplane hangar. If he had been the one calling the shots, the maestro, who had killed him and why? I wished he wasn't dead. Not because he could provide answers. Not because he would lead me up the chain to the man who ultimately gave the orders.

I wished he wasn't dead so I could kill him myself. I still had ten rounds left in the Browning. He would have been worth one or two.

I leaned forward and touched my forehead on the cool, wooden bedpost. Closed my eyes. The house was a bust. I was going to have to be satisfied with finding and killing the triggerman. The bigger answers I sought were slipping away.

"Don't move, or I'll blast you."

The voice, the voice of the man I had hoped to find, came from behind me. I stood up straight. Held up my hands. Remained still.

"Drop the stinger."

I dropped it onto the mattress. I scanned the room for a reflective surface, but there were none. I was blind.

"Very sloppy, Virata Das. My gear picked up your tracker when you got within a kilometer."

"What tracker? I was swept and cleared." Judging by his voice, he was several meters away, probably standing at the door that led into the hall. He took a few steps, I could hear, coming closer. I thought about pulling one of my other weapons and hoping he was a bad shot, but everything else I had was lethal. I wouldn't get the information I needed from a corpse.

"You probably went to some cutter who works out of basement somewhere, right?" he asked. "A guy with a name like Spark or Burner or—"

"Grease," I said.

"Well, from here on out, let's just assume I'm smarter than anyone who calls himself Grease."

"I just came to talk."

"Put your arms down, Rata," Alba said. "This asshole isn't carrying."

I turned around. Jao now had his hands up. My black market beauty stood behind him, one of her Spitfires nuzzled into the back of his neck. Michel stood beside her, bemused. We had agreed to take different paths through Ottavo Colle. Easier to avoid patrols solo than as a pack of mismatched hard cases.

I looked at Jao for the first time in months. He was shirtless and had lost several kilos from an already slight frame; his ribs were now visible through his skin. Eye sockets darkened and recessed. He looked desperate. And he looked dangerous. "You brought friends. Since when do you have friends?" he asked. "That wasn't part of your profile."

Profile?

Alba nudged him towards me with her free hand. I motioned for her to put her weapon away. She lowered it, but kept it out.

"You've done a very stupid thing," Jao said to me.

"You're going to have to be more specific."

"She does a lot of stupid things," Alba chimed in.

He took a step closer to me and lowered his voice as if someone could be listening in. "They're watching the house."

"Who's watching the house?"

"The people who are looking for me. Looking for you," he said. "The people who killed her."

Michel and Alba shifted uncomfortably. "If they want you, why haven't they come to get you?" Michel asked.

"I've been careful. Hiding. The lab is invisible. On any sensors just looks like earth. But you, you just walked in—"

"Just walked in the front door," Alba realized out loud.

"Well," I said. "We're not leaving until you give me some answers."

✝

"Aren't you listening to me? They know you're here. They want to wipe out everyone involved with this. They're probably on their way right now."

I smiled, not believing our horrible good luck. "Good. While we're waiting for them, you and I are going to have a talk. Now, show us this lab."

He led us down the stairs and around the back of them, past the bathrooms and what I figured was the maid's quarters, and to the garden. Alba kept her eye on Jao, ready to lay the Chinese down if he gave her cause. Michel winced every time he stepped over something pretty, rare or expensive looking that had been stomped, ripped or smashed.

The garden was flanked on either side by two huge umbrella pines, their skinny trunks holding up vast evergreen tops that shaded nearly everything. Under them, banks and banks of flowers, overgrown and wild, untended for months.

"Albalonga, my dear," Michel asked as we walked, "since it appears that things are soon going to become less than civil, is there another piece of weaponry hidden on your sexiness that Michel can borrow?"

Alba pulled up the leg of her pants and removed from an ankle holster one of her back-up pieces. One of. I knew from watching her dress every morning she had at least two more on her. She tossed the stinger to Michel. Until that point, he had resisted carrying any type of weapon, but after he caught it, he checked the juice and primed it like he had done it a thousand times.

"*Merci.* Is it—"

"Yeah, Froggy," Alba said, reading his eyes. "That's hack. Each charge is going to sap that batpack five times over. You have three, maybe four throws with it before it bricks."

"I understand, but is it necessary to—"

"That's what they'll be throwing at us," I told him. "Those are the stakes."

He looked at me. I saw fear in his eyes.

"You can go, Michel. I won't think any less of you."

He smiled. "A little less, yes, you would." He slid the gun into his jacket pocket.

The path opened up to a square stone-tiled patio. It was a place made for entertaining. Strong poly tables and chairs, now, like the furniture inside, overturned. Benches situated around two in-ground fire pits. In the middle was a shallow cement pond, holding another waterless fountain, this one topped with a naked baby with wings and a sword. On the cracked and dry bottom of the pond, the skeletons of a dozen or so small- to medium-sized fish.

Beyond the patio, just into the unpaved garden, was a large green plant, with drooping tendrils of red flowers hanging from it. They looked like coral that had been pulled from the sea and co-opted as terrestrial flora.

"Love-lies-bleeding," I said.

"What?" Alba asked.

"The flower. It's called 'love-lies-bleeding.'" My knowledge wasn't from any implant; I knew it from my grandmother's garden in Pujali.

"Pendant amaranth, the tassel flower, the foxtail," Jao said. "Many names, but love-lies- bleeding, surely the most poetic."

Jao reached into the flowers. The plant was still alive, bright and vibrant. I would have guessed it synthetic, but the familiar sweet scent was evident. After a moment of fishing into the deep growth, Jao produced one flower in particular.

✦

It didn't belong there. It only had two petals, like butterfly wings, on either side of its disk. The stem was not natural, but a data cable. He took the fake flower into his hands and pressed a thumb to each opposing petal.

A quiet thump came from the garden behind him. He motioned for us to follow, off the patio, squeezing around the love-lies-bleeding and into the shade of yet another umbrella pine. Beneath it, covered in soft, synthetic moss, was the outline of a hatch with one end popped open a few centimeters. Jao lifted and swung up the hatch and pointed at me.

"Just you."

"All of us," I said in a tone that let him know he wouldn't be giving any orders, in case Alba's twitching trigger finger wasn't clear enough. "We all go down."

Jao thought for a moment, then nodded and stepped onto the first rung of the ladder. I followed, with Alba and Michel behind. It was a short trip, maybe three meters. "Lights," Jao said before my feet hit solid ground. As I came off the last rung and stepped away to make room for the others, the illumination kicked in and showed me the type of laboratory I had hoped to see the night Orso had driven me to the ruins of Fiumicino airport. It was bright white and clean. There were touch-glass screens everywhere, and the terms were more advanced than any I had seen outside of a grav-drone command center. It was quiet and looked sterile, but smelled of food and sweat and general humanness. Jao had been living down there.

Several heavy doors, each protected with printpad security, lead into other wings of the complex. We were standing in what looked to be the hub of the place. One console was comprised entirely of twelve small vid-screens. Each one was running imagery from somewhere on the grounds and inside the house. The front gate, the driveway, the garden, four corners of the lot, two in the upstairs halls and three on the lower floor.

Jao grabbed a raggedy shirt off the floor and pulled it on.

"Why didn't you see us coming?" Alba asked as she studied the security setup.

"As soon as I saw Virata, I came out to warn her. I didn't expect companions. As I said, she was not supposed to have friends."

"What is this place?" I asked, having no virtual recollection of it.

"This is the workplace of the greatest mind to reside in Italy since DaVinci. And the greatest woman, human, that I've ever known. This... place is where she did her work, fed her knowledge, tried to make order of the chaos that was her thoughts."

"This was Amelia's lab," I said.

"Doctor Starr," he said quietly. "To me, she was always Doctor Starr."

Doctor Starr. He had cast aside her married name and spoke with more than just formality and respect. There was reverence in his voice. Devotion. Longing.

Maybe love.

"I have something to show you," he said.

"Answers first."

"I promise you want to see this." He walked towards one of the larger security doors.

Alba started to follow him, but I grabbed her shoulder and motioned for Michel to come close.

"You and Michel stay here and watch the monitors. If he's right, if they're watching this place and they've seen that we're here, they'll come."

"I don't trust him," she said.

"We'll just be in the other room. I know you have my back. But this man has some things to say to me, whether he wants to or not, and he'll be more likely to do so if it's just me and him. Besides. You think I can't snap his neck if he tries something?"

She looked over my shoulder at Jao, then back at me. "Fine."

I kissed her gently on the forehead. Touched her cheek. It made her smile, for just a moment, and her smile made me smile back.

I want to know how she got those scars, I thought. *I want to know more about her.*

Shit. This is turning into the other thing.

"You two just keep an eye out. They want to bring a fight to us, I'm more than willing, but I'd like to have a heads up."

Michel put his arm around Alba's shoulders. "Come. We will keep watch, and while we do, we will swap tales of the many women we have bedded. Man to man."

When I turned around, Jao had already unlocked and swung open the heavy metal door. I went to him, and he ushered me inside. He moved to seal us in, but I grabbed his arm. "No. I can hear them yell; they can hear us yell. Understand?"

Alone in the square and featureless and cold room was a metal box the size and shape of a coffin. I approached it slowly. There was a window in the top of it. I knew what I was going to see. I didn't want to look, but I had to.

Amelia.

My Amelia...

She looked older than she did in my memories. Death had forced her body to relinquish the last traces of youth to which she had clung so tightly. The creases in her face were rough and deep, and her silver hair was thin and brittle. The skin of her neck was folded and loose. Her eyelids were shut, and I longed to see the blue behind them. Was it still there, or had the color of her eyes faded along with the rest of her beauty?

"I thought you would like to see her with your own eyes, not filtered through a foolish man's illusions, at least once," Jao said.

The emotion of seeing the woman I had been tricked into loving was overwhelming. Tears came. I placed both hands on the box but snapped them back instantly. The unit was freezing to the touch. "Is she... are you keeping her—"

"No," Jao cut me off. "This is nothing but dead tissue."

But it was *her* dead tissue.

I wiped my eyes clear with the sleeves of my jacket. It felt like years before I could bring myself to take my eyes from her. When I did, I looked at Jao. He was similarly affected.

"He told you to burn her," I said. "I saw... I remembered him telling you that."

The heart that pumped blood, the lungs that drew breath, the brain that loved me, all ash.

"The Senator and I rarely agreed on things."

"Where is his body? Did you save that too?"

"No. It is wherever the authorities decided to put it. They probably held onto it for a while, then tossed it in the municipal burner."

She was dead, so why had he kept her body in such perfect hibernation? It seemed morbid and profane. And torturous. To himself and now to me.

"Now, Virata Das, sinner-for-hire, proxy of a dead man. What do you want to ask me?"

279

†

There were a hundred things, a thousand, that I needed to know, but at that moment, only one mattered.

"Why do I still remember her?"

"Why wouldn't you?"

"I cut it out. I cut *her* out. But the fire in me. His fire. It's still there. I wake up in the morning next to that woman out there, and every time, I am disappointed she is not Amelia. The money I was promised is long gone, the man I was working for is dead, but the only thing I want in this life is to find the man who killed her and do him the same. Why is she still in there? I cut her the fuck out! All of it! All of you! It's supposed to be gone! Why isn't it gone?"

"Do you want to forget her?"

"Yes."

"Or do you want to forget what happened to her?"

"All of it."

He sighed. "You are having as much trouble with the love I have given you as you are with the hate."

On her hundredth birthday, I bought her a bicycle.

"All of it," I repeated.

"You really shouldn't let anyone tamper with my hacks. They are too sophisticated for most, especially your friend, Grease."

"Why do I still have his memories?"

"You don't. Those memories are yours. Whenever you accessed the Senator's data, you created an image in your own natural brain of the information. The original memories, not being of flesh but of machine, were perfect. Yours are flawed, vague copies, subject to mutation and disintegration, but they are very much yours now. Over time, they will fade and perhaps meld with other pieces of your life, but they will never disappear. I am afraid you are stuck

280

with all of this, no matter how hard you try to 'cut her the fuck out.'"

I roared and grabbed him by the neck. Shoved him up against the coffin and bent him backwards, almost snapping him in half. I pinned his head against the glass while his legs squirmed beneath me. The cold of the freezer caused him pain. He looked up at me with frightened eyes. Amelia, a blind and silent witness.

"You told me you would take them out!" I kneed him in the side. Hard. Not hard enough break or rupture anything, but hard enough to let him know I could if I wanted.

"We lied," he coughed.

I squeezed his throat harder. It took every bit of my will not to finish him. Not to pull Schoolgirl and make a mess of the smooth white floors.

"You lied?" was all I could muster through gritted teeth.

"We assumed the deal would seem more enticing if we promised no lingering damage—"

I stomped on his foot. He howled.

"Everything all right down there?" Alba's voice came echoing from the other room.

"Absolutely," I called back with a tone that told her the opposite but that I had it under control.

"If you kill me, you will never get the answers you came looking for," he said.

I picked him up off the coffin and pushed him as hard as I could across the room. He tried to keep his balance, but after three or four steps, he crashed to the floor.

"I'm seeing other things," I ignored his moans. "Things from his past."

He turned over onto his back. His nose was bleeding. Ligature marks were already starting to appear around his neck. He propped his back against the wall.

"Memories of memories," he said through strained vocal chords. "Things that occurred to him during the blocks of time we installed into you. You may not have even consciously relived them. They could have come to you in dreams. But they were recorded all the same, just like the ones we gave you on purpose. We knew some would leak through, but we had to chance it."

I took a few deep breaths. I wanted to beat him to a pulp for lying to me, for ruining my life, but he was right. I had more questions.

So did he. "Have you... have you found the man?"

"I know who he is."

"But he is not dead?"

"He will be soon. But there is more to it. He was a hired gun."

"Hired? By who?"

"Orso."

He put his head into his hands and shouted. *"Ni ta ma de... Fèi wù chòu biǎozi! Wǒ jiāng sī lièle tā de xīnzàng, wèi wǒ de gǒu!"* He took a deep breath. Recomposed. "So he was one of them," he said, back in the language we had started with.

"One of them?"

"Where is he? Have you found him?"

"His skull was cracked open on the floor of your other lab. How long have you known him?"

He thought, rubbing his neck. "A year. Maybe more. The Senator's previous man had left, and he came highly recommended as being discreet."

"Every time I went to that hotel, there were men with giant guns. Where were they?"

"They left."

"Why?"

"They weren't being paid."

"Why would he stop paying them?"

"Because he was broke."

Broke? I thought. *Impossible. He had promised me—*

"Was he planning on paying me, Jao?"

"No. The man was a liar. Have you not figured that out?"

I sat next to him on the floor, tucked my legs up and leaned back against the wall.

"He wasn't broke. How was he broke?"

He sighed. "Since man first understood the nature of death, he has been on a quest to defeat it. Pharaohs buried themselves with their worldly possessions, expecting to live on. Men hunted for fountains of magical, immortality-granting water and killed each other on quests for a cup that was once used by the carpenter son of their god. They created myths. A paradise in the sky. A never-ending cycle of death and rebirth. Other planes of reality. Planets across the galaxy that we would inherit and explore after we expired. Like those believers of nonsense, I too am sure that immortality is possible. Man does not have to die. Science has the ability to spit in the face of entropy and decay, and erase the one certainty of life. There are many reasons why this hasn't happened yet, but the first among them is that it takes an unending and eternally replenishing amount of wealth that no man in history, not one king, pharaoh or captain of industry, has ever managed to amass. The old fool had spent every bit of his family fortune trying to outrace the end. And it came for him anyway."

I was surprised to not find myself angry. I should have been raging. But I looked at Jao, who was still in pain from what I had done to him, and saw a man tired, defeated and sad. "You cared for her very much," I said. "Admired her.

Loved her, I think. But you had none of that for the Senator. Why?"

"The man had an unsustainable and unenlightened view of immortality. He was so driven and frightened to keep on living, living, living, that he refused to redefine what 'life' meant. Being alive has nothing to do with your heart, your blood, your tissue. The only thing necessary to live forever is your brain. Your brain interprets your senses and allows you to experience the world. Those senses can be simulated. We are solely the collected data of our minds. If that can be harnessed, copied, recreated, then one can live a thousand lives."

I touched my hand to the place behind my ear where the chip had once been.

"In new bodies."

"New bodies, synthetic bodies, yes, in time, perhaps, but no. This..." he waved his hand around to indicate the entire facility, "is all one really needs to live forever. For a century now, man has been trying to make this happen. It was predicted by a great philosopher who, sadly, did not see it happen before he passed. He called this moment The Singularity. The point in which man and machine become one."

"And you figured out how to do it?" I asked.

"What? No. No, no, no. Years ago, it seemed like it was going to happen and happen soon, but the world slowed down. The nations stopped pooling their resources. Men, scared men, got into power and made men like me criminals."

"Men like Kennedy. So the plan was to use his fortune to keep you guys around long enough to figure out how to download yourself into a superterm? And he knew about this?"

"He was aware, yet unconvinced. He was too attached to his flesh to imagine living on without it."

"Who killed her, Jao?"

"You said you found the man."

"You said that Orso was one of *them*. Who's them?"

He looked at me, wheels turning in his head. Deciding what to say and what not to say.

"She called them Project 2:4."

"Amelia did?"

He nodded. "They are an organization, an agency, something. She used to be one of them."

"What do they do?

"All she said was 'They protect secrets.'"

"What kind of secrets?"

"She wouldn't tell me. I asked. Pleaded. But she said the magnitude, the burden, she couldn't do that to me. Wouldn't do that to me."

"Why do you think they're the ones that killed her?"

"Because she was selling something they didn't want her to sell."

"A secret."

"She told me it would provide enough coin to keep our funding going for another decade. Maybe two. 'One last big play,' she called it. A remedy to our money problems, to her husband's reckless spending. Another chance for me and her, and him, to reach our goal."

"You're talking billions."

"Trillions."

"That has to be a big secret."

"A month later, she was dead. She told me they didn't exist, not in any traceable way, and she was right. I have found nothing. Not by any means, any channel. I was beginning to think she made them up."

I wasn't sure how to process what he had told me. What it meant. If it was even true. Men becoming machines. An international clandestine agency? A secret worth trillions of yuros?

My father would have loved this fic-vid.

I had come to Jao looking for answers and had gotten so many that they had birthed new questions. But I needed to know something else. "Jao, why—"

"Hello?" came a lilting French voice from outside. Michel stepped into the room. He looked at the two of us, side-by-side on the floor, the Chinese doctor bloody and bruised, as if he had expected to see it.

"Alba and I would like you to know there are now men with guns walking towards the house," he said. "It may require your attention."

XVII: WITH A QUEEN KICKER

I DROPPED THE MAGAZINE OUT OF THE HI-POWER AND COUNTED. Ten rounds. I popped one out, tucked it away in my pocket and slapped the clip back into the gun. I caught Jao staring at it.

"It's what he wanted," I said.

"He was a barbarian."

"We all are. Don't fool yourself."

The Browning was for backup. I could get three, four shots out of the batpack in my Sprite, and I had a spare. There were five people coming up the drive. Four of them I recognized instantly, even though I had never seen them. The remaining Kings of Roma, minus the two dead men and the one I was actually looking for. In their glossy suits and top hats. Each of them, from what I could tell, with their stingers drawn.

‡

Behind them, walking slowly, seemingly unarmed, was a woman.

"Punch in on her."

Alba slid her finger forward on a touchpad, and the vid zoomed in on the woman. She was taller and had broader shoulders than any of the men. Her gray hair was closely cropped save for a front-to-back ridge on top that looked like a fin. She wore a sleeveless brown dress that ran from her neck to her ankles, covering everything in between.

When the band got closer to the house, three of them fanned out to cover more ground, while the other King, the oldest of them, stopped and waited for the woman to catch up. Alba pulled the image back a little to give us a clear view of both of them. Jao and Michel watched the other screens to monitor the remaining three.

Romulus, the first King. He was probably fifty but powerfully built. He was the god from whose image the other men had been molded. Every feature in them could be traced back to his face. The bulbous nose. The long eyelashes. His face was slightly more angular and hard, a product of age. The man who killed Amelia, the man at the club, the kid Tullus and the three assassins currently trying to work their way into the house, they were all sliced to look like this man. It was his show, the Kings, and I wanted to talk to him. But he wasn't saying anything. He was listening. The tall woman was speaking to him and gesturing, pointing at the house. Giving orders. Taking charge. There was only one way a man like Romulus, a man who insisted that looking at his underlings would be like looking into a mirror, would be taking orders from this woman.

She was the client.

She was paying.

Forget the Kings, I thought. *I want the queen.*

288

"They saw you come in," Jao said, "but they don't know about the lab."

"Orso would have told them."

"He didn't know how to get in."

"So we wait for them to leave," Michel said, not taking his eyes off the monitors, grasping the stinger Alba had given him tightly to his chest.

Jao nodded. "They'll look around for a while, maybe stay a few hours, but they'll eventually assume you slipped out somewhere."

"And you're certain they won't find us?" Michel asked.

"There isn't a scanner in the world able to subvert the shielding I have in here."

While the men discussed how safe we would be if we just sat tight, kept the hatch closed and waited, Alba locked eyes with me. She tapped two fingers on the image of the woman, who had begun to walk, side-by-side with Romulus, towards the house. She gave me a look to let me know she understood, then looked with concern over to Michel and Jao. I shrugged my shoulders. She pointed to her chest, then to me, then back to her chest. *I'm with you*, she was telling me.

Romulus and the woman stopped on the front porch, noting the open door. Two Kings headed inside, one upstairs, one down. And one headed around the side of the house, back towards the garden, back towards us.

"Worst case of things becoming shit," Michel asked, "how much food do you have in here? And, more importantly, is it gourmet? Because Michel only—"

"I'm going up," I said.

"Now that is just nonsense." The Frenchman threw his hands up in frustration. "Why on fuck would you need to—"

"The woman," Alba explained. "The woman isn't one of them. She's the one paying. She's the one that ordered the hit."

"Could be," I corrected. We had no proof. "And I'm not letting her walk away before I get to ask her."

"So you're just going to walk out there now, stingers blazing, like some old American goat-boys?" Michel asked.

"Cowboys," I said. "Alba and I are going out there. You two are going to run."

"Run? Where are we going to run?" Michel asked.

I looked at Jao. "If I can get you to the arboretum," *her arboretum,* "it's a straight but fairly shielded run to the garage. Are there any working carts in there?"

"Several. Wealthy Americans and cars."

"Michel, you get him out of here and take him somewhere safe."

Michel looked hurt. "Rata, I will stay and help. I can—"

"I know you can, but I need this more."

He looked at Jao, then nodded.

"I'm not going anywhere," Jao said. "They don't know the lab is here. I'll be safe."

"I'm not done with you. Not even a little bit."

"I have no more to say—"

"I am *not* done with you," I snapped. "We'll seal the place up so they won't find it, but you are coming with us."

"I will not."

"We could blast you asleep, and Michel could carry you," Alba said, casually pointing a stinger at him. It was one of her make-deads, but he didn't know that.

Jao sized the man up. "He couldn't carry me."

"No, but I could painfully drag you. I promise only moderate to severe bruising."

Jao dropped his defiance, realizing he was going to be pulled out of his hovel whether he liked it or not. "May I grab a few things?"

"Two minutes."

We watched on the monitors as the King upstairs went through the rooms as methodically as I had. When he reached the master bedroom, he noticed something, approached the bed and picked it up. It was my YJ9 stinger, still on the bed from when Jao had made me drop it.

"I forgot that I forgot that," I said. Alba rolled her eyes.

The one outside had made his way around to the garden.

"Time to go!" Alba yelled. Jao came running, a pack slung over his shoulder. We marched back towards the exit. Alba pushed her way to the front and was the first one on the ladder.

"Remember," I said. "These guys are tech-linked, so once we put down the first one, they're all going to know. Once that happens, things are going to go down very quickly. Jao, you get the two of you to that garage and tear out of here."

They all nodded. Alba reached the top of the ladder and grabbed hold of the release hatch. I climbed up right behind her. Michel ran back to the monitors. "He is looking at the patio. Snooping around in the flowers," he called down the passage.

"Let us know when he heads back inside," Alba responded.

"*Oui.*"

We clung to the ladder for a few long moments. I reached up with my free hand and grabbed the back of Alba's thigh. Gently, for comfort. "Just can't keep your hands off me," she said. I couldn't see her face, but I could feel her smirk.

"I want the woman alive," I responded.

"And the others?"

"Make them dead."

"That's my girl."

"He is turning back towards the house," Michel said, running back towards us. Alba pulled the release. The hatch popped open, and, stinger first, she climbed out and into the garden. By the time I surfaced, Alba was already in a crouch, slowly working her way back to the patio. Behind me, I could hear Jao and Michel emerging. I looked back. Jao was on his hands and knees, pressing down on the hatch to make sure it was all the way sealed. Good. I didn't want them to find the lab either.

I came up beside Alba, who was hiding behind the love-lies-bleeding. Through the flowers we could see movement, someone walking around. I pried open a little of the foliage to get a better look. The assassin was still wandering the patio area. He peered into each fire pit, shaking his head each time, apparently not finding what he was looking for. Looking for the lab, probably, with no idea where it was or how to get into it.

The man stopped. Looked right at us. Confused, like he had heard something, or maybe gotten a shiver up his spine. He raised his weapon and slowly walked towards the love-lies-bleeding. I noticed that he wasn't carrying the flashy Beretta stinger that the Kings loved so much; it was a smaller weapon, something that looked more retail. But it was surely hacked. These guys were killers.

Alba and I jammed our stingers forward, through the plant and out the other side, and fired.

✝

The King managed to get out a quiet gasp upon seeing the gun barrels appear out of nowhere and crackle to life, but he fell silent and hit the ground.

We ran out onto the patio, ignoring the body. I pointed Alba towards the back door and then motioned for Jao and Michel to follow me. She nodded and was off. She had never fought on the behalf of any nation but, in the moment, looked like a soldier.

Amelia had cut a trail through some of the wilder parts of the garden that lead to her greenhouse. I sprinted through it, the two men close behind. Halfway there, Jao caught his foot on a fallen log and toppled forward. I ran back and helped Michel get him to his feet. We tried to pull him forward, but he wrested himself from our grasp and went back for his satchel, which had landed in a bush. He grabbed it and carried on, limping.

I came out of the trail first, my Sprite in both hands, ready to blast at anything that wasn't Alba. The rounded arboretum was right in front of us, walls and ceiling of green charge-glass, which let the light shine through while also diverting some of it into the solar cells that ran the house. The glass was a little foggy, but I saw no movement inside. I called Jao and Michel to me.

"That way," I whispered, pointing west towards the main gate. "Get to the other side of those trees. The only thing on your left will be the main wall. No one will see you. Get to the garage. Get out of here. Get safe."

"Come on," Jao said, leading the way. Now that he was out of his lab, the only choice he had was to escape with us. As he ran, Michel looked back at me. I shooed him away to say *I'll be fine*. He didn't believe the gesture, I was sure, but he took it, turned back around and ran to what I hoped was safety.

✝

I climbed the four stairs to the greenhouse. Inside it was hot and sticky, and in my head, I saw Amelia working some soil into a pot, a smear of dirt across her forehead from where she had wiped off sweat. She looked at me and smiled, and I loved her just a little more. I crossed the arboretum to the door to the kitchen. Peered in the window. Saw nothing. Slowly, quietly, I turned the knob and crept inside.

Every turn I took, I took weapon-first. I got through the breakfast room and out into the main dining hall. I wanted to get to the front door, the porch. That's where we saw Romulus and the woman in charge only minutes before.

I dashed from behind a small wall into the dining room and slid across the wood floors, coming to a stop behind the upturned kitchen table, a two-meter-long sculpted piece of driftwood. It would be good cover, and in the corner of the house, no one could get behind me.

I popped around the edge of the table to get a quick look, and I saw her. Alba had her back up against the old-old-looking pillar on the other side of the foyer. Both of her Spitfires held close to her chest.

She saw me. Flicked her eyes upward. There was someone above her, on the second floor, looking down on the entry hall. I couldn't see anyone from where I was. I motioned for her to stay still. I crept back the way I came, through the kitchen and around to the small lift. Kennedy had kept it hidden because he had no desire to announce to company that there were days he was wheelchair bound. I punched the button, and the door immediately opened.

On the way up, just one floor, just a few seconds, I checked my weapon. Two, maybe three make-dead charges left, plus the batpack in my pocket. The door opened, and I rushed out. Down the long railing, I saw one of the Kings, a shorter one, firing his weapon down into the well of the foyer, each time he pulled the trigger, sending a crackle of energy at Alba.

He must have caught me in his periphery. He turned, and I charged. When he lifted his weapons at me and fired, I dove to the ground, landing hard on my stomach. Laid out flat, I fired twice. Neither charge found its mark, and he retreated, ducking into the guest room, from which there was no outlet. The charge on my Sprite was dead, so I grabbed the spare batpack. I went to switch out the power when I saw her. The pack slipped from my fingers, hit the ledge and shattered on the floor a story below.

I didn't care.

Alba was down.

Her body was crumpled behind the column. Her eyes closed, one of her tiny but deadly pistols still clasped in her hand. I couldn't tell if she was breathing or not. Not from that distance.

I was never going to get to ask her about her scars.

I was never going to tell her—

I threw the Sprite over the railing to join its batpack. Pulled the Browning, cocked it and walked slowly towards the corner where Alba's foe had disappeared. I picked up each step and set it down gently. Trained Schoolgirl's sights on the edge of the doorframe, waiting for just one little bit of him to show itself so I could blow it off.

Movement. I fired. A chunk of wall exploded, and the report echoed through the house. I knew the noise had fucked me; there were three other enemies in the house, and I had just struck a signal flare for them. Hoping the shock would have at least given the man pause, I rushed in his direction. When I got less than a meter from the corner, the King stepped out, stinger pointed at my head.

✝

I slid, one foot forward, under his outstretched arm and past him. His stings flew harmlessly in the other direction.

Pivoting on my left knee, I spun and, just as the King turned to face me, sent two searing slugs of lead into his torso. He collapsed instantly, dead before the blood began to show through his suit.

Unless I wanted to jump through a window or off the balcony, which was always an option, I would have to get downstairs to avoid being trapped. I got to my feet and ran back the way I had come. I dared to take another look down at Alba, fantasizing for a half-nano that when I did, I would see her standing, shaking off the grogginess. But she was as she had been seconds before. Limp and unmoving.

Once I got past the exposing walkway, I slowed down, tried to steady my breath, calm my heart. There were still three of them. They could have been in any room. Around any corner. I couldn't see them. Or hear them. But I knew they were there.

I thought about grabbing Alba, getting her out of there, running and living to fight another day. But I needed to know who that woman was. And where was she? For all I knew, she and Romulus were still on the porch, waiting for their minions to finish the job.

I turned the corner to the landing and was immediately proven wrong.

Romulus and I stood face-to-face, having come to the same place at the same time. In a flash, he reached out a large right hand and grabbed my wrist to try to disarm me. I squeezed, and the shot went straight up, smashing a pane in the skylight. Glass rained down on the foyer. Romulus brought his gun up to my face, but I ducked and drove my shoulder into his midsection and pushed. After a few stumbles and staggers, we went tumbling down the staircase.

We wrestled the entire way. He got his hands wrapped up in my hair and pulled. I screamed and went for his eyes. We landed in a pile on the floor, then pushed away from each other and scrambled to our feet.

I looked at his hands; he looked at mine.

We had both lost our pistols during the fall.

I leaped at him. He barely got his guard up to knock away my first two strikes. I tried to go low, but he kicked me away defensively, not doing any damage but managing to put distance between us.

He was by far the largest of the Kings. Solid all the way through. Didn't look scared or nervous. I knew he was pumping all sorts of chems through his ASIS unit, meaning it would take a long time for him to tire, and it would be a lot harder to make him feel any kind of pain. There was no way I could beat him in a straight fight.

I went at him anyway.

I went at him with knees and elbows. With hands shaped like blades and with hands shaped like hammers. With the leg of a broken chair. A large shard of skylight glass.

I went at his eyes, his crotch, his throat, his kidneys.

We said nothing as we fought. He looked so much like Servius. The sick bastard. Turning his sycophants into replicas. They were so similar, it became easy to conflate them in my mind for the sake of killing him.

I went at him with blind abandon. Without regard for myself, only the need to hurt him. I went at him with hatred, for him, for everyone, for what had been done to her, to him, to me, to us.

Strikes went back and forth, most deflected, but some connecting. He was stronger, but I was more strategic. When he hit me, he hit me hard. I felt things in my body give way.

Crack. Bleed. I hit him more often and in more damaging locations. The soft parts of his natural armor. The joints. The cavities. Puncture. Crunch.

I went at him with a sprained right knee, from the tumble down, two cracked ribs, an eye starting to swell shut, and missing at least three handfuls of hair ripped out by the roots.

I went at him exhausted and in pain.

I went at him with a body still aching for the chems that once held it hostage.

I went at him with a broken heart.

As we brawled, I caught glimpses of Alba, across the room, still in a pile on the floor. She was only there because of how she felt about me. And now that I felt the same way about—

I went at him with tears in my eyes. With teeth bared. A growl in the back of my throat. I went at him while my brain screamed.

I went at him dangerous.

I went at him desperate.

And after my fifth stomp to his right ankle finally broke something, after I raked my fingers hard enough across his face to rip off half an eyelid, after I bit his right index finger off at the second knuckle, I went at him hard and sunk a jagged piece of skylight into his neck, right into his carotid. He instantly stiffened and dropped to his knees, the blood escaping his body rapidly and in bulk.

I stepped back from him.

He looked at me with hate, a scathing glare of a man defiantly dying, then fell forward onto his face.

"Fuck..." A disbelieving voice came from above.

At the top of the stairs stood the last remaining King of Roma. I was squarely in the sights of his stinger. I was unarmed, beaten half-dead, sapped of strength and too far away to get to him. He had me.

I was dead.

"Please stop killing people, all of you." The tall woman stood just inside the front door. She too had a stinger trained on me. "I'm getting tired of all the killing," she said. "Come with me peacefully and there will be no more of it today."

My hands were covered in blood. Mine and that of others. For the second time that day, I raised them in surrender.

This time, Alba wasn't there to bail me out.

XVIII: CHAPTER 2, VERSE 4

"LANCE NAIK VIRATA SANYAL. Born Twenty-Nine September, 2101. Kolkata. Greater Republic of India. Volunteered for service at age twenty-seven. Unusually old to be a cadet. Ninth Battalion jump commandos, for which you also volunteered. Commendations for valor, grace under pressure and two for being wounded in the line. Demoted as many times as you were promoted. Served with distinction in Saudi Arabia. Russia. Presumed K.I.A., Neu Berlin, March of 2134, when a gravtrak carrying eight soldiers was hit by enemy ordinance. After investigation, revised to M.I.A. Current status unknown. Possible deserter.

"That about sums you up, correct?"

The woman, the one who had led the Kings of Roma to slaughter and had possibly killed my friends, the friends I only had for what felt like five minutes, sat opposite me in a simple wooden chair. We were in what I could tell had once

301

been a restaurant. The arching stucco ceiling of the small dining room was cracked in a dozen places. There were no windows, leaving the room dimly lit by the old-looking overheads. The few tables and chairs that remained from the place's time as a viable business were broken or shoved against the sandy, fake brick walls. It had been a long time since the place had served anyone, yet somehow I could still make out the faint odor of garlic, which had apparently permeated the walls decades before and was never going to let go.

After I had put up my hands, the one remaining King had picked up the Hi-Power, emptied my pockets, stripped off my jacket and threw it over my head like a hood. I was thrown into the back of a cart and driven around, in circles a few times, for at least a half hour before they dragged me out, into a building, down some stairs and onto a stool. They bound my hands behind my back with a bit of cord.

Every bit of me hurt. My left eye had completely swollen shut. It hurt to breathe.

When they removed my hood, she was sitting there. And despite the gentle and friendly smile on her face, I was going to do everything I could to make her dead, no matter how much pain I was already in. There were two men in the room as well. One was a short, dark African. Sudanese. Maybe Nigerian. He stood with his back against the far wall, playing with the bottom hem of his shirt. He was dressed casually, like the woman. They had no silly uniforms like the Kings of Roma.

The second man sat on the top of a small flight of stairs that lead to the entrance. He was tall and bald.

"Hello, Orso."

The not-dead man forced a grim smile. "Hello, Miss Das."

"You wouldn't believe how happy I am to see you alive," I said, meaning every word.

"Oh, I believe it," he replied with a smirk that let me know he knew exactly why.

My mind flashed back to that night at the hangar, looking down on the debris field that had been Kennedy's lab and what I thought was the body of the Senator's faithful manservant. I'd seen a body, bloodied and beaten, but I never saw a face. I had assumed everything from circumstance, paranoia, a familiar suit and a black walking cane.

I had seen what I had expected to see. It could have been anybody, or any body, lying on that floor. Or not. With all the spare body parts Jao grew in that lab, it could have been no more than a loose collection of flesh stuffed into a nice suit.

I shifted my attention back to the woman. She had recited the facts of my life from memory, and she had my Schoolgirl sitting in her lap.

"First of all, Lance Naik Sanyal, I want to assure you that we are not here to bring you harm. We came without lethal weaponry to apprehend you. And even though you brutally did not return that favor, we do not blame you. Your experiences with the Kings have been most violent. And I apologize for that. We had been told they were reliable and professional, but they have been anything but. We will not be using them again."

"Especially since I killed them all."

"All but one, yes."

"You weren't carrying any make-dead?"

"We were not," the African said.

"Where are my..." *Friends? Comrades? Companions? Allies? Partners?* "... compatriots?"

303

"The elusive Chinaman and whoever that other man was, they got away," she said.

"And the woman?"

"We handed the woman over to The Legion. Turns out she's involved in quite a number of illegal activities."

My heart and stomach held hands in painful free fall. Alba Rocco in the hands of The Legion. She would have preferred being dead. If they found her cache of illegal hack, she would end up that way. I pushed her out of my thoughts. At least she was alive. One mortal worry at a time.

The woman turned my pistol over in her hands. "If they had seen this, you'd already be tied to a crucifix. They tie you, you know? No nails. I've never seen one of these outside of the fic-vids. So loud. Very very messy. The holes you blew in that man..." She closed her eyes and shook her head, reliving the gore I had wrought. "How does it feel the pull the trigger?" She held the weapon like it was meant to be held, slid her finger over the trigger. Held it up. Looked at it like the artifact that it was.

For a moment I thought she was going to point it at me, but she smiled grimly and placed it back in her lap. "I know what you're wondering," she said. "'Who are these people?' and 'if they're not going to kill me, then what do they want from me?'"

When one was training to be a soldier, especially Special Forces and double especially when they were one of the idiots planning on dropping behind enemy lines with a twenty-five percent capture or kill rate, the army taught that cadet how to get through being interrogated. The soldier was told to stick to their name and rank and nothing else. Over and over. Name and rank. Tried and true method that had been used for hundreds of years. Name and rank. Saying nothing but that was a sure ticket to pain and maybe death, so they also instructed how to manage the pain. How to force cognitive dissonance. Compartmentalize. And they told each fighter to look for faith in Higher Powers.

If you are going to die, they would say, *head into the next life knowing you were not a traitor to your country.*

It was easy for the men giving the orders to say, and most of the cadets bought it wholeheartedly.

Cadet Sanyal had not.

The Havildar I had been under, Lal Nagappa, had taught us all those things. He had to. They were in the manual. But he had also endorsed another theory, one *not* in the handbook. He would only give the advice one-on-one, in the quiet hours between training, to the cadets he thought smart enough to understand and use it:

Don't answer their questions; Let their questions answer yours.

I said nothing and let her go on.

"It's very simple. We want you to go back to Bombay and tell your handlers that what you came here to find doesn't exist and that they should stop wasting their time."

Every bit of my willpower went into not letting surprise and confusion show on my face.

Bombay? Handlers? Do they think I'm some sort of—

I flicked my eyes ever so slightly and quickly to the right and then said, "I have no idea what you're talking about."

She smiled, noticing exactly what I wanted her to. "Dead but not dead. Assumed name. And now, pursuing the secrets of Amelia Starr, a woman also dead but not dead, living under an assumed name. Orso here had doubted my theory. Said that you were simply a piece of scum willing to do murder for money. But when there was no longer the promise of money, you kept pursuing. Asking questions.

Digging around. And, when you walked into that house, I knew for sure. You are here for what she knew. But she knew nothing, and we need you tell the Greater Republic not to waste any more of their time in Roma."

I sucked my teeth and said, again, "I have no idea what you're talking about."

The African took a few large strides towards me and sent a strong backhand across my face. A very strong backhand. My face was already raw and swollen; the pain almost knocked me out. But I kept my eyes on the woman, ignoring the man who had hit me.

"If I really am what you think I am, do you really think a little pain will turn me?"

The woman dismissed the man with a wave of her hand. He balled his fists and took a few steps away. "I apologize again, Agent Sanyal."

"Das," I said. "There is no Sanyal."

"I apologize once more, Agent Das. We are not violent people by nature, none of us, and when we commit it, we are simply play-acting."

"Too many dead people around for you to say that."

"We are the good guys. The sooner you realize that, the better this conversation will be."

"This is not a conversation."

"We are trying to help you," she said. "We are an organization that is dedicated to keeping peace throughout the world."

"You've done a lousy fucking job of it."

That seemed to strike a little true with her. She grimaced, then forced as smile.

"I'm sorry," I said. "I've been told that I'm as rude as a Frenchman. By a Frenchman."

PROXY
✝

My joke did nothing. Her visage grew serious. "What you are looking for is not here. It is not anywhere. For the last six months, we have been countering agents from all over the world. They have all given up their pursuit once they realized how futile it was. Except for you. You have been dogged. Which, of course, is understandable, considering the nation you represent. But the world has been defrauded. For your sake, for the world's sake, go home and tell your government so."

"You would just let me walk out of here?" I asked.

"No. We have agents in every developed city in the world. We have contacted the Bombay branch. We will arrange escorted passage for you, and they will assume responsibility for you once you arrive. Once you have delivered your message and resigned your position, we will leave you alone forever."

Home. They were, in their own clandestine and completely misinformed way, offering me a way home. I didn't want to go home.

I knew so little about what I wanted, but I knew I didn't want that.

Besides, I was pretty sure I was home.

I looked at Orso. He stared back at me without expression. I couldn't get a read on whether he believed I was an agent or had just been outvoted by his conspirators.

"But what if I did find something?" I asked. "That something you say doesn't exist. Would you send me back to the Republic then?"

"You are lying," Orso said shortly.

"What you found was rubbish," the woman seemed annoyed whenever the other two chimed in on the conversation. She was definitely the boss.

"I don't think so. It looks pretty legitimate."

"You may have found what Starr was selling, but it was not what she said it was. You would have no idea what you were looking at."

I nodded. "No, you're right. I'm just a soldier. To me it just looked like numbers and squiggles, but why do you think the other man was there? Do you think I'd walk into something like that without an authenticator? When he analyzed what we found, the data we obtained, the look on his face told me all. It was real. It was what we were looking for. And yet you tell me it was nothing."

"It was nothing."

"My man told me it wasn't just something, it was *the* thing."

"He was wrong."

"He's very good at what he does."

"Obviously not. I'm telling you that it's not possible."

"If it's not possible, then why are you worried?"

"The information you were given was false."

"And how do you know that?"

"Because atomic weapons are a myth!"

I battled to remain stone-faced but was sure I failed at least a little. Shock, incredulity, laughter. Had to keep them all down.

"You, of all people, of all *peoples*, should know that," she said.

The Hoax of 2020 had been revealed to the world because of the actions of India. It was the blackest spot we had accrued since gaining independence from the British. To most of our people, it was considered a shame and an embarrassment.

A shame because we were the ones attempting to drop an atomic bomb on Pakistan, willing to bring nuclear holocaust. An embarrassment because we were the ones who first discovered that there had never really been any such thing.

Seventy-five years of living under the impression that man had the ability to make itself extinct had vanished in a day. There had never been an atomic weapon. They were scientific impossibilities. The governments of the world had lied in order to bring about peace by fear. The bombing of old Nippon had been a hoax. The entire lie had been predicated on the belief that no one would dare use these mythical weapons out of fear of bringing about the end of the world. That the threat of annihilation would keep the world from breaking out into more wars.

For seventy-five years, it worked.

India had not been in on the hoax, but it had revealed it to the world. Soon after, we were battling Pakistan the only way we could. With boots, guns, tanks and blood on the sand.

She was right. I of all people, having grown up in the shadow of 2020, should have understood that. And I did.

Atomic weapons were a myth.

But had Amelia claimed otherwise? Had she really put an empty promise up for sale to the highest bidder? She might as well have been trying to sell magic beans or a pack of wild unicorns.

Amelia, my Amelia, had been an international con artist.

I decided to ask my own questions.

"If you are people of peace, like you claim, then why kill her? Because she was selling your secrets?"

"She was selling lies."

"Then why kill her?"

"Because she betrayed us." The African was almost growling. No objection from his leader was going to stop him from speaking out. "Because she pledged herself to us and pretended to die in order to break that promise. She was telling the world that she, and only she in the entire world, knew how to bring them the fictional fire. And she was offering that falsehood to the highest bidder. For money. She betrayed everything we stand for."

"Everything she stood for, before she met that man," the woman added.

"So you killed her."

"She told the organization she was dead over sixty years ago. We just held her to it," Orso said.

"But why her husband?" I directed the question at Orso, but he didn't rise to it. "Why'd the old man have to die?"

"Kennedy was not our wish," the woman replied. "That was paranoia on the part of Romulus and his cadre of thugs. Over-zealousness. They had lost one of their own, and they wanted retribution. We decided to sin on the side of caution."

I let out a long sigh, getting back into character. "So she was lying. All these years of me lying in wait, chasing her secrets, all in vain."

"I am afraid so."

"Project 2:4," I said. They looked around at each other, concerned. "So you are the legendary Project 2:4. We have known of you for years, but to meet you face-to-face, this is very interesting. I've often wondered. What is the significance of the numbers?"

"'And he shall judge among the nations, and shall rebuke many people: and they shall beat their swords into plowshares,'" the African recited. "'And their spears into pruning hooks: nation shall not lift up sword against nation, neither shall they learn war anymore.'"

"Isaiah. Chapter Two. Verse Four," said the woman.

"I don't know what means," I said. I truly didn't.

"It is from the Jewish holy scriptures. It speaks of the end of war. It is the oath we have taken," she explained.

"And yet the world keeps on warring."

"And yet the world still spins," she countered.

"I can't say if any of the allegations you make against me are correct. But I can say, if they were, I would be willing to do what you say. We had suspected Starr was a fraud, but we had to see for ourselves. You understand, of course."

"Of course." She smiled. "May I ask you one more question before we ship you back to the G.R.I.? How did you find them before we did? How did your government know they were in Roma?"

"Candy," I improvised. I was only two steps away from making my break. "We knew the Senator had a fondness for a particular type of American candy. Five years ago, we tracked a large shipment of it to here."

"Candy..." She looked at Orso, who nodded to assure her of the plausibility.

"There's just one more thing," I said.

"What is that?"

"I did find something in that lab, and my authenticator was certain we had found what we were looking for. He was very excited to delve into it further."

The African came over and whispered into the woman's ear. She nodded. "We would very much like to see this data. If her level of forgery was that advanced, it could certainly cause trouble."

"I have a copy on my mobi."

"Orso," she said. "Please bring me Agent Das's communication device."

†

There was a box on an old table across the room. Orso dug into it and pulled out my mobi. Brought it to the woman. "How do I get to it?" she asked, her finger very close to the screen.

"Don't touch it. The moment you try to access it, it will brick forever. Bio-locked. Give it to me, and I'll show you."

The African spoke up. "Giosetta, I don't think—"

She picked up the Browning and pointed it at me. "I've got her covered. Untie her." He loosened the cord from around my wrists. I held them out to my sides to get the blood flowing back into them.

Giosetta tossed me the mobi. The Hi-Power was aimed squarely at my chest, and at that close of range, she wouldn't miss. She had obviously seen enough fic-vids to know to take off the safety. I swiped my finger across the screen to bring up my home page. The battery life was low. I hoped it wasn't too low.

On the home screen was a button.

It read: I AM ALBA'S BITCH.

Didn't I know it.

I tilted the mobiterm just a bit higher and pressed the button.

The woman convulsed as the solo blast hit her. Fell off her chair. I heard her moaning and cursing; there hadn't been nearly enough juice to knock her out completely, but I would have to make do.

I went for the gun, but a booted foot kicked it across the dirty floor. The African launched an uppercut at me, but I leaned out of its range just in time. With a lethal weapon somewhere on the floor, I didn't have time to play with him. He swung again, a cross, but I caught him by his wrist and held on.

Men were always surprised by my—

312

PROXY

✝

He pulled me closer to him and drove a knee up into my stomach. My cracked ribs screamed, but I used the closeness to slam my forehead into his. He let go of me and stumbled back against the wall.

Orso jumped on my back, but I was expecting it and used his momentum to flip him over me and into his friend. They went down in a tangle.

While they were wrestling to stand, I crouched and brought a hard fist across and down onto the black man's face, landing right below his eye and most likely cracking his skull at the socket. I grabbed his head and twisted as hard as I could. I heard the snap and dropped his lifeless husk to the floor.

Orso had managed to half-stand. Before he could get his bearings, I made my hand flat like a blade and chopped him in the windpipe. He slammed back into the wall and collapsed.

I turned around to see the woman, Giosetta, dazed from the low-power stun blast and pointing Schoolgirl shakily at my chest. "Killing us doesn't change anything." She sounded much more timid than when I was at her mercy. "What you are looking for doesn't exist. Do not believe her lies."

"I don't care." I took a step forward. "About any of this. About you, your secrets, your project. All I want is to find the man who killed Amelia Starr and end him."

Turned out there were five of them, at least.

Three down, two to go.

"I'm not a secret agent. I'm not here for your secrets. I am not Virata Sanyal.

"I'm just a proxy."

She pulled the trigger.

Giosetta had known enough to take off the safety, but—

It has only a single action, Michel had said, *so you have to cock it before you fire the first shot, but after that, you can just pull and pull and pull until it goes click.*

Her moment of confusion over the gun not firing gave me ample time to close on her, knock the pistol from her hand and send a side-kick into her gut that threw her violently into the table. The box with my stuff hit the ground and spilled. Some yuro chips, part of one of Alba's earpieces and, most importantly, my jacket. I grabbed the nine-millimeter off the ground and pointed it at her.

"They know you," she said, now sitting with her back against the wall. "We're everywhere. All over the world. You do this, they won't stop until they find you. We are doing good work. We are the good guys."

I did what she had not: pulled back the hammer.

"Do your orders come from up high? Whose call was it to kill Amelia Starr?" I asked.

Her upper lip stiffened. I had to hand it to her. She knew what was coming, and she wasn't crying. "It was ours. The three of us."

That was all that mattered to me.

The report didn't make me flinch. I was getting used to the loudness of it all. Unfazed by the carnage it created.

After the echoes of the gunshot faded, the only thing I heard in the room was heavy and unhealthy wheezing. Orso was siting, his back to the wall, suffocating but not yet dead. I knelt beside him as he struggled for breath. I had crushed his windpipe. He had very little time.

"I'm sorry I killed you before we had a chance to catch up," I said. I knew he couldn't talk back, but I had things I needed to say. "When you and the old man hired me to find her killer, did you see this coming? Us, here, now?"

Terrified hate shone in his eyes. It was getting harder to breathe. The sounds coming from him were disgusting but nothing I hadn't heard before.

"At least take comfort in knowing that you were right. I don't know a fucking thing about what Amelia was doing or selling. Bombay thinks I'm dead. I'm just a desperate and stupid bitch who needed the coin. Not like you. I want you to know that I understand. Here I was thinking you were a traitor, but you weren't. Not on your end. Not to you and your friends and your obsession with history's greatest fairy tale."

His eyes fluttered as he fought hard to get some air into his lungs. I hoped he would fight as long as he could. He wasn't going to survive; prolonging it would just mean more pain.

"You were a spy. I get it. But if you know anything about war, you know the punishment is the same for both." I stood. "I would love to stay here and watch you die, but I want you to die alone.

"Goodbye, Orso."

I gathered my stuff, including the completely drained mobi that had saved my life. Keeping the pistol in my hand, I climbed the stairs to a landing and what was once the cash register. Another set of stairs lead to a door at the top.

I pulled on my jacket and hid my weapon, then opened the door and headed out into the street, whatever street it was, with one word on my mind:

Alba.

PROXY

‡

XIX: FOUR FAVORS

I EMERGED FROM THE RESTAURANT onto what the locals called Via Del'Inferno. It hadn't always been called that, but somehow over the years, it had become a two-block stretch of Hell. It was as far west in the city as one could get before hitting the river and lined with orphaned and shuttered businesses. The only people on the street were vagrants and addicts who were either on or craving their next hit of hypnometh or Dragoon or the amped-up version of chryo they had started calling Wicked, which sounded both delicious and nightmarish to me. They hung out in doorways, argued on corners. There were some amongst them who looked like they didn't belong, not there to use but to sell.

It was a sad sight, this block of people circling the drain. Like I had been. Like I did. The only difference between me and them was that I had managed to pull myself out before I drowned. For the time being, at least. I had thought myself free of the stuff before.

The block reminded me of those first few nights I had spent sleeping in the Circus.

The Circus.

The words of a dead boy echoed through my mind:

Serv's a spinner. He'll take anything for a tweak or a twist, but he loves the hypno.

He's probably sleeping in the mud at the Circus or sucking dick for coin.

Or dead. Probably dead.

I headed down the block, not sure where I was going. I couldn't go to Alba's and had no idea where Michel and Jao were. I needed to find a place that would let me throw my mobi on their juice-pad long enough to be able to get a message to them. I wasn't going to find that on Tweak Street. I needed to get back towards the City Center.

I examined the face of every person I passed. Looking for Him. Servius. There were a lot of troubled people in Roma, and the odds of seeing him right there, right then were not in my favor. But I looked. There couldn't have been more than two dozen, but I still searched and found myself disappointed when I turned the corner.

Another three or four blocks east, I found a cafe near the Campo de' Fiori that let me charge my gear for twenty minutes. I gave them a hundred denarii to cover that and a cup of coffee.

I sat at a table outside with my cup and let myself breathe for a moment. The adrenaline of the past several hours had faded and left me with an exhausted and useless body. And pain. All-encompassing, violent, crippling pain. Romulus had taken a lot out of me, and as a result, taking out the three non-fighters in the basement had been much more difficult than it should have been.

I missed the chryo. I would always miss the chryo, though. I would miss it after a near-fatal fistfight; I would miss it when I woke up in the mornings feeling perfectly fine. It was part of me, and the most I could hope for was to keep on missing it and never find it again.

My ears were still ringing from firing the pistol. The first time I brought the coffee cup to my lips, my hands were shaking so badly I had to put it down. I had never been more tired in my life. I closed my eyes, stayed still in my chair and focused solely on my breath. On the rising and falling of my diaphragm. In. Out. In. Out. I wanted everything else to fall away. In. Out. In. Out.

Om...

I heard my father in my head, reciting the mantra, letting it resonate in his throat.

Om...

He had often grown frustrated with me when we attempted to meditate. I didn't have the ability to stay still for more than one or two minutes, and I would fidget. Then, when I got really bored, I would talk. He would shush me. I would quiet, and then a few minutes later, it would happen again.

It hadn't taken him too long to give up on my spiritual side. It would be a few more years before he did the same for the rest of me.

Om...

After a few minutes, I opened my eyes. I didn't know what I had expected to happen. I was just as tired, just as desperate, but my head hurt a little less. And my hands had stopped shaking.

One by one, I ticked through my problems.

Sarkis and The Sindeketa. They were looking for me. The message from Isra had proven that. And there wasn't much I could do. I had killed one of their own, Sarkis's only cousin, and staying out of Pakitown was not going to protect me from them. Nothing Safia Gondal proposed was going to keep them inside their own borders. I could leave Roma. There were Paks everywhere, but, as Michel had pointed out, at least I'd have a head start.

The Project. I didn't know what to make of that. If they were lying, then they were maniacs. Atomic weapons? Who believed in atomic weapons? They had claimed not to, but their obsession with Amelia's research, their eagerness to see what was supposedly on my mobi, said otherwise. Fanatics. But if they were telling the truth, then Amelia had been a fraud and not the person I thought or wished her to be. It didn't make me love her any less. That big bitch and her two cronies discovered that. But if they truly were an international conspiracy, and if they had told others about me, then that was another group of people with cause to hate me. Another reason to run, but also another reason why it didn't really matter.

Servius. If I had to stare into the eyes of every junkie, tweaker and untouchable in Roma, I would find him. There was nothing that could sway me from finding him. And I had just figured out where I was going to start.

Alba. It was easy to say that she had known what she was getting into, that she had volunteered, but she hadn't. Volunteered. The way she felt about me gave her no choice. At first, I had played on it, used it, but things changed. I changed. The idea of her in the hands of The Legion was crushing, especially knowing the Caesar's policies on gunrunners. Despite all the other life and death problems, it was Alba's fate that weighed on me the most.

The owner of the cafe brought me my mobi. "Your twenty minutes are up," he said. "Now get back to Browntown."

I left my untouched coffee on the table.

Before I could contact Michel, I saw that he had already messaged me.

An address and a unit number.

Testaccio. It was going to be a long, painful walk.

You knew you were approaching the old neighborhood known as Testaccio when you saw the pyramid. Some old-old Roman had built himself a scale replica of an Egyptian tomb and had himself buried in it. Behind the pyramid, which long ago had been built into a city wall, was a cemetery for non-Catholic foreigners who died in Roma. Beyond that were the streets of Testaccio.

It was an artists' community, the only one of its kind in Roma. A group of people desperately clinging to the last gasp of Roman art, be it cinema, paining, poetry, sculpture. It was also the only place I knew where the different races mixed without conflict. The walls were covered with graffiti and murals expressing anti-Caesar sentiment. It was a different place than any other in the city. The residents called themselves Neo-Bohemians.

The building Michel had directed me to was a tall brick structure on Via Galvani with a butcher's shop on the ground floor. There was a call box, but the front door was cracked, so I entered. Number one-two-six, his message had read. First floor. End of the hall. It wasn't a bad building, at least not by my standards, not from the looks of the hall. No animal shit. All the lights worked. No bodies, living or otherwise, collapsed in the doorways. No shouting,

☥

screaming or fucking. And not a communal bathroom in sight.

There was no intercom or touchpad for door one-two-six, so I knocked. There were a few long beats, which I assumed were used to check the digital peephole. I stared directly at its lens. The door opened, and I was immediately in the embrace of a Frenchman.

I found myself hugging him back. Hard.

So this is having friends, I thought.

It felt like he was never going to let go of me, so I pushed him off. He held me at arm's length and looked at me. "You're not dead," he said. "How are you not dead?"

"1990 Browning Hi-Power Practical. It's a sexy little tart, does the job, but it does snap back and bite your hand every time you fire it."

He pulled me inside. It was a modern apartment, with all the conveniences. Full-wall vid-screen, currently displaying a huge map of the city. Two brightly colored S-shaped sofas and a full-touch low table like Bijan's. A kitchen loaded with traditional components as well as a replicator for making quick synth meals.

"Michel, where are we?"

"Welcome to my home," he said.

On a short table sat a figurine of a small boy, his arms spread out to his sides. He held a planet in each upturned palm, creating a human bridge between the two distant worlds. The imagery was well known.

Michel was a Child of Epsilon.

I didn't know what I expected Michel's home to look like, but a clean, sensible, normal place had not been it. Everything I knew about Michel d'Arme I knew from what had come out of his loud, flowery, braggart mouth. There should have been rubber cocks on the tables. Empty bottles of *vino* smashed on the floor. Blood stains. Other stains. Wild animals. Dead whores. Something. Not even the wall art was erotic. It was…

Photos.

Family photos.

Flat, animated images mounted to the walls. One was of Michel, a beautiful brunette showing supernatural legs out the bottom of a short skirt and two children. A boy of six and a girl of maybe four. They were in a park somewhere, sitting on a bench, each parent with a kid in their lap. At first they were still, a perfect portrait, but after a few seconds, the boy started to squirm in Michel's lap. He tried to hold onto him, but the child fell, out of the bottom of the frame, and by his mother's horrified expression, it was clear he landed hard. The little girl began to applaud in joy. Michel threw his head back in laughter.

Then the image reset, and they were a perfectly posed family once again.

There were several vid-pics on the walls. The children, at various ages, playing ball in the street. Michel walking with the girl perched on his shoulders. And a dimly lit one, close and intimate, of Michel and the brunette sharing a sweet but serious kiss, then turning towards the cam, towards me, and smiling.

I turned from the wall. Michel was watching me take in the images of his family.

"Did you both get out?" I asked. "Jao?"

"He is safe. He is, but—*merde*. Albalonga. I am so very very sorry. She was—"

"She *is*," I said. "She still is."

"She is alive?"

"For now. The Legion has her."

He muttered to himself in French and then sighed. "For the likes of her and me—"

"I know."

"We have to help her." He clearly had no clue how to do so.

"I'm working on that. Do you have that extra clip of bullets you were going to sell me?"

He shook his head. "I left it in Alba's storage room. For—"

"For safe keeping," I said. I couldn't chance going back there and would have to make do. "Where's Jao?"

He nodded towards the hallway. "Last door on the right."

We got halfway down the hall when I heard a small voice behind me. "Papa?"

The little girl was beautiful and a little older than the latest of the images I had seen. Her bright yellow dress was nearly long enough to cover her bare feet. "Who is this?" she asked.

"This is my friend, *mon ange.*"

The door opened wider, and the woman from the photos appeared, grabbed her daughter by the waist and picked her up. She was even more stunning in person, with eyes of vibrant green and a body, though hidden under casual clothes, I could tell had destroyed more men, and women, than cancer.

There was an awkward moment and then Michel said, "Virata, this is my wife, Antonia."

I didn't know what to say, so I didn't say anything. She smiled, but she didn't mean it.

"And this little *poupée* is Dione." Michel took his daughter's hand in his. "Our boy Simon is around here somewhere."

324

"He is hiding," Antonia said. I had wondered if she would have an accent like Michel's, but she was Italian. "He is afraid of the man."

"That is why Virata is here," Michel replied.

"Good." She did not want me or Jao in her home for one second longer.

Before Antonia could close the door, little Dione looked at me and said, "My mama's prettier than you."

She wasn't wrong.

"And you have jam on your coat."

The blood on my jacket, from more than one source, including myself.

Antonia closed the door with a little extra gusto, if not an outright slam. Michel and I went to the end of the hall and stopped outside the last door. "You need to take him away from here," he whispered. "I cannot have him in my house. Surely you are seeing why."

"I am."

"And you are never to come here again. Michel has made a terrible mistake. I fooled myself that I was still the man of my youth. That I still craved adventure. I had tried to walk away from you, but I was so fucking... curious. I wanted to know you. What your world was like. But now that I know, I cannot follow you. It was stupid fucking stupid for me to help you. You are seeing what I have at stake."

I looked back towards what I assumed was his bedroom door. "I am."

"So please, take this man and never come back. I take risks every day. A smuggler's life is not like a baker's. But I am safe. *Très* safe. And you, Virata Das. You are not safe. Promise me."

"I promise."

325

He leaned forward and gently kissed me on the lips. Just for a moment, then pulled back. Stared into my eyes. "I hope you find what you are looking for. This justice. Vengeance. I hope it doesn't destroy you. But I have very much fear that it will."

Michel had kept Jao in a spare room, bound and gagged. I untied him and walked him out without another word to my French friend.

"Where are we going?" Jao asked when we hit the street.

"I have a place you can stay," I said. "Maybe. But while we walk, and it's a long walk, you talk."

"We're going to just walk? Exposed? They are looking for you, looking for me," he complained.

"They're not looking for anyone. Not anymore."

I told him what had taken place in that basement. About Project 2:4, about what they told me about Amelia and about the secret she had claimed to be selling.

"Atomic weapons are a myth," Jao said. He was dumbfounded by it all, at least acted like he was. I didn't know what to think of Jao. Part of me wanted to believe him; Amelia had trusted him, maybe even loved him. And a lot of what he had told me gelled with what I learned from Project 2:4 before I killed them. But he wasn't telling me everything. I knew that.

"I have one more answer I need from you," I told him.

"I've told you everything that I know."

"I doubt that. You can answer this: why me?"

He stopped walking. "I'm sorry?"

"Why choose me? You said you had a profile. So you would have known how fucked up I was. My vices. How unreliable, how deep in bad shit I was. Why choose me?"

"There were other candidates. Ones that also met all of his requirements."

"What requirements?"

"He was very specific. He wanted someone in dire straits, someone with combat ability and experience, someone connected to the underworld. With ambiguous morality. And he wanted a beautiful woman."

All I could think to say was, "What for?"

"I won't pretend to know. But after he met you, he called off the search."

"Why?"

"He said he liked your jacket."

"What does that mean?"

"I have no idea."

It was a half-hour walk to Grease's shop, and by the time we got there, I was hobbled with pain. It was early afternoon, and the 'jock was just waking up. "Jao, this is the famous Grease."

On cue, Grease scratched his ass. "What the fuck is this?"

"The first time you cracked my head, you admired the hands of the man who had done the work." I grabbed one of Jao's hands and held it up. "I brought them to you. He's going to stay with you for a few days, and in return, he's going to teach you a few things."

"I am not," Jao said.

I took Jao aside. "This man knows how to hide things and how to be quiet. Look around you. Everything in here fell off the back of a gravtrak. You teach him a little of what you know, teach him how to do his job better, and he will keep you safe."

"I won't stay here."

"Where else are you going to go? It's just a day or two. I have a few more things to take care of, then I'll come back for you. Then we'll figure out what to do next. Okay?"

The two men sized each other up. Jao looked around at Grease's gear in disgust.

"The first thing we have to do," he said, "is clean up this shithole."

Safia Gondal was the most successful and, some would say, only up-and-up businessperson in The Esquilino. She was also a woman with vision. She wanted The Orphanage to be something more than a bandits' den, a place for criminals to hide after stealing and killing in the outside world. She thought it could be a home, a place for the displaced. A city-state within a city-state. A living, breathing community where the Paks could prosper. A place that traded with the Romans instead of relying on New City smugglers to provide everything. She wanted her people to coexist and interact with Roma while still having a home of their own to sleep in at night.

Not a criminal fortress, but a sovereign neighbor.

The Sindeketa hated her.

The people, the good people, of which there were plenty, loved her.

That love kept her in power. Kept her alive. Despite the dangers, Gondal continued to keep regular and public hours at her original business, a grocery on Via Carlo Botta called Safia's. First, a grocery. Then, a retail chem-center. A cafe. Another grocery. Two decades later, a dozen businesses, but she still worked the counter at the original location three days a week, and the people came in all day to say hello.

This didn't mean she was stupid. I arrived at Safia's minutes before closing, completely unarmed. Every one of her shops was guarded by expensive anti-weapon portals. Only her personal guards were allowed to carry, and they only had off-the-shelf stun wands. No one was allowed to die in Safia's.

It had been hard to leave Schoolgirl at Grease's, not only because I was walking back into Pakitown without any hack, but because she had become such a comfort to me. Felt right in my hand. I savored the ache in my shoulder, the blisters on my skin where the hammer would reach back and bite me. Of all the shit Kennedy had done to me, I would never forgive him for turning me into an American.

I passed the sensors and entered the store. Another thing that set Gondal apart from her peers was that she had spent the coin and modernized her businesses. The inside of Safia's looked like the food-shops I remembered in Kolkata. Like I assumed they were also in Paris and London and Beijing. She had managed to keep it small and traditional looking. It was a symbol to the people that she was one of them. But the gear was new. The shelves reached the ceiling, way out of arm's reach, but featured automatic retrieval at the push of a button. In addition to the fresh and frozen food offered, she had a robust aisle of replicators and meat printers. Synth chow was cheaper to produce, therefore cheaper to buy, and almost, kind of, nearly tasted somewhat as good as the real thing.

Before the planes had stopped flying, Roma had intentionally not modernized. To do so would have been foolish and irresponsible. Nearly all the coin being made had come straight from the pockets of outsiders coming to take pictures of the ruins of the old-old Empire. Held in stasis, it had been unequipped to handle the dissolution of worldwide tourism.

329

They had not modernized in order to make money and keep their city alive. When The Crunch came, they couldn't, because the money went away. And it was killing their city.

The only thing in Safia's that came from the past was the cash register, a bronze relic that made loud mechanical sounds when Gondal pressed the buttons. She loved using the machine, serving her customers and taking their coin.

But this night she wasn't there. A much younger Pak girl was behind the counter, counting the contents of the drawer, getting ready to head home. I stepped up to one of the guards. His hand didn't even flinch towards the stun wand hanging from his belt. He smiled, actually smiled, and asked, "Can I help you?"

"I need to talk to Safia," I said.

"Senator Gondal is not seeing anyone else this evening. Perhaps Tuesday."

"She's going to want to see me." I tried to be a little more forceful.

"Oh, she surely will. Senator Gondal makes herself accessible to all residents of The Orphanage. She cares about what you have to say. Your needs. Your problems. She believes the people of The Esquilino—"

"Save the speech. Let me see her."

He kept his smile firm. "Perhaps Tuesday."

"This place is cammed up, right?"

His eyes glanced ever so quickly down to his weapon. I was a question or two away from making him draw it, which was not what I wanted. I backed away, nodding. His smile returned. I scanned the room, looking for signs of make-vid gear. I wandered casually into the replicator section, but no one was fooling anyone. The guards knew I wasn't done, and I knew they were watching. In the back, though, above a synth machine that advertised fake beef "So Good You'll

Hear it Moo!" a vid unit was mounted on the wall. I took a few steps back to make sure it could see me, then crossed my arms and stared at it, locking virtual eyes with the person on the other end.

After thirty seconds, I felt like an idiot. Standing with my back to the rest of the mart, staring into a corner. I was just about to move when the guard I had spoken to said, "The Senator will see you now."

I nodded at the cam and followed the guard down the frozen aisle to a door in the back. He swiped a key card and pushed the door open. Motioned for me to go inside first.

Gondal's office was fairly sparse, with two chairs sitting opposite a modest living-surface desk. The light was dim, and the walls bare. Gondal looked up from her desk at me. She did not smile.

"Senator, I don't think—"

"It's alright, Raza." She opened a desk drawer and brought out a stinger, a new-new looking Hornet Max, and set it on the digital glass. "Leave us."

The door closed behind me.

"You know who I am," I said.

"You watched me from the shadows. Stood over his shoulder, dead-eyed and obedient. His supposed enforcer. His Cleopatra. You're Bijan Wur's whore."

She wasn't wr—

No. She *was* wrong.

"I'm the woman who killed him."

She didn't seem surprised. "That is the rumor. Have you come to turn yourself in?"

I shook my head. "Not quite."

"Are you here to kill me?"

I held my hands out to my sides. "I am unarmed."

"From what I hear," she said, "that wouldn't stop you."

I didn't answer. I wasn't there to hurt anyone.

"I need a favor."

That surprised her. She nodded for me to go on.

"I heard you say you had a man in The Legion. Was that bluster, or was that true?"

"I don't bluster," she said grimly.

"They have a friend of mine, a special friend of mine, in custody. I want her out."

She smirked. "You want her out? Is she one of us? And by 'us', of course, I don't mean you. One of," she pointed to her chest, "*us.*"

"No. She's not one of you. She's Roman."

"And I should help her why?"

"You shouldn't. Which is what makes this a favor."

And a long shot, I thought.

She leaned back in her chair. "What are her crimes?"

"They're too numerous to count."

"Give me the gist."

"She sells hot gear."

"Weapons."

I nodded.

"Make-dead hack?"

"Sometimes."

She stood up, turned away from me. "You are asking me to use my clout with The Legion to have them free a murderer?"

"I never said she was—"

"Every piece of lethal she put on the street was intended to take a life. That blood is all on her hands. And you dare to come in here and ask me for this? You. You who I owe nothing. You're not even one of us. My people, this place, The Orphanage, it all exists because of you. Your people sent us screaming from our home, took our land and killed

332

thousands of us. We are forced to roam this world without a nation to call our own, being looked at by everyone with pity and disdain. *You* did that, you Bhindi bitch. You. And you ask me for a favor? You walk into *my* store, the place where I do my best to serve *my* people, and ask me for this?"

When she was done yelling, crying, ranting and slurring, all justifiably, I said, "Yes."

"Why?" she asked, exhausted. Perplexed.

"It's the only play I have." The Queen was down to her last good move.

"I am not India," I told her. "I am less welcome there than you are. I believe in their silly gods less than I believe in your big one. I have cut the path of my life on my own, until recently not caring who got in the way of my knife. But someone close to me has been cut, and I need to help her. I don't have enough money to buy off a Legionnaire. And I don't have the firepower or stupidity to storm the walls holding her, and I don't know how to stage a jailbreak. So I come to you, on my knees, knowing you have the pull to make it happen. I don't expect you to say yes, but until every avenue is exhausted, and even after that, I have to keep trying."

"She is that special to you?"

"Yes."

"And by 'special' you mean..."

"Yes."

"And what made you think you could walk in here and get me to help you?"

"Because I have something to offer in return."

She sat back down. "What could that possibly be?"

"Sarkis Wur."

The words hung in the air between us. She said nothing, but her entire posture and demeanor shifted.

I went on. "I know what you want to do with this place, and I think it's right. I lived here, just down the street, for years, and it was miserable. But you, you know what the future of The Esquilino could be. I could tell when I heard you speak, when I was standing over his shoulder, being his whore. But none of it's going to happen with The Sindeketa running everything."

"Killing Sarkis," she whispered even though no one could hear us, "will not be the end of them. They are everywhere."

"But if the head is removed, and with Bijan already gone, the rest of them will scramble for power for months, maybe even years. That's how Sarkis took control in the first place. While they're fighting each other, you could use your power, your influence and the good will these people have for you, and build The Orphanage that you really want. By the time the hard cases settle their differences, there will be no place for them."

She exhaled, actually listening to me, it seemed. I hoped. "Even if what you say would happen were to happen, the amount of effort it would take—"

"You will be surprised by your strength. And so will they."

"No one has more to gain from Sarkis being gone. They'll know it was me."

"Not if it's done by the crazy Bhindi bitch that killed his cousin."

She let that bit sink in. There would be nothing to link it to her. She was not a woman of violence, I knew. But great leaders had to be able to eat sins for the betterment of those they lead. I was wagering Alba's life on Safia Gondal being a great leader.

"No one ever sees Sarkis, no one talks to him" she said. I had her.

"I thought you spoke to him about Bijan. That day that you—"

"Sometimes I *do* bluster," she said with a smirk.

"Doesn't matter. Since I turned Bijan into meat, he's been looking for me."

"To kill you."

"Probably."

"So your plan is to kill him first?"

"Yes."

The minute of silence that followed felt like forever. The wheels in her head spun as her eyes began to well with water. When she closed them, it sent quiet tears streaking down the sides of her face. When she opened them again, they were cold and resolute.

"Do what you say you can do, and I will help your friend."

I stepped out of the shop and sent Isra a message:

TELL SARKIS I'LL BE AT YOUR SHOP AT NOON
TOMORROW FOR MY NECKLACE

And then added:

WHICH I KNOW YOU DON'T HAVE

It was a full twenty minutes before I got a reply. I could only imagine the back and forth between the Vulture and the gangster.

SARKIS JUST WANT TALK

So did I:

FACE TO FACE

A minute passed, then:

HE SAY NO GUNS

I wasn't entirely sure what that meant.

NO GUNS ME? NO GUNS US?

335

The reply came quickly this time.
NO GUNS JUST TALK
I didn't believe that, but I had no choice.
FINE NOON

That night I did exactly what I had promised not to and returned to Michel's house. The front door was locked this time, so I had to use the call box. He answered, I replied, but the door did not unlock. A minute later, it opened, he stepped out, wrapped in a robe, and closed the door behind him.

"You cannot come here again. I told you not to. Do you understand me? Not again. Not near my wife. *Ma famille.* Not near me. You promised me."

"I know," I said. "And I'm sorry. But I don't have anyone else."

"You don't have Michel anymore, either."

"I need two last favors. Then I'm out of your life. Gone for good."

"I don't believe you."

"Forever. I promise. Please. I have a way to help Alba. I have a— But I can't do it alone. And I need to save her, Michel. She's—" My voice quivered. "You know what she is."

He rubbed his temples. Forced a sly smile. "You and I could have been something beautiful, something *très* fuckable, but, alas—"

"Alas your wife, children and the fact that I find you zero-zero attractive?"

"In another life, perhaps?"

"There is no other life," I said, channeling Kennedy.

"Not at all attractive? Michel? Not even just a little?" He wanted me to throw him something.

"Nope."

336

He smiled. "*Merde.* I had thought maybe—"

"Nope."

"You are very rude," he said. "Are you sure you are not French?"

"Your wife is sexy, though."

"*Oui. Oui*, she is."

He looked at me, up and down, as if for the last time.

"Okay. What are the two favors?"

XX: AUGUSTUS

"HELLO, HALA. HOW'S THE ANKLE?"

The man scowled at me as he patted me down but said nothing. He had apparently done nothing to get out from under The Sindeketa, even after I removed Bijan from his life. It seemed like years since I had gone to his shitty restaurant and beat him and his cousin bloody. Now he was doing grunt work for Sarkis, even though a man like him wasn't built for it. He couldn't fight. He couldn't shoot. But he was good fodder, and no Wur had ever turned down an indentured servant.

He nodded and let me pass into Isra's hockshoppe. The musty smell and low light were the same, but the old lady was not hidden in her blast-proof cage. Hala joined three other men, all Paks, standing off to the side. Two of them were obviously muscle, much more intimidating than the

339

former restaurant owner, who was still limping a little from his run-in with me.

I knew the last man, even though I had never seen him before, not in person, not on vid or pic, was Sarkis Wur. The boss of The Esquilino. While Bijan had been objectively, technically attractive, his younger cousin looked as if nature had taken Bijan's features, scrambled them and reassembled the pieces as an actual handsome man. He dressed like a man of the street. Loose-fitting pants and a canvas jacket over a sleeveless shirt. There were a few light scars on his face, more of the looking tough kind than the disfiguring kind. His hair was black, like it was supposed to be, and he spoke like a Pak criminal was supposed to speak:

"We been looking for your ass all over, Virata."

"I tend to avoid ambushes," I said, entering the room and instinctively heading towards the opposite side of the shop.

"Bijan used to always talk about how fine you were, but I don't see it."

I could barely open my swollen right eye. "Once you get past the bruising, I'm a goddess."

Without taking his eyes off me, he asked, "She clean?"

"She ain't carrying," Hala told him.

"But she's still a danger, ain't she, Hala?" Sarkis smiled. "Ain't you?"

I shrugged my shoulders.

"Then maybe you stay on that side and we stay on this side while we have our little parley."

"How do I know you're not armed?" I asked.

"You don't. Learn to live with that shit."

I nodded. There was a wooden high-backed chair amongst Isra's stuff. I touched it.

"Mind if I sit?"

"Sit the fuck away."

I turned the chair around to face them and sat. I was right next to the enormous old-time synthetic wood chest of drawers that Isra had never been able to sell.

"Before we get into this," Sarkis said, "I just want to make sure the facts is facts. Are you the bitch who killed my cousin?"

I tried to keep an eye on all four of them, looking for any twitch that would tell me they were about to do something. "I am that bitch."

"I saw what you did to him. Cold. Caved in his fucking face. Real cold. Heard you did it with lead. You must have wanted him dead-dead to bring lead."

I wasn't sure why they hadn't tried to kill me yet. They knew I didn't have anything on me, and they sure as hell did. "He did you pretty dirty, didn't he?" Sarkis asked.

"He did her dirty every night," one of the other thugs chimed in, eyeing me. "I heard he even made her take it in the—"

"Shut the fuck up, Amir," the boss said. "You talk when I say you talk, and just to let you know, I ain't ever going to say you talk."

Amir winked at me. I was going to enjoying killing him the most, I thought.

Sarkis continued. "Just to get all this tough-fuck tension between us out the way, I want you to know I didn't come here to kill you. I came to thank you and reward you."

The fuck...?

"Erasing that punk was a service to me, and I believe in paying people for their service. I know what kind of man my cousin was, as to say, he weren't one. He earned for us, but no more than any other man would. Coin sharking is the job we give the stupid ones so they stay out of the way. Not one man worse off for what you did. The story of my cousin and me is a twisty fucking ride, but it was only going to end one of two ways. Either I was going to kill him, or he was— No. There was only one way."

"He wanted me to kill you."

"Do you think you could have?"

"Yes."

"Why didn't you?"

"There's still time."

He smiled. "Ever since my father died, Bijan had this stupid fucking image of me and him. Antony and... And some fucker from the old-old times."

"Augustus."

He shook his head. "Octavian. I think it was Octavian. Anyway. It was in the old man's wishes that I be in charge, even though I was just a kid. Bijan didn't like it all too much, thought he had put in more time and gotten more shit done, which to be fucking honest he kind of did, but we put our shit aside so we could squash all the other Pakis trying to muscle in. I might not even be boss if it weren't for him. It wasn't until later when he told me how things went south with those old-old fucks that I realized someday me and him was going to come to a head."

"Why didn't you kill him before now? Why let him speak for you in the Senate?"

"'Cause I don't give a fuck about the Senate. Bunch of Pakis trying to be shit they not be. Let them Pakis pretend to run things while the real men go and do the real things. What do I care if he plays politician and dyes his hair and wears a dress and rubs shit on his skin to make it light like a white man?"

I knew it!

✝

"My father loved the fuck out of him. He used to be smart, you know that? Back in the day, when helped me be boss, he was sharp as fuck. But over the years, all the money and the fucking and the daze just sent him over. Playin' like he was a real-blood Roman. Fucking shame. But he was family, and you only kill family when that family makes it the only thing left to do."

He thought for a second, then asked, "Why'd you have to kill Kalb, though? That fuck only had like half a little boy brain."

"We didn't get along."

"Fair enough. Not a woman in The Esquilino that got along with Kalb."

I was growing antsy. "If you're not going to kill me, Sarkis, why are we here?"

"Bijan told me you was smart too, but you real thick up top. I already told you that already," he said. "To thank you and reward you. The thanks is obvious, but here's the reward: we're writing you off. You got to leave The 'Town. You don't belong here in the first place. But your debt is gone. What you owe us, we'll consider payment for offing the freak. The Pakis won't come after you. I'll make sure of that. Just go the fuck away, and we be done."

I was stunned. Sarkis had a reputation for being fair, measured and, at least compared to his cousin, sane. But what I hadn't expected was him being, in his own, perhaps twisted way, decent. "You're going to let me walk away?"

"You never deal with us again, though. We won't loan you one coin, you got no business in The Orphanage. Ever never again. And maybe you want to get out of Roma. This place ain't been nothing but bad luck for you. May not be your town."

Agents in every developed nation in the world, the woman had said. The Project would be after me, if they were for real. Not because I had shot three of them, but because they were convinced I knew or had something that I didn't. If they were for real, and both Jao and Amelia had believed them to be, they would be coming for me.

But Sarkis was telling me I was square with The Sindeketa. That my debt was null and that I never had to step one foot in The Orphanage ever again. I could start over, zero-zero, which was better than I had been in a long time.

Clean slate.

Reset. Hard reboot.

Alba would stay bottled in a Legion cell. When they nabbed her, she was carrying lethal hack, which was bad enough. But she was known, and if they had managed to find her place and her cache of smuggled and stolen gear, she'd be a goner. They wouldn't care about the mobis and hot 'plants, but the crates of stingers, some cherry, some make-dead... They would come down hard. The only way she would ever see daylight again was if they decided to bring her out to Sant'Angelo and put her on display.

A year ago, it would have been simple: I would have shaken Sarkis's hand and walked out of Isra's shop and into a new life. Six months ago. Three.

I could do it now. Shake his hand. Leave the shop. Take with me just my memories... and the memories of others.

Virata Das. Deserter. Addict. Whore. Slave. Hard case. Bruiser. Desperate and dangerous. She would have done it without blinking.

Virata Das. Grieving husband. Free woman. Friend. Lover. Avenging proxy for a dead old fool. Could she?

I had killed for country. Killed in self-defense. I had been willing to do it for money. And for revenge, with one more to come. I had killed for my manumission, my freedom.

But I had never killed for love.

"Sorry," I said. "No deal."

I jumped out of the chair and took cover behind the black wooden dresser, the one with the reliefs of Ganesh carved into the sides. I pulled open the third drawer from the top, and there it was, right where it was supposed to be.

My Schoolgirl.

Favor number one:

"I need you to go to Grease's in the morning," I had told him. "I'll message ahead and tell him it's okay for you to take the Hi-Power. There's a hockshoppe in Pakitown called Isra's. You've never been there, so your face won't mean anything to her. It's supposed to open at nine, but she's a slow and lazy cow, so the shutters usually go up a half hour after that. You show up, you wander around the shop, be your usual charming and weird self, and you buy something. Something stupid, something little. I don't care. In the middle of Isra's pile of junk is a giant black chest of drawers. You can't miss it. It has carvings of a stupid-looking elephant man on the sides. It's been there forever. The drawers face away from the front door. When you're browsing, I need you to slip the gun into the third drawer from the top. Then buy your thing, then get out. Can you do that?"

"*Oui.*"

I cocked the hammer and came out from behind the chest and fired. One of Sarkis's men dropped, Amir, the one with the big mouth, and I dove back behind my cover. They had already drawn their stingers. I heard them hum to life, but they had no line of sight on me.

I hopped out the other side and fired again. It caught Sarkis in the shoulder. He screamed, grabbing at the wound, but didn't fall.

Hala ran for the door. I let him go. He didn't want to work for them any more than I had. It wasn't his fault he was there. I had planned on letting one go, anyway, having promised Gondal that the hit wouldn't be traced back to her.

Go tell everyone, Hala. Go tell everyone what you saw.

And who you saw.

I got back behind the dresser as Sarkis's last remaining thug took aim and fired. I heard the stinger discharge three times, but I was safe behind the heavy hunk of man-made wood. Sarkis was hurt, but I wasn't sure if I had taken him out of the fight. If I hadn't, they would soon try to flank me.

Heavy footsteps, rushing towards me. I braced against the dresser with my back as someone slammed into the other side of it. It tilted, causing several of the heavy drawers to slide out and knock me on the head before crashing to the floor.

I pushed back as hard as I could, aware that the struggle was leaving me open to the other shooter. The man I was pushing against was grunting, straining, doing whatever he could to topple the dresser and crush me.

I had to guess which way the other would be coming, and I guessed right. When the other thug, not Sarkis, came around the side to take a shot at me, I blew a hole in his chest.

"Bitch!" I heard Sarkis yell from the other side of the bureau.

PROXY

‡

I reached behind me with the gun and stuck it into the dresser, through an empty cavity that seconds ago had held a drawer. Only one layer of thick synth wood between me and him. Enough to stop a stinger blast, but not a bullet.

I fired.

He screamed.

All pressure from his side of the dresser vanished. I steadied it, then came around. Sarkis was on the ground. My shot had caught him in the stomach. He was writhing in pain, swearing and praying in Urdu and Italian.

I aimed at his head to finish him off. He stared me down.

"Why?" he choked out. "I was letting you— Why would you—"

I pulled the trigger and braced for the boom.

But got a click instead.

Empty.

Sarkis's stinger was still clasped in his hand. I knelt next to him and, careful not to touch the weapon itself, took his hand and pointed the weapon at his temple. He tried to resist, but all the strength was leaving him. I wrapped my finger around his, which was on the trigger.

"Why?" he asked one more time.

I applied pressure to his finger and stung him point-blank in the side of the head. His end came less violently than his cousin's had. There was no blood, no spray of gore out the back of his head. After taking the stinger blast, he convulsed, then fell still.

Why? he had asked.

There were many reasons why I shouldn't have killed him.

And only one why I had.

Even if I had decided to never see her again.

347

XXI: VENDETTA MASSIMO

IN THE ROMA OF OLD-OLD TIMES, the Roma of Empire, the Roma whose remnants had once brought tourists to its streets, the Roma glorified by men like Bijan, Villano and the historians of nearly every century, its people and leaders enjoyed few things more than they enjoyed public games. Contests of speed, strength and violence. They would pit men, nearly all of them slaves, against each other. It rarely mattered which combatant came out of the spectacle alive, as long as one of them did not. They called these slaves, these men conscripted to do senseless battle, gladiators. Some became famous, beloved, heroes. But most died young, hopeless and violently. They were still slaves, even the heroes, and they killed and died for the amusement of their betters.

The ancient Romans also enjoyed races. They would strap wheeled carts to a brace or two of horses and cheer them on as they circled a dusty oblong track. The drivers of these carts, also men owned by other men, would attempt to ride and guide their chariots faster than the others for seven laps. Like their gladiator kin, many of them died in their pursuit of glory, for part of the contest was the elimination of the other charioteers by violent means. This gave the masses what they so wanted from the sport: thrilling competition, spectacular collisions and crashes, and death.

The largest and most famous arena for these games was the capitol city's own Circus Maximus. A half-kilometer long and a fifth of that wide, it was built in the shadow of Roma's first hill, Palatine. From their backyards atop the founding mound, the wealthiest Romans and, later, the Emperor himself, could watch the races while the unwashed masses packed the bleachers below. Horses and men, going round and round and round, fighting to be first, fighting to win, fighting to survive, only to end up, like anything traveling in circles, back where they had started.

I had spent my first two weeks in Roma sleeping on the same land. The Circus Maximus had devolved from a symbol of Roman pride and excess to an abandoned field to a public park and, now, to a tent city for the downtrodden. A half-kilometer of spinners, freaks, whores, homeless and worse.

I had been hanging around the Circus for over a week. The people there didn't know me, so they didn't trust me. Not knowing that I had once, for a brief time, been one of them. Not knowing that I had been walking the line between them and the others for as long as I had been in Roma.

Not knowing that, after years of fighting to be first, fighting to win, fighting to survive, I had come right back to where I had started.

Like I had been doing for a week, I walked, slowly, amongst the wretched. Tried to ignore the needles sticking out of young women's arms. The starving children. The unmistakable screams, both male and female, of people being forcibly fucked in more than one hole, coming from more than one tent. None of it existed for me. It had taken a few nights to tune it all out, but I could do it. Do what I needed to do. See what I needed to see.

Faces. I needed to see each and every one of their faces.

I couldn't go around asking questions or showing a sketch of the man I was looking for. I would be pegged as a Legion informer and probably killed just in case.

I just had to look.

Every night, scan every face. Not stare. Never stare. Just glide through the Circus, down one hundred-meter row of tents and up the next. Trying to get a glimpse of the sleeping. Walking by fucking couples and getting a good look at both participants, for I didn't know what type of fuck my target preferred.

Within a day of taking out Sarkis, my mobi had buzzed. Not once but repeatedly, in a dash-dot-dot pattern. I looked at the screen. I had expected to hear from the Ghost-ID it showed me, but I had not expected to have to hear her voice.

"We don't talk on the Ghost. You know that. You taught me that."

"I'm out," Alba said. She sounded good. Tired, but good. "I don't know how you did it, but thank you."

"I'm glad you're safe."

"One minute they were fitting me for a cross, and the next they were telling me I could go. I know a pulled string when I see one. There's no one else in the world who would do that for me, whatever it was that person had to do."

Like double-down on her death sentence, I thought.

351

†

"Where are you?" she asked.

"I'm gone."

"What do you mean, 'gone?'"

"I'm sorry." *I'm so sorry.* "But I'm leaving, and you can't come with me."

There was a pause, and then, "Rata, I don't— Meet me at our spot on Cavour. We can talk about this."

"I put you in danger," I said. "And for nothing."

"It wasn't for nothing."

"I won't get you killed again."

"I'm still here—"

"But I have a question."

"I will find you, you know I will. Just come meet me. You don't have to—"

"What happened to your face? How did you get those scars?"

"I'll tell you," she said, her voice cracking, "when you come meet me."

That wasn't going to happen.

"Goodbye, Alba."

"Don't do this. Rata, please, don't do—"

I disconnected, then logged out my old GhostPass and entered another I had bought from Grease. Completely different number. Unreachable. No one around me was going to be safe, not for a long time, not ever. Before I met Kennedy, I hadn't had any friends. Now, I couldn't have them.

Not even her.

Each night I covered more ground, went over some of the old. With an old-time American handgun in one pocket and a single lead bullet in the other. Never said a word. Tried to look chemmed out and disengaged, all the while running a slower, less accurate, low-tech version of the face recog software I had seen used in battlefield AI. One face at a time. It could take forever.

I had one advantage. I knew what he looked like, and he had no idea he was being hunted.

I didn't know if Servius was there, but I felt, deep inside, that at some point he would be. Spun out on hypno, unemployed and, by the word of his old colleague, absolutely tweaked and twisted. The Circus was the place where everyone in Roma who hit their bottom eventually found themselves. Maybe not every night. If one was lucky, they could find safer, warmer places to flop. But every cadger, twitcher and for-rent cocksucker spent their fair share of time sleeping beside their fellow untouchables.

He would, eventually, come to the Circus.

I would, eventually, find him.

I took my time. Eight days, half of them in the rain, to that point. Many more, if necessary. Many more days, many more weeks, months, years. I would spend forever amongst the dying and diseased if that's what it would take to find him.

But on the eighth night, I discovered that forever wouldn't be necessary.

The Circus was divided along its entire length by a slightly raised hump that acted as a central lane looking down on both sides at the sad tents and fires. I began that night as I had each one before it, walking the ridge, scanning the scene, before stepping down into the rabble and hunting face-to-face and tent-to-tent.

I stopped.

Ten meters away, three men and a woman stood around an old wine cask that was burning straw, paper, wood and whatever else people had shoved into it to make it release as much heat as it could. The woman was Chinese and ancient.

The tallest man was an African with skin like slate who was so skinny, his cheeks met in the middle of his mouth. Next to him stood a Sicilian runt who, even dressed in rags and pumped full of Dragoon, swaggered like he owned the place.

The last man was shaking, from the cold or from a tweak or from both. Twenty-five, if that. A bulbous and wide nose that was flushed red. Raggedy blonde hair, down past his elbows and a fully grown beard that was missing certain patches of connecting hair, which made it look mangy and unfinished. His hands nervously drummed on the lip of the burning barrel.

It was him.

It wasn't Not Him this time.

It was Him.

Servius.

I pushed down my emotions for a few long moments, knowing that soon I would have no control over them. I reached my left hand into my jacket and grabbed the final nine-millimeter bullet. The sudden appearance of a firearm at the Circus would have caused chaos, so I slowly took the Browning out of my other pocket and, using the darkness and the front of my jacket to hide it, slid that last round into the chamber. Pulled back the slide, cocked it and held it down against my leg.

I stepped down from the ridge and started to advance towards him. I got close enough to see his pretty lashes, his light-blue eyes, but I could also see the dark bags under those eyes. He had lost more than ten kilos, and his softness had been replaced with the hard and sharp face of a chem fiend.

He looked up at me and nodded a greeting. He had no idea who I was. He had no idea what was coming for him. Who was coming for him.

But my face gave me away. Seeing him, really seeing him, had given my entire body over to the rage. To the flames. He must have seen the fire behind my eyes. The bile dripping from my mouth. He didn't know who I was, but he could tell I meant harm.

He ran.

I whipped the gun up and aimed at his retreating form. I could have drilled him right between the shoulders, but in the dark, a moving target, with a true projectile weapon, I could have just as easily missed. Most likely missed. Besides, I needed to talk to him first.

So I ran too.

He took off south, barreling over anyone in his path. Stumbling over people sleeping in the dirt, collapsing tents. Stepping on people. Knocking over children. He was fast, agile, but I also knew he was no longer 'planted and would eventually run out of steam. I would catch him. And he knew it.

In the dark I caught my foot on something—a person, a crate, a log, whatever—and went flying. I landed face-first in the mud and felt the air shoved out of my lungs. I quickly got to my knees and realized I had dropped the gun. I groped around in the darkness, knowing every moment was more time for him to get away. I found the barrel, grabbed it and resumed my pursuit. I had lost ten, maybe fifteen seconds.

I hoped it wouldn't cost me more than that.

I got sight of him. He was heading up the steep embankment that led from the Circus to the street above, not entirely in control of his body. His arms flailing and constantly trying to regain balance.

He was headed south, towards Aventine Hill. In the founding myth of Roma the wolf-suckled twins Romulus and Remus competed for leadership of their city by a contest of augury. Romulus stood atop the Palatine; Remus, the Aventine. They waited for signs to come to them. Who should lead this new city? While the augers, in the form of birds, came first to Remus, an overwhelming number of them came to Romulus atop Palatine Hill. Romulus became the first King; Remus was outcast, killed and shit out of luck. The story was why we lived in Roma and not Rema. It was the story of the first loser of Roma.

It was fitting that the men and women who no longer found themselves welcome in Roma proper had migrated to the valley between its two founding hills. If they could not be Romans, they would be Remans, the descendants of the brother who lost.

When I reached the incline, Servius was only halfway up and slowing down. I pumped my legs, my calves burning. I gained on him easily. Grabbed at his upper arm with my free hand, got hold and pulled.

He yelled in surprise and then went tumbling back down the hill. He rolled several painful-looking times and crashed at the bottom into the thick, dark mud.

I slid down after him. He had managed to pull himself upright.

"Don't move," I yelled.

He stood still, keeping all of his weight on one foot, having injured the other in the tumble. I trained the Browning on him and approached slowly. "What do you want from me?" he asked in a strained and shaky voice. It was the first time I had heard him speak. His voice was higher-pitched than I had expected. I had wanted something ominous, sonorous.

I want you to know why this is happening...

I took each step deliberately, squaring his head in the pistol's sights.

"What the fuck is this? I didn't do nothing to you!"

Why I am doing this...

I said nothing, which unnerved him even more.

He rushed at me, gnashing his teeth to avoid the pain in his broken ankle. When he got close, I brought the gun around in a sweeping backhand arc, catching him on the side of the head, spinning him and knocking him to the ground before he could touch me.

Servius rolled over onto his back. Looked up at me with hateful, no, terrified eyes. I placed a boot on his chest to hold him down.

"Get off me! Get off me! What are you doing?"

"I want you to know why this is happening," I said. "Why I am doing this. Why you are beaten, bleeding, and why there is cold steel pointed at your head."

He wanted to struggle, but he was exhausted and hopeless. His fate was in my hands, and he knew it. "I also want you to know that in a few seconds you will be dead, and everything you are and were and were going to be will cease. I am going to erase you. I don't care what you believe, what toxic mythology you have governed your sad little life by."

"What the fuck are you talking about?" he mumbled. "What did I do to you?"

"I have been to the other side and want you to know that there is no other side. Just this one. So when I pull this trigger, when I drive your brains through the back of your head—"

He was wearing the necklace. Amelia's necklace. DNA wrapped in amber set in platinum. Nested in the tuffs of hair on his chest. I leaned down and took it into my hand. Looked him in his yellowed eyes.

"Why do you have this?" I growled.

"What?"

"This necklace. Why do you still have this? You could have sold it."

"I thought—"

"You thought what?" I screamed. "Why do you still have this?"

"I..." he thought for a moment, then in an almost childlike voice said, "I thought it was pretty."

I snatched it off him, breaking the chain. I placed the barrel of the Browning under his chin. "What is your name?" I asked, quietly.

"Servius."

"What is your real name?"

"Servius."

I shook my head. "What does your mama call you?"

"Tonio. My name is Tonio."

"Tonio," I repeated. A plain name. "Tonio, I want you to understand why this is happening. This is happening because you took the life of a woman named Amelia. She was my wife. She was brilliant and beautiful and strong and better than you in every way."

None of it was registering on his face.

"I don't know who you're—"

"My name is Virata Das—"

... Robert Caden Kennedy. I have been a juvenile delinquent, a businessman, a—

"I have been a soldier, a traitor, a criminal—"

... a criminal, a leader, a celebrity—

"A chemhead, a whore and a murderer. But most importantly—"

... the husband of the most remarkable woman in the world—

"The husband of the most remarkable woman in the world."

You killed—

"You killed her. Do you remember me now?"

"No." Of course he didn't. He had never met me.

"Do you remember shooting an old woman outside of Navona? Three months ago?"

He searched his thoughts. It felt like an earnest attempt, but he came up blank. Shook his head. "No."

Tears were running from his eyes down across his temples. His lips shaking; eyes darting back and forth.

"You don't remember her?" I asked.

"No, man. No. But if I did, I'm sorry. It's what they—- It was orders. I don't remember. I don't— If she was someone to you— I don't— I'm just trying to get by. Like you. Please don't kill me. I didn't do nothing to you. Please!"

He wasn't wrong. He had been hired to kill her; I had been hired to kill him. We were both bad people, sinners-for-hire, hard cases that did what we needed to do to cut our paths through the world. We had both been slaves to the chems we pumped in our bodies. His head was a mess. Mine wasn't much better. I had pulled myself together, but only barely. I understood him. I felt for him.

He and I were the same. Twins. Suckled from the same she-wolf.

But we were standing on different hills, and for some unknowable reason, the gods had chosen me.

I stuck the barrel of the Browning in his mouth. I had to force it between his teeth, but it went in. "I didn't do nothing to you..." he pleaded one more time, despite the steel in his mouth.

I angled the barrel towards the soft palate roof of his mouth.

"I know," I said quietly. "But I *loved* her, and you *killed* her."

I honored my promise to the old man and kept my eyes open when I squeezed the trigger.

A child screamed behind me. I turned from the now headless body. Lined up along the edge of the Circus, all staring at me, were a dozen people. The crying little girl had her face buried in her mother's dress. Every one of them looked horrified. Some were holding their ears; the report of the gun, a sound I had grown used to, had terrified and hurt them.

I looked at the Browning. The empty husk of machinery hung limply in my hand. It was spent, impotent and no longer felt like power. The nickel plating was scratched, the blued slide faded, caked with dirt, stained with blood. It was an ugly, scarring and sad thing; it had been from the start. I was disappointed in myself for ever being seduced by it. For coming to love it, rely on it.

Like Michel had shown me, I pulled Schoolgirl apart—

Fuck. I had even given it a name.

I pulled the thing apart into several pieces and tossed them off into the darkness, to hopefully rot in the mud, but kept the firing pin. I held it tight in my hand, determined no one would ever make the weapon whole again.

The people continued to stare at me. I walked towards them, leaving the Aventine and Tonio's corpse behind me. As I approached, the line of bystanders parted, letting me pass. They were frightened. Frightened of the noise they had heard and frightened of the violence they had seen and frightened of the woman who had brought them both.

I continued past them, back into the Circus, back towards Palatine Hill.

Wear the chip.

360

PROXY

‡

Kill the guy.
Walk away...
Just walk away.

XXII: DEJAH

I slept for three full days in a ten-denarii pod flop, a place that rented you not so much a room as a coffin with a mattress in it. I slept hard and long and well. When I emerged, I ran to a trattoria and devoured everything they put in front of me. Then I waited for the message. Two days and twenty denarii later, it came. I checked out, everything I had stuffed into my duffel.

An hour later I walked into Grease's place, where I found him and Jao having an argument. Scattered on the table were a dozen different implants, many of them taken apart into pieces. Jao was taking a component from one and connecting it to another.

Grease paced back and forth behind him. "The gear is fine," he said. "It's fine... It's... It's fine, you yellow bastard. It's fine. It works."

"You make fine components, you idiot. You just put them together all wrong."

They both noticed me at the same time. Jao dropped his patchwork 'plant and came around the table to me. For a moment I thought he might hug me and was relieved when he simply put a hand on my shoulder. He looked at me, studying my face like he had never seen it before. His eyes began to glass over.

"You did it."

I ignored him and called to Grease. "Did Michel leave a package for me?"

"Yeah," Grease said and walked to his desk.

"What did it feel like?" Jao asked me in a whisper.

"Has she come by looking for me, Grease?" I asked.

"Every day for a while, but it's been a few days now."

She would eventually give up. Stop looking. And forget about me. She would try to find Michel, but if she did, he wouldn't talk. Grease didn't even know where I was going.

Over the past three months, I had loved and lost two women: one to death and the other in an attempt to protect her from the same.

Grease handed me a plain envelope. I peered into it. A handwritten note, an ID card and some sort of stone pendant. I tucked it in my pocket.

Favor number two:

"I need to disappear. I want a certain handsome contrebandier to arrange transport for me. To Paris, to London, to anywhere."

"When?"

"I don't know. Hopefully two days, probably two weeks, possibly two years. How much notice will you need when I'm ready?"

"Not much. I will need to make two identities. I will need thumbprints from both you and--"

"Just me. It'll just be me."

"Tu es sûre?"

"Yes, I'm sure."

"I will need a print from you because once my man on the other side of the trip delivers you safely to French ground, you will be on your own. And in Paris, your papers are your life."

"No problem."

"Do you have a name you want to go by, or do you want Michel to make up one especially extra sexy sounding?"

"He said everything you need or need to know is in there," Grease said. "That's all he—"

"Virata!" Jao snapped like a child not getting enough attention.

"Did. You. Find. Him? The killer?"

Tonio, I thought. *His name was Tonio.*

"I did."

"And?"

"It's over."

His whole body sighed. He stumbled backwards, caught himself on the wall and found the nearest chair. "What did it feel like?" he asked with a trembling voice. He was shaking.

"I don't know."

"I need to know. You found him. You killed him. You avenged her. Did it help? Do you feel better?" It was easy to forget that there had been two men who loved Amelia.

"Now that you know he's dead, do you feel better?" I asked.

It took him a long moment to answer, as if he was doing an inventory of the emotions flooding his brain and assessing each. He shook his head. "No."

I looked at Grease. "Can you give us a minute?"

"You're kicking me out of my own den?"

"A minute, Grease."

After he stepped out, I knelt down next to Jao. "What are you going to do?" I asked him.

He shook off his shock. "As far as I know, they haven't found the lab. I need to get back there and get out what I can, then find another place to set up. I need to continue the work. We were so close. I can't let all of that rot."

"What are you going to do with her body?"

He hadn't thought of that. "I don't... I don't know."

I got up to go. He stopped me.

"You're sure you won't stay?"

"I'm sure. I don't care about... any of this. Not her work, your work. Not the reasons why, the bigger questions. I don't care what Amelia thought she was selling, and I sure as fuck don't care about The Project."

"They care about you now."

"Maybe, but they're not going to find me. I'm starting over. None of you exist for me anymore. Not you, not The Kennedys, not the Kings, not..." *No*, I thought, *not even her.* "None of it. I'm power cycling. When I boot back up, all this, all of you, will be fucking ghosts."

"He was right. You have a mouth as filthy as hers."

My knees cracked when I stood. There wasn't a place on or in my body where I wasn't hurting. It was to be expected, the pain, after what I'd been through, but there was something deeper to these aches. I was walking a little gingerly. It took me a few extra seconds to sit down. My bones were creaking. I was always tired.

The whole thing had aged me, stepped me a few paces closer to the grave.

And I was okay with it.

"I don't want to live forever," I said to Jao. "All your work, it's an empty quest. The whole point of living is that we die. It's the only reason any of this means anything. I'm not going to lock myself in a bunker with you and try to unlock the secrets to immortality. I'm going to go out there and live the remaining time I've got left. With two international cabals after my head, that's not going to be much."

Jao took a deep breath and went to the corner of the room where Grease had set up a cot for him. He knelt and slid his bag out from underneath. Dug around in it, found something and came back to me.

The thing he pressed into my hand was square, metal and cold. It was a small tin with a hinged lid. Inside, I knew without looking, were candies, each of them a brown and green striped disc. Months before, an old and heartbroken man had offered me one, and I had refused.

"I don't—"

"Please," Jao said. "Just something to remember us by. The Senator was wrong about a great many things, but I promise you his love for these things was not one of them."

I nodded and put the tin in my pocket.

"May I ask you one other thing?"

I was ready to get out of there, but I told him he could.

"All of this time, all of this chasing around. You found out why and who and turned that who into ash. But, in all this searching, I wonder, not that it means anything, but did you ever find her necklace?"

A platinum sphere. Her DNA suspended in amber.

"No," I lied.

And left.

I got a block away from Grease's and stopped and sat on the curb. I pulled out the envelope and opened it. The note was simply a time and a place. That night, an hour to midnight, at a bakery in Testaccio.

The new ID card marked me as an Indian national with a five-year visa to work in France. It came to life when I pressed my thumb to it, and I was able to scroll through the extensive and completely false travel records Michel had programmed into it.

My new name, as I had requested, was Dejah Thoris.

Princess of Epsilon Eridani.

The last thing in the envelope was a pendant made of bone. On it was written, in Devanagari, the holy word *Om*. I turned it over, and on the back was a price tag. Eight denarii. I had wondered what Michel bought that morning at the Vulture's.

I held the gift from my friend tightly in my hand. I looked around. Roma. I had hated it for so long but realized I was going to miss it. I took a moment to hear its sounds, smell its smells. Touch the old brick on the building I was leaning against. Say goodbye.

I looked around—

And there she was.

Alba had come to Grease's one more time.

I ducked behind a trash bin and peered over to see her. She hadn't seen me. She went straight to the 'plantjock's shop. It hurt to watch her. I wanted to go to her. I wanted to kiss her and tell her I had to go and walk away in slow motion like they used to do in my dad's favorite romance vids.

Instead, I took one last look at my black market beauty and walked away.

PROXY

☦

EPILOGUE

I HALF-HOPED MICHEL WOULD BE WAITING for me at the bakery, but he wasn't. I was greeted at the door by a short Roman with a wispy mustache. "I was told to come by a mutual friend," I told him. He let me inside. Even though it was long after closing and hours before the ovens would fire back up, the place smelled of fresh bread. I followed him through the kitchen and out to the back alley where a truck was waiting. Behind the electric cab was hitched a cargo trailer.

"There's a false wall in the front of the trailer," he told me. "You and the others go behind the wall. You can breathe in there, there's light, and there's food. After you're in, we pack our cargo behind you and, if all goes the way it always goes, you won't come out until we're safe in France."

"Are you putting this thing on a ship or a train? Driving the whole way? How are we getting there?"

"You don't need to know that. You just got to trust us."

"I don't trust you," I said.

"Then trust our mutual friend."

Twenty minutes later, I was sealed in behind the false wall with my fellow travelers. A man, a woman and a twelve-year-old girl. All Roman. The space itself wasn't bad. Four mattresses, barrels of water and several crates of dry goods and cured meats. We wouldn't be eating well, but we would be eating. We were bathed in the soft glow of four lumos strips stuck to the walls. I hoped we'd be able to dim them when we wanted to sleep.

The four of us waited in silence while we listened to them loading the truck on the other side of our wall. Entombing us behind crates and crates of who-knew-what. I wasn't sure why we were afraid to speak, but we had somehow made an unspoken pact to hold our breaths until we got onto the road.

An hour went by and then the noise stopped. We heard the back door of the truck slam shut. Five minutes passed. We began to move. Even then, no one talked. The man fell asleep. The woman and the girl held hands and closed their eyes. The mother began to pray.

The girl's right eye popped open. She saw me catch her and instantly shut it again. Her mother continued mumbling, something about blessing us and our travels.

The eye opened again, this time slowly. I smiled at her. She smiled back.

The mother finished her prayer. "Amen."

"Amen," the girl parroted and opened her eyes.

"Daddy got crucified," she said with a child's bluntness.

"Constance, do not tell this woman—"

‡

"He killed his friend," she went on, ignoring her mother. "He killed his friend who was also mommy's friend."

"Why did he do that?" I asked.

"He went to the war, and when he got home, he was crazy."

The mother smacked little Constance on the hand. She pulled it to her, stung, but it didn't dissuade her from talking. "Did you go to the war?" she asked.

I looked down at the faded patch over my right breast. "Yes."

"Did you come back crazy?"

"A little bit, yes."

She smiled. I reached into my pocket and pulled out the small tin of candies.

"Is it alright if I give your daughter a treat?" I asked.

The woman nodded. She was fighting off tears, but she wasn't angry. She was terrified.

I popped the tin open with two fingers and held it out to Constance.

"They only make these in America," I said. "They are very special."

She took one, popped it in and rolled it around her mouth to savor it. "Aren't you having one?" she asked, her words a little garbled.

"Sure. I'll have one."

The candy hit my tongue and began to dissolve. It tasted of mint and chocolate with maybe a whisper of—

Oh, Jao, you son of a—

I remember. Days. Years. Decades.

I remember my life.

My name is Virata Sanyal.

My name is Virata Das.

My name is Amelia Starr.

I'm a deserter, a traitor—

... a scientist, a professor—

... a hard case, a sinner-for-hire—

... an author, a philosopher—

... and the proxy of a dead old man.

... and the wife of an amazing man.

My hand in his. The feel of his lips on my cheek. I remember laughing. And crying. Red wine at sunset. Dipping my toes in the Tiber. The smell of roasted chestnuts. Waking with my head on his chest.

"I am become Death, the destroyer of—"

I remember fear. Doubt. Mistrust. Injections. Surgeries. Implants. Transfusions. The cold metal of operating tables. The chill when the anesthetic hit my blood.

I want to live forever.

I remember the moment of discovery. After years and years of work and research, I found their secret, got inside of it and learned how it worked. I remember the cold, hard decision of what to do with it.

"Our nuclear weapons are meant purely as a deterrent against—"

I remember becoming the most dangerous person in the world.

I remember the pain. Intense, shriveling agony. The music floating out of the piazza behind us. The taste of rust in my mouth. I remember Caden's face as he lowered me to the ground. He spoke, cried, pleaded, but I couldn't hear him. I couldn't hear anything.

"... all been deceived and I, for one, am grateful for that deception!"

I remember his eyes. He looked scared. He must have been so scared. I'm so sorry.

I don't want to die.

"...been shamed and embarrassed and today I regretfully resign as your Prime—"

I remember the darkness closing in on me like an iris. I remember my heart beating and then not. I remember blackness.

"... unmistakable evidence has established the fact that a series of offensive missile sites is now in preparation on that imprisoned island. The purpose of these bases—"

I remember something else. I remember it. The secret.

The reason they killed me.

"Balad biha qanabil zar-riya hiya balab ziyada an ma yalzam!"

I remember. I know.

"...tear down that wall!"

I know what they wanted the world to forget.

I know how to split the atom.

She knew how to—

"Miss, are you okay?"

Three faces stared at me. The man was awake. The woman had taken my hand in hers, like a mother. The daughter was standing on her seat, backed away from me, scared.

"You're crying."

Dampness on my cheeks. My brain was exploding, and I didn't know who I was. Couldn't remember my name. I was two places at once; I was nowhere at all. Two people at once; no one at all.

Who was I now? Where was I then?

"Miss?" the woman asked one more time.

The only thing that came to my lips was the last coherent thought that had passed through my mind.

"I know," I said in voice that sounded both familiar and foreign.

"I know how to bring the fire."

‡

ABOUT THE AUTHOR

**CHAD J. SHONK is the award-winning
writer of the increasingly popular
independent film *Dakota Skye*.**

**A product of the great states of Ohio,
Georgia and California, he currently
resides in San Francisco.**

***PROXY* is his debut novel.**

VIRATA DAS WILL RETUN IN...

HOMME FATALE

SOMETIME IN 2014

IN THE MEANTIME, VISIT **JUSTAPROXY.COM** FOR FREE DOWNLOADABLE CONTENT SET IN THE WORLD OF *PROXY* FEATURING SOME OF YOUR FAVORITE CHARACTERS.

ALSO CHECK OUT **CHADJSHONK.COM** FOR UPDATES AND INFORMATION ABOUT UPCOMING RELEASES FROM ANTITHESIS PUBLISHING AND MEDIA

FOLLOW ME ON TWITTER **@CHADJSHONK**